HELL IS A WORLD WITHOUT YOU

A NOVEL

JASON KIRK

Shutdown
Fullbooks

PRAISE REPORT

"**Divinely savage, emotionally pure, and devilishly funny**, *HELL IS A WORLD WITHOUT YOU* took me back to my days as a hopelessly confused church kid. I absolutely adored this sweetly subversive romp with every fiber of my being."

— **BRIAN DANNELLY**, co-writer / director, *Saved!*

"It's funny, but also compassionate, romantic, and optimistic. Open-hearted, it rings with the specificity of the personal while evoking the universal. **Whoever you are, you'll find some of yourself in it**."

— **WILL LEITCH**, author, *How Lucky* and *The Time Has Come*

"No book I've read has better or more lovingly depicted the Evangelical terror of the 2000s. **I loved it**, even when it made me remember times I wish I could forget."

— **JANE COASTON**, Opinion writer, *The New York Times*

"A magic trick: a portrait that feels almost tactile in its specificity, yet **utterly universal**. You'll be thinking about it for a long time."

— **CLAIRE McNEAR**, author, *Answers in the Form of Questions*

"**Hilarious, big-hearted, and deeply humane**, it transported me right back to a world in which spiritual crises can be faced at Pizza Hut. The miracle of *HELL IS A WORLD WITHOUT YOU* is that it sees both sides of that equation with equal clarity and tenderness."

— **BRIAN PHILLIPS**, author, *Impossible Owls*

"Almost astonishingly accurate. Comical, endearing, and purely hideous. It is unlike anything else I've read about the Evangelical church: **unshakably critical, yet unshakably empathetic**."

— **JON BOIS**, creator, *17776*

"Genuinely funny, with **real laughs to be found in its painfully accurate depiction** of a pious world. It's a deeply funny book."

— **DREW MAGARY**, author, *The Night the Lights Went Out*

"A sweet, wry story that will be familiar to so many of us. **A crisis of faith that rings with uncommon truth**, shot through with surprising humor and kindness. I loved this book."

— **ANTHONY OLIVEIRA**, author, *Dayspring*

"Relatable af. **I felt like I was reading my own teenage Evangelical diary**. A hilarious way to feel grateful for the people who helped us leave the harmful parts of our faith behind."

— **APRIL AJOY**, co-host, *Evangelicalish*

"**An enthralling coming-of-age story, equally as engaging as it is hilarious**. A sweet yet biting portrait of extreme religiosity. A refreshing debut from a unique and imaginative writer."

— **ZITO MADU**, author, *The Minotaur at Calle Lanza*

"Humor, heart, and attention to details. Engaged me as both a former pastor's kid and a current scholar of religion. A message vital to our moment. **It will make you laugh, cry, think, and maybe listen to MxPx, whether you've been to youth group or not**."

— **MIKE ALTMAN**, Professor of Religious Studies,
University of Alabama

"Devastatingly funny, heartbreaking, and incisive. Will resonate with readers regardless of background. **I love every single one of these idiot church kids, and so will you**."

— **VICTORIA ZELLER**, author, *One of the Boys*

"Leaving the faith can be lonely. Even though Jason Kirk tells the story in a novel, it seems at times as if he wrote the biography of many of us. Sometimes this book will leave you laughing or crying, but **at all times it will leave you feeling a little less alone**."

— **MASON MENNENGA**, host, *A People's Theology*
and *The BlackSheep Podcast*

"As Jason Kirk juggles dozens of voices, it's **so quick and funny and smart**, you almost forget he's trying to square the unsquarable contradictions of hardcore Christianity."

— **TOMMY TOMLINSON**, author, *The Elephant in the Room*

"I'd never before read a book so in tune with what it's like to grow up Evangelical: self-hatred, fear for your soul, and trying to impress your date by recommending a Christian replacement for Sublime. **Deeply funny and deeply felt**. The good, good shit."

— **TYLER PARKER**, author, *A Little Blood and Dancing*

"Will remind you what it was like to be — or be classmates with — the religious kids. **At turns cathartic and cringe**, Drops you into all the horror, humiliation, and humor."

— **BLAKE CHASTAIN**, author, *Exvangelical and Beyond*

"If you were raised Evangelical (or are curious about what that world is like), this book from an honest, brilliant writer is **the one**."

— **JONATHAN REDDING**, author, *One Nation Under Graham*

"I have read Jason's book, and by 'read,' I mean 'had my team explain it to me.' Please let the record show that I was the first to say that it either **shifts the paradigm** or is extremely problematic."

— **MATTHEW PIERCE** in *Evangelical Thought Leader* mode

"Deeply fascinating. Witty, sad, and compassionate. A bitingly funny and insightful coming-of-age tale. **Highly recommend**."

— **READERS' FAVORITE** review, 5/5 stars

"As funny as it is unpredictable, **it's for anyone** who's ever felt disappointed by an institution or struggled to reconcile inherited ethics with nuanced realities. (And anyone who experienced formative moments via AOL Instant Messenger.)"

— **RYAN NANNI**, staff writer, *The Messenger*

"In between artfully woven portraits of adolescence, **Jason has constructed something extraordinary**: a compelling case for the existence of a better world. This book is for anyone who hopes or even believes that world might someday be real."

— **HOLLY ANDERSON**, writer and editor, *Channel Six*

"As a non-Evangelical, I had no idea what it's like. It's a terrifying galaxy, and Jason writes his ass off about it: **beautifully, angrily, and with deep empathy** for people stranded on Planet Jesus."

— **SPENCER HALL**, writer, *Channel Six*

This is a work of fiction. Names, characters, places, and incidents portrayed or mentioned are either products of the author's imagination or used fictitiously.

Cover art by Emily Mahon.

Published in the United States by Shutdown Fullbooks, New York, NY. For media requests and all other inquiries, reach out via jasonkirkbook@gmail.com.

Additional quotes from:

- Robertson, Pat. *The New World Order*. Word Publishing.
- Wiese, Bill. *23 Minutes In Hell: One Man's Story About What He Saw, Heard, and Felt in That Place of Torment*. Charisma House.
- Kimel, Aidan. *Destined for Joy: The Gospel of Universal Salvation*. Independent.

Library of Congress Control Number: 2023914729

Paperback ISBN: 978-1-7354926-4-3

Ebook ISBN: 978-1-7354926-2-9

Hardcover ISBN: 978-1-7354926-5-0

Librarians, as well as bookstores and others interested in bulk purchases, please visit ingramcontent.com.

To my best friend
since we were children,
former AIM user moshngrlMLE

CONTENT WARNING

This novel references elements of religious trauma, including existential dread, familial shame, intrusive thoughts, pervasive guilt, purity culture, self-harm ideation, systemic bigotry, toxic positivity, and unresolved grief.

Also included are things many church people secretly enjoy, such as cuss words, alcohol, and canoodling.

HELL IS A WORLD WITHOUT YOU

If I say, "Surely
the darkness will hide me,"
even the darkness
will not be dark to you

— Psalm 139

PART ONE
THE BOOK OF FRESHMEN

Your eye makes you sin?
Better to gouge it out
than to have two eyes in Hell

— The Sermon on the Mount

ONE
THE BEAUTIFUL LETDOWN

EARLY SUMMER, 2000 A.D.

I DIDN'T KNOW WHETHER MY DAD HAD SPENT THE PAST 2,360 DAYS IN ETERNAL conscious torment, but I knew I wanted to play pickup football.

So there I stood in swim trunks on a weedy field, staring up at rising seniors and recent graduates. Beneath the judgmental sun, I emphasized how close I was to age fourteen, and all these years later, I remember asking them a version of the only thought I'd ever had:

"Please choose me?"

They didn't need me. They had full teams already. They could've told me to go find the other freshmen beside the lake. But those huge people gathered to rustle my hair anyway.

"You're with us, 13.9-year-old," said a behemoth in a shirt with a modified Mountain Dew logo that read, "Jesus MEANT TO DIE for you."

One buzz-cutted enemy recommended we play shirts vs. skins, making his girl-woman teammates roll their eyes. *I'll never get away with jokes like that*, I thought.

Hoping to become worthwhile, I fervently volunteered to perform the kickoff, promising I'd eaten Iron Kids bread that morning. When my elders laughed, I so nearly understood why, I felt my social skills leveling up.

The camp's only popular sophomore, the pastor's visor-wearing son, asked, "Gonna be a JV kicker, Iron Kid?"

Ignoring that JV assumption, I bragged about having been a middle-school football player (albeit a mere punter, the guy whose only job had been surrendering the ball).

My camp elders teasingly debated my qualifications until counselor Sara Beth, a seventeen-year-old volleyball player with Rosie Perez dimples, told me, "Kick it deep, Isaac!"

I blushed, swooned, flexed, and recoiled with revulsion, having fallen prey to her smile, eye contact, and everything else. All my life, I'd been trained by Christian men to resent anyone my eyes wanted. Wanting was sinning.

A second time, I let my eyes admire her, even while an internal voice I believed to be the Holy Spirit warned me, **"GUARD YOUR HEART! OR REGRET BOILING WITH YOUR DEAD FATHER FOR ALL ETERNITY!"** I believed that voice's assessment of my soul, but had always hoped it was speaking hyperbolically about Dad's. He'd died when I was eight. Car accident. Or not an accident.

Oblivious to how much I deserved damnation, my teammates fanned out. In the fallen world, I stood center stage, and my enemies lined up as if I couldn't kick very far.

Now to convert my doubters, I vowed. *Blast the ball all the way to Target!*

Despite believing Jesus had been mutilated in order to forgive my glances at Sara Beth, I snuck a third. **"REGRET!"** Fourth glance. **"STOP KILLING JESUS, YOU PIECE OF SHIT!"** *Sorry.*

The pastor's son knelt, holding the football for me. Nobody had ever taught me how to kick off, but I'd watched my middle-school team's kickers practicing behind the bleachers. It was basically striding, stomping one foot, then swinging the other, right?

Facing the giants, I leapt, planted one foot so hard my ankle twisted, and thudded onto my butt. *Prepare for judgment,* I feared.

"Dude, you okay?" the pastor's son asked, holding the side of his head. "Kicked me in the darn ear."

I apologized, scrambling to hop one-footed while mumbling excuses about my socks.

"We just had a real-life 'why the ear, man?'" someone shouted. The pastor's son laughed, but didn't get it. I laughed loudly, emphasizing I recognized Fight Club quotes. *Sorry for sneaking R-rated movies.*

As the sun spotlit my frailty, I hurried to try again. I limped, hopped, planted my injured foot, and fell sideways into hard dirt. Worst of all, I yelped.

Everyone gathered, looking down at me. Sara Beth surely hated me, which meant I'd die alone. But when she squatted beside me, she only said, "Let's carry Iron Kid into the shade." I felt addicted to undeserved acceptance and suspicious that my social debt would soon come due. (Fifth glance. Even bigger debt.)

I knew acknowledging my pain wasn't right, especially as the man of my mother's house. Jubilation and indignation were the only acceptable feelings for 13.9-year-old men of God.

The seniors rested me on a picnic bench, then dispersed to keep playing. A husky man sat, tucked Kurt Cobain-length hair behind his ears, and side-hugged me.

"Stud, your ankle's way broken-ish," said youth pastor Timmy.

"Nah, I just dunno my own strength," I scoffed. "I can carry sixteen folding chairs at once."

A grin puffed his Santa cheeks. Mostly shaven and holding half of a hot dog, he was highly aged — like twenty-six.

I wished I looked less tough, so he'd hug me forever, then realized that would've sounded like a same-sex-attraction thought to anyone observing my brain. I'd never had one of those thoughts, but chastised myself anyway.

"Cast that demon outta his ankle, Timbo," shouted a senior from the field.

Timmy laughed and winked at me. As my breath stopped, he waved his hand, murmuring, "Your ankle feels rad. Jedi mind trick."

Everyone laughed because that wasn't a crazy church that believed in healing people. It was a sane church that believed humanity is doomed, except for people who'll survive by agreeing with sane churches.

Timmy looked closer at me. "Yo, now I recognize you. You're his mini-me!"

I flinched, wondering what he knew about Dad.

But Timmy said, "Mister Eli without the beard!"

Phew. Me and my twenty-two-year-old brother, Eli, shared Mom's black hair and Mediterranean nose, plus Dad's hazel eyes. Eli actually played varsity, though, a fullback with a goatee even as a freshman. Later, he'd become so godly that a lady quit college to marry him. He'd started volunteering as Timmy's second-in-command, so I was tagging along despite being a member of a different church.

Handing me a hot dog, Timmy encouraged me to join his church for real. "Get plugged into our family, stud."

That'd require convincing Mom to let me stop attending her downtown non-denominational megachurch, where nobody knew I existed. (As a lifelong church kid, I'd visited many other congregations too, including the hardcore Calvinists beside the Pizza Hut, after which I'd hidden under my bed, hoping God would *forget* I existed.)

From the field, Sara Beth looked back and gave me a premarital thumbs up, and I felt led by either satanic lust, social acceptance, or divine encouragement to make that place my church home. Sixth glance. *In Hell, demons will pop my eyeballs like Gushers — unless I earn Heaven by popping them myself first.* Seventh glance.

"Maybe the Spirit's not the only thing calling you to join us," Timmy chuckled, as if I was just a normal kid crushing on a camp counselor, not a degenerate committing sins foul enough to get me flicked like a loathsome spider into endless agony.

And then we all shot Super Soakers.

That perfectly clear central Pennsylvania night, dozens of campers gathered at the cabin beside the moonlit lake. They parked me, my swollen ankle, and my stomach full of hot dogs beside Timmy on the porch as underclassmen rapped about spoiled food.

Seniors were mocking the way youth pastors always mangled Neo-is-like-Jesus movie references. "Teens, know who can change your ... final destination?" said Sara Beth, making me view her as a gospel-ridiculing jezebel. But once Timmy laughed at her mimicry, I discerned that she remained wife material.

Mom had encouraged me to make friends at camp, though I already had plenty at school, including the kid I'd eaten lunch with throughout seventh grade. We'd spoken at least twice. (Punters weren't popular.)

As junior campers horsed around with sophomores, Timmy strummed his guitar. I sat still, wary of jostling my half-digested hot dogs.

Eventually, everyone gathered, facing Timmy.

Like an earnest Jack Black, he sang a Rich Mullins song about learning to follow God. Kids joined in with eyes closed and palms raised toward stars. Bodies swayed infectiously as shoulders sought shoulders to brush against. The last lyric repeated, fading into the forest's katydid choir.

For three reasons, I'd always attended churches: Mom required it multiple times per week, I didn't know how else to seek friendships, and I was horrified, especially since Dad's death, to have been born into a universe that involved everlasting damnation. (But attending was the bare minimum. The million other requirements included saving America from liberals, defending humanity from Satan, and tithing toward church-van transmissions.)

"Bros and lady-bros, God's working on our hearts tonight," said Timmy, strumming more gently. "I sense something moving within us."

Looking at singing faces, light and dark shades of moon-blue, I felt fired up to ace the whole checklist.

"Moment of silencio," said Timmy, eyes glimmering. "Just breathe the Spirit in. Biiig breath ..."

Only bug noises and muffled chuckles decorated the darkness. A stern-faced girl whispered, "Thank you, Jesus." Something raised my palms heavenward along with hers.

We filled our lungs with not just the breeze, but with each other's breaths. Biiig breath ...

And like a trumpet blast, I farted.

Seniors exploded in laughter, then howled the story of my failed kickoff. One of my day-old nicknames morphed into "Charlie Brown Pants." I shoved laughter forth from my scalding face, certain the mob had been lulling me with kindness, eager to pounce.

But Timmy bumped my elbow and winked. He cut his voice through the giggles, freestyling about farts being preferable to pukes, sharts, and turtleheads. Soon, everyone sang along with his gassy "Hey Jude" parody. Even I, the unclean defiler, was allowed to sing. Accepting fist bumps from people who'd laughed, I felt chills.

"If you got a hand, hold a neighbor's hand," Timmy said, so I and my new friends hurried to obey. "This week, we'll get our hearts supercharged, but for a purpose: so your secular-school friends will see the Lord's joy in you. They'll want what you got! Don't let your light fade after camp ends!"

When goofy Timmy got serious, even the Slipknot-shirted senior listened. Pastors, prophets, and authors always made God sound complicated, but Timmy's mission was simple: Be so relentlessly cheerful that nobody goes to Hell.

Wiping a tear, he told us, "Beloved, I believe you'll lead the world-changing generation that'll free captives from all-consuming fire."

Beneath the wooden bridge, where the noon sun couldn't see me, I let cool mud soothe my wounded ankle. I could hear people by the lake blaring the Christian rock band Switchfoot.

"Inviting myself into your secret club," said Josiah, my visor buddy from pickup football. He stepped into my shady muck.

The lanky sophomore with KFC-tan limbs and Penn State shorts offered to introduce me around. I said, "You look like a quarterback. Sorry, that sounded fruity." He was nonchalant about being a Christian private schooler, even though that made him holier than a public-school wretch like me.

Then he asked, "So, what's your testimony?"

Church terminology for your personal story of Christian conversion. I'd always hated that question. *Sorry.*

Christians loved cheering for each other's thrilling testimonies about Jesus lickety-split saving them from lives of theft, arson, and even agnosticism. Earlier that morning, Josiah's father, Pastor Jack, had testified about being the grandson of a Buffalo bootlegger, which had led to dangerous adventures before "accepting Christ outside a den of iniquity." Jack had then driven overnight to seminary, promising God to "pack pews or die trying."

I'd heard testimonies all the time. Sometimes, they were about avoiding Hell, seeking good Jesus feelings, or wanting to go somewhere cool like Heaven or Beach Fest. When I was nine, Mom had taken me to father-son banquets where pro athletes had testified about finding Jesus during season-ending injuries. At middle-school assemblies, born-again bodybuilders called the Power Team had testified about out-dueling satanic wizards. At the megachurch, one sweaty speaker had testified, "Don't be like me, paying child support from before Christ changed me. Slippery slopes! Fellas, could you resist the Devil if that vixen beside you tore your jeans off right now?" (I wasn't sure. I was in third grade.)

Lacking a sufficiently inspiring salvation testimony, I told Josiah, "Mine's boring."

"It's all God, buddy," he said with a future pastor's smile and fragile Ben Affleck eyes, bumping knuckles against my arm. "Hit me."

Well, at age four, I'd said a salvation prayer at my cousins' church, plus a different one at the megachurch when I was eleven and other salvation attempts at Christian pizza parties, illusionist shows, and dirt bike races. Too young for penny contracts with the Columbia Record Club, but old enough for eternal pacts with the Omnipotent. *Which pact counted, though?*

"I've always been a Christian," I shrugged. "I mean, nobody's born one, even if your parents are, duh. You gotta ask Jesus into your heart and know you mean it, obviously."

(I didn't have blessed assurance, but could certainly spout Christian lingo. Sadly, this was a sin called "talking the talk but not walking the walk.")

"Listen, if somebody put a gun to your chest, maybe you'd doubt where you'd spend eternity," Josiah said, and I was embarrassed to have made him worry. "Having no peace of mind stinks."

He set the scene for his own testimony story. Hundreds of thousands of husband-fathers, the Promise Keepers, rallied at the Washington Monument, where a shameful little Josiah had asked God to remove the sinful thorn from his side, turning him from a twelve-year-old abomination into a patriot worthy of becoming a husband-father. Feeling instantly aligned, the pastor's son had even heard God speak blue-sky thunder.

"A new man, raring to take this nation for Christ," he said. From the other side of the creek, I coveted his peace.

Counting nails in the bottom of the bridge, I listened to my heart, thump-thump-thumping toward Judgment Day. Having only ever heard the heavens speak of "**REGRET**," I decided to follow Josiah until a sunrise sang to me.

"Hey 13.9, wake up," whispered a senior, rustling me awake. "We gotta go pee on the Target."

Code for something important, I assumed, scrambling to find my shorts in our dark cabin. On autopilot, exhausted from hours of wailing singalongs and sunburnt sports, I followed the giggling boy-adults into the night. Shushing each other, a dozen of us herded down a woodsy gravel path.

It wasn't code, actually — anyone who didn't scamper across the street and decorate Target's poorly lit back-corner brick wall was a "pussball," per my elders. My ankle was killing me, but I hobbled urgently.

"The Bible says men are people who pisseth against walls," explained Josiah, the only other underclassman invited. The pastor's son possessed obvious social rank, so the older kids must've viewed me as his sidekick and / or their wobbly mascot.

Minutes later, I was back in my bunk, half believing I'd dreamed about being included in grown-man business.

After another afternoon packed with activity, Josiah walked me toward the sunset campfire, where marshmallow-roasting juniors were quoting Office Space. Youth pastor Timmy was strumming again, smiling at the chatter floating past.

"Well, 13.9, I gotta go do pastor's-kid stuff," Josiah said, "so you're stuck with this weird ginger."

He meant his freshman cousin, Sophie. Sitting on a log, she play-thwacked his thigh. He straight-armed her forehead, mostly gently, then left.

A pastor's niece? Outta my league, so whatever. Besides, I was basically married to Sara Beth. Sitting next to Sophie, I deployed my primary social skill: requesting her testimony.

"When I was six, Uncle Jack asked if I was ready to be baptized," she said, "so I prayed what he told me to say." Sadly, she'd then backslid at the library by reading Jurassic Park. "Bad secular stuff we shouldn't be curious about. Not just evolution, but girl dinosaurs that do boy things."

(Five feet away, a Sunday school teacher laughed at someone quoting an R-rated movie's line about threesomes.)

Though I'd been taught conservative gender roles, I was confused by a scabby-kneed tomboy worrying about dinosaurs upholding them. So I asked the obvious question: "How'd you read a movie?"

Believing I was joking, she laughed — *freckle explosion! Make it happen again!* — before complaining about Hollywood's inaccurate adaptation, not that she'd seen it. As my depraved eyes fell prey to her frizzy ponytail and slim muscles beneath sun-pinked arm skin, I tried my other social skill: asking about school.

"Homeschool," she said apologetically, unsure whether the new kid would make fun of her. "My sisters were, too. I'm the runt cousin, following the path."

"Runts stick together," I said, offering a fist bump. She brightened, thanks to my social ... sorry, *God's* social skills shining through my disgusting flesh.

"My folks are kinda sick of homeschooling, so I have time to learn whatever I want," she said. "That part's cool! Not that learning's cool."

"You haven't missed much in public school. Just boys comparing new armpit hairs." *Another freckle-explosion laugh!*

Across the campfire, Timmy sang "Big House," an old Christian rock-ish song about Heaven's accommodations. Sophie joined in with sincere hand motions — while older guys did let's-go-smoke-stuff head nods. Timmy grimaced, aware his audience was wavering.

As night fell, black clouds blocked the stars. When Timmy left to help elsewhere, remaining seniors described his mishmash accents: "Like if Adam Sandler was from Miami or something. World's biggest dweeb. I love him." *Hmm. Noted.*

Sophie's eyes watched a sophomore, the youth group's best rapper, some deacon's square-jawed son in a Duke polo. *I'm not jealous,* I assured myself. *My heart belongs to Sara Beth.* Regardless, I leaned close and baby-squawked like my idea of Miami Sandler, "Bro, when you got baptiii-eee-iiized, how'd the pool shmell?"

She scrunched her nose, no longer looking at the Dukie. Success.

"I have to clean it," she said. "Otherwise there's algae. Josiah gets to do boy stuff, power tools and preaching. But I get to do sign language!"

I learned that her Sunday-morning job was translating her uncle's sermons with her hands for the ASL section. Instead of asking an obvious followup, I Sandler-honked, "How do you clean algae-a-heeeeea?"

She jutted a pouty lip. "They want me to kill it with spray, but I release it in the creek like Free Willy. Sorry," she said, before mimicking some groaning geezer's voice, "that movie's environmentalist propaganda."

She then unloaded algae facts like she couldn't stop. Veering perilously toward evolution, she argued algae was vital to Genesis 1's creation story "if you read between the lines." We did little algae voices, pretending to warn algae children against upsetting the all-powerful redhead who might destroy them despite loving them. I proposed we liberate baptismal algae to a haven named Algae-querque, and she snort-laughed. *Talking to a girl isn't a sin if I eventually marry her (and Sara Beth), right?*

"Yoohoo, dorkballs," shouted an unseen counselor, startling me, which confirmed I'd been sinning. "We're meeting Mister Eli by the cabins."

I limped through the woods on my bum ankle, following flashlights toward whatever my immense brother had cooked up — he'd warned me of his plans to "jolt this stagnant youth group." The cabin lights, warm yellow the night before, had become strobes scratching witchy shadows everywhere. Anticipating an intense sermon, I filtered through the crowd toward the previous night's safest spot: the porch.

And rumbling forth from the cabin door, boots tromping along creaking boards, was my prophet-bearded brother. At the sight of the upright lion, even eighteen-year-olds and crickets ceased chattering. In the crowd's strobe-lit ocean of wide-open eyes, I couldn't spot my new friends. Worship night's serene smiles were long gone.

The volunteer assistant youth pastor growled, "Boys and girls, we're done wasting our fleeting time. We're going to talk about certainty."

I'd never known anyone who preached Hellfire harder than Eli did.

He told us to line up, pointing toward my corner. Four tall guys emerged in Scream masks, placing metal buckets along the porch's far side. (Some sermons, called "object lessons," involved props and crowd participation.)

"Your whole life, you've heard six is the Devil's number, the Mark of the Beast," said the strobe-lit Eli. "You've heard associating yourself with 666 will *lower* you to Satan's level. Nope. Your predicament's even worse than that!"

Man, that huggy-huggy youth group wasn't ready for Eli. He hadn't always possessed Hell Mode, but after Dad's death, my brother had become the man I was supposed to be, ignoring everything but saving souls.

Standing close to the stage backfired; I was second in line. *Wait, I'm behind Josiah! I feel sa– … err, I hope his presence makes* others *feel safe. I feel safe regardless. I'm a God-trusting Christian soldier.*

"Six isn't the number of Satan," said Eli, holding up sharp metal. "Six is the number of humanity. Which day'd God create us on, huh?"

Sunday school veterans murmured, "Sixth." I limped onto the porch as a Scream guy handed me a baggie full of metal: long nails, six of them.

"So if six is supposedly the Devil's number," said Eli, jabbing nails toward the crowd, "but actually *our* number, what's that signify about us? We're already as low as Satan, deserving the same eternal fate."

The white-black-white forest offered no rebuttal, only echoes of Eli's voice.

"You were born into a system with only two options," he said. "You can either reject this world entirely, or ride it into never-ending fire."

My brother pointed downstage at the labeled metal buckets. "The Catholic cult says there are seven deadly sins. Nope. Plenty more than seven, all equally damnable."

Aw man, a confessions game, I realized. At most churches, that meant writing your sins onto paper and tossing them into campfires. I'd done weird versions, but never with strobe-lit Scream reapers.

"Ohh, but Eli, I've never murdered," said my brother, waving limp hands, mocking feminine sinners. "I don't deserve Hell, right?"

Behind me, reapers kept handing out nails.

"Nice try, slick," said Eli, tromping toward buckets. "Matthew 5 says whoever's angry with his brother risks damnation. Ever thrown a tantrum? Guess which bucket that is? Do we hide behind vague words like wrath, or call anger what Jesus called it?"

He held a bucket high like Goliath's severed head.

"Murder," my brother read from its scrawled Sharpie ink. "Thoughts are actions! Still think there's no blood on your little hands? Still think you're unblemished virgins?"

Someone fired up a loudspeaker, shattering the night with the sounds of screams. Kids recoiled. I winced because Eli had gotten that audio file of a Siberian tunnel to Hell — authentic, according to one Christian TV network — from my computer. *No wait, that's good! He's warning souls against joining this damned choir, and I helped! Except I hear Dad wailing. Er, he's in Heaven. Right?*

"Each nail in your hands is a confession," Eli barked, pointing at those of us on stage. "We repent, and only then have we earned happy-clappy time. One by one, we're gonna drop each nail where it belongs."

My brother tipped the bucket in his hand, revealing what'd been taped at the bottom, catching our nails: a printed-out picture of Jesus' bleeding hands.

"Even if I'd been the only sinner, he would've died," Eli said, lip quivering. "Therefore, I killed him. To acknowledge that or not is the only choice we ever get."

He set Murder back between Harlotry and The Appearance Of Evil.

"I'll confess out loud, but you can skip that part," he said, dropping nails into buckets — clang, clang, clang — while reciting his sins.

Pastor's-kid Josiah stepped forward, wordlessly clanging five nails. The nearest reaper watched the sixth nail fall into a bucket, then muttered, "Dude, take this seriously. Got bad aim?" Josiah, flustered, reached down to move his sixth nail from one bucket to another, then hurried around the corner into the woods.

Passing me as I limped to confess, Eli bellowed at everyone, "Get scoured now or devoured later." When he patted my shoulder, I worried the crowd would think he was taking it easy on me.

You can guess where I dropped my first nail. I'd been taught God had designed men to always look once, but in my diseased desire, I'd constantly chosen to look again. My mind was such a lust sewer, I pictured the nail skewering my eye like an olive.

Clang. Adultery.

Two. After years of wallowing in atheist MTV and satanic Sonic games, I'd done nothing to lead my generation toward seizing America for Christ.

Clang. Worldliness.

Three. I'd never hugged a non-Christian girl, but daydreaming about unbelievers was as impure as impregnating one.

Clang. Unequally Yoked With A Heathen.

Four. Never sharing the gospel at school had risked damning my classmates. How many times had I failed to spread the good news of God letting his Son be slaughtered?

Clang. Ashamed Of Gospel.

Five. I didn't have enough nails to confess all the times the Holy Spirit had screamed, **"YOU'LL FOREVER REGRET DOING THIS,"** and I'd done it anyway. Masturbation? Duh. Gambling? Yes. Peeing on the Target? Annihilate me. Drinking? Never, but I'd laughed at beer commercials, which counted.

Clang. Rebelliousness.

I'm the Jesus-murdering shitstain whose actions degrade the universe by the minute. Puncture me with cyclone claws. Almost every bucket begged for my last nail, but one was undeniable.

Six. Six years, five months, and twenty-two days prior, God had needed another angel, yet I remained sick with jealousy, resentful of predestination, and emasculated by emotion. As Siberian Hell screamers throbbed in my ears, I still wished God would scrap perfect plans, choose the unchosen, and give back my father.

Clang. Coveting.

Church can't just be hugs, light, and snacks, I thought. *The whole awful world is counting on us. I have a testimony at last, but only if I remain this red-lined until I die.*

I felt pressure-washed, hoping I'd finally become an "on-fire Christian" (an emotionally overwhelming level beyond born-again). Behind me, I heard Eli confronting more weaklings with rock-hard reality.

As I limped along the path around the lake, something snuck past the Hell howls, un-tensing my chest. Under moonbeams, through breezy trees, among sobbing freshmen and whispering seniors, I heard guitar strums. Timmy's voice led living creatures in a new song.

Once I entered a clearing beside an old shack, people gave me hard-earned hugs. We formed a semi-circle around Timmy, who sat criss-cross on dark blue grass, all of us somewhere between broken and buzzing (except for the hard-hearted deviants cuddling in passionate piles, creeping toward their next confessions).

I no longer heard Hell, just guitar, sniffling, flirting, scolding, and whispered arguments about Eli. A little old woman shuffled out of the shack, distributing plastic cups of lemonade. Some kids sang with Timmy, swaying and finger-snapping. Others stood to help the woman.

I felt too dirty to join the "Lean on Me" singalong. But as campers whooped and laughed, I felt a head-to-toe shimmer. *Radiant light invading me? I don't deserve it! Gimme more nails!*

A lanky sophomore arm wrapped around me. With leaking eyes and swollen cheeks, Josiah pulled me near and said, "Snuggle up, tough guy." My godliest friend considered me non-disgusting, and my prideful flesh gobbled up the praise.

"Gang, right now, you're feeling God working on your hearts," Timmy cried out. "Let's bow heads and close eyes. If you're ready to pray with a counselor about killing your old self and becoming brand new, put up one hand. Nobody will see but m– ... Yes! I see that hand! I see ... praise God! Hands!" He was cackle-weeping. "We'll keep singing all night!"

I peeked to see Eli crying on Timmy's shoulder and lots of hands raised like an army's spears as weeping seniors led salvation huddles. One senior, hurrying toward us, was Sara Beth.

She collapsed, hugging Josiah from the other side, which gave me a jealous pang. He squeezed her arm as she sobbed about dumping all her confession nails into Stumbling Block, the term for women who sin by being wanted. My heart was so high on fellowship, I didn't blame her. I soared until I didn't want to gouge out my eyes anymore. **"YOU'LL REGRET THAT."** *Sorry. Too high.*

I hoped I wasn't happy because of fake crap like other friends joining our hug pile. I hoped I'd instead found authentically permanent joy.

In that moment, the deal finally seemed simple. To feel that loved forever, I had to always copy Josiah, Timmy, Eli, Pastor Jack, one million Promise Keepers, the Power Team, the True Love Waits guys, Billy Graham, James Dobson, Jerry Falwell, C.S. Lewis, Pat Robertson, Rush Limbaugh, Rich Mullins, George W. Bush, the guys who'd peed on the Target, and father-husband-patriots like the Apostle Paul and Jesus.

Easy peasy, since God had already told all those men to tell me the same things.

TWO
NOT OF THE WORLD
SUMMER 2000

There I sat on AOL Instant Messenger, in love with a 15/F/Nashville. When she told me her weekly routine, which included a lot of stuff about horses, I asked:

> SHARKSWITHRABIES: wut ab0ut church?

> FatBoySlimShady42069: fuck no!! church is for turdbuglrerz

Dang, she'd seemed pretty, I lamented. *Oh well, Christian M's can only marry Christian F's anyway.*

> FatBoySlimShady42069: what'z a church boi week like?? u been to church a zillion times????

Hmm, have I? Time for a math project. Along the way, I'll give you a crash-course tour of what I'd learned during my fourteen years in various conservative denominations/non-denominations.

SUNDAY

"Wanna hear some math?" I asked Mom. "I've been to church like fifty Sunday mornings per year. Already 700 times total."

"Well, you reached that 700 club way faster than I did," she laughed in our '92 Chrysler minivan, bought when her and Dad had expected to produce an abundance of kids. She was driving to her downtown megachurch, which I'd secretly decided was no longer mine.

She'd grown up in Southern California during the '70s Jesus Movement, when semi-hippies invented Christian rock. She'd been a total hippie, though, meaning she'd preferred weed over war (until Jesus fixed her). After moving east, she churched Eli and I heavily from the beginning — and tried to drag Dad along, too. He'd resembled white-messiah paintings, but her Greek-bronze skin was like Revelation 1:15 Jesus'.

At most churches I'd attended, Sunday morning meant laughing at the pastor's usual jokes, worrying about Bad America's persecution of Good America, tithing my lawn-mowing money, being warned against churches that interpreted the Bible non-literally, and singing songs whose lyrics appeared on a big screen I'd nicknamed "the HumbleTron." Then everyone was invited to the altar, either to get saved or to rededicate by publicly admitting failures. I needed to do that again soon because, mere days after camp, my radiant glow had dimmed to a flicker.

Also each Sunday, there was youth group, which the megachurch's snowboarding youth pastor called Inspiration SuperHisWay 3.0: Rzrgnx (pronunciations varied). It mostly consisted of singing along with men dressed like Carson Daly, then breaking into boy groups and girl groups. While learning how to focus on Jesus instead of girls, boys wondered what girls were learning about, then tried to read candy-glossy lips from across the room. That led to *falling in love with her and her and her and h—*

"Isaac, how would you answer that question?" my group's teacher interrupted.

"Jesus," I assumed.

"Bingo."

... and her and her ...

Adult church + kid church equaled 1,400 lifetime sessions for me so far.

Plus 650 Sunday nights. Those were so mellow that when the pastor at my cousins' tiny church said The Little Mermaid mind-controlled Ellen DeGeneres into gayness, he was wearing shorts.

Driving home past billboards of the megachurch pastor's gleaming smile, I almost convinced Mom to let me join Eli's medium-sized church, which fed my soul the best, you know? Coincidentally, people there liked me.

MONDAY

Smoke flashed above a thousand jumping teenagers. On the megachurch warehouse's stage was Skillet, which had been Christian Nirvana, but had become Christian Nine Inch Nails, part of Evangelicalism's never-ending project: constructing a facsimile world designed to consume the original. (Everyone thinks DC Talk was Christian Nirvana, but that was just one song. DC Talk had gone from Christian MC Hammer to Christian U2.)

I secretly loved secular music, but had enjoyed the bonfire at my cousins' little church, where we'd destroyed all our sinful stuff. In went Harry Potter books, "C U When U Get There" CDs, and Forrest Gump tapes. As white dads blew Jewish shofars, garbage bags burned, and sixth-graders mooned each other, I'd torched a Madden game because James Dobson's Breakaway Magazine said sixteen-bit cheerleaders would make me lust.

My schoolmates had seemed surprised whenever I'd mentioned going to church on weekdays (while secular middle-schoolers did things like cocaine and welfare). "At church, I get high the old-fashioned way, while you smoke stems and seeds," I'd said, citing things rappers disliked.

I didn't know whether Eli's church did stuff on Mondays, but did know it'd ignite my soul-saving passion better than the megachurch warehouse, where I liked loud noises but lacked friends.

Also, my classmates claimed MC Hammer and U2 were Christians. *Then why don't Christian merch stores sell their albums, dumbass? Sorry.*

TUESDAY

Once, I met a Catholic. After I rebuked his Mary witchcraft, he explained his made-up holidays that have perfume names like Ascension, Conception, and Epiphany. So I explained holidays about Jesus: Christmas, Easter, and Thanksgiving, when God gave this land to Judeo-Christians like Thomas Jefferson.

Speaking of, something I knew I'd miss about Mom's megachurch was its oomph. On Tuesday, July 4, 2000, we sat watching fireworks crown its thirty-foot Jesus statue.

People sang along to Christian every-genre musician Carman's "God in America Again," a song about our Judeo-Christian country having been great until 1960s Supreme Court stuff turned high schools into warzones of condoms and astrology. (Middle school had lacked those things, except for the kid who'd detonated salsa-filled rubbers and the goth girls who explained the moon's emotions. High school sounded scary.)

Near the song's end, Carman preached about how Christians should storm the White House until Americans stopped going to Hell.

In a star-spangled hat, Mom cheered the White House plan, which would involve terminating adulterous Democrats (because "character matters"). Eli, wearing Charles Barkley's Olympics jersey, preferred Hell stuff. I figured they went hand in hand.

WEDNESDAY

At the megachurch, girls could wear whatever to weeknight youth group, unless the youth pastor discerned armpits were too sexy. At my cousins' fundamentalist church, girls couldn't show their shins. I hoped Eli's church didn't forbid Sara Beth's modest summer attire.

Bathroom break.

Back from jerking off, full of fresh **"REGRET,"** I prayed for the strength to join Eli's church without succumbing to Sara Beth's cruel near-nudity.

I'd long ago stolen an uncle's six-inch stiletto knife, then kept it hidden in my backpack. Sometimes, after sinning, I warned myself, "Pop goes the eyeball!"

I practiced on grapes, slicing away their skins while imagining my eye-stuff glooping down my cheeks in my pitch-blackened shower, my skull lightening as its sins trickled down the drain forever. I believed suicide would be one sin, but it'd prevent so many others. Cold, hard math.

Anyway, Wednesday church was usually fun. Obstacle courses! Eating live goldfish! A pretend funeral? This kid Zack read his friend's suicide note, which listed times Zack should've shared the gospel. After Zack cried, "Why didn't I tell him about Jesus?" the casket burst open. The dead kid screamed, "I'm burning in Hell, thanks to you," and then we played red rover.

In the kitchen, I asked Mom, "I've been to like 600 Wednesday nights, right?"

She laughed at my chart of attendance stats. Only one Wednesday had involved four gunmen storming in and threatening to kill a seventeen-year-old unless he denied Christ. Mom still didn't know about that.

Eli sure did. Years prior, he'd been that seventeen-year-old.

THURSDAY

In elementary school, I went to Awana meetings at a neighbor's church each Thursday. There, we learned to tie rope knots, shoot BB guns, and pledge allegiance to the Christian and American flags.

"What was Awana, like, for?" I asked Mom in our mint-green Pine-Sol kitchen, beside big photos of smiling kindergarten me and smiling preteen Eli.

She looked up from cutting coupons. "Bible trivia? I have ribbons you won."

Oh, right. One year, the final question was about the Bible's rivalries between brothers. Cain vs. Abel, Ishmael vs. Isaac, Jacob vs. Esau, and Joseph vs. everybody (and that was just Genesis). Sixteen-year-old Eli had celebrated my victory by putting me in a headlock and joking about adding to the list.

At the megachurch, Thursday was a church day, just like every other day. Softball leagues about First Timothy 4:8, buffets about John 6:51, movie nights about Neo being Jesus …

Twenty-two-year-old Eli preferred his church's focus. "Did Jesus command us to build Upward Basketball gyms or to save souls?"

"You're mad your church can't afford any gyms," I laughed. He laughed. The thing his church did afford: friendships.

FRIDAY

Josiah invited me to his weekly Men's Accountability Group for men ages thirteen through sixteen. At our Pizza Hut buffet meeting, after we prayed that our personal pans and Mountain Dew would "nourish unto our bodies," it felt weird when it was my turn to finally confess JOing. But once I admitted I'd fallen prey to immodest knee socks stretched around sinister soccer-girl calves, everyone hugged me like I'd been jumped into a gang. *Confessions = hugs! Keep confessing!*

Nearby was an upperclassman accountability group, where seventeen-year-old Christians laughed about sinning. *You think JOing is funny, you frost-tipped generation who played GoldenEye instead of making America Judeo-Christian again?* I vowed to never become a jaded senior who considered freshmen naive.

Otherwise, Fridays were for remembering.

One Friday, long ago, imperialists butchered an innocent drifter, so we call it Good Friday.

And, on a Friday in 1993, sunrise blinded Dad as he was driving. Hours after that, my cousins' pastor said in an ice-cream-man voice that I shouldn't cry, because Dad was "finally happy as can be, partying in a big mansion." So I never had.

If my hero's enjoying perfect happiness, then he must've been delighted to leave eight-year-old me behind. Wanting him back is heartless of me. Imagine depriving someone of gold streets, offering nothing in return but pillow forts.

I learned lucid dreaming for two reasons: to see boobs without leaving internet evidence, and so that, when I dreamed the sound of Dad's garage door opening, I could say, like the angel in All Dogs Go to Heaven, "You can never come back."

SATURDAY

As the world's only Bible-believing monotheists, Saturday was the one day without religious services. (Excuse me, "relationship-with-Jesus" services.)

Usually. Several Saturdays, I'd been handed anti-abortion signs and told to stand in parking lots, feeling productive for angering strangers.

Other Saturdays, we did overnight kid parties at the go-karts arcade. My main church lock-in memory: Playing Tekken against some kid who told me arcane secrets about R-rated movies. Wild Things sounded like everything English teachers claimed Shakespeare was, but I feared it'd make me JO myself unconscious. *Lord,* I prayed, *safeguard my computer from Wild Things. Unless my wife wants to watch it with me. Once we're seventeen.*

Other times, multi-day church events lasted through Saturdays. At one youth retreat, I remember teams racing across a parking lot, slurping flat Coke from a tub, running back, spitting it into another tub, and repeating. Nobody won. Too many kids puked. Then we made beaded bracelets to use as tools for explaining salvation.

What's there to explain? Salvation's already easy to understand. Right?

ONE SATURDAY IN PARTICULAR

"Okay, I've attended 3,000 church events," I said, showing Mom my lifetime tally. "With all this experience, can I pick which church I attend?"

"You don't like my choir singing?" she teased, looking up from clipping coupons. "Hmm. You did come home from Eli's camp abuzz, even if they let you hobble all week on that mangled ankle!"

She worked at the hospital, so she was a geek about boring junk like bone fractures. Big deal; I'd convinced grownups my leg was fine so I could stay with my new friends.

"At Eli's church," I began, "my non-purpose-driven life got edified into souled-out Kingdom materi–"

"Pouring it on thick," she cackled. "Those camp girlies were that cute?"

"I'm co-leaders with the pastor's son. I could help Eli help Brother Timmy, who's godly ..."

"Junior, you have your daddy's poker face. What's your sweetie's name?"

Name? Singular? My soulmates from camp week were named Anna Grace, Bethany Grace, Charity Grace ... whatever, give Mom a detail and move on. "Her name's Sara Beth, okay? She's godly."

Mom said she'd consider it while I ran an errand. I biked to Pizza Hut and back, pedaling with my walking boot and balancing boxes on handlebars.

It was enough for our guests: Eli, who'd finally moved the last of his garbage out weeks earlier, plus Josiah and some girl he was courting (AKA pre-engagement, minus perversions like kissing). In our driveway, I saw two familiar cars, including Eli's crappy Jeep.

"... and I hear Isaac has his first lady-friend," Mom was chirping in the kitchen. First? Ridiculous. In fourth grade, me and a neighbor had stood only four feet apart and licked our palms while making peripheral eye contact, a slippery slope to STDs.

Peeking through fake ferns, I saw Eli wearing work khakis. "Bout time the boy took interest," he said, Hank Hill style, as if his confession game hadn't revealed I was a sex addict. And I saw Josiah smiling at someone around the corner.

"What are the odds," Mom said as I approached in stealth mode, "of another gal sharing your name?"

"Must be a um, new kid?" said the voice from my most lucid dreams. Sara Beth, my least attainable crush (besides Halle Berry), was courting my so-called best friend.

Well, duh, the pastor's son was two inches taller than me and a sophomore only a few hundred days younger than her. Of course a Christian F liked the Christian-est M. Like she was gonna wait for me? Half her friends would get married the following summer, presumably to watch Wild Things without me.

As my snoopy mother, ruthless brother, supposed buddy, and ex-wife spotted me lurking behind plastic foliage, I asked Earth to swallow me (Numbers 26:10). I knew Sara Beth would tell every girl how pathetic I was, ensuring I remained Mommy's widdle roommate until Eli mercy-killed me as Josiah eulogized me, complete with a laugh track.

But Eli took the pizzas, Mom hugged me, and everyone confessed their own ambitious crushes from age fourteen. Sara Beth: "I drew MS Paints of the singer Seal as a cowboy." Josiah: "I smuggled a Spice Girls album." They promised there'd be a Christian F for me, but only if I remained a steadfast Christian M forever, just like the author of I Kissed Dating Goodbye.

SHARKSWITHRABIES: pleeeeeeeeeeeeeeezzzz never tell anybody

MyPlaceInThisWorld (Josiah): Hmmm.

SHARKSWITHRABIES: shoot me instead

MyPlaceInThisWorld: I'm kidding. Not a word.

SHARKSWITHRABIES: swear?

MyPlaceInThisWorld: Matthew 5:34-37. ;) This means we can trust each other. Deal?

SHARKSWITHRABIES: yeah tell me your deepest secrets

MyPlaceInThisWorld: I'm scared I'll never be a devoted father like my dad.

SHARKSWITHRABIES: i meant cool secrets about boobs

ANOTHER PARTICULAR SATURDAY

Years earlier, I'd helped Dad install our basement's giraffe-print carpet, which we'd selected because it'd made us laugh.

That basement had always been Eli's room, even during college. But as he'd finally moved out for good, it'd become mine.

"Don't forget," Eli, handing me an old rifle stock, "never aim at something you're not prepared to kill."

The Siena lineage had included Grandpa hunting deer and Dad refurbishing antiques, so I'd heard those safety rules forever.

Focusing hazel eyes on mine, Eli said, "Those with power must protect others. Fire can warm homes or burn them down. Guns can defend children or hurt innocents. Christians can save souls or start wars."

"Cut out that peacenik brainwashing," Mom groaned, appearing downstairs to drop off extra Board Game Moms Night tacos. "It's still Fourth of July week!"

"Wars kill," Eli shrugged. "When people die, most go to Hell. War's unacceptable. Cold, hard math."

Once, fourteen-year-old Eli and six-year-old me had huddled in that basement, watching night-vision Iraq footage. Like playing Missile Command but cheering for the missiles. I'd asked why it was okay to bomb people if "thou shalt not kill." He'd said, "They started it." I'd asked, "Are they going to Hell?" He'd said, "They deserve to."

After Dad died a couple years later, Eli stopped liking war. Seemed unfair. War hadn't killed Dad.

"There's more to church than Hell, Hell, Hell," Mom said in her sour-gorilla Eli voice. "Music! Potlucks! Hugs! We have other callings too, like defending the unborn!"

Crunching a taco, I mumbled, "Do aborted babies go to Hell?" I'd always loved asking Eli questions that forced his literalist brain to crunch Bible verses like code.

"Well," he sighed, like he was sharing a disappointing baseball score, "the Bible says *all* have sinned, which might mean unsaved babies g–"

"Oh for the love, innocent cherubs go to Heaven," Mom shouted, on the way back up to her friends. "You two are so morbid!"

Whenever anyone discussed babies, Eli got weird. Church adults whispered about how he'd been married for three years but somehow hadn't impregnated his wife.

"If aborted babies go to Heaven," I asked him, confident his ruthless logic would lead somewhere delightfully taboo, "wouldn't abortion be good?"

(My cousins had once snitched on me for asking that, so their youth pastor had explained to me "the age of accountability," the idea that people only need salvation once they're old enough. I'd said, "Duh, Romans 9:11 says babies haven't sinned. How many freebie years do we get, though?" He'd said, "The age is different for everyone. Play it safe. Get saved." I'd said, "I am." He'd said, "What's the problem, then?")

In my basement, Eli replied, "Whenever a Christian threatens an abortionist, I think, what if that abortionist sends a thousand souls to Heaven, even if he's sacrificing his own? Technically heroic, if you buy the accountability theory."

Cold, hard math. I pictured a conveyor belt dumping fetus chunks onto golden streets. How to tell Mom I'd vote for abortion-hungry Democrats in order to keep rerouting souls directly to Heaven?

The walls still bore Eli's teenage posters, like Bone Thugs-n-Harmony, Reggie "Minister of Defense" White, and Judge Dredd (but I'd have to trash either the Elvira poster or my eyeballs). His closet was full of Ghost Rider comics, plus books about battling demons for real.

Scooting onto my yellow-and-teal-plaid couch, I heard Mom blaring Rush Limbaugh replays upstairs for her rowdy coworkers. *I can't believe she lets them drink wine. Drinking is the stupidest sin. Drinkers deserve to die in car wrecks before their children become car-wrecking drinkers.*

"By the way," Eli said, reading bodybuilder forums on my computer, "thank you for tone-setting at camp like a man. That confession exercise was ... a little rough. I got yelled at."

"By Timmy?" I asked, puffing my pecs like a man, then deflating pride back out of my flesh.

"No," he scoffed. "Pastor Jack. Guess some parents complained. C'mon, kids got saved! If someone's in a burning building, should I encourage them to leave, or should I shove them out? Jack asked me to convey the reality of Hell without scaring away visitors. Now there's a puzzle. Oh, and he said to be nicer to Catholics. They shouldn't have turned salvation into colonial pyramid schemes, but whatever."

Upstairs, Limbaugh was yelling about global elites. Not the Catholic kind, but the purple-haired kind.

"With your leadership potential, it stinks you're missing football," Eli said. "JV would let you catch up, once your ankle's better."

"Maybe I'll skip this year," I said, realizing practice had started three weeks prior. "Gonna be busy with church friends."

He nodded approvingly. And Mom returned, unloading more tacos.

"It's weird hearing non-Christians talk about global elites," I said. It was also weird that we treated Limbaugh like a pastor even though he'd said the abominable Jesus-was-just-a-wise-philosopher heresy. "Rapture books warn about creeps who control the world's money, and Rush admits it's true."

"End-times crap?" Eli yelled, looking at Mom. "Sounds like Isaac's still reading that Bible Code garbage of yours."

"Well, we're in the last days," she yelped. "Be polite to the tacos lady, or she won't bring you any more!"

He grunted, "We're here to guide people outta Hell, not worry what some pinhead's conspiracy spreadsheet says about Magog's black helicopters. That Antichrist crap made me psycho as a kid."

My brother was so weird that he barely believed in the Rapture. After he went home, Mom rummaged through closet boxes and handed me a book, The New World Order by Pat Robertson. THE NEW YORK TIMES BESTSELLER, it bragged, though I'd always been taught the Times was for pinkos.

"This opened my eyes," she said. "The Left Behind books are timid, compared to what you'll learn from the 700 Club grandpa."

I read. Upstairs, her friends played Trivial Pursuit at max volume. I ate tacos. Of the many Illuminati explanations I'd learned from Christian books since age five, Pat's was the most alarming. Past 3 a.m., I hammered Mountain Dew.

According to Pat, an ages-old messianic cabal has infiltrated militaries, corporations, and governments, crusading to remodel the world despite already having overseen centuries of slavery, war, and pollution.

Fortunately, Pat explained, that cabal will be stopped by Christians.

OH, NOW IT'S SUNDAY

I shambled upstairs into staggering light. Mom was lacing her sneakers for a normal workday, despite Pat's description of baby-harvesting liberals stealing America like never before.

As my bleary eyes battled my caffeine-rattled hands, I read Pat's words to her: "'The blending of the pro-Soviet, monopoly-capital globalism of the Establishment, the Establishment foundations, and the Establishment media — particularly when coupled with secular humanism, radical communism, the human ... s-e-xuality movement, and New Age religion — makes a potent cocktail in America's high schools.' Yikes, that's where I'm going!"

Mom rubbed her temples. "Angel, I wish I could homeschool you. Mothers shouldn't be out there providing. Look at you, shaking from neglect ..."

After Dad died, she'd worried about going broke, but her job as a sonographer meant weird hours, which made her worry about doing too many gender roles. She said, "I hate how lonely I leave this house. If you'd prefer your brother's church this morning, great. And I'll see you tonight," she said with a twinkle, "at our new church home."

THREE
GOTTA CATCH 'EM ALL

FALL 2000

School had always been stressful.

Not the studying part. Relatives had nicknamed me "Sponge" because I easily absorbed information, ignored study time, and got Bs anyway.

Not the social part, either. Invisibility was fine, I insisted.

The stressful part? Inhabiting a secular building.

Attending public school and church youth group meant straddling universes with separate adults, rituals, lore, field trips, homework, sins, and ... final exams.

The gap was so wide that, at middle school, I'd claimed I was dating a cheerleader from church — and vice versa. But one universe's normal behaviors were taboo in the other. (Don't play the Notorious B.I.G. at church or Christian rap at school. Maybe bridge the divide by pointing out the Supertones, the biggest Christian ska band, covered a Metallica riff.)

Turning fourteen, I prepared to enter the ultimate astrology-and-condoms warzone: public high school, where men of God had always warned me I'd either get brainwashed by secularism (and go to Hell) or become such a flagrant Christian that I'd get shot just like Columbine's legendary martyr (and go to Heaven).

Was there a middle option to just be a nice guy? Nice try. That's called being lukewarm (and going to Super Turbo Hell).

So millions of children understood this with all our hearts: ♫ You're nobody 'til somebody kills you. ♫

Facing those options, I spent the last night of summer listening to

"Creeping Death" at full volume, amped to win my entire school district for Christ. Or else. *Now we enter Armageddon.*

(Armageddon means a place of war. Don't be fooled by the Bruce Willis movie, which is about Liv Tyler's belly button vs. Revelation's second trumpet, not about Armageddon. Sometimes title drops are only partly right.)

Day one. I stood by myself, watching the cafeteria's groupings assemble like anthills.

If nobody notices me, nobody can persecute me. Luckily, in my short-sleeved plaid button-up and baggy jeans with hammer loops, I blend in with all the guys and maybe-lesbians. Rush Limbaugh says lesbians are ugly, but I've snuck way too much Xena to agree. **"REGRET!"** *Sorry.*

I felt a shoulder tap. Gabe, the blue-eyed rapping Duke fan from my new church, was apparently also my schoolmate. In a bright orange Sonicflood shirt, he asked where we should sit. *Help! A way-too-obvious Christian! He'll get me shot by people who listen to Tool!*

I tumbled into the nearest open chair. The nerdy kids at that table were laughing about things that included me. Well, I'd been noticed, but at least I'd evaded association with Gabe, though I felt burning **"GUILT"** for sacrificing my brother in Christ to the cafeteria's slings, arrows, and shotgun shells.

"Gnarly walking boot," said the largest nerd, wearing a raincoat indoors.

They were sorting piles of Pokémon cards. *Hey, I know cards! My Shaq rookies will buy Mom a house one day.* Plus, I'd watched the Pokémon cartoon until Mom had banned it for depicting evolution and, even worse, the character Misty's midriff.

"Dank," another nerd commented. "Now we can play two games at once."

And, behold, the third Pokémon nerd, whose powder blue hair and dark brown skin captured my eyeballs so hard that I thought of a quote about Hell from Event Horizon: "Where we're going, we won't need eyes to see."

As Bobbi Birdsong taught me how to play Pokémon, her brown eyes laser-locked me, cracking my brain's code. We debated which planet was the coolest, but she was too Advanced Placement to stick to just our solar system.

When I said the most romantic thing imaginable — "Dank hair" — she asked, "Close enough to Rei Ayanami's?" With no idea what that meant, I said, "Probably." She laughed.

I knew I shouldn't score her AIM handle without knowing where she'd spend eternity, because adults had constantly warned me against dating Hell-bound infidels. *But I want to.* **"LOVE IS DESTRUCTIVE,"** snarled my angelic counselor. **"IDIOT ISAAC, BEING MANIPULATED INTO OBEYING UNSEEN FORCES! DISGUSTING!"**

Wait! I'll make up for this! After I convert this table, I'll ride the momentum. One conversion per day. Easy! Be bold, persuasive, and charming. By next summer, I'll have led my whole freshman class to Christ. That's enough, right?

At church, sons of honchos hogged the seats around Josiah. I sat on their perimeter beside Gabe, apologizing for "accidentally" dissing him in the cafeteria.

"Ain't no thang," he said, fixing his ice-blue eyes onto various girls, who smiled back, proving he was a pervert. "Ay, your mom seems nice. Where's your dad?"

So difficult to avoid being asked that. "Died when I was eight."

"My b, that huffs dong. At least he's in Heaven. What happened?"

Whenever I revealed details, church people lost confidence in Dad's afterlife whereabouts, so I always changed the subject. "You know Pokémon Bobbi at school? Her butt's so cool, honeymoon-wise."

Gabe did a double-take and ranted about the ancient kingdom of Israel collapsing because King Solomon had touched non-Christian butts.

Ugh, this handsome idiot's right. **"TOLD YOU,"** my God-voice boasted. *Well, love doesn't give up that easily.*

"I have a question," whimpered Bobbi in a Pokémon Misty costume. "But only a man of God could answer it!"

"Woman, I'll explain theology to you," I thundered, voice not cracking. "Ask!"

"Well … once I'm your helpful housewife, will Father God let you touch my butt?"

"Yes, once Father God crowns me as your steward!"

"Oh, I surrender all!"

[Romance set to Santana guitar solos.]

What a bizarre dream. Santana?

During lunch, I almost told Bobbi to get saved, but she persecuted me by describing something as happening "eons ago," as if there had ever been that many years. **"COWARD, THAT'S ANOTHER GOSPEL-SHAME NAIL THROUGH JESUS' WRIST BONES. YOU'LL REGRET THIS IN FIERY TORMENT FOR ... YEP ... EONS!"**

A week later, seeking an explanation for daily being martyred by a 105-pound anime nerd, I asked my history teacher, "Is the New World Order real?"

"Hulk Hogan's gang?" replied Coach, flexing in his skintight polo. "What-cha gonna dooo, brrrotherrr!"

"No, like, public schools helping the one-world government. Pat Robertson sai–"

"No X-Files for me, brrrotherrr," said Coach, a brainwasher. Some kid called me a "conspiracy buttlord," oppressing me even further.

You ever feel like a misfit, but worry you're not a big enough misfit to save the universe, because the only people who fit sufficiently poorly are those who get garroted by agnostics, so you wanna stop being a misfit, even though that'd make you the buttlord who got all your history classmates damned forever? Well, do you?

"I love this imperfect world," Pastor Jack rasp-boomed throughout the half-full sanctuary. Stocky in a plain blue suit and backed by a blue-flowers screensaver on the HumbleTron, he extolled lovable creations like clever chameleons and dozing bears.

The gentle Casio keyboard signaled it was almost time for the altar call.

"But I don't belong to this world of doubt, promiscuity, drunkenness, rebellion, and single-parent homes," he said, making me hang my head, ashamed to lack male role models. (Fortunately, that was Pastor Jack's role.)

"Jesus prepares a better place for us," he said. Unlike some preachers, he didn't promise Heaven would feature endless buffets and everyone becoming able to dunk like Michael Jordan. "That's speculation. The only guarantee is eternally joyous community."

From the youth group's back corner, I watched Sophie's hands translating her uncle's sermon, her red hair braided like a crown.

"Our earthly lives are answers to one question," Jack rasped. "Do we let this world coax us into eternal tragedy? Or do we disciple each other, so we may disciple the world?"

In church-mouse mode, Sophie was certainly pretty, but whenever we played Sunday afternoon softball, her aggressive base-running made me want to cheat on Bobbi before I could even disciple Bobbi into marriage material.

"Who's desperate to fill a void?" Jack preached, holding his big hands out wide. "The folks outside these walls, chasing money, power, women, and toys? From personal experience, that life's dreadfully lonely, a temporal sample of Hell. I've never felt the lick of everlasting flame, yet I've sensed what Hell is. Father God, Hell is a world without you!"

Jack's preaching included hints of semi-forbidden concepts about Hell being a stubborn separation from love rather than a literal prison for the undead. Still, he never denied envisioning an inferno of pitchfork-wielding demons, the image that consumed my mind every night.

"On the contrary, who's sampling the joys of Heaven?" he continued. "Within these walls, we are, by the grace of Father God. And all God's men said ..."

As people murmured, "Amen," I nodded, agreeing that we were the happiest. Being the happiest helped recruit converts! The only problem: I sucked at being happy.

"But attending on Sundays doesn't make you a Christian any more than standing in a barn makes you a cow," preached Jack. "If you're ready to finally belong, won't you walk?"

The choir cooed beneath his bellows, and congregants slowly sang along. I hobbled up the outer aisle in a herd of remorseful teens, who merged on our knees with Marriage Ministry members (adults) and Singles Ministry members (adults who'd graduated high school four months prior).

"The Lord's still drawing you near, so we're gonna sing one more verse," rasp-thundered the voice above me. "Brothers and sisters, in this world, we're exiles."

I'm sorry, God, for several things and everything. Gimme a new chance, which requires me to believe certain things are so true that it'll let Jesus change me into someone he prefers. Or however you'd rather me word that these days. Amen.

"We're called to love a world that's allergic to love. To become misfits."

Kneelers held hands as everyone blanketed us by singing, "I surrender all, all to thee." Sophie followed her uncle, comforting kneelers until she sniffled in his arms. I felt ashamed to have added to their burden. I pressed my face into worn-down carpet, wishing for visions or voices, anything that'd verify God was aware of my rededication.

And the father of my flock, strong hand gripping my shoulder, preached, "In my house, there are no misfits."

There! That's the receipt! Now spread this at school. Stop hiding your light! Invite at least one classmate to church per week. Sure, the rest are Hell-bound, but something's better than nothing. Right?

Since 1990, Christian students nationwide have participated in an annual early-morning event called See You at the Pole. At public schools, renegades gather to defy the one-world government by doing liberal-banned school prayer around flagpoles.

I remember my fifth-grade book report on Foxe's Book of Martyrs, a gory Renaissance history later modernized by DC Talk. It celebrated first-century Christians being de-brained, thrown into kilns, and bagged among scorpions. *What an inspiring reminder to proclaim our beliefs so loudly that we get drawn and quartered! It's so hard to give your life, though. Even seventeen-year-old Eli failed that test.*

Standing at the flagpole, I prayed another regular prayer: *Dear Jesus, please help me share so much hope that some beardy cultist jabs a semi-automatic rifle into my chest. I'll avoid Hell if I get dismembered by pacifists, incinerated by environmentalists, or de-eyeballed by my own knife, right?*

Longing to be strangled by lesbians, I loudly recited Psalm 24 beside my school's deeply anti-Christian HOME OF THE CRUSADERS: STATE CHAMPS '89 sign. Dozens of classmates were "praying," wearing Five Iron Frenzy shirts, and inviting me to Fellowship of Christian Athletes meetings. Either they were CIA informants, or ... my school wasn't actually controlled by a Jesus-hating government. *Hmm.* **"YOU CAN'T SECOND-GUESS YOUR ELDERS' WARNINGS! YOU'LL REGRET THIS!"** *Sorry. CIA, definitely.*

I gritted my teeth, determined to invite the whole cafeteria to church.

I'll get thrown into a CIA kiln. Too MFing bad! Otherwise, Bobbi will get killed by five Oakley-wearing atheists with SKS rifles, then spend eternity in the kiln that never stops doing whatever kilns do!

In fired-up desperation, I boldly unzipped the hoodie covering my old DC Talk shirt that said "freak" in grunge font, meant to boldly imply

"Jesus freak" without having to say so. Unfortunately for souls awaiting the gospel, my shirt just made people think I liked Korn. (I did. *Sorry.*)

Labor Day. By then, Dad might've been burning for six years, eight months, and 18 days, and I'd never done a single thing to keep anyone from joining him.

Hassling Eli, I quoted firearm safety advice from OutKast's "B.O.B." and said, "You wouldn't know that song, buttlord. You're old."

"Boy, I introduced you to rap in the first place," he chuckled. He hadn't always been a lion-bearded zealot. The person who'd taught me the wonders of explicit lyrics, he'd once lost a Doom II bet with his friends and gone streaking, before he'd gotten scared straight.

Maybe that's what I need.

It's been a month, and I haven't ignited a single global revival. If I'm such a crappy Christian that I go this whole semester without leading any classmates to eternal life, I don't deserve my temporary life.

FOUR

BE MY ESCAPE

HOLY-WEEN 2000

"THE DAY YOU WERE HANDED THIS BOOK, YOU GAINED THE ANSWERS TO ALL OF life's questions," the man said, waving a leather-bound KJV (the Bible for gray-haired preachers). "B.I.B.L.E., basic instructions before leaving Earth, okay?"

He had a soul patch, so it felt uncool to remember whether his name was Dave or Tony.

Dave-Tony was youth pastor Timmy's boss (or whatever), a mid-forties former pastor from a big, faraway church. Pastor Jack preferred him over Timmy, according to intel gathered at Josiah's birthday party, which had mostly been attended by the Dynasty, the nickname for children of deacons, directors, and denomination hotshots. Some, like Josiah, had never seen PG-13 movies. Others enjoyed being overheard ranking cigarette brands.

At Dave-Tony's Bible study, kids brought paint-splattered NIVs (for teenage preachers), watered-down Message Bibles (for middle-school preachers), and pleather-bound NKJVs (for slightly cool adult preachers).

My black Amplified Bible, handed down from Eli, suggested every verse could mean multiple things (for wishy-washy fence-sitters).

Dave-Tony only banned the NRSV (for man-hating feminazis), which used the ridiculous term "children of God" instead of the obviously correct "sons of God." Coincidentally, Dave-Tony's group was almost entirely boys.

That evening, we began studying the apostle Paul's letter to the Romans, often considered a foundational explanation of Christianity.

We took turns reading verses. I had verse 13, about the importance of converting Gentiles. (Sore subject.) Another lap, and I had verse 26: "God gave them over to degrading and vile passions; for their women exchanged the natural function for [that which is unnatural / a function contrary to nature]."

I missed something. Lesbians are foundational to Christianity? Man, I wish! **"YOU'LL REGRET THAT."** *What? It's two girls. Multiple, dawg.* **"STOP ADVANCING THE GAY AGENDA."** *But Paul said God allowed it.* **"NO. GOD HARDENED PHARAOH'S HEART INTO SINNING, REMEMBER?"** *You sound like the Calvinists beside the Pizza Hut.* **"IT WAS THE PLAN."** *Lesbians are the plan? Approved!* **"YOU'LL REGRET THAT!"**

Focus, Isaac. Reread this chapter I've read a hundred times. Where's the concrete eureka that'll correct my soul at last?

"This chapter says people with reptile idols should get murdered," chuckled some kid. "Should I throw out my old Ninja Turtles?" His knucklehead friend found that hilarious.

Dave-Tony sighed, "An idol is anything that replaces God's truth, okay? Secular MP3s, environmentalisticness, dope, unsaved girlfriends ..."

To atone for my lesbian agenda, I emphasized that women only date men, saying, "Unsaved boyfriends, too, right?"

"Why, you visiting San Francisco?" said Dave-Tony. Everyone laughed like I'd farted. I grimaced. He chuckled, "No unsaved boyfriends, right, Miss Sophia?"

Sophie nodded, shrank as eleven males grinned, and clutched her flowery Girl Bible (for non-preachers).

As another knucklehead blurted something else, Dave-Tony looked annoyed by all of life's questions. *Why are we dicking around? We'd never give Timmy crap like this. We'd be terrified to goof off around Eli.*

"It's simple, folks," Dave-Tony huffed, about to explode. "Christians are different from the world. Eat, sleep, dress, and live differentaneously, ok? Become men of God and Proverbs 31 women," he said, referencing the chapter usually described as if it encourages women to be subservient housewives.

Sophie cleared her squeaky throat. "Eat different? In Acts, God said all food's okay, even Chick-fil-A sandwiches that hurt very nice birds who were filled with the breath of the Spirit in Genesis 1, so maybe secular love songs aren't ba–"

"Stop justifying garbage," Dave-Tony barked, making my lip curl.

"Paul said sinners 'worshipped and served the creature more than the Creator.' Now, a love song about a human, is that about a Creator?"

"Maybe both," said Sophie, biting her fingernails. "Like, there's this K-Ci & JoJo son–"

"Dangerous thinking," Dave-Tony growled. "Slippery slope from Amy Grant to 'Murder Was the Case' to cross-dresser movies."

"I just think maybe it's not the worst thing," the pastor's niece said, summoning mana, "if people love people. Like, any people."

All eyes snapped toward the blushing girl staking her vague claim. Per stereotype logic, the oddball tomboy was admitting to liking girls, but I'd seen her gazing at older boys (not that I was insanely jealous).

All eyes snapped to Dave-Tony's face, a cartoon steam whistle about to explode.

"It's time to go," said Josiah, clapping his Bible shut loudly enough to jolt Dave-Tony's attention. "Our movie's starting soon."

We grabbed Holy-ween costumes from our backpacks, then crossed the lawn toward the Hell house, our haunted house meant to scare visitors toward salvation. (Holy-ween was similar to Halloween, except we depicted the Devil as being VERY EVIL, rather than merely very evil.)

"He got flustered," Josiah told his cousin, "but if your folks knew somebody's been sneaking you secular CDs, they'd make you find pants that fit."

I thought Sophie's tights fit stupendously, completing her butterfly costume, but apologized to the Almighty for thinking so, making sure to threaten myself with self-lobotomy.

They both said, "Love you, technically." She plopped onto a rock near the woods, and he was called toward the lawn's big projector screen.

I sat beside the unhappy butterfly, trying to make her laugh.

But she sniffed, "Sorry. I shouldn't have defied a leader guy. I'll never do that again." Beneath her headband's antennas, her red pigtail buns looked perfectly messy. "And I shouldn't make Josiah stick up for me. When Uncle Jack became pastor here, elders told Josiah to change the world someday. Simba's gotta hold everybody accountable, including me."

Confused by her over-the-top guilt, I said, "Your wings are cool."

Perking up and flapping them by pumping her arms, she said, "I'm a butterfly ... on Noah's ark!" (Holy-ween costumes must be biblical.) She'd never been allowed to trick-or-treat, so I handed her a pebble. "Rock candy." She pretended to bite it and asked about my cardboard sword. Israelite sword-guy costume.

"Don't the grownups know what *ween* means?" I asked.

She finally laughed. *Whoa, she knows what penises are? Me saying "ween" probably made her imagine them lustfully. I'm sorry, Lord of Hosts.*

Across the lawn, little King Davids played soccer vs. bird-winged angels. But seniors loitered around the Hell house in Gladiator and Toy Story cowgirl costumes. *How do they always know which rules they can ignore?*

"Anyway," Sophie said, sitting criss-cross. "Everybody knows my family, but what about yours?"

Uh-oh. I broke out my "Mom isn't Greek enough for her wacky Greek parents" jokes, which usually bailed me out of having to say anything else.

But persistent Sophie said, "And ... you don't have to talk about ...?"

For months, I'd dodged that question, but her voice was a brook across smooth stones. I reached into my moneyless wallet and handed her a photo of eight-year-old me building a model airplane with a tattooed guy in a purple Randy Savage tank top.

"You have his friendly eyes," she said, tensing her bold eyebrows.

I cleared my throat. "He was an airplane mechanic, which seemed pretty cool."

She nodded. Her eyebrows asked me to trust her.

"He drove drunk, one time. Christmas party, 1993." She caught her breath and touched my wrist, even though he'd died dirty. "He'd said some really sad stuff before then, so people think he might've hit the tree on purpose," I whispered, the part I'd never said out loud. One grownup had preached about the Columbine shooters' worst sin being suicide, because they could have atoned for everything else.

Sophie gave me a pinkie swear without specifying what she was promising. I waited for her to say the thing super-churchy people had always said, upon hearing my details: that his death should motivate me to evangelize [so nobody joins him in Hell, where he'll be forever, deservedly].

But Sophie bowed her head, antennas and all, nesting her fingers around the photo. A water drop struck her knuckles. Something old rustled within me as another tear fell from her face. Something begged to be unearthed. *Shake it off, Isaac.*

"I've never lost anyone," she said. "My heart can't imagine ..."

Cramming myself into myself, I returned her unspoken pinkie swear, wordlessly vowing: *I'll never let anyone silence you ever again.* She lifted my photo, delicate like a communion wafer, and asked, "What was he telling you?"

"I messed that plane up," I laughed. "I worried he'd get sad, but he just got glue thinner. He was like, 'Anything that can be built can be rebuilt better.'"

"That's beautiful," she said, her sharp chin trembling.

She turned the photo over. I flinched, but let her see what he'd written: "To my lil engineer: keep learning rules (so you know which ones are bullshit)!!!" Cussing? Encouraging disobedience? More evidence he was fallen.

We took turns pointing out shapes in the golden sky's purple-pink clouds, but her gray eyes kept checking my face. Smoothly, my social skills changed the subject. "Do homeschoolers have non-church friends?"

She blinked. Whoops. She grinned. Phew. "Nobody ever asks! People assume we're hermit freaks. I have neighbors, math group, field trips …"

"The Homeschool Illuminati."

"Shh, don't tell," she whispered, pretend-sinister. Those sunset-silver eyes made me feel like I'd tricked her into being too beautiful. *I could lie on my back and let my six-inch knife fall straight down like pinkeye drops. If it plunged through my brain like a bullet through Jell-O, I'd never again pollute such a perfect creation.*

"And I ran homeschool cross-country for two years," she continued. "I miss it."

Loneliest thing I'd ever heard, which was saying something.

We talked about a goofy Christian punk song, Relient K's "Marilyn Manson Ate My Girlfriend." When I pointed at a cloud shaped like Batman, she gasped, "A seraphim." I felt like Neo, baffled by Morpheus' grasp of things unseen.

"Wanna play?" I said, nodding toward a group of kids playing soccer.

"Aww, I gotta help with Heck House," she said, side-hugging me. "But … you have a friend. Me, I mean. Though you must have plenty already."

Smelling sunshine on her forehead, I said, "This sky is ours, foxy."

This what is what, who? I'd meant to say she looked/smelled as mysterious as the sky, that God had established the same heavens for her as for Dave-Tony, or whatever. *Since when do I call her the word that means "sexy" when old people say it? I suck at this!*

I blushed so hard it hurt, her face turned fuchsia, and I stammered, "Foxes have red hair, you see."

Framed by purple-gold clouds, she giggled, "You too, mister," which almost made sense.

Butterfly wings bounced away. *Scored her AIM handle! Almost held her hand, thanks to my tragic backstory! Imagine a wretch like me marrying the pastor's niece, Aladdin-and-Jasmine-style, and/or marrying Bobbi, Halle Berry, and/or Sara Beth!*

The movie on the big projector was Left Behind, whose Antichrist was less convincing than the book version's. Still, it was one of the most impactful Rapture movies I'd ever watched while sitting outdoors.

Everyone applauded actor Kirk Cameron's post-credits message about making our secular friends see his movie once it hit theaters, forcing liberal Hollywood to keep paying him to make Christian movies.

I should've asked why she quit cross-country. I should've walked her to the Hell house. I shouldn't have revealed my fatherless broken home, the kind of non-nuclear family Church Dynasty kids are warned about. Errors like that are how you get left behind.

FIVE
THE WAR ON CHRISTMAS
CHRISTMAS 2000

Church Dynasty kids always got big pageant roles. As a deacon's daughter, Sara Beth played Mary, permissible because Josiah claimed they'd never passed first base. By that standard, my socks weren't qualified to play Mary.

"I got dragged onto stage as Mary in eighth grade," Mom said, doing a clasped-hands pose. "Little too meek and mild for me. The donkey had more lines! Heehaw!"

Josiah was playing a lanky Apostle Paul, spreading the gospel as a fugitive. (Our Christmas pageants told the entire New Testament story, in case any attendees died unsaved before the Easter pageant.) During his speech from First Corinthians, he impersonated his dad, gazing pensively at middle distance.

Sophie's Intolerant Liberal Professor villain had one line: "Happy holidays, you born-again bigot." Ricardo, volunteer drama minister, told her to ham it up. When I suggested she channel Ursula the sea witch, she sneered so hard, my socks trembled. I felt glad that her fake purple hair, fake nose ring, and real butt were on my anti-Christmas side. **"YOU WILL OBVIOUSLY REGRET ALL THIS!"**

Nope! I'm method acting!

Playing the sergeant of a demon squad trying to abort Jesus, I commanded six rectangle-shaped eighth-graders, each named Caleb. Quite an org chart for our forty seconds of stage time, but Ricardo envisioned attendees loving "campy" scenes that poked fun at conservative reputations. (I don't think the subtext registered.)

We even had our own herald, a pretty freshman named Paisley Grace — who greatly preferred her nickname: "PG," like "peachy." Church women always asked her how grateful she was to have been missionary-adopted from India as a baby. The youth group's best singer (*and Sophie's secular music source, but don't tell anybody*), she had emo-angled hair and theater-kid exuberance. I was, of course, in love with her, but so were my Calebs, so I chose — mercifully, IMO — not to compete against them.

I noticed a pleasant light-to-dark skin tone array among my Calebs, though as a demon, I preferred racial disharmony. Some of them played sports, some played instruments, one ceaselessly beatboxed, and all six were SpongeBob addicts. During pre-pageant music, they applied each other's demon-goth guyliner while guffawing, "Dude, kiss me."

"How come we play 'Rockin' Around the Christmas Tree'?'" asked one as we admired PG's main rehearsal, a secular medley. "It's got cussing."

"No it doesn't, numbnuts," said another.

"Yes it does, crackwhore," said the accuser. "PG says f-asterisk-c-k-ing pie. She's so hot."

"*Pumpkin* pie, gaywad," said the advocate. "I said she's hot first."

"Privates," I uttered with grim gravitas, "dissension aids the Heavenly enemy."

"Here it comes," yelped a Caleb as they leaned toward the stage to listen.

Then, half of them, believing they'd heard PG sing something naughty, quivered with adoration. The others blinked, refusing to believe that their future wife had sinned. All six looked at me for a verdict. Months earlier, I'd been Josiah's newbie tagalong. One semester later, I was proudly in charge of wrangling block-headed oblongs.

"She said pumpkin," I rumbled, "but it does sound like the fudge-word. Everyone said she's hot at the same time."

"Well, we should avoid the appearance of evil by not playing secular music," protested a Caleb.

"Appearing evil is our job, dorkhole," I thundered, voice barely cracking. "But, uh, remember the despicable Peter's vision in the appalling Book of Acts? God made everything clean. That includes Christmas music."

"All Christmas music?" asked a Caleb. "What about 'All I Want for Christmas is You'? The video, dancing in the slutty dress? That's bad!"

"I whacked it to that yesterday," shouted the beatboxer, "and hated myself. Then, the one with her evil twin in the theat–"

"Yes, 'All I Want for Christmas is You' is Christian music," I interrupted. "Who's the only thing Christians should wan–"

"Jesus," the Sunday school veterans replied.

"Do another, Sarge," laughed one. "'Frosty the Snowman.'"

I thought for a second. "Frosty was molded from nature. That's an Adam reference. 'He'll be back!' This song's about the second coming! Boys, *any* song can be godly."

Wait. I, Isaac Siena, Jr., almost believe this thing being said by my character. Well, God made the notes, writers, and singers, right? **"FOR ALL ETERNITY, YOU'LL REGRET EXPOSING CHILDREN TO SECULAR INDOCTRINATION!"** *Man, I'm a demon, but you're the Grinch.* **"ENOUGH!"** *Sorry.*

The irritating Caleb said, "It's still bad when Christians make secular music, though. You know …"

Oh, not this again.

"… my dad said Amy Grant's going to Hell for being lukewarm," he squeaked, referring to the chart-topping Christian singer who'd written love songs without Jesus words. Christian stores often banned her.

As other Calebs condemned her for "wiping her butt crack with the institution of marriage," I wondered: *Why do we treat her and the Sixpence None the Richer lady like traitors for singing mostly Jesus songs, but cheer whenever a secular country man sings one? Is that … s-e-xism?* **"REGRET!"** *Sorry.*

"Amy Grant's not worthy of Hell," I growled, seeking to calm the Calebs. "For too long has she prais–"

A heavy palm thumped upon my shoulder, and I stared up into the Darth Maul contacts of a mighty senior demon.

"Amy Grant's going to Hell," grunted the 18-year-old, "because she said premarital s-e-x isn't always life-ruining. Third Day's message board said so. So stop slobbering on her lukewarmness. Jesus said it's better to have a millstone around your neck than to lead your younger brothers astray."

---

g00dbyeskyharb0r (PG): every song's redeemable?? (╭ʘ_⊙)

SHARKSWITHRABIES: ¯\(°_o)/¯

g00dbyeskyharb0r: wut about ♫ TOO CLOSE ♫, the bonerz song

SHARKSWITHRABIES: it'z about avoidin bonerz by leavin space 4 Jesus

g00dbyeskyharb0r: lmfbo wut about ♫ BCUZ I GOT HIGH ♫

SHARKSWITHRABIES: adam + eve blazin stickyicky b4 original sin happend

g00dbyeskyharb0r: kk wut about ♫ SYMPATHY 4 THE DEVIL ♫ ᕙ(˵Ó﹏Ò ₎)ᕗ

(Yes, demons are allowed to type about "bonerz.")

I investigated. LimeWire claimed "Sympathy for the Devil" was by either Led Zeppelin or Joan Osborne. Regardless, I was disgusted to discover its title wasn't a joke.

SHARKSWITHRABIES: nebbermind, we cant redeem literally EVERYTHING

g00dbyeskyharb0r: yr brother said we deserve hell as much as satan!! do u think so??

SHARKSWITHRABIES: ya

g00dbyeskyharb0r: do u think melody grace is purty???? (๑σ ₃ σ) ♥

SHARKSWITHRABIES: ya

g00dbyeskyharb0r: nu metal is so played out!! !!!!

SHARKSWITHRABIES: ya

g00dbyeskyharb0r: shud i dye mah hair neon green????? ($_$)

SHARKSWITHRABIES: ya

g00dbyeskyharb0r: if we can b saved, can satan???

SHARKSWITHRABIES: lol

SIX
FEAR IS WHAT KEEPS US HERE
NEW YEAR'S 2001

I'D ALWAYS BEEN TERRIFIED OF THE RAPTURE, THE EVER-LOOMING MOMENT when Jesus would teleport authentic Christians away, letting the Antichrist enslave everyone else.

Church people always told me to eagerly anticipate our exit. So even before 1995, when the Left Behind novels finished mainstreaming the Rapture, I'd consumed Christian media that predicted my childhood would include the apocalypse.

I was driven by one question: *Will I make the cut?* Thanks to Rapture movie tropes, whenever I saw a pile of Mom's clothes around the house, I worried she'd abandoned me to Hell on Earth. (Even scarier scenario: If I *did* get raptured to Heaven, I'd be stuck with my virginity forever.)

Some Rapture prophets picked specific years, often 2000. So when that year only had thirty seconds left to prove them right, I pressed play on Pennywise's "30 Seconds 'Till the End of the World." If Christians were correct about 2000, the Rapture would happen during that song. But our crappy internet buffered, so the MP3 never finished.

"Of course a secular song failed," chortled Josiah, seconds into 2001.

"For all you know, it's a Christian punk band."

"Oxymoron," said the pastor's son, though I'd played him examples of not just Christian punk, but Christian death metal like Living Sacrifice. Josiah was clueless about *any* pop culture, even the Evangelical kind. (Meanwhile, youth ministers like Timmy approved of loud Tooth & Nail

Records music, recommending we replace Blink-182 with MxPx's older albums, the ones full of God lyrics.)

I trusted Timmy, especially because I was suddenly running low on trustworthy grownups.

Since the famous Christians who sold zillions of books about the year-2000 Rapture are officially incorrect, what else are famous Christians incorrect abou– **"STOP QUESTIONING MY WISE MEN, OR YOU'LL REGRET IT AS MILLION-POUND DEMONS PUKE SCABBY GUTLOADS OF HOT PUSS DOWN YOUR THROAT 24/7/365 FOREVER, YOU CRUEL LITTLE FREAK!"** *Sorry. You know, it'd be a lot easier if I could just force myself to never doubt. Hey, why is belief the most important thing, anyw–* **"STOP QUESTIONING!"** *Sorry.*

In my basement room, Josiah and I returned to my enormous yellow-and-teal couch. I'd built wooden displays for Eli's old rap stuff, like his Gravediggaz posters and Geto Boys autographs, from before he'd chosen Christian college. I'd hidden my Bill and Ted's Bogus Journey, Bedazzled, Spawn, and Devil's Advocate posters behind sports stuff once Mom complained. (Not because I'd fixated on Satan movies, but "because of Hollywood's agendas." Yeah Mom, red-leather Elizabeth Hurley was turning me gay.)

While she was working overnight, she let me invite my Men's Accountability Huddle (our name changed frequently) to a New Year's sleepover, but only Josiah showed. He brought the only secular culture of which he approved: a college football video game and a Monday Night Raw tape — minus the match between underwear women. (I preferred Madden and hadn't watched much wrestling since Dad's passing. He'd told me, "Dusty Rhodes is the baddest motherfucker because he fights for the little guy. Don't say motherfucker.")

"The Undertaker's a hero even though he killed his brother or whatever?" I asked Josiah, surprised to learn the devilish character had become a biker. "How do wrestlers decide who's the bad guy?"

"They don't care who gets cheered, just that butts are in seats," he said, glancing at his pager. "Hmm, I sent my folks a 'happy New Year,' but no response."

"Musta got raptured."

"We'd be gone, too," he laughed.

A half-hour passed. Dark talons descended into my mind. "You sure we'd be gone too?"

"Of course. All born-again Christians leave."

"Like, how sure?"

Josiah glared at me. "This sounds like doubt. Nip it in the bud."

Within an hour, we were partly pretending we weren't afraid we'd missed the Rapture, partly planning our end-times survivalist strategy.

Eventually, in a goofy 3 a.m. panic, we hurried to my front porch. I pointed at college dudes in a snowy driveway, proof that the Rapture hadn't happened. They were howling in drunk laughter, lighting a Roman candle clenched between naked butt cheeks, Jackass-style.

"Oh, like those guys would be raptured," Josiah scoffed. "Jesus was like, 'Nope, don't need anybody from that neighborhood.' Golly, maybe we missed the Rapture *because* we were scared to miss it. The power of doubt. See?"

My doubt's so strong, it contaminated the pastor's son. Soon we'll be guillotined by Al Gore, the Demon-crap Party election-denier settling for the job of Antichrist. This sucks!

We went downstairs to check AIM, because seeing church kids online would prove the Rapture hadn't happened. We clicked through away messages, hunting clues within passive-aggressive song quotes — as if PG posting AFI lyrics with / | \(;..;)/ | \ emoticons was apocalyptic code.

I was legitimately freaked out to realize the stoic Josiah couldn't hide his worry about the Tribulation, the forewarned seven years of post-Rapture carnage. We competed to laugh the hardest, thereby proving our lack of fear.

By 4 a.m., we'd gathered peanut M&Ms, Mom's Glock, and Doritos in my basement tent, with the TV blaring CNN in case the Rapture was so obvious, even liberals had to acknowledge it.

We were studying crucial information, including The Late Great Planet Earth, the 1970s' best-selling "non-fiction" book, whose film version was narrated by Transformers actor Orson Welles. Millions believed the book had decoded Revelation's warnings about thermonuclear Illuminati harlots. *S-e-xy!* **"REGRET."** *Sorry.*

"Like we were warned, everyone's gotta join the Antichrist's mystery religion or be tortured," Josiah concluded, tossing it aside. "If we join, we'll go to Hell within seven years. Duh."

Re-skimming other Rapture books we'd read years prior, we compared predictions about China invading the Mediterranean, pools of blood hundreds of miles long, and "Western Europe, the United States, Canada,

South America, and Australia" fighting for the Antichrist in the Middle East. Having mastered geopolitics and depleted our Mountain Dew, we rolled into our sleeping bags.

I semi-confessed, "I always prayed the Rapture wouldn't happen until after I had s– … some fun on a road trip. Well, that proved I was too selfish for Heaven, apparently."

"Tomorrow, we start working to rejoin God's team," he said, rolling away.

"Sara Beth's raptured," I said, nestling toward him. "You're single now. We're apocalypse husbands, amigo."

"Not Satan's team," he snorted, too devout to pretend-flirt like a normal sleepover person. "Actually, she's breaking up with me anyway."

Whoa! How nonchalant! She's back in my league!

"She's sweet, lifelong friend, all that," he yawned. "But we realized the pastor's son marrying a deacon's daughter was cutesy stuff, masterminded by our moms. Also, she wants kids by the time she's twenty. Not it! Also, she's raptured."

Oh right, that's why she's outta my league.

As he pretended not to be heartbroken, I pretended to snore, but felt dark talons descending again. By then, I was 51% afraid the Rapture had happened, but 49% afraid of something worse: *I kinda doubt it ever will.*

We braved a late-morning bike ride through snow and Tribulation. Josiah pulled his house key from a porch rock because his dog, likewise left behind, needed to poop. Josiah's house, slightly bigger than mine, had an old chandelier we could trade for ammo.

Despite the Rapture, we'd passed normal traffic along the way — which proved I'd always been surrounded by heathens, you see. But someone with Mom's code paged me good morning. On Josiah's TV, the South Carolina Gamecocks were playing the Ohio State Buckeyes in a stadium with 60,000 un-raptured fans, and coaching the Gamecocks was a Christian named Lou Holtz. Therefore …

"Nobody got raptured, duh," I said, sneaking leftover casserole to Bundles, Josiah's chunky bulldog. "College football sucks. You're so old-fashioned. Hey, the Cocks scored. Cocks!"

South Carolina led, 3-0.

"You were scared," Josiah grinned, crunching Doritos. "Gamecocks."

"I felt sorry for how scared you were, so I pretended. Cocks."

"We were 5% scared," we agreed, doing our handshake.

South Carolina led at halftime.

"Russians know they're in Rapture books, right?" I asked. "If Russia only invaded Israel as a haha-we're-doing-Rapture-stuff prank, would it still trigger the Rapture?"

"Somebody said it'll happen once everyone on earth has heard the gospel. So, could you prevent the Rapture by locking one person in a soundproof room?"

The Rapture was starting to sound ridiculous. **"REGRET!"** *Sorry.*

"Man, if we were raptured, we'd realize it way faster than people do in Rapture movies," I said. "Like in every zombie movie, nobody's seen any zombie movies, you know? Cocks."

"Gamecocks. I haven't seen any zombie movies."

South Carolina led, 10-7. We heard the garage door, a car pulling in, and Bundles barking. We clenched our fists, expecting secret police.

Oh, Josiah's dad, home for lunch. The Rapture definitely hadn't happened. Yet.

"You fellas planning a heist?" said Pastor Jack, salt-and-pepper hair ungelled as he surveyed the Levant maps littering his coffee table. I shook my pastor's hand with impressive firmness.

Hugging his dad, Josiah said, "We were studying Rapture stuff, just for fun, and w–"

"Hmm, come with me," said Pastor Jack, nodding us toward his upstairs study. His broad desk was surrounded by floor-to-ceiling shelves packed with books, framed diplomas, and Formula One memorabilia. He rummaged, muttering about somebody disorganizing his stuff.

"Oh, I bet Sophie was in here," he chuckled. "She mixes stuff up to prank her uncle. Not like a teenage girl reads this dense material."

Apparently unaware Sophie's homeschool-bookworm powers had conquered even The Silmarillion, he handed us scholarly Revelation books, ones without explosions on their covers. :(

"Before studying prophecy, know this," he said, pointing. "As Christ instructed, we shouldn't scrutinize global squabbles for clues about his return. Remember how many predicted it in Y2K, 1999, '94, '88, the 1930s, 1844 ..."

"Pat Robertson predicted 1982, but he was wrong," I said, hoping to impress one father figure by betraying another.

Jack nodded. *Success! Sorry.*

"But you preach Antichrist stuff," Josiah said.

"Well, we must apply scripture to the present," our pastor said, tilting his head back and forth. "But to challenge America's anti-Christian forces isn't to presume a supervillain called *the* Antichrist is ascendant. Besides ... okay, want something too off-topic for the pulpit?"

Arcane secrets!

"Loudmouths claim the books of Daniel and Revelation are specific warnings against today's European Union. Well, earlier Christians said that about Muslims, popes, Lutherans, Ottomans, Napoleon, Gorbachev ... How'd that go? You fellas scared of Ottomans?"

"I'm, like, half-Greek," I said, proud to have intimidated whoever.

Jack even claimed 666 was probably a reference to a long-dead Roman emperor, not some futuristic global dictator. Our confused expressions delighted him. *The biblical Antichrist isn't an inbound Lex Luthor? Jack's testing whether academic crap can deceive us, right?* **"REMEMBER EVERY RAPTURE MOVIE DEPICTING A PASTOR WHO REGRETS BEING A DOUBTFUL SMARTASS?"** *Right.* **"I'M SO PROUD OF YOU!"**

On the stairs, Jack pointed at our coffee table mess. "Anyway, I just hoped you boys weren't worried about this stuff."

We hadn't told him how scared we'd been twelve hours earlier, but he cared so much about resolving our dread that he'd denounced half the Christian bookstore.

Unworthy of the heresy, I chased that huggy feeling anyway, asking to see his Charger, as a fellow car guy. He brightened again, led us past his daily-driver Taurus, and showed me around his semi-restored 1970 Dodge.

"Fear's not always bad," my pastor said, his gray eyes on me. "If a rifle's pointed at your heart, fear could save your life. Do whatever that gunman says! Other than denying your beliefs, of course."

He turned to Josiah and said, "I work seven days a week because of fear. Every Sunday morning, I'm terrified I'll see empty pews. I'm scared God's commissioned me to help change the world, but I'm failing to change even this town."

Fully acquainted with the guilt of letting my cafeteria friends slip into damnation, I couldn't imagine the agony of feeling that about something much bigger.

"I fear I'm pulling punches," said my pastor, "instead of getting butts in seats."

> SHARKSWITHRABIES (me): the undertaker's
> father figure is the little guy with the urn, right

MyPlaceInThisWorld (Josiah): Paul Bearer.

SHARKSWITHRABIES: do you think one day the
undertaker said "i declare him my father figure"
or did he fill out a form or what

MyPlaceInThisWorld: I think he just knew.

SEVEN
WHAT IF I STUMBLE?

SPRING 2001

The day before spring break, all but two Pokémon-table people were absent. Bobbi, sporting a pink sundress and sneaky smile, showed me a card, delicately holding its sides with her neon nails.

"The error version," I gasp-shouted. Charizard was cool, but Error Charizard was awesome.

"Shh! Gonna buy my folks a house with this thing."

I vowed to bring her a protective card case. During a congratulatory hug, she leaned her head on me, giving me a new sensation I could've only described as my heart splooging. Louder than ever before, the thing within me screamed, **"SEIZE THIS MOMENT, OR FOREVER REGRET DAMNING HER!"**

Aw man. This tenderness is a satanic distraction. "If you love someone so much that you let them go to Hell," Eli had once told me, "then you hated them all along."

Mustering everything I understood about love, I cleared my throat. "Hey, you know how Ash saying, 'Charizard, I choose you,' gives Charizard purpose? Well, Bobbi, there's someone who wants to choose y–"

She made a buzzer noise. *I can't even finish my intro without persecution! Spreading the gospel is impossible!*

She said, "Charizard's stubborn."

Oh right. "I meant Pikachu."

"Sure. Who's choosing lil ol' me?" She even fluttered her eyelashes.

Aw man. Literally the last thing I wanna say right now is … "Jesus."

She sputtered a laugh. As I rambled, her smile faded. "Ugh, you're religious? Seriously?"

Stay cool. I planted a gospel seed. Give it time. Don't correct her on Christianity being a relationship, not a religion.

Wait, just drop it? Just drop the Ashamed nail into Jesus' hand? Just drop a loathsome spider into flames?

"Church is good."

"Church is bullshit."

Uh-oh. "My church is easygoing. We have fun. It's a God thaaang."

"Can you stop?"

I sure want to! But what if a turkey-fryer explosion sends her to Hell? It'll be my fault. I was dying to double down while also yearning to relent.

She leaned back, crossing her arms like a back-row kid challenging a substitute teacher. "If God's real, why don't we ever see him? God's fake shit for dumb-dumbs."

My brain overloaded as my semi-wife revealed her final-boss form: my first-ever atheist. *Stay cool,* I thought, straining to remember atheist-defeating scripts about transitional fossils. *I've trained for this.*

"They hate people like me at church," she said, slumping forward.

Guessing she assumed my church would mistreat her because she's Black, I said something statistically true at the time: "My church is almost as diverse as this cafeteria. You know, the thing about dinosaur fossi–"

"Isaac," she hissed, "I think I like girls, okay?"

Brain crashing.

She glanced around, wide-eyed. "Please don't tell."

Brain rebooting. Say words. Any words. "I so don't hate you. Actually, I love you." *Like … love-love you, I think.*

"Love the sinner, hate the sin, huh?" she sneered, like my assigned line had hurt her before. I thought about conversion therapy, the practice of sending gay kids to facilities meant to turn them straight, and felt cowardly for hoping nobody would send Bobbi away to one.

When Christian leaders were enraged by gay people, they'd sometimes wished someone would punch "feminized" men, but rarely specified anything about lesbians. Therefore, accepting her orientation felt … easy?

I said, "Bet I'm a worse sinner than you."

"But I'm the one going to Hell?" she challenged.

"Well, there's only one verse about girl-girl stuff, in Romans 1," I said, too excitedly. "And maybe it's actually about lizards. I don't care who you like!" A lie, but only because I wished she liked me. *Hey, what if I go with her to conversion therapy? Like, just in case it works, makeout-wise?*

"Don't care? How'd you get *politically correct?*" she said, mimicking some old guy's blustery voice.

"Umm, my mom loves Elton John," I said — not that she'd ever acknowledged his orientation. "He made Lion King. He's my dawg."

The whole time, regret **screamed** about my failure to condemn her atheism. *Shut up. Please. I'm scared to lose my best school friend. Sorry.*

"Great, your mom might endure me," Bobbi said. "Bet your church wouldn't."

I told her the name of my church. She groaned. I sank.

Rotating her can of Tab on the table, she said, "I might tolerate superstitions if it meant finding adults who've survived being me. How many of your women priests or whatever could I be honest with?"

Actually, there are no women in charge who are straight! Because there are no women in charge. Stalling, I told her my youth group had a turntable, Timmy didn't nag girls about tank tops, Brother Ricardo seemed 99% gay, and Pastor Jack had almost declared the Rapture fake. Cool church!

Bobbi watched my struggling expression and said, "Exactly."

"SEE WHY THE BIBLE SAYS WOMEN SHOULDN'T SPEAK?" *Yeah. Wait, biblical women speak constantl–* **"HOW DARE SHE DISRESPECT YOU, A WHITE MAN! CALL HER AN AFFIRMATIVE-ACTION BIMBO!"** *Wow, that'd feel powerful. Wait, why do you sound like Rush Limbaugh someti–* **"WHY DO YOU SOUND LIKE A PUSSY ALL THE TIME?"**

The cafeteria chattered like normal. *Man, let it go. Jesus was just a friend sometimes.*

But what will I say if she's killed tonight by a Pennsylvania tsunami, and Eli, Pastor, Timmy, and Josiah ask whether I fought for her soul?

"You know, church has lots of pretty gir–"

"I'm not going, you Bible-thumping bigot!"

Unless I summon perfect words from the Spirit right now, my friend will be torched forever. My year-long crusade has accomplished nothing but driving at least one soul away from salvation. As of now, the universe would've officially been improved by my self-annihilation.

"I'ma go read about the Big farking Bang," she said, standing and wiggling her fingers like tongues of flame at our table's rubbernecking neighbors. "Hot stuff, coming through!"

At the Pizza Hut buffet, our Men's Accountability Summit had grown twelve strong, including my six Christmas Calebs.

Each week, another Caleb summoned the courage to admit that his "unspoken prayer requests" had always been about chronic masturbation addiction. Then each Sunday, we'd inform adult men, who'd praise our shame and encourage us to keep them updated.

Hang on. We wouldn't cheer Bobbi for revealing she thinks about girls, so why do we call ourselves courageous f– **"REGRET!"** *Sorry.*

"Gimmick time," Josiah said, scanning eyes. "Everybody likes to compete, right? Sports, video games, whatever, we keep score." He pulled a notepad from his backpack. "Well, now we have an accountability leaderboard. A LeaderLord. Dumb name."

"Awesome name," the non-Calebs alleged.

"We'll track our weekly progress toward Christlike masculinity," Josiah said, filling in statistics beside his name. "This week, I missed the chance to invite two neighbors to church, let four lustful thoughts become lustful actions ... and so on. Got it?"

"Josiah, strategery question," shouted a Caleb. "How do I stop liking premarital boobs?"

Startled, but not surprised, Josiah sighed. "It's about taking your thoughts captive, like Paul said. Outsmarting temptations. Like, I Sharpie over things on CD covers that've stolen my eyes."

"Genius. Wait, *your* CDs? The Gaither Vocal Band has boobs?" said a Caleb, seeking high fives.

Josiah rolled his eyes and said, "Isaac, your turn. Miss any witnessing opportunities this week?"

"My school has a thousand unsaved souls," I mumbled at the floor. "I missed a thousand."

"I'll ... put you down for two. Miss any quiet times?" (Church code for meditating ... on scripture. Meditating on anything else was a gateway to demonic practices like doing yoga at Magic: The Gathering tournaments.)

"Nope," I answered.

"Nice. Any lustful actions?"

"Like 800,000."

The non-Calebs gasped. The Calebs laughed.

"We're only allowed four jerk-offs?" I asked. "Yikes. I hit four just reading a Christian comic book. It has nurse cleavage. I'll impale my eyeballs and keep shoving until I kill the demons in my head who told me the Holy Spirit wanted me to be racist during Pokémon."

Josiah blinked, overwhelmed, until a Caleb smashed the silence by shouting, "I accidentally installed Tomb Raider naked mods. Yanked it 'til nothing came out. Then, I felt so crappy, I promised to evangelize the South Pacific, Nevada, and London."

"I did a trillion pushups as punishment for lusting at Heather Grace's eyes," shouted another. "I mean boobs. *Eyes* sounded gay. Feel my pecs."

"Isaac," shouted another, "what's the Christian nurse porn called, so I can avoid it?"

EIGHT
COVENANT EYES

MAY 2001

"Happened upon something we need to discuss," Eli said, grabbing pages from the printer beside my computer and tromping upstairs. I scrambled behind, worried he'd discovered my Christian-nurse MS Paints.

He smacked the pages onto the kitchen table, where Mom was reading yet another Christian-frontiersman romance novel.

"Your son typed something concerning," he said.

"One of my two sons?" she said.

He pulled up a chair and glared at me.

"These are computer chats?" she said, pointing at something I'd posted. "Language, Isaac."

> SHARKSWITHRABIES: creed effing sucks

And I realized which conversation Eli had printed. Uh-oh.

Sophie, overcoming shyness while inheriting the graduating Sara Beth's den mom role, had been encouraging youth group connections during the three days per week without any church. She'd used our dozens-strong AIM buddy lists for a group project.

It'd turned out to require First Chronicles attention spans, so it'd ended up just me and her. Every night, we had tested a music genre. Punk, ska, industrial, backpack rap, whatever. For each, we'd downloaded five secular MP3s, plus Christian counterparts, seeking the genre in which Christian musicians were the most competitive with their secular peers.

I explained that to Mom, and that we hated Creed because heathens assumed the only Christian bands were Creed and some '80s glam thing called Stryper.

"The concerning parts are later," Eli grumbled.

"I have things handled, son," said Mom, making eye contact with him until he left.

Her forehead wrinkled as she read. "Okay, angel. Who were we chatting with?"

"You might not know them," I lied. At church, Mom's choir spot was right behind where Sophie stood while translating sermons into ASL.

"Girl screen name narrows it down. These are Christian bands you're discussing? Ghoti Hook, Tonéx, Plumb …?"

I nodded. "We deleted the secular MP3s."

"Yeah right, like I'm deleting my Fleetwood Mac," she laughed, because even though she hated Hollywood enough to boycott Disney, she wouldn't give up secular music. "So, this page here …"

SHARKSWITHRABIES: christian rap's good bc it's made by not just white ppl

OneGirlArmy86: i love christian rappers who christian rap in spanish about being nice to girls! i dont like songs about shooting demons with guns!!

SHARKSWITHRABIES: whats wrong w spiritual warfare, do u like demons >:-)

OneGirlArmy86: hehe 0:-)

OneGirlArmy86: i dont like guns or thinking about certain things

SHARKSWITHRABIES: whats wrong w guns

OneGirlArmy86: i dont wanna argue with u :(:(

"I used to sound like her," sighed Mom, as I felt embarrassed by Sophie's bleeding-heart instincts. "Voted for Jimmy Carter, embarrassingly. Anyway …"

SHARKSWITHRABIES: have you read This Present Darkness by the Christian stephen king

OneGirlArmy86: no, just his kid books about being stuck in dungeons

SHARKSWITHRABIES: it's about angels and demons battling. so metal, with some detective story about a professor who does satanic yoga

OneGirlArmy86: yoga's my #4 favorite exercise :)

SHARKSWITHRABIES: SATANIST lolol

OneGirlArmy86: pshhh it's just stretching!! i tried to get PG into it cuz she's from india but she said it's too much like PE class hehe. i think she thinks it's bad to learn about india. [shrug] anywho if you like evil swords vs good swords.......

OneGirlArmy86: mmmaybe read LOTR with meeeeeeee before the movies start :)

OneGirlArmy86: if your mom asks, explain cs lewis's friend wrote it!!!

SHARKSWITHRABIES: but it's ginormous

OneGirlArmy86: only 400 pages :) for the first of three parts :) technically two of six :)

SHARKSWITHRABIES: youve read this HOW MANY TIMES?

OneGirlArmy86: you've watched fight club bazillionteen times!! :-P

SHARKSWITHRABIES: yeah but its about spiritual warfare, which is impt to think about

OneGirlArmy86: the only spiritual warfare i like is buffy :)

OneGirlArmy86: ill watch pokemon if you watch buffy :)

OneGirlArmy86: also im grounded for watching buffy :(

SHARKSWITHRABIES: watch the pokemon episode where ash lets butterfree go. i felt sad. this unmanly msg will self destruct

OneGirlArmy86: trading secrets :)

SHARKSWITHRABIES: speaking of, when you witness, how do you accomplish anything

OneGirlArmy86: whatcha mean

SHARKSWITHRABIES: how do you get people to church? im sucky at it haha lol

OneGirlArmy86: im megas*cky at it. i pretend its ok to be "a friendly light." PATHETIC excuse

SHARKSWITHRABIES: do you ever tell ppl theyre going to hell

SHARKSWITHRABIES: r u there

"*You're* grounded," Mom said, grabbing a pencil for notes, "two weeks for Fight Club. Isn't Pokémon that show with a half-naked redhead? Three weeks. Plus more weeks if you make me figure out your friend's name on my own. Hmm … a sporty tender-heart who's cute enough to make a boy read books for fun …"

I hated how easily Mom called my female friends cute. To agree that I found them attractive would've made me feel like a pervert undeserving of eyeballs or existence.

OneGirlArmy86: my turn to say a secret?

SHARKSWITHRABIES: yep

OneGirlArmy86: secret secret secret

SHARKSWITHRABIES: promise

OneGirlArmy86: im NOT some homeschool weakling

OneGirlArmy86: ive snuck ACTUAL stephen king and WORSE

OneGirlArmy86: but i CANT think about h*ll

OneGirlArmy86: i block it out

SHARKSWITHRABIES: how

OneGirlArmy86: if i said somethig my family would make me listne to them explani its real

OneGirlArmy86: i wont listen!!!! im bad im sorry im letting ppl go there bc it crushs my heart

OneGirlArmy86: i cant EVER thinkabout people going

OneGirlArmy86: and me getting some reward foreveer

OneGirlArmy86: and them begging theythink i can heelp them and wonder why i dndt savethem

OneGirlArmy86: on stage at church i use the wrong words on purpose!!!! IM AWFUL!!!!

SHARKSWITHRABIES: maybe everyones wrong about how hell works

OneGirlArmy86: call me pls !!!

On the phone, I'd been so weak, wanting Sophie to feel happy more than I'd wanted to be correct about the afterlife.

"Okay, so she's unwell," said Mom, rubbing her temples. "Did you call her?"

Answering would've meant phone records could reveal Sophie's number, breaking my vow of secrecy, so I stared at the table.

Mom sighed and crossed out her note. "I'm overlooking things — once. The infinitely bigger danger is you doubting what men of God have taught you. Everyone's wrong about Hell, angel?"

Always dead-fish defenseless against Good-Cop Mom, I almost confessed the worst thing: Sophie and I were afraid we might *go* to Hell. But I said, "We dunno exactly what happens after we die, so can't we just trust G–"

"We know. Hell's for whoever chooses Hell. Basic stuff, Awana Bible champ."

"It's okay to feel bad for Hell people," I mumbled, imagining the heartsick agony of looking up from Hell and seeing my mama smile back from distant paradise.

That's what I was always told I'd do if I made it to Heaven: grin down at everyone, including my tormented father. *No! I don't wanna exist in an eternal-torture universe! Let me the fuck out! If killing my body could permanently delete my soul, I'd keep stabbing my face until my arm went limp!*

Mom flipped to the last page, after Sophie and I had reached post-sadness giddiness and returned to ranking music genres.

OneGirlArmy86: BEHOLD the genre christians are best at: METALCORE!!

SHARKSWITHRABIES: omg i have another secret to confess

OneGirlArmy86: nooo i cant handle another :*****)

SHARKSWITHRABIES: i kept hoping youd get into punk or something. i never imagined the sweetest kid would like bloodfire snotmonster music

OneGirlArmy86: its intense and spooky and HONEST and RARRR!!!

SHARKSWITHRABIES: ur the awesomest. i wanna hug u haha lol

OneGirlArmy86: :#) okie hehe lol

xSHARKSWITHRABIESx: screen name update

xOneGirlArmy86x: RARRRRRRRRR!!!!

xOneGirlArmy86x: g2g! jesus loves u! :) [hug][hug][hug]

xSHARKSWITHRABIESx: jesus <3 u! [hug][hug][hug][hug]

xOneGirlArmy86x: [Away message: Zao - Autopsy]

My stomach turned, remembering how I'd felt while writing "i wanna hug u." **"TOLD YOU YOU'D REGRET THAT, NEEDY LITTLE CONTAMINANT!"**

"What ever happened to serenading ladies with Stevie Wonder?" sighed Mom. "Headbanger music's supposed to make her less scared of Satan? I blame Jimmy Carter."

"I'm happy we like the same music," I said. People at school found the idea of Christian metal hilarious. Well, everybody needs music, even weird church kids like me, Sophie, and PG.

"We," Mom cooed. "Adorable. What are these Xs around your names?"

"It means we're straight edge. Loud-music people who never do drugs."

"Oh, for the love! Keep making stuff up and we'll have a book club."

We laughed about the last time she'd whipped my bare butt, trying to obey Christian parenting expert James Dobson's instructions to beat me into motionless silence. Frustrated by my yelps, she even raised his book like a club, but threw it across the room, cradled me, and bawled about being unequipped for a father's job. It was funnier in hindsight.

"On the bright side, I love you treating girls as humans, not decorations," said Mom. "You cheered her up! She gotcha talkin' feelings! But I also see why Eli felt led to inform me. Angel, I'm sure she's sweet, but nobody's sweet enough to deny the gospel for."

"Gospel" means "good news." But how could any news be good if it involves souls being punished forever? Something refused to add up, and for the first time, I wasn't sure it was my fault. **"REGRET!"**

"Eli sucks," I snipped at Mom.

"Language! And hey, your brother oversteps because he cares. Hell's real, which means he's the best defender your gang has. Right?"

Ugh. Fine.

Still wondering which of my friends was heretical, Mom read again, spotted some giveaway detail, and shouted, "Pastor Jack's cherub niece is scared of the Bible?"

I'd always assumed my fear of Hell had arisen because Dad might've gone there. But Sophie's super-churchy parents were both alive, so that theory went poof.

Whatever caused her fear, maybe it was why my gentlest friend got into loud music. After all, I'd always liked violent movies and stuff. The bleaker the world got, the sooner we'd get raptured, unless the Rapture was fake or we missed it or whatever. So bleak it up!

Mom hugged me, told me to "cheer up," and dismissed me. I felt even less capable of telling her about the lying-awake-at-night terror that made me want to hurt myself, the ultimate cheering-up failure.

Once, I'd woken her to tell her about a nightmare. She had blamed Freddy Krueger, but hadn't known I'd been having the same dream for years. I kept seeing Dad's body in the heart of the sun, and I kept floating toward him.

End-of-semester school status: Made no friends. Saved no souls, but drove some away. I was a long way from summer-campfire euphoria.

After eating lunch in six minutes (again), I began shuffling toward the library to ponder Matthew 12:31's horrors (again). *Don't damn me, just destroy me.*

"Jesus Boy, sit."

Crap. I'd avoided Bobbi's table for months. For a while, I'd thought about offering her evidence that God was fine with her liking girls. For example, the apostle Paul called lesbians "unnatural," but said the same thing about long-haired men. *Well, long-haired male lions are natural, so maybe lesbians are too!* **"YOU'LL REGRET DISREGARDING AN AUTHOR OF GOD-BREATHED SCRIPTURE!"** *But …*

"Now we have enough folks for five games at once," Bobbi said, with eyes laser-lockier than ever. I greeted the kids I knew, met the ones I didn't, and wondered how much they hated me. She handed me crappy Pokémon cards, her experimental deck. *Don't damn me, just destroy me.*

"Do you think the Bible's flawless or whatever?" she said while we shuffled.

I nodded, accepting the ambush as fair.

"So Methuselah lived 900 years for real?"

I'd been warned about atheists who'd memorized the Bible just like Satan had. Deep breath. "Methuselah lived 969 years because Noah hadn't invented alcoholism, and the flood's water was still in the sky, blocking harmful UV rays."

She blinked hard and maybe smiled. My designated retorts sounded like creative jokes. "How'd they fit brachiosauruses on the ark, huh?"

"Maybe eggs, like Jurassic Park," I said, rolling with it. Genesis never said otherwise.

"How'd they prevent eggs hatching? They sailed for forty years or whatever!"

"Like half a year. Not sailing, just floating. There was water up to Mount Everest. Plenty of ice for preserving eggs, like Demolition Man."

"It was freezing? How'd they keep lizards warm?"

"Hmm. Hippos snuggled them?"

She went *aww*. "How'd they find all kazillion beetle species?"

"Maybe they all came from two beetles, like all dogs came from two wolves."

"That's evolution!"

"Totally different."

"How?"

"Evolution's just a theory. Dogs aren't a theo–"

"I seriously can't tell if you're screwing with me," she said, slapping the table. "Most fundies are knuckle-dragging morons. You just confuse me!"

"Speaking of dragons," I said, reaching into my backpack, "your Charizard case has been in my bag since ..."

"There's a verse about the sun going down and scurrying back for the next day. That's inaccurate."

"That's poetic. Even science teachers call it sunrise."

"But every verse is supposed to be literal."

"No, Jesus taught lessons with made-up stories."

"Can't Noah's ark be a made-up lesson?"

Hmm. One point for Bobbi. Even though I wanted to believe Noah's flood had happened as described, it felt negotiable. "It's all true. Parts aren't literal."

"Who gets to choose which parts are?"

"I dunno," I said, too tired to remember my assigned comebacks. "Smart guys."

"YOU'LL REGRET SURRENDERING!" *Probably. Anyway, I'm permanently atoning tonight. See ya there.*

Bobbi watched eight kids banter over card games, then laser-locked me again. "I know they brainwash you into capturing souls, but that's not gonna work at this table."

Brainwash? Capturing? Should I tolerate that? Would it matter? As if I could damage the cause any worse, as if me dying won't clear space at Bobbi's table for an actual Christian to get the job done?

She held up a palm and let me press mine against it. *Why should her soul be the one in danger, when she's already a better friend than me?* **"MY SWEET ISAAC, THERE IS NO GREATER LOVE THAN TO LAY DOWN YOUR LIFE FOR YOUR FRIENDS. COME HOME, MY SON."** *Okay.*

"I'm so excited to argue with you every day," Bobbi said. "Just don't expect me to believe Bearded Sky Genie will give you a harp for saying enough Hail Marys. Deal?"

"I don't believe any of that newspaper-cartoons-about-Saint-Peter's-pearly-gates stuff," I sighed.

"Well, you believe I'm damned, but you're not, right?"

My stiletto knife was in my hand, clicking open and shut and open. Mom was working graveyard.

I answered the phone on the first ring, and Sophie, making her weekly rounds through church freshmen, said, "Since we're straight edge now, let's become root beer connoiss–"

"Can we pray, like now-ish?"

She gasped. "What's wrong?"

Men had always warned me against confessing sins to girls, which could generate dangerous intimacy, but the only friend who'd ever mourned my dad was the person I trusted most. So I sinned by confessing, "I suck at everything. Doubts. I let all that summer-camp passion die. Bad thoughts. Can't share the gospel. My eyes look at p– ... pretty bad music videos. I'm not bringing God to America again."

I rambled. She listened, exhaled, and asked in her sun-shower voice if I was ready. Sure. Then maybe I could tell her that I was undecided between that knife and the Glock upstairs. *After a trillion years in eternal Hell, I'll have made zero progress, so why not get started?* That way, the next day would be the first since 1986 without Isaac Siena misrepresenting Christ to the nations.

"Dear Jesus, please make the best sunrise ever," she prayed, "and give it to my best friend as soon as he's ready."

Wait ... best? C'mon, her best friends are all named Grace. I grazed my knife against my closed eyelid, stretching the skin enough for the light to intensify. My phone was silent.

"Was that all?" I asked.

"Sorry, I could babble, but I don't pray out loud much. Guys always say grace. I'm a dork. Sorry."

"Stop always randomly apologizing. You think you're bad or something."

"Sorry," she laughed.

We talked a little longer. I struggled to explain. She gently suggested I try having more faith. *Great idea, faith girl.* We discussed a sophomore who was dating a non-Christian. We prayed for either his soul or their breakup. Then we imagined all our friends camping on a beach. In my filthy mind, it was just the two of us. Fortunately, I was one jab away from ensuring I'd never ruin her.

"I'm sorry I couldn't help better," she yawned. "If you have bad dreams, call me? I'd answer before it wakes my mom. I still owe ya one! Please know Jesus loves ya, mister."

"Foxy, I know Jesus loves you."

On the cover of that old Christian novel This Present Darkness, bleak clouds devour a dusky town, foreground trees are creeping death, and demon talons descend all around. Nighttime was when I felt it most.

In my life, I'd attended 3,200 events at a half-dozen churches. Passed catechism tests all through Awana. Read so many Christian apologetics manuals that my devout mother laughed at the pile. Studied the whole Bible cover-to-cover twice, memorized chunks, done daily devotionals, and loved correcting adults' scripture references. Won awards for beating other children at explaining popular Western Christianity.

But I couldn't figure out what we believed.

Does salvation from Hell happen by way of asking, receiving, believing, confirming, grace, works, wonders, fruits, dying to self, killing our flesh, the Name, the Law, sacraments, sacrifice, forgiving people, letting Jesus appease God and/or Satan, canceling money debts, sinning no more, letting the Spirit make us sin less, healing diseases, handling snakes, rebuking demons, screaming the gospel until we got martyred, praying secretly, giving everything to the poor, joining the 144,000 undead saints beside the Living Creatures, getting good judgments recorded in the Book of Life, saving the world, being hated by the world, fixing the world's governments, or …?

And if I didn't know which, how could I guarantee I was saved? And *can* we choose, or were most of us created for Calvinist Hell? I'd never agreed to exist, let alone pass the age of accountability, yet I sat one breath away from flames unless I guessed correctly whether we're saved by asking, receiving, believing …

"Call doubt by its real name: the Devil in our mind," a pastor had once said.

Well, if Satan's stuck in my skull, my afterlife destination will be the same as his, right? Satan can't possibly be saved, right? That's something God can't do, right? It's impossible even for God. Right?

By contrast, Matthew 12:31 was simple: "Blasphemy against the Spirit will not be forgiven." Push button, get instant Hell. Easy. So I dreaded what'd happen if my brain said, "I, Isaac Siena, Jr., officially blaspheme the fucking Holy Spirit."

That's already blasphemy! After all, it's my brain, right? I should lean over the toilet and scoop my brain into it, right? That's more rational than accepting damnation, right? Jesus said to lay down my life, right? It's time, right? With this six-inch blade in my hand, quivering so close, all I see is silver blur. If I fall forward, it'll plow all the way through the back of my skull, not only martyring me, but maybe even aborting me before the age of accountability. Mom won't find me until I've bled out, but with my last thought I can repent, in case Catholics are right about suicide, right? This might be how Dad went out, and you said he's not sad anymore, right? Laying down my life for failing to save Bobbi would count for something, right?

"RIGHT."

There I sat, war raging in my mind. I tried praying, singing Veggie Tales songs, punching the top of my spine, reading Derek Prince's demon-assassination manuals, barking at demons as their sergeant, everything.

Only one thing distracted my brain from daring itself to curse God. Watching the scrambled Spice Channel could be forgiven; blaspheming the Spirit couldn't. According to Jack Chick tracts, on Judgment Day, I'll stand public trial with my dead grandparents among the trillions stuck watching God's surveillance footage of me jerking off. That's what I thought about while jerking off.

My alarm rang. I'd fallen asleep in the bathtub. My algebra final was in one hour. Well, I'd wussed out at 1:39 a.m. by closing my knife, blighting the universe by leaving Isaac Siena in it. I thought I'd been strong enough to take up my cross, die to self, and wash in a fourteen-year-old's blood.

But there was a heart I couldn't bring myself to break.

She'd called me her best friend.

I caught my brother's football. I punted it back. Repeat.

"Think the Sixers can beat the Bucks?" he asked.

"Yeah. Are you finally researching minivans like a baby-maker?"

"Hmm. Whatcha gonna major in at college?"

"I dunno. Mechanic stuff, like Dad. How can I be 100,000% sure I'm not going to Hell?"

Eli's arm, wound up to throw, dropped to his side. He strode forward, glancing around like I'd spoken loudly. He thumped a big arm across my shoulders, his beard brushing my ear, and pulled me toward a park bench.

"Everybody needs reminded sometimes," he said, eyes zeroed in on me. "You're like me. Blueprints guy. Clear directions. So, back to basics. Whoever believes in Jesus shall not perish, but have ..."

"Eternal life."

"And do you believe?"

I dunno what believe means! Believe Jesus lives in my heart? Believe every interpretation of every translation of every poetic Bible verse? Believe everything said by thousands of denominations across thousands of years? Believe believing is the point?

I said, "Yeah."

"So you've affirmed that out loud, as commanded in Matthew," Eli said. "After that, we follow his commission to spread the gospel. That's the entire playbook."

But I unloaded worries about Paul's verses describing salvation like some sort of universal gift, despite James saying we had to *do* stuff, and Matthew writing the thing Eli quoted, but also that we're saved by charity, and ... Eli looked shaken.

"You sound like Dad," he said, lip quivering. "He spun his wheels, treating complexities like contradictions. I believe salvation is eternal, but Jesus said, 'Not everyone who calls me Lord will enter Heaven.' Isaac, our father doubted so much that it's clear he never trusted to begin with. So ..."

Eli exhaled like a beast groaning from a cave.

"... I don't want anyone following him. I'm convinced Dad died unsaved."

There I was, standing above a canyon, looking down, and realizing I stood on nothing. In Eli's voice, my fears sounded like certainties.

"You're old enough to hear it," he rattled, wrapping me in big arms. "I'm too weak to bring it up with Mom."

I muttered some helpless rebuttal.

"What were Dad's fruits?" he said. "A saved person doesn't bail on the mission to save souls. At church, he went through motions, barely attending, acting like a good parent ..."

"He was good," I heard myself saying.

"Except he never, not once, warned us about Hell. What kinda parent abandons his kids to flames? Isaac, right now, he's crying out, begging us to keep young people from following him!"

Our father. Absorbed into something like the sun. Beyond the end of time.

"So, I'm rough with your friends," Eli said. "I screw up. I've apologized to the girls, for how I've judged their clothes. Jesus said *we're* responsible for what our eyes do. In the Sermon of the Mount, he told married guys: I'd rather you pluck your eyes out than wrong your wives."

Eli didn't even know that was the verse I'd twisted into my excuse to hurt myself. (Yep, the eyeball verse isn't literally about self-harm. The punchline: I'd known that the entire time.)

"You were Dad's guy. Not many younger brothers get the junior name," Eli said, sitting me upright.

People were staring at the sniffling gorilla. Sure, he was being odd, but anyone who claims to believe in eternal damnation yet doesn't react hysterically is either an all-time sociopath or a God-damned liar.

"Dad still loves you," he said. "He's got a job for you."

I told Eli about the knife, my yearlong obsession. He squeezed me like an avalanche and demanded I call him any time things got bleak.

"If you ever try to damn my baby brother, I'll fucking kill you first," he said. "Stop laughing. I'm not joking."

"I know. That's the funny part."

Pacing my room, I realized my luck. Josiah had adopted me. Bobbi found me worth forgiving. My family loved me. Pastor Jack was my interim dad. And Sophie ... *I'll never be worthy, but I'll die trying.*

I dropped my knife into my trashcan. Clang.

Days later at church camp, leading my beloved Calebs to pee on the Target, I worried that I believed something wonderful: People wanted a wretch like me to keep breathing.

I've asked you to choose me. But if I'm unchosen anyway, then maybe after a trillion years in Hell, I'll find him. After another trillion, maybe we'll find a way out.

All of us.

Duh, that's not what eternal means.

But isn't it okay to say maybe?

What's it hurt to hope?

What's wrong with sympathy for literally everyone?

"Boy, there's a reason it's called forbidden love."

PART TWO
THE BOOK OF SOPHOMORES

Sinful passions,
aroused by the law

— The Epistle to the Romans

NINE
ECHOES IN ETERNITY
JUNE 2001

Save her soul, so she'll dump the point guard for me.

Alexa Giovanni — so popular at school that classmates even complimented her braces — randomly stomped into Wednesday night church, flicking her dirty-blonde hair like a force field. She'd been my coolest classmate since kindergarten. Back then, I'd drawn pictures of her enchanting scowl, while she'd only talked to second-grade boys.

At church, though, I was more popular, and the only person she (kinda) knew. Everyone would see me being the first to hug the visitor. *Treat her like a sister in Christ who's not in Christ. Once she's in Christ, ditch the sister part. Foolproof plan, one of these times.* I proceeded, jutting my pecs like the seniors who said "tight-tight" instead of "cool."

But Sophie had already taken her by the elbow. Outraced by den-mom instincts!

"I'm adopting ya, beauty queen," squeaked the homeschooler in hand-painted overalls.

"My motherfucking douchebag dad's punishing me with a cunt-ass year of this cocksucking church bullshit," grumbled the Joe Dirt's-hot-sister lookalike — as I once again fell in love.

Sophie, shaking cuss words from her ears, noticed the Playboy bunny suntan tattoo above Alexa's low-riding cutoffs. "Cute rabbit! What's your favorite book?"

Yikes. It was like watching a cartoon hamster try to saddle a shark.

Alexa curled blood-red lips and snarled, "What the fuck are you, a sexy farmer?"

Huh. Kindest thing she'd ever said.

As the newcomer was hug-mobbed by girls middle-named Grace, she didn't smile, but almost smirked. It seemed possible she'd like it there, where I was a cool guy. Rumors said she did stuff with cool guys. **"OBVIOUSLY, YOU'LL FOREVER REGRET DAYDREAMING."** *Instantly regretted! But no worries, she's only here until next summer. Not enough time for anyone to get into doin'-stuff trouble!*

Eight nearby youth groups sent busloads to our church's compound, where "PAINTBALL WAR" chants surged across the lawn's sea of hugs.

Me and the bros had trained by spraypainting camo onto our jorts and telling Josiah the plot of Gladiator. We were ready.

In the crowd, the Graces hug-mobbed Alexa again, convincing her to wear one of their baggy tracksuits. *Phew! Running around in a tube top would've been dangerous! Also, she could've gotten injured.*

Timmy parked the church van, which was loaded with lukewarm hot dogs. Older bros chanted his name because our youth pastor was quitting to join a traveling praise band. In a huge group hug, he tearfully announced that the day's winning team would pick which band we'd invite to Harvest Season, our November festival day. I'd miss him, but was distracted from sadness by Alexa's alluring sneer.

Graces had argued that Eli's wife should replace Timmy, but deacons reminded them women couldn't preach the resurrection gospel, which seemed weird, becau– **"YOU'LL REGRET BETRAYING BIBLICAL GENDER ROLES, YOU FATHERLESS SON OF A WOMAN!"** *Sorry.* Eli himself could've saved souls by taking Timmy's spot, but he was busy selling real estate.

I was on Team Eagles, headquartered on the camp bridge where I'd befriended Josiah a year earlier. I hugged my way through my army, which included two Calebs, Sophie, and four Graces. Alexa ignored the rosters, following Sophie while side-eying huggers. Our enemies were Team Warriors, based beside the main sanctuary.

"Glad we're not on Team Warriors," Sophie said, red hair in snug braids, hugging a Caleb.

"Josiah's team would be fun," I said, hugging a Grace.

"No, war is sad," she said, hugging two Calebs.

"War is fun," I said, hugging two Graces.

In our huddle, Alexa said, "Ladies, if this huggy shit's unavoidable, let's hug *them*," then flashed her tongue piercing toward some shirtless megachurch seniors. Graces giggled and danced their eyes up and down. What a terrible influence, corrupting everyone into liking guys cooler than me.

Round One. The shirtless morons stampeded straight ahead. Alexa followed, girls followed her, I followed girls, and Calebs followed me. We became Team Eagles' B Squad. A shirtless moron charged back with the enemy flag. In 95-degree heat, dozens quit to wander toward hot dogs.

Round Two. Our shirtless morons, riddled with bloody welts, quit. When the wayward B Squad spotted scoundrels making out, we joked about it, but assured Alexa that those sins were entering Heaven's permanent record. She called Jesus perverted for watching. Saving her soul seemed impossible, but trading mine for some action began to seem feasible. We lost Round Two. Tons more people quit.

Round Three would decide Paintball War. With bruises on tired legs and sweaty armor peeled away, the remains of B Squad regrouped in the creek bed. As Sophie explained ant facts to an anthill, PG and the last Caleb sat in the storm drain tunnel's opening.

"We're gonna lose," wheezed PG, so exhausted that her emo bangs dangled over *both* her eyes. Caleb, built more for power than endurance, was too weary to beatbox.

I expected Alexa to quit and go lick shirtless morons, but she tightened her long ponytail and barked at PG, "Listen up, Whichever Grace, the motherfucking B Squad doesn't lose. I fucking hate losing."

"I frickin' h-word it too," squawked Sophie, popping upright and trying to scowl.

"But we tried all the smart ideas, and they sucked farts," wailed PG, slamming her forehead into Caleb's arm.

Freshman Caleb, leaned upon by a pretty sophomore, clenched himself in place and stammered, "Then let's try dumb ideas?"

Say no more. I pulled handmade maps from my shorts, pointing from our tunnel to the storm drain beside the enemy flag. "We'll be up and down before they know it."

"The freaking underworld? Eww!" said PG, whirling so quickly to peer into the dark tunnel that Caleb almost toppled over.

He pulled a flashlight from his cargo shorts, leveling up from Final Caleb to Best Caleb.

"We'd get in trouble," giggled Sophie with roller coaster eyes.

Alexa, the deciding vote, popped bubblegum at her. "Baby, you need trouble. Fuck it. We're tunnel rats!"

"The Christian rap group?" I said, gaining hope that Alexa would fall in love. With Jesus.

"The Christian fucking what?" she said, advancing our first conversation since kindergarten. "No, some Vietnam shit my dad said. Tunnel soldiers."

"We'll be Christians hiding in Roman catacombs!" said Caleb.

"We'll be Gandalf choosing the Mines of Moria!" said Sophie. "Not Frodo. The movie's wrong. Sorry."

"We'll be freaking megadoomed," sighed PG. "But if you guys are going … fiiine."

Suiting back up, PG demanded a group hug ("in case we don't make it"). Sneaking into the dark metal tube, she encouraged hand-holding ("since you guys seem scared").

"Yo, can y'all explain some church shit?" said Alexa, her semi-whisper echoing behind me. "Why do weirdos go cry up front? Yesterday, some girls cried during stupid-kid church, stupid-geezer church, *and* stupid-night church."

"That's the rededication cycle," PG said too loudly, clinging to light-source Caleb's arm. "First you get convicted and broken, which means feeling more ashamed than usual. Maybe you skipped PE because pushups are cruel and unusual, heard someone talking about drinking and didn't spaz, believed God can use evolution, gossiped in retaliation about that b-word Kinslee Grace, or other hypotheticals. But then you rededicate and feel great!"

The Graces rededicated frequently.

"Church has fuckloads of rules," Alexa snarled. "Yesterday, some crypt-keeper handed me a dress code while staring at my boobs."

Lord, please let these ladies discuss boobs for this entire ten-minute walk, amen. Honestly, I like girls so much, I'd listen to them talk about anything, even Jesus! **"FIRST TIMOTHY 2:12! WOMEN SHOULD BE SILENT, FEMINIZED SHE-MAN!"** *Sorry.*

"Ugh, Timmy's leaving, and Dave-Tony's dress code is back," groaned PG. "No, I won't wear a sports bra! Freaking suffocate me!"

"That's the only kind I've ever had," mumbled Sophie.

"Wait, you're *that* much of a jock?" said Alexa.

"No, like … it's important to dress mindfully, guarding our brothers-in-Christ's eyes."

This is so hot. First Timothy was an idiot. Women should talk constantly.

"You're smooshing yourself all day just so boys might jack off less?" whisper-squawked Alexa. "They won't! Right, Isaac?"

Never mind, First Timothy was right.

"I don't judge anyone who dresses normal," said Sophie. "Sorry."

"Girl, I'ma acquire you a whole new wardrobe. If they give you church detention, I'm taking it instead."

"Aww, majorly Christlike," said PG. "The detention part."

"Church rules change sometimes, at least," said Sophie, oblivious to Alexa's shoplifting offer. "Our seventh-grade youth pastor banned dancing. That backfired! I felt bad for him."

"Like you've ever danced, Saint Virgin," Alexa snorted.

"I'm not a frickin' Mennonite, Britney Abercrombie!" Off-the-charts sassy, by Sophie standards.

I looked back into the storm-drain light and saw flashes of Alexa's ponytail. "Gah, you're strong," she cackled. "Why the fuck are you whirling me?"

"Swing dancing! Me and Josiah won bronze in sixth grade."

"Sooo homeschooled. Dance normal! Here, hump my ass."

A play-slapping scuffle broke out. The quickly subdued smoker cooed at the tomboy, "It's hot when you bully me." Between that duo and artsy PG holding onto lunkhead Caleb, I was suddenly surrounded by weird friendships.

We heard a shouting gun skirmish above ground. Alexa whispered, "Is it your pastor's-niece job to fix the crying re-whatever kids? Kneeling with them even though you're miss innocent?"

"Pshh, I sin constantly," whispered Sophie, sinning by lying.

"Then, after den mom Sophie fixes your anguish," PG shouted, echoing as we shushed her, "you delete the external hard drive of secular MP3s you'd been building since your last re-dedication. Then you're happy enough to sit up front!"

"The kids up front always jump while crying," Alexa laughed.

"Those are on-fire Christians," Caleb mumbled. "I'm not on-fire enough to jump-cry, because I suck."

I knew I'd better fix him before Josiah heard that kind of pouting, because whenever the Calebs acted backslidey, they became my Calebs, not our Calebs.

Signaling to turn right, the big boy pointed his flashlight at graffiti.

"When you're on-fire rededicated, it feels grrreat to jump-cry," shouted PG. "Christian music effect!"

That was when emotion-soaked worship choruses blasted sparks throughout your skin while you stood hand-in-hand with radiant-faced friends who were falsetto-breathing "Open the Eyes of My Heart," swaying their hips against yours, and wiping mascara tears onto your black shirt. (For some reason, it was often followed by teenagers sneaking out to grope each other.)

"After a while, most jump-criers backslide to middle rows," PG babbled, yelling away the tunnel's darkness. "They drag their accountability groups along, feeling bad about not feeling the right kind of good, then feel the wrong kind of good until they feel bad enough to try the right kind of good again!"

"Careful," said Sophie. PG saying the quiet parts literally loudly was risking our paintball mission *and* making church sound bad to Alexa's lost soul.

Caleb snapped his fingers, hushing us as we reached our exit. Looking up into blinding sunlight, he asked me, "What's the plan, Sarge?"

"Uhh, boost each other up, swipe the flag, and escort the thief home."

Sophie climbed out, reporting camo-friendly foliage and enemies with their backs turned. Husky Caleb squeezed through next. Alexa and I prepared to boost PG, but the emo girl hung her head.

"I'd slow you down. I'm in awful shape." Looking up at smiling faces and Alexa's perma-scowl, PG huffed so hard she stomped one Converse. "And I'm depressed Timmy's leaving. He taught me guitar and everything. Just leave me here to rot ..."

After a silent beat, Sophie told her she was perfect. Caleb struggled to compliment her without lusting. And I glared warnings at Alexa so she wouldn't say anything mean.

But she sparked a cigarette, offered it to PG, and said, "I'm staying with you, PG-13. You listen to Hed PE?"

Huh, that was nice. Regardless, I planned to fix Alexa's soul, dating status, love of corny nu metal, and potential lung cancer, in that order.

"Wait," Sophie whispered as I climbed, "when we grab the flag, let's pass it down, then run around as decoys! Leave them the flashlight, Caleb."

Once I said, "Good idea," the freshman obeyed.

The three of us masked up and snuck behind bushes, closer to the flag's bike rack. Whispering, Sophie taught us a couple ASL hand signals. Caleb hid, ready to cover us.

We crept to the bush beside the flag, and then … heard boots thumping pavement. Caleb was sprinting and firing. Fool of a freshman!

Six Warriors spotted us. He eliminated one, but got shot. Enemies ran in his direction, hunting phantom Calebs, but more enemies emerged, raining red paint. From behind the bush, we returned green fire, totally outnumbered.

Before I could say anything badass, Sophie scurried around our hedge of protection and slid behind the bike rack, covering me. I scrambled, dropped my gun beside her, grabbed the flag, and bolted while she dual-wielded our weapons. From the storm drain, Alexa reached out, maybe standing on PG's hands, as paintballs zapped my shoulder, thigh, and butt. Eliminated, I tossed the flag as I fell.

It plopped inches from Alexa's hand. She gritted her teeth and lunged. Red paint splattered her mask. She jolted, slipped down, and screamed cusses.

Enemies surrounded the drain, worried about her landing. From below, she barked, "Before you come get your flag, pray for my fucked-up elbow." As I walked away, she kept delaying them by claiming that Jesus was repeatedly amending the stipulations about which of them should retrieve their flag.

Someone flicked paint off me. Sophie, grinning with pride about being our most-painted soldier, handed back my gun.

"It's kinda mean, how dumb Alexa makes boys," she laughed, unzipping her sweaty jacket. "I feel weirdly drawn to protect her, even though you two have bajillionty friends at school. And each other?"

"Next time, let me get shot. Running away was so unmanly."

"Girls can get shot just fine, thanks! Besides, I'm a smaller target, and you're faster."

"You run cross-country!"

"Pshh! Years ago."

"You're in awesome shape," I said, instantly realizing how it'd struck her ears.

She blushed magenta, yanked her jacket closed, and apologized for letting me glimpse an inch of bare shoulder while praising her fitness. Her whole life, she'd been told bra straps transform boys into uncontrollable lust monsters. But even as a teenage pervert, I didn't understand why youth pastors considered any straps unbearably hot. **"WELL, IN THE LAKE OF FIRE, YOU'LL REGRET DISCREDITING HER SAFEGUARDS!"** *Sorry.*

Nearing the creek bed, we complained about Green Day's "Church on

Sunday," a song describing something impossible: a good person in love with a non-Christian.

Caleb appeared, bragging about having discovered a shortcut to the camp bridge, not exactly life-saving info worth risking Paintball War for. He was his goofy self again after trying to be a cool hero for PG.

Behind us, we heard an uproar. Once Alexa's ruse ran out, three enemies had stampeded right past PG, who was strolling through the creek bed, wearing their flag like a bandana scarf. That badass had traversed the darkness by herself.

So they'd assume she'd also been eliminated, we escorted her to base. Victory airhorn.

Alexa's sneakers thumped to a stop beside us. She flung aside her jacket and delivered sweaty tube-top hugs to me and non-me people. *Her soul (and body), sanctified any minute now!* But she displayed hands covered in Sharpie phone numbers from megachurch guys, offering to share with PG and Sophie. *She'll corrupt souls (and bodies) until I die alone!*

Following flag-bearer PG toward victory food, zipped-up Sophie greeted the sunset with hands spread wide, releasing unseen doves. With both our guns slung over my shoulder, I reached for her outstretched fingertips and tried a celebration.

"No," she said. "Bad dancing!"

"Oops."

"Boys spin girls, silly goose. If they want. They don't have to."

We laughed through an awkward stumble, which ended with a spirit-refilling hug. My arms fit over her shoulders like puzzle pieces, she smelled like salty Starbursts, and golden-hour sunbeams blinged her gray eyes silver as I tucked a loose hair behind her ear.

"REGRET." As my fear of corrupting Sophie deepened, somebody yelled, "They told me and my boyfriend to leave space for Jesus, but that pastor's niece is over there dry-humping!"

We definitely weren't, but we jolted apart like negative magnets. Anyway, my heart clearly belonged to Alexa, the girl admired by normal people, such as me.

We reached the crowd on the lawn. Muddy, bloody, and painty, Alexa barked, "Are you not entertained, bitches?"

"Team Eagles, Paintball champions," Timmy bellowed with maximum vibrato, beckoning toward his hot dog supply. He asked Alexa not to cuss, and I was proud she didn't call him a fuckhead. His final act as our youth pastor: bequeathing his guitar to a bawling PG.

We hugged our enemy soldiers, ate, and traded war stories. I loved every face. I thought back to a few weeks prior, when I'd wanted to shove a knife through mine. I felt bone-deep gratitude that I hadn't.

Josiah pointed across the lawn at buildings speckled green and red. He stood to assist the grownups hosing off our mess. We followed our rising junior leader.

"Somehow, church is dope," Alexa garbled through a mouthful of food, skipping arm-in-arm with Sophie. "Somebody said there are beach trips?"

"Next summer! Beach Fest!"

"Gah, let's ruin so many church boys by then."

---

hearitinmyghost (Bobbi): how's summer, Jesus Boy

xSHARKSWITHRABIESx: AWESOME! how bout u Charlene Darwin

hearitinmyghost: ready for school, Virgin Larry ...

xSHARKSWITHRABIESx: Christopherina Hitchens, ur ready for WHAT??

hearitinmyghost: i miss my friends, Pope Wrong Paul The Worst

xSHARKSWITHRABIESx: oh right, school friends. sorry, Generally Incorrect With Jill Maher

hearitinmyghost: too far!! ... what's "AWESOME"

xSHARKSWITHRABIESx: we won PAINTBALL WAR today. lol alexa giovanni showed up

hearitinmyghost: PLLLLLEASE say you shot my third grade bully

xSHARKSWITHRABIESx: she's fun!

hearitinmyghost: 9 outta 10 drunk jocks agree!!

xSHARKSWITHRABIESx: huh guess u dont wanna hear about her wearing mostly paint

hearitinmyghost: ... ... go on xSHARKSWITHRABIESx: see! you'd like church lolll

heariitinmyghost: lmaooo ... turn HER into a nun rofl!!

xSHARKSWITHRABIESx: thats the plan!!!!!!!!!!!!

xSHARKSWITHRABIESx: what if rumors about her are fake

hearitinmyghost: lmao u got it baaaad, tiger

hearitinmyghost: yo ... play diablo 2 with me ... im boredddddddd

hearitinmyghost: help me MURDER SATAN ...

xSHARKSWITHRABIESx: downloading! give it 19 hours

hearitinmyghost: be a paladin ... he tanks damage ... protects his friends with jesus auras 0:-)

xSHARKSWITHRABIESx: hey do u like this quote by gladiator's dad

xSHARKSWITHRABIESx: If there are gods and they are just, then they will not care how devout you have been, but will welcome you based on the virtues you have lived by. If there are gods, but unjust, then you should not want to worship them. If there are no gods, then you will be gone, but will have lived a noble life.

hearitinmyghost: maybe ... do u??

TEN
UNDISPUTED

SUMMER 2001

BOASTING PILES OF VIDEO GAMES AND CLOSE PROXIMITY TO PIZZA HUT, MY basement became the summer base for my church bros. Playing Tony Hawk 2 from noon until dawn, we piled on my enormous yellow-and-teal couch, where the retort to being called "fruity" was to flirt until the accuser flinched. Mom fortified her new sons with endless granola bars.

For my fifteenth birthday, we invited all the Graces to stay until their curfews. The couch bore twenty-four people who'd pooled money to buy me Gran Turismo 3, because whoa, they cared about me?!

I revealed my presents for them: create-a-wrestlers modeled after them in Josiah's left-behind copy of WWF No Mercy.

"Josiah, handsome-ish, dorky button-up. When you enter, it says PASTOR'S KID. PG, your guitar's a weapon. Sophie, lemme change your hair to your new bangs. Calebs, you carry folding chairs like good youth group boys. Alexa couldn't make it, but this skirt is, whew, accurate …"

Instantly, they were challenging each other, forming alliances, editing themselves, and discovering I'd created Satan (plus his archrival, Christian singer Carman). Two hours vanished.

"Hang on," I said during goodbye hugs, un-wadding paper from my pocket, unsure how to intro my drastic tonal shift. "I, uh, made a list of Bible girls who preached without getting in trouble. Because maybe a lady *could* be our youth pastor? Ummm, Miriam was a prophet." Nervous, I jumped around my list, from Old Testament liberator Deborah to Paul's lady-friends and back. "And Mary Magdalene was the first to preach the resurrection. In Proverbs, there's this wisdom goddess named ... uh ..."

"Whoa, whoa, whoa," said Gabe, the annoying junior with ice-blue eyes and a deacon father, non-dead. "Female biblical duties are things *besides* speaking. Goddesses are New Age bullsqueeze!"

You see, at Dave-Tony's Bible study, we'd reached First Timothy. In that book, Paul says girls must shut up (*sorry Paul, I respectfully disagree*) and have boring hair (*fuck off, Paul*). So I'd searched the Bible for, um, contrary opinions. After all, Dad had once said, "Women are strong, despite their piss-poor skeletal mass. Calling women weak is weak. Don't say piss-poor." And I was still annoyed at whoever let a donkey outshine Mom's pageant Mary decades earlier.

"BUT GABE SOUNDS LIKE YOUR MALE ROLE MODELS! YOU'LL REGRET THIS!" *But I'm quoting the effing Bible!* **"JUST LIKE SATAN IN MATTHEW CHAPTER 4!"** *Fine! I'll stop reading the effing Bible!* **"NO, YOU MUST LIVE BY GOD'S WORD, SAYS MATTHEW CHAPTER 4!"** *Sorry.*

Meanwhile, a spirit of confusion consumed my friends. Someone said, "The Bible says ... girls can and can't speak in church? Happy birthday?" People shrugged, then hugged, a common combo.

I walked my platonic friend Sophie toward her dad's car, griping about my own randomness.

"Well, I liked it," she said. "I'll say so next time."

"Since Paul told you to be quiet, I'll crush him in No Mercy."

She asked if I wanted arcane secrets from her uncle's bookshelves. *Always! Whisper girl-noises into my earhole!*

"Paul mayyybe didn't write First Timothy," she said, meaning its introductory verse is inaccur– **"DENYING BIBLICAL INERRANCY? YOU'LL REGRET THIS!"** *Sorry.*

We agreed to co-found Video Games Church, a weekly Bible study (with video games) on my enormous couch, filling my basement with exciting-haired priestesses while dipshit Gabe grumbled with Dave-Tony.

As we walked, Sophie hummed a song I recognized as "Sympathy for the Devil." We laughed, realizing both of us had learned the same blasphemy from music nerd PG. We signed *request* and *prayer*, ASL words she'd taught me. They flowed together, normal-friend code for "see ya on AIM."

I circled her dad's car, observing its bumper stickers: three Buffalo Sabres logos and one "IN EVENT OF RAPTURE, VEHICLE UNMANNED." He'd once taken her to a purity ball, where fathers promised to guard their daughters' virginity. *Imagine Mom vowing that about mine! Awkward city! She couldn't even keep me from watching Wild Things! Sorry.*

I mouthed, "Mr. Primrose," to him and shook his hand like I was hammering nails. He patted his heart, tapped his chin, and tapped his chest: "Happy birthday." Leaning in, I asked her how to tell him thank you. She showed me, giggling because it was kind of like blowing a kiss.

Back inside, Calebs were irate because Carman had lost his Hell in a Cell match to Satan. So they created Satan's real archrival, an olive-skinned man with long hair, a beard, wide-armed poses, no fear of bleeding, and a 3:16 shirt.

"Is this blasphemous?" one asked.

"Not yet," Josiah said, sprawled across the couch.

"What about when I said Proverbs has a wisdom goddess?" I asked.

"Wisdom personification. Vocab word."

"Put Jesus' skill points into defense," said one Caleb. "Tanking damage is his entire gimmick."

"No, we're gonna kick Satan's butt, you pussy," I said.

"Hard to picture Jesus fighting anybody, you cock gobbler."

"Carman danced for our entertainment despite being Italian," said another Caleb, "and you're letting Satan get away with killing him, you peace freak?"

"Whoop Satan's butt," said Josiah. "It's Satan, you fairy."

We cast Satan through tables and slammed ladders into Satan's skull. It was funny the first, second, and hundredth time. But no matter how many elbows we dropped, the bell rang, the menu screen loaded again, and Satan was as good as new.

At 2 a.m., we microwaved grapes and flung fruit-goo at each other until Mom woke up yelling. Once everybody was snoring, I dug through my Bible while plagued with a horrible vision.

Know how Satan, the heavyweight champion of the fallen world, gets his ass kicked all the way from Matthew 4 through Revelation 20, when he's finally thrown into Hell?

Well, here's the problem: In Revelation 21, even after Satan's damnation, the menu screen loads again.

ELEVEN
MY CHEMICAL ROMANCE

AUGUST 2001

"As we plunge into the guts of another school year, when the world grinds against us the hardest," newly assigned youth pastor Dave-Tony told the Wednesday night crowd, "we're gonna refocus on preserving ourselves for biblical marriage, okay?"

I'd taken Timmy for granted. He was cool because he didn't mind being dorky. Dave-Tony was always stumbling into gruesome wordplay, freaking out about the sin du jour, and — worst of all — creeping out Alexa.

"Now, I could plug the boring stuff, pointing out the Bible insists we avoid abortion, premarital affection, teen pregnancy outside wedlock, and homosexualism. But lemme titillate you with the benefits of waiting, okay?"

Dave-Tony called his wife onto the stage, wiggling his eyebrows at her golden hair and obvious physique. "Here comes the pastor's-hot-wife routine," whispered somebody.

"Because my beautiful trophy and I waited," Dave-Tony said, "God rewarded us with an X-rated honeymoon slam-packed full of ..."

Eww. Hip-thrusting and grunting, he catalogued their pent-up eruptions. She looked mortified, while he seemed to think the crowd was snickering *with* him. I'd heard church leaders overshare all sorts of bodily details, but never that many at once.

"That's God's insta-passion promise," he said, wiping his forehead as our jaws unclenched, along with our buttholes. "Wedding night, all your switches flip. Gentlemen, start your engines! But only if you've waited, okay? Otherwise, that marriage is ice-cold snoozeville!" Sinners pretended that sex takes practice, but men of God assured us: just get married, then get instinctual.

Dave-Tony preached a parable we'd all heard many times, one about tasting a piece of bubblegum already coated by another man's saliva. "Nobody wants used stuff," he said, adding a loogie-hocking noise. "Gals, reward your husband with something flawless! And guys, that monster between your legs isn't yours, okay? It's Jesus', until he gives it a garage to park in!"

And he described a bride horrified by her groom's ex-girlfriends lining up to claim slices of his heart. "She'd earned her white dress, but he'd surrendered his purity to disease-rotted, purple-haired fleabags!"

And he told the Coca-Cola parable, about sipping a drink, but swallowing a stranger's backwash, bacteria, and vomit, the long-awaited lesson from the Coke-spit game we'd played as vacation Bible school nine-year-olds.

Premarital sex was constantly presented as the only truly permanent sin. As we all sat one slippery-slope makeout away from detonating nukes in each other's shorts, I felt disgusted by bodies near me, as if they'd mercilessly designed their own femininity in, well, No Mercy.

"You might remember, last year at camp, Mister Eli had everyone confess nails into sin buckets," Dave-Tony said, making people wince at the memory. "We tallied those confessions. Lust stuff blew everything else away, okay? Blew hard! We're tainted, okay? And last week's lock-in confirmed many of you are way too deep in that taint!"

Really? Me and the bros spent the lock-in wrestling with our jeans on. Why'd the bad kids sin during the overnight post-puberty party? Weren't they afraid of being caught in storage rooms at 5 a.m. by outnumbered grownups who'd needed fifty coffees just to reach midnight? Glad me and my friends will remain chaste forever, unlike the befouled seniors.

"Next," Dave-Tony continued, listing new rules, "no more boy-girl front hugs. Only side hugs. Squashing breasts releases chemicals, just like dope, increasing the female's dangerous potency, okay? Next! If it jiggles, strap it down!"

Snickers erupted, but seeing girls slump with embarrassed faces made me feel sad. **"YOU'LL REGRET CRAVING THEIR IMMODESTY!"** *Sorry.*

"There's a book our young men are gonna read," Dave-Tony continued, "about the battles we endure against temptatious imagery, even in this room right now. And a book for our ladies, about how dating's no way to find Prince Charming." (Every new youth pastor assigned I Kissed Dating Goodbye like it wasn't already the fifth gospel.)

Finally, he raised a wallet-sized card. "Do you agree with the world that you're too weak to control yourselves, surrendering to STDs, sodomification, and dope? Or are you bold enough to select the sexier path? If so, come sign a purity pledge."

The first to walk forward was dipshit Gabe, proving the whole thing was wack. Then again, Josiah was among the upperclassmen walking forward. Juniors followed him, along with everyone else.

According to the cards, exemplary Christians commit to NO KISSING UNTIL WEDDING, NO DATING UNTIL ENGAGEMENT, NO TOUCHING SKIN, and more. Imagine being the only one not checking any boxes! Might as well wear a shirt that said DISEASE-ROTTED! We did a group prayer, emphasizing that the fates of America, the universe, and even our honeymoons depended on us upholding our celestial contracts.

After a (heated) game of boys-against-girls dodgeball, we lingered beside a hallway table. Someone was selling silver purity rings, the kind worn until the wedding night.

"All this shit, just to avoid church-girl abortions," barked Alexa, glaring at gasping grownups. "They could just make everybody watch health class videos! Babies are grody."

"You big weakling! Babies are rewards for guarding our hearts," Sophie said, ignoring Alexa's eye-rolling groan. The pastor's niece slipped on a new ring. "Mine's inscribed on the inside, just like the One Ring to Rule Them All!"

"Perfect," said Alexa, blowing a big pink bubble. "Let a guy carry you up a hill, then roll around in the dark until you ditch the ring!"

"Aww, you read that far, Precious?" Sophie said, clutching Alexa's forearm. "Your cool friends are gonna dump you, nerrr-rrrd."

"CliffsNotes. That counts. Now we gotta see Fast and Furious again. You pwwwomised."

"Oh no, anything but more Paul Walker," Sophie giggled, fanning her blushing face. I felt jealous, not that I cared.

"Ooh, let's try Dave-Tony's chemical hugs," Alexa said, wrapping Sophie tight, looking through red hair at me. "God yes! Isaac, she wants to chemical-hug you, I bet."

We'd both hugged friends all day. What was one more? After a sheepish side hug, Sophie latched back onto Alexa from behind.

"For reals, do you two try to look like girlfriends?" PG asked, on break from recruiting some Calebs to start an emo band. "Not that there's anything wrong with that ... is a thing people say." *Ooh, time to impress them with my biblical lesbian knowledge. The Book of Ruth might be about lesbians! Hey, has anybody noticed King David kinda had a boyf–* **"REGRET!"** *Sorry.*

"Don't gotta try," Alexa said, making their prom pose more offensive by raising her arms high enough to reveal her whale-tail.

She kept basking in attention until a muscle-shirted senior lumbered past, bellowing, "I can't wear virgin rings. Guess why."

"Nah, these rings are tight-tight! Shorties fiend for yoked virgins with Mustangs," bellowed his puka shell friend as Alexa preened her hair and Sophie fanned body spray. "Snap, they got tribal virgin rings. What's the card say about butt stuff?"

Alexa followed those 1990s-scented deviants, but grinned like she counted on being halted by her favorite homeschooler. On cue, Sophie grabbed the taller girl's wrist and tugged her toward Dairy Queen. Arm in arm, they sang "Can't Fight the Moonlight." Cutest friendship ever. Marrying them both sounded ideal, but unfortunately, Christians outlawed biblical marriage.

"Pastor said butt stuff can't possibly involve love," bellowed Puka Shell as juniors snickered and an adult hissed. "That means there's no love to give away too early. Virginity loophole! My history teacher said, in Spartacus times, being the butt-pounder didn't count. Ergo factor, butts are freebies!"

"My neighbor's chiropractor's cousin said Mormons say monster-in-punani doesn't count unless you pound. Way intimate. Also: flannel PJs, commando. Mad friction, pimpin'."

"Another loophole is wrapping her panties around your monster. No condom means no premeditated sin! Major girth upgrade, son. Yo, this one time at church Beach Fest ..."

"Blood, anything goes at Beach Fest. Oh, another loophole ..."

What BS. Bad kids have cheated purity ever since MTV invented lust and Bill Clinton invented lying. A couple years ago, I even found a list by veteran church teenagers, explaining the partial virginity percentages you can retain by doing everything but punani-pounding. Percentages? Loopholes? Pretending first base isn't adultery? Pathetic bullcrap that tricks used-up people into thinking they're still lovable!

G00dbyeskyharb0r (PG): hai hansummm ♥‿♥
would ya like to take a surveyyy

G00dbyeskyharb0r: platonically hansum

xSHARKSWITHRABIESx: kk mah byootiful ... sister
in christ ✞

I clicked her link, which took me to a message board. After Dave-Tony had asked us to withhold pledge details from opposite-sex friends (since discussing purity would arouse purity-jeopardizing chemicals), one of our smartasses had created a workaround.

"YOU'LL REGRET BREAKING THE FIRST RULE OF VIRGIN CLUB." *I'm not! My pseudonym's informing other pseudonyms about my sacred oath to resist premarital makeouts, non-Christian dating, and stuff that never tempted me anyway.*

Easily identifiable posts revealed PG's promises matched mine, even Alexa had checked some boxes, and Sophie was a nun in a bunker guarded by Terminators on an undiscovered planet patrolled by Death Stars.

Tenth grade started with the annual See You at the Pole school-prayer gathering.

Still wary of the event's oxymoronic "public-school Christians," I unveiled my sophomore uniform: tight black jeans and black T-shirts of loud Christian bands none of those secular perverts would know. (Never mind that my first choice, Project 86, had been on MTV for a year by then.)

"Radiohead hasn't done a studio version of 'True Love Waits' yet," said some kid standing beside me.

I shrugged, looking at my new silver ring's emblem of suffering and shame, the cross upon which cops assassinated Jesus because finger-banging would happen 1,972 years later at Beach Fest.

"That means," Radiohead Kid said, "true 'True Love Waits' waits."

TWELVE
EXTREME DAYS

SEPTEMBER 2001

A bunch of Tuesday nights in a row, the whole crew filled my basement for Video Games Church. With no clue how to run a Bible study, we'd chatter until a Caleb blurted something like "non-Christians should be banished to San Francisco," which made me scold him until Josiah reeled me back in. PG played poppy emo versions of worship songs and even worked up courage to write her own. Sophie spoke without nerves, explaining that Jesus' lack of human father meant "he kinda didn't have a boy chromosome, maybe," making the faces of Calebs and Graces twist in thought until Tekken Tag happened to the sounds of TobyMac.

Well, somewhere on the list of bad things caused by terrorists was our Tuesday streak ending. Living basically in the middle of where the four airplanes ended up? Yeah, things felt quite Revelation.

On the phone, Sophie and I decided to hang up and check on other friends. She felt "responsible for so many hearts," and I felt the same, but less mushily.

"Jesus loves you, Ize," she said like usual.

"Me and Jesus love you, Soph."

"... sorry ..."

"..."

"... hang on ..."

"..."

"Closed my door. Um, I love you too!"

Got a little too fired up by patriotism. I love lots of people. Watch.

"Hey Josiah, I love you," I said, finally getting through. Church girls clogged his phone line on regular days, let alone on 9/11.

"Hey man. Love you too. You okay?"

Apparently, when the second plane hit, Josiah's teacher quoted the Bible's "be strong and have courage." Then Josiah prayed with kids in the halls all day.

"Oh right, at Christian school, you're allowed to pray," I said.

"Hey, what really happens when you pray at public school?"

"Uhh … nobody … seems to care," I realized. *Wait, why have church guys always said the government banned prayer at school? Nobody except telepathic Professor X could stop prayer. I'm about to be screamed at for doubting my elders, so I'll stop.* **"GOOD CALL."**

"Pray with people tomorrow, dude," said Josiah. "Also, if you make my cousin sad, I'll tap you out." *What? Random.*

Mom finally got home. We wanted national revenge, but all we could do was hug, lock doors, and thank God our president looked cool in tough-guy hats.

hearitinmyghost (Bobbi): crazy to think the people who attacked NYC are fundies

xSHARKSWITHRABIESx: omggg todays not the day for this

xSHARKSWITHRABIESx: if you were raised like me youd believe like me

hearitinmyghost: hmm … what about vice versa?

xSHARKSWITHRABIESx: sure! for a while

hearitinmyghost: then u'd grow out of believing what u were taught?

xSHARKSWITHRABIESx: yes just to annoy the christian version of you

hearitinmyghost: [hug?]

xSHARKSWITHRABIESx: [hug] <3 u Know-It-All

hearitinmyghost: <3 u Jesus Boy

I emailed the Calebs, "i love you morons." One responded with a P.O.D. quote. Weird thing about 2001: Five years after that Christian rapcore band's minimum-budget second album had an error version tainted by porn audio, they spent weeks battling NSYNC for TRL #1. (That was no longer the weirdest thing about 2001.)

> LetsTalkAboutLexBaby (Alexa): if you hurt my precious ill assassinate you

> xSHARKSWITHRABIESx: wtf

> xSHARKSWITHRABIESx: u ok? <3

> LetsTalkAboutLexBaby: yeah. u? <3

> xSHARKSWITHRABIESx: if u need to talk, im around <3

> xSHARKSWITHRABIESx: checkin in haha <3

> LetsTalkAboutLexBaby: i need help

> xSHARKSWITHRABIESx: call me lmao <3

> LetsTalkAboutLexBaby: if anybody asks, say i was home online all night thx :-*

I emailed "I love you" to old youth pastor Timmy.

> g00dbyeskyharb0r (PG): omfG u WUV sophii?? ima play guitar at ur weddn!!!

> xSHARKSWITHRABIESx: i luv u also

> g00dbyeskyharb0r: u jus luv her not WWWUVVV her?? booooooooooo!!! i hoped armagddon made u confess feelinz bc ur skurred erbody gon die 2moro

> g00dbyeskyharb0r: kthxbai lubb u 2

> xSHARKSWITHRABIESx: call me if ur skurred haha (″˘ ³˘)(˘ ε˘ ″)

The only explanation for everyone knowing what I'd told Sophie: The CIA was monitoring me.

> xSHARKSWITHRABIESx: hey dude, been a while. love u

> BadBoys5318008 (Amir, my former football teammate, a lowly kicker hoping to score touchdowns): too long man!! scariest ish ever. love u bro!!

Lying in the backyard, I couldn't hear any highway sounds. I kept trying to picture Jesus retaliating, but everything was dead clouds and silent stars. Mom called me inside.

"Stay strong, Isaac," growled Eli on the phone.

"Okay. I love you."

"Love you, buddy. This was bound to happen, after America bombed those people for years. Unsaved people on both sides are gonna die. Our job's getting more urgent."

Eli's opinions always surprised his peers. Despite his beard and Oakleys, he sometimes grunted about Jesus being "a socio-anarchist, not that it matters, because our only mandate is to boycott Hell."

"Christians don't blow stuff up," I said, hating Eli's anti-American politics more than ever before. "Other than those '90s fake Christians whose hearts were in the right places or whatever."

"Who says they were fake? Was there a net gain in souls saved?"

"The CIA's listening, dummy."

"Hey, CIA, you must accept Christ. Over."

"Man, you can't say America deserved this. America helps people."

"Buddy, watching those towers fall, numbers ran through my head. Hell's population soared," he said, catching his breath. "I don't fear death. I fear *unsaved* people dying. It might even be rational to eliminate anyone who endangers the unsaved. Foreign, domestic, friend, foe, family, whoever."

"Hey, CIA, I dislike terrorism," I emphasized, peeking out the window for unmarked vehicles.

"You're awesome," he chuckled. "Don't get distracted by guys using tragedy to sell Rapture books. And don't waste time rooting for empires. Babylon, Rome, England, America … empires fall. Keep souls outta Hell. That's the mission."

"Man, rotten.com posted guys jumping from the towers," said a guy in shop class. "I printed it. Didn't know what else to do."

"Bombs over Baghdad," said another. "The terrorists came from literally Babylon! Freaking biblical!"

We'd grown up pampered, never ducking under tables for nuke drills like our elders, just dinky little active-shooter drills. So fifteen-year-old men like me had to step up, as Josiah had advised.

"When the Old Testament says Babylon, it means *Babylon*, not Iraq or America," I told my worried classmates, trying to recite Eli's utterances and Sophie's heresies from Pastor Jack's pulpit-unfriendly library. "In Revelation, Babylon means Rome, which is gone, except it has soccer. Psychos told everybody the Bible predicts nuclear war, but they're just selling books."

"The Bible says we're getting nuked?" groaned shop class' only girl. "That bites fat dong!"

Really, it felt like the proto-Left Behind doomsayers had been right all along. Rough time to be a smartass, to say the least.

At a special weeknight service, with all kids and adults crammed into one safe place, Pastor Jack preached, "We must radiate love, now more than ever." *But how's that gonna punish villains?*

Once we got home, Mom cranked the volume on Fox News. *That's more like it!*

"The pagans and the abortionists and the feminists and the gays and the lesbians who are actively trying to make that an alternative lifestyle," said Jerry Falwell, our pope, "all of them who tried to secularize America, I point the finger in their face and say, you helped this happen."

Hoping for rah-rah, I just felt gross. That famous Christian was telling everyone that I believed tragedy happened because Bobbi agreed with me about girls. I couldn't think of any gay guys I knew, but wanted to think they were okay anyway, even though that'd mean unwinding five Bible verses, not just one. **"YOU'LL ETERNALLY REGRET EXPANDING YOUR GAY AGENDA!"** *But Falwell's embarrassing! I can't respect a guy scared of Teletubbies!*

Then he said terrorists had "given us what we deserve" for "throwing God out of the public schools." *So the attacks were my fault for not smuggling God back in? That's more like it! Wait, who was strong enough to evict God to begin with? If Falwell's right, liberals are mightier than Professor X or even Galactus. Man, what's in that purple hair dye?*

By then, I sat taller than Mom, so her head rested on my shoulder. Her guy Pat Robertson nodded at Falwell, blaming the Supreme Court, agreeing God was in detention, and marveling at the inbound apocalypse.

"Still think the Bible Code's a scam?" she said.

"Nah, Revelation's got false prophets. And both these guys whiffed on Rapture predictions."

She glared at me, two tears streaking down her cheek, and walked to her bedroom, chin jutted high. Carman's "God in America Again" blasted from behind her door. I heard her call her semi-boyfriend and dump him for missing church and failing me as a role model.

The world needed a man of the house.

THIRTEEN
WHAT IT IS TO BURN
NOVEMBER 2001

WINNING PAINTBALL WAR HAD EARNED US THE RIGHT TO PICK WHICH Christian band we'd invite to Harvest Season, according to our ever more dearly missed youth pastor Timmy. But we'd never filled out forms or whatever, and then 9/11 had further distracted everyone from forms or whatever.

So we nagged the loathsome Dave-Tony into keeping Timmy's bargain, then decided Alexa should pick the band, as we hoped to nudge her toward exploring the Christian MP3s that'd save her soul. But she refused to download anything because guys at school burned CDs for her anyway.

Somehow, Sophie talked her into joining Harvest Season setup day, where we planned to play Christian bands until Alexa liked one. And with Harvest Season in two days, PG's emergency band of Calebs would just cover whichever group won Alexa's favor. Foolproof plan!

Everyone greeted each other with sneaky and/or non-sneaky front hugs, except me and Sophie, who side-hugged. Inside joke, maybe.

After six hours of setup work, we convinced a senior to teach us how to use the sanctuary's sound equipment, promising to only play music from Christian stores.

Ten of us crammed into the audio booth, confident we'd find bands Alexa could tolerate. Then she'd get saved, meaning I could date her, meaning she'd ruin me at Beach Fest, giving me a dramatic testimony about atoning for Beach Fest. Foolproof plan!

"Lifehouse is Christian! They sing about Jesus like he's their boyfriend," Alexa snickered, unaware that Christian youths had always made that same joke about awkwardly intimate worship songs.

First, Josiah played her the goofy Newsboys song about Hell-bound souls not deserving breakfast. She spat thirteen cuss words. Sophie played Relient K, every church girl's favorite band. "Punk sucks," Alexa groaned. A Grace played Steven Curtis Chapman. "Grocery store music," Alexa grunted. Best Caleb played Pigeon John. Alexa was shocked to find herself calling a Christian rapper "pretty fun," but she didn't want to hear Calebs attempt hip-hop at Harvest Season or anywhere else.

From the sanctuary floor, people yelled requests. At the controls, Caleb flipped through ZOEgirl, the Insyderz, Delirious?, Element 101 ...

"Just not loud-ass enough," said Alexa, smirking at disappointed faces.

"How loud-butt you want?" I asked, grabbing a CD that'd out-decibel her nu metal.

"Don't do it," Sophie said, squeezing my arm. "Wait. Do it! Yes!"

Amid distorted noodling, a wraith shriek froze the sanctuary. Some hands covered ears. Other bodies leapt with delight. Another howl struck. Josiah was mortified. Sophie was nervous-giddy. PG cackled. Caleb squirmed. Hammers fell, drums blasted, and some kids sprinted into the sanctuary's instant mosh pit, while others speed-walked out in disgust.

"WHAT THE FUCK IS THIS," a wide-eyed Alexa yelled in my face.

"BLACK METAL, WHICH IS ABOUT BURNING CHURCHES IN NORWAY, BU–"

"THIS BAND BURNS CHURCHES IN NORWAY?"

"NO, THIS BAND ATTENDS CHURCHES IN TAMPA."

Underoath wasn't incredible back then, but they were sure as shit better than Alexa's beloved Crazy Town. Originally an Evangelical band playing Christianity's most off-limits sub-genre, Underoath had just begun transitioning toward mainstream metal.

"NOTICE THEY SNUCK GODLY LYRICS INTO" the song stopped "SATANIC CHURCH-BURNing ... music ..."

Silence. *No fair, that song had six minutes left!*

All eyes swung to the sanctuary's center, where the beast snarling toward me was Eli. At the sight of my angry brother, everyone vanished.

Oops, I'd been waving devil fingers beside Alexa, who'd been torso-thrusting in a Slytherin hoodie, unzipped over her bare navel. She fled, too.

I plopped into the desk chair to face the music.

Eli's bearded face boiled olive-red. "Boy, what's wrong with you? Satanic *what*? In the *sanctuary*?" As my brother roared, I was embarrassed to know that people outside the booth could see me shrinking. He accused me of ruining a night when people might've gotten saved, an act that made me responsible for souls.

Panicking against such an accusation, I searched for the song's lyrics, showing him the lines about making black metal for Jesus.

Eli stood up straight. "Huh." He read again, then left.

Something rustled from behind my chair. Sophie emerged and planted an illegal front hug. *Chemicals!*

"I picked that band," she said. "I should've spoken up. Gosh, he's scary!"

"I picked that song. Doesn't matter. Somebody might yell at Alexa next, so w–"

"Oh, crêpe," she cursed, leaning into the hallway, eyes darting. "Let's hurry!"

We slipped into an empty hall and crouched beside the front door, peeking outside. On the lawn, kids were playing pickup soccer.

"How'd you lure her to volunteer day, anyway?" I whispered.

"We're friends, duh," she shrugged. "Saturday, we spent five minutes at some drinky Halloween party, dressed as each other. Sunday, people yelled at me. 'Alexa's a jezebel, a W-word, and ... gasp ... a Harry Potter reader!' She's actually sweet! She takes good care of her dad! I hope she gets saved soon. She's not an anything reader."

Distracted from all that by urgent mental images, I asked the baggy-flannel tomboy, "You wore a tube top?"

Blushing beneath her bangs, she said, "With a T-shirt under." We gazed into each other's eyes forever (like three seconds). *Who is it I have a crush on? Oh right, Alexa. Crap, we gotta find Alexa!*

By the lawn's edge, we spotted her letting a senior arrange her hips into kicking form as Dave-Tony appeared, mid-rant. We ran to help. Alexa had never gotten saved, so if he upset her into finding a way to leave, I'd have no idea where she'd spend eternity after being forgiven for what she'd do with me at the Beach Fest she wouldn't attend if Dave-Tony made her leave. Hurry!

Dave-Tony shrieked so much that the soccer kids stood still. We yelled for his attention, but the situation worsened as a Ford Taurus parked beside the lawn.

Shit. Pastor Jack stepped out, and Dave-Tony spindled toward him, blaming "Miss Midriff" for Satanism polluting the holy place.

I stopped beside Jack and panted, "It was my b."

Sophie told her uncle, "No, my b."

"*My* b," said Best Caleb, emerging from the lawn crowd. "I pushed the button."

"It's on me to lead, Dad," said Josiah. "The b was mine, whatever that means."

"The whole thing was about my b," PG insisted. "B is for band."

Moshers claimed they'd egged on the b. Soccer people wanted in on whatever the b was.

But Dave-Tony kept chirping in Pastor Jack's ear. Lips curled, Jack looked down his nose at Alexa, who jutted her chin up at him in silence.

And behind us boomed a heavy voice. "I become all things to all people, so Christ might save them." We turned to see Eli, his concrete forearms crossed. "Guy called Apostle Paul said that. I believe 'all people' includes rascals who listen to loud racket."

Look at that powerful ally with a skull full of Bible verses. Believe me, I knew how much it sucked to oppose him, whether in backyard football or debates about Purgatory ("not biblical," he'd always argued). The manly man of God plopped his paw onto my shoulder, so we all stood taller.

Skinny scrub Dave-Tony kept squealing up at Jack about belly-button piercings and Harry Potter. Who you gonna side with: Dave-Tony or the guy who could eat Dave-Tony? Might makes right, pal!

Before our eyes, Pastor Jack changed shape, like John Arbuckle puffing his chest near pretty veterinarians. Jack rolled his sleeves and clenched his jaw, a daily-driver Taurus becoming a roaring Charger.

"As your shepherd," Jack rasped, bass-boost activated, "I've got far bigger concerns than Christ's soldiers enjoying some rambunctious worship. Cartoons aren't on my radar when God's chosen nation is at war. Now, do my troops want doughnuts or not? Father God's enemies will be sick to realize attacks on New York City won't stop Harvest Season!"

We ate it up, plus the doughnuts, then joined the soccer game, which by then felt a little too French.

Sophie asked me how to kick, so I told her, "You kick fine. Trust me, I was a middle-school punter."

A senior in an Uncle Kracker hat pulled me aside. "The girl who dresses like you wanted you to touch her hips, genius. You scared 'cause her uncle thinks he's Jack *Bauer* now?"

Psh. Seniors think they know everything.

"Thanks for, like, having my back," Alexa said, quietly accepting group hugs. "Maybe I wouldn't trash a CD of whatever Jesus music sucks the least ass."

LetsTalkAboutLexBaby (Alexa): u guys didnt have to burn me TEN cds

xSHARKSWITHRABIESx: it was our whole tuesday night project!

LetsTalkAboutLexBaby: FINE i like the vampire song by blindside

LetsTalkAboutLexBaby: is "stars" really PG?? shes dope

LetsTalkAboutLexBaby: u guys make me feel accepted :*)

xSHARKSWITHRABIESx: [illegal front hug]

LetsTalkAboutLexBaby: [sex]

xSHARKSWITHRABIESx: roflmfaooo hahaha

LetsTalkAboutLexBaby: jesus fucking christ, audio adrenaline sucks

---

PG and her Calebs named their "Norwegian metal" band Skull Hill, but Harvest Season arrived before they could learn anything about metal or Norway. As families carved pumpkins, Skull Hill played weird emo covers of Christian musicians — Jars of Clay, Amy Grant, Grits, etc. — who'd been accepted by mainstream America.

Next up, preaching truths about mainstream America's rejection of all Christians, was Pastor Jack in a tough-guy ball cap. *No more Mr. Nice Church!* He said born-again men of God had to retake America, defeat religions that wanted to conquer America, and defend our president's enemy-punishing Christian values. *Gimme a hell yeah!*

"First time I've ever gotten quote-unquote political on church property," he said, cutting off a U-S-A chant. "And now every demon in Hell and the Middle East is quaking! That rising beast of Revelation has stirred Father God's sleeping-giant army!"

Goodbye to dorky crap about the Antichrist being a metaphor! Everything's a metaphor until 9/11 happens! Chest inflated, chin high, Jack preached awesome stuff like, "Before Christ saved me, I went to three different jails. I'm ashamed to say the other men went to three hospitals." *Now that's the goshdang gospel!* "God in America Again" played as fireworks blasted. All around, huge cheers rose for the song's lyric that claimed the Founding Fathers believed non-Christians weren't Americans. People pumped their fists at Jack, my father figure.

In the bounce house, watching a pumpkin festival become WrestleMania, Alexa said, "Jesus was cool. The red words rip ass."

She read the Bible?! Sophie, jumping nearby, latched a hand onto her unsaved friend's shoulder. *It's happening!*

"Red words are the main words," said the jumping Josiah. I prepared to stop jumping, land on a knee, and propose. Patience.

"So explain something, you fundie freak," she said, spinning toward Josiah. "Jesus hated violence, but your dad wants war. What the fuck?"

Uhh, better keep jumping. His grin vanished. Sophie's other hand grabbed his shoulder, forming a bridge of black and pink bracelets.

"Turn the other … cheek," said the smartass, slapping her own jeans butt. "Seems simple to this heathen. Too complex for Simba?"

"You want them to get away with killing Americans?" he shouted, no longer jumping, only bouncing in place.

"America probably attacked itself," she spat, making me and even Sophie scowl. "Christians cheerleading war? Where's that in the red ink?"

"That red ink says, 'I did not come to bring peace, but a sword,'" said Josiah during another U-S-A chant. "Alexis, you should study before you pipe u–"

"My name is Alexandra, you fucker! Where's it say regular humans can swing swords, let alone shoot guns? This church wants countries to burn because some government says so! Jesus hated the fucking government!"

Meanwhile, on the loudspeakers, the Carman song promised God would punish America because gay people had left the closet. Husbands on the lawn preached along with him. Josiah gritted his teeth at Alexa.

"We're preaching spiritual war," I argued, trying to calm a fight, mad at the bleeding-heart name-caller but wondering how the new girl was so easily unearthing things from my own mind. Like: *How can Christians keep saying we deserved it, but we gotta avenge it?* **"REGRET!"** *Sorry. You're right. After all, who's Revelation Jesus condemning with fire swords, if not al-Qaeda?*

Surely Revelation Jesus wasn't condemning Rome itself, because the modern Rome is … **"REGRET!"** *Sorry.*

"Once we realize," strained Sophie, "we all breathe the same Spirit, then w–"

"Not your New Age crap again," said Josiah, sliding out and brooding toward the popcorn stand. Alexa stormed toward the nacho stand. They shouted, "No, *I'll* lift *you* up in prayer," at each other. *Hey, at least Alexa's praying!*

I was a paragraph into a Revelation question before I noticed Sophie's wet eyes reflecting blue and red fireworks. Hand on her sagging shoulder, I routed her toward a bench and offered her Mountain Dew, startled by how much she was chastising herself for not fixing their fight.

She talked. I realized den-mom status was a burden, especially for an introvert, especially when every day was 9/11. I couldn't carry it for her, but I could … offer a piggyback ride?

Navigating the crowd like that, hoodie arms and warm legs snug around me, Aladdin was proud to be seen. Yet Jasmine was being *watched.* She wasn't supposed to premaritally touch any boys, let alone squeeze limbs around fatherless weirdos in ripped black jeans.

Under flashing purple smoke and loudspeakers begging Christians to capture the Capitol, we snuck from warzone to corn maze, where we got so lost that nobody knew the pastor's niece was crying into the chest of a devil-music riffraff whose mystery-gushing heart was realizing … every love song had always … been about hiding beneath fireworks … while holding tight … to a raspberry-scented miracle.

Oh. Duh.

This is what that feels like? Whoa.

Wait. Help. Uh-oh.

"YOU HAD ONE HEART, BOY. YOU'VE JUST GIVEN IT AWAY FOREVER. LONG AFTER THE LAST SUNSET, YOU WILL STILL REGRET THIS."

Dammit. Not her. Shit.

BigDog699999999999 [Best Caleb]: [confession secrecy zone] just JO'd about corn maze rumors and lady marmalade video. mostly corn maze rumors

xSHARKSWITHRABIESx: tmi

xSHARKSWITHRABIESx: what rumors

BigDog699999999999: MAKEOUT CITY!! mostly seniors. also matthew snyder and alexa. pg and some jerk! both stoltzfus brothers and alexa. idk whats true. me n hannah grace were blameless but deserve rumor attention. and another rumor...................... ?????

xSHARKSWITHRABIESx: nothing happened. but [confession secrecy zone]

BigDog699999999999: spare no detail. type x-rated adjectives so i can pray accurately

xSHARKSWITHRABIESx: dude i think im like in love or some wack ish like that

BigDog699999999999: just tell her "girl im da library, so check out mo b dick" (im teaching myself hiphop as you can see)

xSHARKSWITHRABIESx: sophie's such a better person than me. she'll marry some pastor. i just sighed OUT LOUD wtf

BigDog699999999999: ok good you're done saying "i like alexa" while googly eyeing sophie

xSHARKSWITHRABIESx: i feel PAINFUL STOMACH GRAVITY but weve KISSED STUPID DATING GOODBYE and the pastors niece cant hold PINKIES. WHAT if i lead her freaking ASTRAY FROM GOD. caleb my whole stupid everything hurts SO BAD I JO about me and her FALLING INTO A VOLCANO so we can SHARE ONE MELTED-TOGETHER BODY in heaven. IS THAT WEIRD

BigDog699999999999: nah, let it out

xSHARKSWITHRABIESx: i cant stop listening to THE GOOGOO DOLLS

BigDog699999999999: tmi

FOURTEEN
CALL ME ISHMAEL

DECEMBER 2001

At school, I had one person per class to joke with, knew enough rap references to join general convos, and had found the cafeteria metalheads, who liked my CDs until I revealed they were Christian. I refused to ruin Norma Jean for them.

Some classmates knew my beliefs, probably because of my backpack's loudly Evangelical patches, which I often hid in embarrassment so nobody would persecute me. (Then I felt ashamed of embarrassment, so I added more Christian patches. Repeat.) People apologized for cussing around me, even if I explained that Psalms is a curse-fest. Some debated me about Bible stuff. I won, unless it was Bobbi, because she copied Carl Sagan, who cheated by writing worship poems that used "the universe" to mean "God."

Meanwhile, I'd admitted there really were other outspoken Christian students in that supposedly secular cesspool, but their bright-eyedness made me feel like a depressed fraud.

In the hallways, I was supposed to be everyone's unquenchable source of Christlike joy. Even when I was down, I forced myself to smile, smuggling God into demonic strongholds so 9/11 wouldn't happen again.

Amir, an old middle-school lunchmate and former football teammate, got moved into my tenth-grade PE class despite being a junior. He'd always been pretty popular — dating girls, wearing cool sneakers, and trading rap mixes.

A week prior, someone had bumped him into the lobby's big trophy case. He'd turned and looked, but only to make sure no glass had broken. He'd laughed. **"MOCK HIS FALSE GOD! DEFEND AMERICA!"** I'd laughed. **"GOOD BOY."**

Another day, I saw him find a note somebody left for him, then trash it as two girls snickered. In PE dodgeball, somebody said, "On three, counter-terrorists win," and six kids threw at Amir. He batted one ball away, got hit, walked away, and got hit again. He laughed, so I laughed.

He was a tall junior football player (kickers count as football players) with an impressive goatee, a sick zigzag in his fade, and dark eyes that made girls look twice. His wannabe bullies were milk-fart sophomores. *He'll be fine.*

Time to head upstairs for Mountain Dew, even though I had plenty downstairs.

On one hand, I couldn't believe Mom still played board games with alcoholic monsters. On the other hand, whenever I accidentally wore nothing under an unzipped hoodie, sometimes one of the tipsy women would mutter something that made Mom shoo me away from them, confirming I was the sexy danger man. *Exciting! Wait, why is this fun for me, but church girls have to feel evil for wearing gym shorts?* **"YOU'LL REGRET THIS!"** *Which part?* **"WISHING YOUR FRIENDS DRESSED WHORISHLY!"** *That's not what I said.* **"REGRET!"** *Sorry.*

In the kitchen, two milfs spewed gossip about another milf. (By "milfs," I meant "average-looking forty-year-olds in the same building as my room.") Another complained that it was taking forever to fix Afghanistan, two whole months after we'd liberated it. When the tallest milf yelled, "The president should just inspect everyone who looks like, ya know, them," the glasses milf agreed.

Mom, preparing Trivial Pursuit, looked up at her half-drunk friends.

After 9/11, she'd lined our yard with more American flags than anyone else in our neighborhood, had me install a bigger bronze cross on our front door, and added another patriotic bumper sticker to her minivan every few days. That night, she was wearing a bald eagle sweatshirt. But just like Jesus, her skin was olive.

Her star-spangled cactus earrings shimmied as she said, "Everyone?"

The spirit of fear went deeper than I'd realized. Everyone was scared of being attacked, but some were also scared of being lumped in with the attackers. Well, if lumping was causing fear, who was doing the lumping?

I zipped my hoodie up — *show's over!* — because Mom's friends were no longer milfs. They were lumpers.

Coach Watkins, busy flirting fruitlessly with the volleyball coach, always let us call our own fouls. We never played rough, since bleeding at 9 a.m. sucks. Except that, one day, Amir grabbed a rebound and landed on someone's foot, yelping, "My bad."

"Call the foul," said Amir's teammate, making a bunch of Muslim jokes. My teammates called him a pussy for *not* calling a foul. That was a new one. Then he got fouled again, a shoulder into his chest.

"Bullshit," I realized out loud, calling a flagrant foul on my own teammate. A rules debate began. Coach Watkins yelled at me for "cussing in a classy lady's presence." Everyone argued, but I'd overheard a deacon's meeting before, so I knew how to filibuster until the bell rang.

Another day, during our one-mile jog, Amir ran ahead of a group calling him names.

On the news, Billy Graham's son had called all Muslims "wicked." But, just like I'd never bombed the Olympics for Jesus, Amir had never hurt anybody. Jesus demanded that we hang with "the least" of society, and that's what those losers believed Amir to be. **"STOP CALLING BILLY GRAHAM'S SON A LUMPER!"** *But he is!* **"YOU'VE BEEN WARNED AGAINST CONDONING FALSE RELIGIONS!"** *Sorry. Wait, am I sorry?*

Gabe, my Paul Walker-looking nemesis, jogged alongside the bullies and asked them to watch their language. *Lukewarm effort, pretty-boy fence-sitter!* I out-Jesus'd him by running beside Amir and beaming a Christlike smile.

Somebody called me a terrorist sympathizer, so I turned the other cheek over my shoulder and yelled, "You're all shit-fuck lumpers."

Then they said stunning things. Thirty seconds earlier, they'd viewed me as a Bible-thumping cracker. Suddenly, I'd become a semi-swarthy jihadist. *I'm the least of society?* I felt unzipped. *Exciting!*

Coach Watkins sent Mom a note, so she grounded me from everything but Christmas pageant practice. Fine, Jesus wouldn't say "shit-fuck." That word hadn't been invented. But after all my cowering at school, that'd been my first-ever religious persecution. *Proud of myself! Shut up.*

On AIM, I apologized for not speaking up. Amir wanted to talk NBA and Star Wars, just like in middle school. And we talked life goals.

> xSHARKSWITHRABIESx. itd be cool to fix machines. idk. college is billion years away

> BadBoys5318008: my mom didn't like college. pops did but he's an electrician anyway lol

> xSHARKSWITHRABIESx: what about u? D1 scholarship and then what

> BadBoys5318008: haha yeah right

> xSHARKSWITHRABIESx: u got this playa

> BadBoys5318008: nah maybe meteorologist!!

> xSHARKSWITHRABIESx: so u find lightning for your dad, then he puts it into houses

> BadBoys5318008: exactly!! what u doing for christmas break

He called it Christmas break instead of winter break, and he did that for me.

I mentioned the pageant, telling him I'd been promoted to Pro-Abortion Demon Colonel. In the fight scene, my job was to react to archangel Gabe's pathetic sword swing like I'd taken a Stone Cold stunner. I'd ad-libbed that, and people had cheered, so drama minister Ricardo had kept it. (My demon scene was only fifteen seconds that year, making room for America stuff. For once, no adults complained about our pageant's Harry Potter references, because 9/11 had stolen witchcraft's thunder.)

Confused, Amir asked what demons had to do with Christmas. Semi-explaining, I bragged about "my girl friend" Sophie playing the Lecturing Starbucks Employee who screeched about Christmas trees' feelings. She'd ad-libbed a rant straight from FernGully. People had complained, so Ricardo had kept it.

I had to fulfill Jesus' demand to hang with Amir. Since I was grounded, the pageant was the only one place I could invite him. I promised him that my Demon Calebs had fun debating whether Frodo or Neo is more like Jesus. For some reason, Amir was hesitant to ask his parents if he could assemble with fired-up theocrats doing patriotic demon wars.

Before first period, I walked toward the flagpole beside the HOME OF THE CRUSADERS sign. Amir and I did our handshake. Before we performed a different kind of ceremony, I figured I should learn things.

"How long have you been a Muslim?" I asked. "Is there, like, a moment when you get saved from … not being one?"

"Well, I shoulda told you," he said, looking over his shoulder. "I'm, like, not."

I'd never felt dumber. He explained performing prayers from his mom's Sikh tradition, while his dad was more into Muhammad Ali than Muhammad. "She doesn't push me, and Pops is hella lapsed, so I'm remixing stuff, I guess."

"Why not tell those dickheads this?"

"I asked that once. Mom said don't correct them. Know why?"

I thought. "Because that'd say it's okay to bully actual Muslims?"

"Basically. We have Muslim classmates, but they're smaller than me. I can take the heat."

There I was, parachuting in to help for five minutes so I could consider myself Christlike. Meanwhile, Amir had never signed up to be a paladin, but tanked damage daily.

We asked each other about God and stuff. My role models always hated the idea that we shared a God with any other religions, but I couldn't find evidence that Amir was describing some *other* Nice Scary Being. **"REGRET!"**

"It's weird," I said. "I have to believe God talks through the St. Louis Rams' quarterback, but I'm not allowed to think God talked to somebody in the desert a thousand years ago."

"Yeah, I ain't telling the Man Upstairs what he can't do."

"I guess I'll just keep cussing at your dumbass lumpers without cussing."

He paused and grinned. "It's not all bad. The wannabe-rebel girls suddenly like this straight-A's barely-a-football-player! Fine-ass Lacie Messerschmidt was like, 'Let's make my Puritan-ass dad worry how my thong got in his car.' Yooo, chill, Lacie," he said, singing some Sisqo before saying, "Hey, what's your best move with Christmas girl? You got my back. Lemme level you up."

I rambled, wildly exaggerating the sins I'd attempted.

The junior explained, "Be patient, make her happy, cuddle afterward, and maybe she'll let you go further next time. It ain't just about the ending.

Everything that happens beforehand matters too. It leads to jackpot eventually, believe me! Yo, let's do a strip club once we're eighteen. Get it? See you at the pole!"

I liked how Amir talked like I wasn't a Puritan, just somebody with buttoned-up pants. Eager to try his system during my honeymoon, I asked God to arrange my marriage soon, like before Beach Fest.

"You know, anybody could wear that," Amir said, tapping my black WWJD bracelet. "Muslims, Sikhs, everybody likes JC. That'd blow some minds, or confuse scrubs into shutting up."

I handed it over. "In case you wanna try."

He protested taking my "sacred bracelet," as if my backpack didn't contain a spare.

As snow lazily flurried, we turned east and prayed for our persecuted classmates. May their lumpy oppressors get dickwarts, inshAllah.

---

xOneGirlArmy86x (My girl-friend): "In the beginning was the Word, and the Word was with God, and the Word was God. Through him all things were made."

xOneGirlArmy86x: so the Word-Spirit that became Jesus was there before creation

xOneGirlArmy86x: it made judaism and christianity and "ALL things"

xOneGirlArmy86x: including all RELIGIONS???

xOneGirlArmy86x: then Jesus says He's "the only Way." can't ways have lotsa paths??

xOneGirlArmy86x: is that wacko?? skurred to say this out loud hehe

xSHARKSWITHRABIESx: but im an audio learner :):)

xOneGirlArmy86x: hehe callin u :):):):)

FIFTEEN
BE A FAMILY MAN

VALENTINE'S 2002

JOSIAH HAD TO SKIP OUR EVENING ACCOUNTABILITY WAR ROOM, SO I WAS IN charge. He always struggled to keep the Calebs focused, but from watching Dave-Tony, I was confident that I knew what not to do. Having engaged interfaith councils at school, I could surely corral my sweet knuckleheads.

At the Pizza Hut buffet, I placed my copy of Every Young Man's Battle, a best-selling Christian book, beside our third Mountain Dew pitcher. Dave-Tony had assigned us everything but the last chapter.

"World's horniest book," said one Caleb as others nodded. Okay, off to a rocky start.

The book's about learning brain hacks so powerful that a fifteen-year-old can walk past beach volleyball without ogling anybody. Five Calebs scrambled to speak, alarming Best Caleb.

"The author could just explain how to reprogram ourselves, but nooo," said one, unfolding papers, the first Caleb to ever take notes. "My sanctified imagination's in tatters after he typed a zillion words about lusting after teenage string bikinis, cheerleader boobs, jiggly-glistening joggers, stepsisters, sister-in-law crotches …"

I interrupted, knowing he'd never run out of quotes. You know Dave-Tony youth pastors who try to be relatable by talking way too openly about desire? Yeah, that book is the epitome.

Best Caleb was annoyed, wanting me to enforce serious discussion. Great idea. How?

"This book is basically Dave-Tony's dress code crap," squawked another Caleb. "Girls can't wear shorts, only capri pants? Capri pants are hot, dummy! Astronaut suits would be hot! Dave-Tony sucks. At least when Pastor Jack brags about drilling *his* milf, he pauses to defend America's freedoms."

They were giggling but genuinely perturbed. I tried discussing the book's least Al Bundy material, the parts about slavishly micro-analyzing your every thought even while asleep. (You know, simple stuff.) But the Calebs retained control as Best Caleb slumped in frustration.

"The book's *if you see boobs, you're robbing them from her future husband* thing ... bro, boobs change when looked at, like the quantum light thing?" yelled one. "Boobs have visual acuity based on movement?"

"Wait, how's some time-traveling husband own them? Aren't they her boobs?"

Whoa, that fits Dad's girls-are-people speeches! Signs and wonders! Caleb wisdom! With big-brotherly head nods, I encouraged them to continue. *I'm great at this!*

"During the part about how me boning this author's daughter would dishonor him," said another, "I'm like, imagine my mom writing, 'My faith-based womanhood depends on nobody porking my son.' That'd suck for my mom, 'cause look at me, baby."

"I like the chapter about how fapping isn't a major sin, unlike me porking your mom."

"All sins are major," I said like an attorney advising against crime that'll happen anyway.

"Someone said fapping is gay because it's a guy touching a ween," said another Caleb. "Someone else said it's murder because it blasts a zillion babies face-first into a T.J. Maxx catalogue's photos of capri pants."

"What a way to go," cooed another. "Which is worse, gayness or murder?"

"Murder," I managed to interject.

"At school, if you're not chasing girls down halls, screaming GIMME S-E-X like Jimmy Kimmel, you're gay," said another. "At church, if you're not sad about liking boobs too much, you're gay. Everyone's gay, especially since the Twin Towers fell."

"Book Man says instead of fapping, wait for a wet dream," said another Caleb, citing advice I'd heard from a half-dozen Christian men. "Nature's loophole! Satan never sees it coming."

"This book says to have Longest Wet Dream Streak contests. Are you bad enough dudes to dream wetter than me?" said a Caleb, doing Morpheus' bring-it-on gesture.

His neighbor retorted, "Ryu from Street Fighter says, 'Don't fight for victory. Fight to improve yourself. Victory will ... come.'"

They were honk-laughing. Could Josiah have steered things back on course? Could anyone?

"The book's parable about me being a sumo wrestler, and my lust's another sumo wrestler, and we're bumping jiggly-glistening bellies to the death?" said a Caleb. "My man-parts got tingly. Talk about a sumo surprise."

"When this book argues church girls are just as horny as guys, I'm like, great, now I'm never thinking about anything else. Hugest stumbling block imaginable, pervert."

"It's called diddling, you virgin," said a virgin, grabbing the notepad. "Let's rank church girls by how much they probably diddle."

"Alexa'd say she's number one, but she lies to mess with us, which rocks," said a Caleb, tugging his collar.

"No, it's true," said another. "She's a sk–"

I punched his arm in time. Alexa finding out I'd let someone say that? Last thing I needed.

Best Caleb chimed in, arguing PG surely hadn't diddled, as evidenced by her singing voice's purity.

"You know who's the X factor in the bad-girls ranking?" one said. "Isaac, I bet y–"

"You idiots would explode if you discussed this for thirty seconds," I said, snatching the notepad, ignoring my brain's instant top-ten list. "Does describing our friends like that fit *accountability group*?"

"Substitute teachers should be fun," a Caleb pouted. "If girls are so horny, shouldn't there be Every Lady's Battle books about not staring at balls?"

"Every Lady's Battle would be like, MY FELLOW AMERICANS, I TOO ADMIRE JIGGLY-GLISTENING BALLSACKS, BUT JESUS SAI–"

"Stop yelling," I whimpered, respecting Dave-Tony for having gotten anything done ever. No way was I gonna tell them that the same male author had indeed co-written Every Young Woman's Battle, or that I'd learned bits about what girls were taught. In middle school, they'd had to play Sleeping Beauty while a Prince (future husband) defeated Demons (non-husband people with disease-spewing penises).

"Listen, I'm terrified I'll lead Serenity Grace into sin," said a Caleb. "I wish some book could out-jiggle my Lust Sumo, but this young man's battle rages on."

"Wait, are the arcane secrets in the last chapter?" asked another.

"That chapter's about, um, not becoming gay," I said. "Which isn't how it w–"

The Calebs guffawed about needing that advice, because, after all the jiggly-glistening talk, they wanted to JO together. At church and school, everyone always joked about being gay. Per rumors, the only gay kid in church history had been renditioned to rehab, and that'd happened before 9/11 inspired Jack to preach about gay people getting us all anthraxed.

Looking around, I felt worry. What if a gay person overheard our commotion? If we made that person think Christians were homophobes, we'd offend them toward Hell. I whispered, "Maybe quit these jokes."

That made the Calebs whisper jokes about me being gay, but at least they were whispering.

"I despise myself," blurted Best Caleb, silencing everyone. "I sucked at making this book fix me. Every day, my sins make the nasty world even nastier. So, every night, I pray to get crotch leprosy until my monster rots away and I'm free of this poison."

The other Calebs looked around, exposed. I felt scared, because that kind of self-disgust had once made me try to knife myself in the face. I felt some sort of duty. I mumbled second-hand advice that I knew was empty.

"Good effort, Sarge," said a Caleb. "Let's play Street Fighter, Sumo Guy vs. Sumo Guy. Evenly matched in power, jiggliness, and respect."

---

xSHARKSWITHRABIESx: prayer requests? HA SAID IT FIRST

xOneGirlArmy86x (Sophie): GASP! CHEATER! IT WASNT TIME!

xSHARKSWITHRABIESx: too bad lets hear em

xOneGirlArmy86x: hmph! fine

xOneGirlArmy86x: just unspoken for me pls :-/

xSHARKSWITHRABIESx: r u ok

xOneGirlArmy86x: idk :-/

xSHARKSWITHRABIESx: r u wearing capri pants

xOneGirlArmy86x: uh yeah why

xSHARKSWITHRABIESx: brb

xSHARKSWITHRABIESx: back. what if ur prayer request's only kinda unspoken

xOneGirlArmy86x: i look around the mall and everywhere and see people holding hands and its valentines and i snuck romeo + juliet 50 trillion times and i think about somebody constantly and idk if we'll be more than friends in a gazillion years when we're allowed to court because they could just go date somebody whos allowed to be normal :(:(:(:(:(:(

xOneGirlArmy86x: OOPS

xOneGirlArmy86x: DONT READ

xSHARKSWITHRABIESx: ok

xOneGirlArmy86x: [Away message: FORGET I EXIST]

I stared at my computer.

I'm gonna spray rainbows from my stupid pukehole.

If this isn't about me, I'll die alone when I'm super old, like twenty-nine.

If this is about me, I can't confess my Galactus-sized crush on her — even bigger, Shaq-sized — because her celibacy vows are so severe that they forbid several kinds of eye contact.

At the following week's Accountability Fight Club, I said, "Caleb, I told my mom somethi–"

"You told her I suffer from cartophilia," he groaned, slapping his rectangular forehead, "which means I'm in love with Carmen Sandiego? You bented-dick Arnold!"

"Sounds like last week's meeting went well," Josiah said, elbowing me.

Actually, I'd told Mom about my guys discussing how to think of girls. She'd been in the middle of complaining about men getting promoted over her and about choir ladies scolding her in 1997, 1999, and last September for not marrying anybody she'd semi-dated, as if she'd chosen my fatherlessness. I constantly discovered people had opinions about my parents.

"She suggested something for us," I said. "First, tell me which Street Fighter character you most respect."

"Street Fighter II? Hyper, Super, or Turbo?" blurted a Caleb, sputtering pizza. "EX series? Street Fighter III? First, Second, Thir–"

"I don't care. Gimme a character."

They huddled and agreed: "Guile."

"Rad. Weird-haired Army guy. So ..."

"Air Force guy."

"Rad. What if instead of doing Dave-Tony's thing, disgusted by girls, and instead of doing the world's thing, being brainless Jimmy Kimmels, we treat girls like they're Guile?"

"Staying away if they're crouched, because they're charging flash kicks?"

Treating them respectfully, but sure, that too. Best Caleb tested "Isaac's Hot Mom's Guile Plan," ordering cheese sticks from the pretty cashier.

"I saluted her," he said, returning. "'Ma'am, I respect your professionalism.' Foolproof. Except she laughed, so I'm in love. Tell your mom it was worth a shot. Your mom's also worth a sh–"

I punched his arm.

"This respect thing seems like a good plan," said another, "but what about when girls *want* their boobs honked?"

"Hey, does Uday Hussein's name spell 666?" shouted the most off-topic Caleb.

"Isaac, when ya gonna sprout a pair," shouted another Caleb, "and ask Sophie to leave space for Jesus with you?"

I reiterated my most common excuse: "Can't take her anywhere until I can drive," plus bigger roadblocks.

"If you're scared, say you're scared," six virgins chanted, certain that the pastor's niece wouldn't date until after she'd married some televangelist and immaculately conceived a quintuplet praise band.

Oh yeah? You think I'm not good enough? I'm not, but how dare you agree.

"In this life or the next," I said, studying my red cup's Mountain Dew light beams like a crystal ball, "I will see her whole-entire sports bra."

Calebs gasped at my starry-eyed ambition. Josiah punched my arm so hard, I didn't swing back. *My forbidden soulmate has a big cousin I'm supposed to confess my thoughts to! Life sucks!!!*

"I think the perfect woman would have PG's butt, Sophie's hair,

Alexa's fruits of the Spirit once she's not going to Hell, and Isaac's mom's butt," said a Caleb, and everyone punched each other's arms for five minutes.

"Not to sound gay, but I agree ladies should be respected," said a sweaty Best Caleb. "Except the Bible acts like girls are … uh, you know … property."

Josiah half-choked on Mountain Dew, then quoted his dad's explanations of God-programmed dominant-man households. He explained that Paul said genders have different roles but are equal in Christ.

"Guile ain't the only guy with different versions, huh," said a Caleb.

"Um, all scripture's equally God-breathed," Josiah said, quoting Paul to defend Paul. "If Paul's messages seem contradictory, we gotta study harder."

"Huh? Oh, wasn't listening. Busy thinking about jiggly-glistening sumo in capri pants."

SIXTEEN
BRUSHED RED, LIVING IN BLACK AND WHITE

APRIL 2002

IN THE WOODS BEHIND CHURCH, NEAR OUR CAMPGROUND, LIVED AN OLD woman named Miss Esther, Timmy's grandmother.

Forever ago, before our church was even a shack, her family had moved up from Appalachia. As shopping centers emerged, her land had suddenly become valuable. After Pastor Jack arrived in 1993, his church had bought most of it.

She kept only her house's central acre, but had willed it to Jack. Meanwhile, she'd worked for years as the church's lead custodian — first in, last out — plus always made lemonade for teenage wanderers. Our adopted grandma.

One day, Miss Esther shuffled in between Alexa and a red-mad Dave-Tony, asked to see photos of the troublemaker's one-eyed rescue pit bull, and said, "Lean your ear down here, Puddin' Pie," handling the situation, whatever it was, with a whisper. Alexa grumbled, "Yes ma'am."

Miss Esther let Sophie teach her non-satanic yoga.

"We hold our hands like this … and we breathe in …"

"Sugar Dumplin', know what I call this?"

"Nuh-uh."

"Naptime."

Miss Esther told Josiah it was okay to just be Josiah instead of worrying about being the Dynasty's future father-pastor-husband. She repeated it until he cried.

She told me, "I miss my daddy too, Gumdrop. He was a traveling preacher whose hiney got ran outta town a time or three. Last thing he told me, forty-nine years ago next February, was that the Lord's gonna restore all things, Acts 3:21. Now, what do you suppose *all* might mean?"

"Hiney," I replied, practicing her accent.

But at eighty-six, Miss Esther was no longer able to trudge a hilly quarter-mile. On Sundays, the church shuttle cart arranged a stop just for her, but she protested, "If somebody misses their moment 'cause the trolley was toting my lazy bones, I'll never forgive myself."

Jack preached about wanting to keep paying her, telling everyone she'd replied, "Spend my salary on hungry babies instead," regardless of the tithes pouring in. (Amid the post-9/11 revival, we suddenly needed three Sunday morning services to fit everybody.)

And then, chemotherapy.

When we learned, there was crying, prayer, and guitar. At Pizza Hut, Josiah said we should raise money to tithe in her honor. Glaring at him, Alexa said it should feed hungry babies. How to raise money? Calebs proposed selling tickets to a six-Caleb wrestling match. Graces listed nice things to do for Miss Esther. And they shrieked when Sophie said, "I can't let her be bald alone."

As PG left my house to pick up Graces for Video Games Church (and Calebs began the forty-minute round-trip walk for two-liters), I heard my clippers buzzing in my bathroom. Because thoughts murder Jesus just like actions murder Jesus, I blasted Tony Hawk 3 at full volume, drowning out shower sounds.

Water stopped, and Sophie called through the door for PG.

I somehow communicated the situation. We were each alone with the opposite sex, semi-breaking my parental rules and annihilating hers. She asked, with infinite umms, if she could borrow a hoodie in order to cover the clothes she promised she was wearing.

Dreaming and dreading, I rummaged through my middle-school clothes upstairs, found a black zippie hoodie, and figured a lapsed Buffalo Bills fan wouldn't mind the L.A. Raiders logo (from my weird phase when I'd rooted against local teams). Back downstairs, the door unlocked, opened for a hoodie handoff, closed, and opened for real.

I saw black jeans with ripped knees, her Underoath shirt, and my hood over ... red bangs almost to her eyebrows. *Phew, she didn't do it. Then again, my Shaq-sized crush would've been cured if she'd adopted Shaq's hairstyle.*

"Miss Esther insisted I donate hair to kids with cancer, and keep some for myself," she explained, gnawing her fingernails. "Holy gosh, I'm freaking out. Tell me this was dumb. I'll move to a cave in Idaho."

"Lemme see." *One glimpse of her skull, and we'll be just friends! Problem solved!*

"Be honest," she said, wincing, squeaking, and revealing … huh.

"How honest?" I asked.

"Completely. Call me hideous."

I couldn't hide my goofy smile. With long bangs and short red hair on her freckly scalp, she looked punk-rock adorable. So much for a haircut changing anything.

"My family's gonna call me a circus freak again," she said, yanking the hood back up, finding security in *my* hoodie. "I'll be on stage like this, translating Uncle Jack's altar calls, distracting people from getting saved! I'm so ugly, I'm endangering souls!"

Total opposite problem, lady! I sought the obvious solution: rummaging for a comic book. And I made her stop whimper-flailing long enough to look at a post-apocalypse scene starring a bloody warrior with more tattoos than hair.

Staring at the smirking Tank Girl, she gasped, "This … chick … is … awesome!"

In that haircut and *my* lawless silver-and-black hoodie, the undateable saint looked like she'd been claimed by the fatherless wretch.

Claim me back! "Gimme a bracelet," I said, "and this hoodie's yours."

She raised her shaky wrists' mishmash bracelets beside my face, rambled about one bringing out my eyes, and slid pale green beads onto my wrist, her shuddering fingers rushing witchy chemicals throughout me. Our silver rings screamed that we were slippery-sloping into demonic pregnancy orgies, so I swing-dance twirled her away, chasing safety.

She spun back into an illegal front-hug (*oops*) and pouted, "I've always gotten yelled at for hating floofy dresses. They'll kill me for looking this boyish!"

Flirting was deadly. So, innocently reassuring my nervous friend who was pressed against me, I said, "If you're boyish, I'm freaking gay."

Oops. She looked up with roller coaster eyes. *Quick, how do you un-confess illegal attraction?* Blushing, she reached around my arm to fidget with her hair, but found her scalp and hid a gasp-laugh against my chest, tightening a hug we believed to be verging on eternal regret.

Men had constantly explained ladies to me, but nobody'd ever warned me that ladies *want* things, rather than just wanting to prevent guys from acquiring things. I realized this by realizing a particular lady wanted … me. **"YOU'LL REGRET BEING HER VIRGINITY'S KRYPTONITE, YOU MANWHORE!"** I was a satanic test of her no-kissing pledge, worsening the difficulty by grazing filthy fingers across her head's peach fuzz.

Heartbeat racing, my fingers found goosebumps on her neck, her eyes fluttered shut. I heard her swallowing nerves. And, tasting breaths from the freckle-lipped mouth of a lunging viper, I said, "I'm cutting my hair too! For Miss Esther!"

Flee into the bathroom. They say cold showers fix everything. Dreams became spikes splintering Jesus' wristbones, Matthew 5:28. But dread was also embarrassing, because I knew Jesus was my excuse for cowardice. *Awesome, there are red hairs in here! Pervert, make it a freezing shower. Wimp. Psycho.*

Flesh mortified and clothes on, I stepped out. Graces filled the enormous couch, chattering about Britney Spears and cheering my new mohawk.

"Rock 'n' roll hair, dude! I ever tell you I saw the Clash?" Mom said, walking downstairs with pizza. "And hello my ladies, who's hungr– … nnnNNNOOOoooOOO!"

She shoved boxes into my chest and pawed at Sophie's mostly buzzed head. Sophie stared at the floor, still shell-shocked by what she'd perceived as my rejection of her sinfulness. Mom recovered and called her brave, but threatened anyone who might cut Harmony Grace's long curls.

Josiah and a dozen dudes arrived. Calebs whispered, "Get any, coward? Better not have."

I bragged, "Almost. Never."

They said, "Nice! Don't."

"The bad news, which you'll somehow like," Amir said, after I sort of told the story, "is you were nowhere near tapping that. But I believe in you, playboy! Mohawk looks sick!"

"I'm one to talk, but just kiss her," Bobbi said during lunch. "Jesus."

"She feels slutty for hugging you," Alexa said at my locker. "You're such second-graders! Obsessed with marriage! You're such 40-year-olds!"

"You're a legend for getting that greenlight," said Gabe, who spoke differently at school than at church, "but a pussy for not taking it."

Everyone assumes I'm unaware it's silly to agonize over my crush liking me. If we could kiss like normal people, don't you think we would? What makes everyone assume I chose a brain full of medusa demons vomiting abortion gore?

For a while, our youth group was small enough for its entire goth-jock spectrum to mingle without school-style cliques. But as the church grew, divisions formed.

My usual basement crew avoided scaring lost souls with songs that mentioned Jesus too much. We played a game: Someone called out a verse, I dug up a verse that arguably contradicted it, and Sophie proposed a weirdo resolution. And then we played video games for hours, laughing and trash-talking, because it was called Video Games Church.

But Gabe's crew plastered their cars with the dorkiest Christian stickers and parroted Dave-Tony, Pastor Jack, and Eli. Josiah had to hang with them sometimes. Sophie managed not to, except that she sometimes looked at Gabe and hid her skull from him.

One day, the beautiful moron strutted into my basement, followed by three unsaved upperclassmen from our school.

"Figured the fun-times Bible study would be better for these newbies than Dave-Tony's hardcore mode," Gabe told me. "Good-lookin' crowd!"

He might be older, bigger, more righteous, more talented, and more Paul Walker-lookin' than me, but I'll be damned if he beats me at spreading the gospel. Maybe literally, LOL.

"Why the gay-for-Jesus cult mohawk?" said some classmate. "Punk hair's allowed at church?"

"Me and my girl-friend cut our hair," I explained. "She covers her head with a shawl at church. Anyway, Miss Esther ..."

"Your girlfriend's bald? You homo! Does she go here?"

Rubbing my temples, a habit I'd inherited from Mom, I said, "Homeschool."

"Yooo, 'Saac is banging some three-eyed Westboro Craptist werewolf!"

Gritting my teeth, I grabbed my wallet's photos and found one from the Five Iron Frenzy concert, when she had long hair.

"Fine, your Mennonite band-camp cueball's cute," he conceded. "What, you two get horned up reading Bible verses?"

Tempted to brag about surprisingly flirty exegetical phone calls, I said the most passive-aggressive thing available: "I'll pray for you." (I then felt bad and prayed for him.)

I couldn't avoid the Jesus Boy role. With endless misdeeds to compensate for, like pondering girl smells during science class, I raised my hand. "Coach Ramirez, why worry about the sun eventually consuming the world? The Son's already consuming the world's sins."

And English class.

"Miss Blanchard, once Democrats start burning books, they'll include the B–"

"Isaac, there's a Bible on my desk. No one's picking on you."

"Yeah well, ever notice Siddhartha tries all the religions, but not the relationship?"

And history class.

"Miss Madson, this book The Case for Christ has thirteen unbiased experts proving the gospels are history. Jesus was either Lord, a liar, or a lunatic, and doing psychology proves he wasn't crazy. Boom."

"Were those thirteen unbiased experts non-Christians?"

"No, why? Boom."

And the nurse's office.

"I'm doing forty days without movies, music, internet, games, TV, comics, sports, hugs, porn, food, sleep, a–"

"Do you understand why you passed out?"

"It's called dying to self."

And health class.

"Coach Jackson, shouldn't mid-birth abortion be banned?"

"Lord, help me. The rest of us are discussing the pancreas."

"Unborn babies have panc–"

"Siena, I'm not getting sued, shot, or fired for discussing that. I gave you the informational pamphlet last week. Here, have a stack of pamphlets."

"You should play ball again," Amir said at some gym assembly, wearing headphones, Detroit Pistons shorts, and flip flops with socks. "Our only punter's graduating."

Still just the kicker, he dreamed of playing wide receiver, meaning he could use training help. *Hey, rejoining the team would triple my friendships, shine Christian light, and be un-mysteriously guilt-free!* I proposed two-man summer workouts.

"Hells to the yes," he said, slapping my palm. "Speaking of … Coach Jackson!"

Amir waved him up from the gym floor. Coach saw me and grimaced until Amir said, "Mighta solved our punter situation."

"Well, I never make promises," Coach said, squatting behind us. "And, Brother Siena, speaking to just a couple spiritual fellas, lemme say I understand. My church really wrestles with that issue you've brought up."

You're telling me there are Christian grownups here? Paid by the government? Please. Besides: "How could Christians wrestle with that issue? It's babies."

"Ohhh, believers disagree on everything," Coach said, wringing his hands, maybe flashing his wedding ring's cross. "Considering ninety percent of Americans believe in God, that's however many million opinions, right?"

"You mean ninety percent *don't* believe in God, right?"

He told me other things, contrary to what I'd been taught, daring me to look them up.

---

xSHARKSWITHRABIESx: did u know lotsa denominations say abortion's ok, and.....

xOneGirlArmy86x (Sophie): [christian drumroll]

xSHARKSWITHRABIESx: ....for a while even southern baptists did

g00dbyeskyharb0r (PG): < (^_ ·) ゝ

BigDog699999999999 (Best Caleb): wut

MyPlaceInThisWorld (Josiah): Bullcrap.

LetsTalkAboutLexBaby (Alexa): lmfao

xOneGirlArmy86x: but wait, there's more

xOneGirlArmy86x: priests can end pregnancies. numbers 5:20-28

While they read those verses, **"YOU'LL REGRET THIS"** ran rampant in my brain.

BigDog699999999999 (Best Caleb): wutttttt

g00dbyeskyharb0r (PG): ('◉⌓◉')

BATMAN69FOREVER (Caleb #2): wuuuuuuuutt

Wario4Prez69 (Caleb #3): wawawawaaaaaaaaa

LilBigDaddyBoy69 (Caleb #4): que

69ALLMADDEN69 (Caleb #5): noreaga - superthug lyrics

ManicHedgehog (Radiohead kid): ◆♒♋⧫

Proverbs6verse9 (Caleb #6): WÜT?

xSACREDxDOOTIEx (Deuteronomy Grace): :brain asplodes:

MyPlaceInThisWorld (Josiah): Pump the brakes, folks.

LetsTalkAboutLexBaby (Alexa): LMFAOOOOOOOOOOOOO

xSHARKSWITHRABIESx: ditching my mohawk now

SEVENTEEN
THE SPACE BETWEEN

MAY 2002

"Come outside," Sophie said. "It's snowing."

"It's sixty degree–"

"Shhhhhhhh."

I laughed, walking my cordless phone into the cloudless night, accustomed to her sensing mystical wonders I couldn't.

I asked, "Know how grownups say, 'Leave space for Jesus,' whenever people dance? What exactly does that mean? How many cubits?"

"Like exactly how much space would leave room for Jesus' body?"

"Yeah, to the inch, how close can people be without sinning?"

"Hmm. Well, Jesus was short, but pretty strong," she said. "How many inches deep is a normal guy's chest?"

I held my hand alongside my ribcage in the window's reflection. "Mine's like a hand length, front to back. Is that how it works for everybody? How deep's your chest?"

"Sir," she scolded, like how she usually spoke to Alexa.

"You asked me first, sorta."

"That's kinda different!"

Maximum romance! She acknowledged our chests are different! I'm the sexy danger man! **"YOU'LL REGR–"** *Please go away. I'll feel triple guilty later, okay?*

"Ancient Christians debated whether Jesus still has his body," she said. "If he's just the Spirit now, people could smoosh super close and still leave space."

"Thank you, whoever discovered Flat Jesus. Like the masks in Face/Off."

"In what?"

"Wait, Jesus lives in our hearts! You aren't the Soulcalibur guy whose heart dangles outta his chest, and neither am I. If our literal hearts don't touch, we're leaving space for Jesus even during front-hugs," I said, mastering theology.

"Great, let's just explain this to Dave-Tony's spies. Oh, can I confess a daydream ..."

Wow. Please. "Whatever."

"On Sunday, Uncle Jack kept preaching the world is fallen trash. And I know what that means, but I love God's creation. I let myself imagine a shadow sermon, calling the world breathtaking. I thought, girls can't preach, huh? Well, I could say so much. That'd be bad ASL ethics, so I won't."

"Well, bad can be good."

"What do I do if he's wrong?" she whispered.

"It's hot when you're competitive," I said, feeling my face catch fire. "Church softball, Mario Kart, whatever. To win against you, I have to *try*. Well, don't let even Pastor Jack boss you around. March off stage if you disagree with him. Dare you."

My heart pounded through infinite silence.

She giggled, "I like it when you're blunt."

Now there's a greenlight!

"So, I wondered about space because we're 9.1 miles apart, b–"

"How'd you know that?"

"MapQuest."

"You're on the computer? You stranded me outside?"

"I looked it up earlier, 'cause I'll get my license soon. And 9.1's too much space, I think?"

"Yeah. Pretty breezy out here. But your hoodie's warm."

"Duh, it's snowing," I said, inhabiting our 66-degree daydream. She was humming. Those 9.1 miles were no distance at all. *Here goes. Boldest thing I've ever done, other than cussing out Satan every few nights. Squeeze out the words like ketchup:* "Wanna girlfriend-boyfriend it up? Tons. Cool beans?" *Nailed it.*

She stopped humming. Uh-oh. I said, "Sorry. I ... like-like you."

"I like-like you majorly," she said, and I fist-pumped at my reflection, cool like Tiger Woods. "But ... I dunno if, um, girlfriend-boyfriend ... is, like, Christlike ... especially because ..."

"We'll figure out how, like we solved the space-between thing," I said, beholding my reflection's ugly dork. "Half the upperclassmen backslid from their no-dating cards!"

"But they aren't Pastor Jack's final niece," she said, gentle but devastating. "I get watched closely and gotta be the example. I'm sorry, Ize. I'm not worth drama."

We competed to take blame for the awkwardest hangup ever. I'd always been scared around her, the last person I'd ever wanted to ruin, until I'd tried anyway.

The daydream was alluring, but the sky had made itself clear.

EIGHTEEN

THE PLACES YOU HAVE COME TO FEAR THE MOST

SUMMER 2002

PG, EMO HAIRCUT AT A SUMMERY ANGLE, SAT BESIDE ME ON THE BUS AND played guitar with three Calebs across the aisle. Their band, now called Exploding Judas, considered itself "pre-calc mathcore," but they were doing normal Third Day covers.

Two more Graces crammed into our seat to sing along, and another sat on my lap. The still-growing girl pile played a game, randomly matching their names with boys' last names and then imagining the honeymoons. Buried beneath bodies, I laughed at my name's results. It might seem weird, how quickly I'd become nonchalant around (most) female contact, but church world was relentlessly affectionate (in a feverishly chaste way), especially during Beach Fest.

In the back rows, seniors were straight-up making out, and the bus hadn't even reached the highway yet. Everyone was ignoring Dave-Tony's warnings about lock-in sinners getting riled up by fellowship. *Well, they can do what they want. At least me and my friends will make it home with our purity intact.*

Thousands of teenagers, mostly from tons of van-sized youth groups across the country, poured toward the gigantic beach tent. My old downtown megachurch arrived in two buses.

By day, everyone gathered for comedians who joked about almost sinning, goofy skits about avoiding temptation situations, and heart-bursting singalongs.

Once our blood was supernaturally buzzy, we mingled with our brand new friends under easily avoidable supervision, especially as grownups lost track of room assignments. By night one, Dave-Tony's dress code — T-shirts on girls, even in the ocean — lost to the megachurch's. "If they're wearing two-pieces, so are we," announced Alexa, with Graces following like self-conscious ducklings.

Night two. A genius from Omaha snuck her room's microwave into our hallway, where multitudes enjoyed 3 a.m. burritos. Someone claimed they'd seen weed, so Dave-Tony materialized. Everyone dispersed in sarcastic panic before falling asleep cuddling, as a joke.

Night three. We tested Dave-Tony's spidey sense, yelling weed lyrics while running past his door until he wearied of materializing. Microwave anarchy!

But someone yelped, "Mister Eli's coming," and everyone scattered in genuine panic.

Downstairs, I told Omaha Burrito Girl, "Everyone's weird about my brother. But he only yells about real stuff like Hell, not made-up stuff like burritos." After hours of watching ElimiDate in the lobby, OBG wrote "•.☽° Rebekah Grace (Phil 4:13) ｡•✧" on my hand.

Some juniors and seniors kept sneaking off together, with rumors of third base and worse. The smallest churches had one adult per kid, and the megachurch had a backup van of full-time grownups. But our group, over-extended by our church's rapid attendance surge, had unsupervised rooms.

Luckily, my friends will never do beach sex.

Final evening. Eyes closed in the big tent. Nobody could leave for dinner until they'd heard a personal word from God, then repeated it to a grownup, like a CAPTCHA.

Hearing people leave by the minute, I felt something beyond jealousy: stubborn resignation.

I don't think I'll ever hear God. **"YOU ... wait, I'm not God?"** *Maybe you are, but all you do is yell at me. God's not yelling at these people hearing nice things. Either they're all lying, I'm the worst, or you're not God.* **"Uhh ... YOU WILL REGRET THAT!"** *I know. Please stop yelling at me. It hurts. I'm scared all the time.* **"IF I'M NOT GOD, YOU'D BETTER HURRY UP AND**

HEAR FROM HIM BEFORE ETERNITY BEGINS!" *That's what I'm trying to do.*

I waited so long, I heard feet not just leaving, but then returning.

Someone knelt beside me. "Go eat, chief," Eli said, patting his Bible against my arm. "God gave you a million words in this book."

So I slumped toward sunset, passing crowds goofing around like hearing God's voice had been NBD.

"What'd God say?" I asked the board shorts-wearing Calebs who were following superstar Josiah, that morning's junior speaker with a sermon about saving it for marriage.

Best Caleb hoisted hot dogs. "My soul heard 'hungry.' My soul's right here," he said, poking his belly. Sometimes he was brilliant.

Outside the tent, some spiky-haired megachurcher told Alexa, "I sensed the word 'her.' I said, 'What's that mean, Father God?' Father God told me to look, and I saw ... youuu."

"Amaziiing," she sing-songed with jazz hands. "But there's so many *her*s here! Hey, if Dad God tells you my name in the next five seconds, I'll do beach stuff to you. Ready, go!"

Stammering, he pled, "Father God, I just beseech you right now, Father God. Abba Papa Daddy God, I just ..."

"Alexa," I said, semi-jokingly flirting with my non-girlfriend's friend. "Hey."

The spiky-haired dork repeated Alexa's name, palms exalting Heaven.

"That doesn't count unless Isaac's God," she snickered, further punishing her suitor by calling me "too somewhat cute to be God."

She walked with me, trading adventure tales. I tried to make Microwave Hall sound illegally sexy. She'd allegedly tried mushrooms with an adult from Lexington.

I asked, "How many people heard God's actual voice, you think?"

"Everybody but this defective bitch," she said, pointing thumbs at herself. Passing crowds, I recognized greedy shame in the eyes glancing at her tied-up Mudvayne T-shirt. Drawn to something beyond her skin for once, I turned one of her thumbs toward another defective bitch: me.

"Yeah, right, Bible club leader," she snapped. "I'm being fucking vulnerable, dickhead!"

"I can't even imagine hearing God," I admitted, to Alexa of all people. "But everyone's always so certain. Receiving evidence. Dreams, visions, signs, feelings ..."

Sunset exposed amber in her dark eyes. I'd always seen her as a supermodel stuck waiting out adolescence, but I suddenly saw a kid stuck being lanky, noisy, and shiny. As we joked about our paths diverging since kindergarten recess, I noticed our, like, friendship. Well, instead of turning Alexa into a good Christian, maybe a fellow bad Christian?

"That spiky-haired dork's trying it again," she said, pointing. "Just let tonight's horny-Jesus-music concert work its magic, dork! Speaking of, I told Sophie that music will make her jump you."

I shrugged, doubtfully.

Alexa said, "She was like, 'What I want doesn't matter.' It's sad!"

"It's about what God wan–"

"It's about what brainwashers want," she hissed. "Men hate girls having the power to choose anybody besides whichever random loser wants to turn us into Dave-Tony's trophy wife. Well, if we can't learn who we like, we can't choose! Don't you see? The Matrix is gonna destroy Sophie unless you go down on her tonight!"

"On it," I laughed.

"For real, one beachy hookup will deprogram your minds," Alexa said, miming the Matrix being unplugged from her spine. "Poof, all better!"

"Your hair's grown enough to move in the wind," I said, running fingernails across red turned moonlight-purple.

"That tickles nice," Sophie said, her eyelids tranquil. A while back, she'd cut the sleeves off my Raiders hoodie. It'd become an unzipped vest over her swimsuit. No T-shirt on the pastor's niece? Anarchy reigned.

The black ocean roared, swallowing our legs by the minute. My heart felt breezy-electric after the huge singalong an hour before.

"What'd God tell you?" I asked, assuming she wouldn't have to lie.

She inhaled and said, "'Chaos' has been on my heart for a while." Sea breeze adjusted her upheld fingers and clacked her beady bracelets. She swayed, freckled starlight-blue, in her element, where I was clearly unworthy. She sat back, palms on sand, and wondered why Genesis 1:2's Lady-Spirit had chosen to harness chaos. "What about you?"

There's nobody I would've rather lied to. "Silence."

Bangs blowing in the breeze, she said, "What'd God mean by 'Silence?'"

As usual, she was ignoring my attempted confession. I scooped wet sand and let it plop into fleeing water. Waves raged beneath wandering stars, for whom endless night is reserved.

"Sit criss-cross," she said. "Hands out." I put my hand under hers.

Fingers laced. "Closed eyes. So Elijah went to Mount Sinai, where everyone heard God, right? But Elijah heard silence and got sad. Turns out, God spoke *as* silence. So … c'mon, take a big breath in …"

And the ocean roared. *Into a welcoming terror, we could swim forever, maybe to a little island. Non-satanic yoga's okay otherwise, because we're holding hands while she's pantsless. And as the ocean roars, do you hear what I …*

"Hey criss-cross and apple sauce," shouted some older bro behind us. "If you're breaking curfew, at least come get fucked uuuuup!"

"Oh shit, Pastor Jack's niece," yelled another bro. "Wearing a beach hoodie? Slippery slope to Goths Gone Wild, ma'am!"

Alcoholics! Demons! They faded away, hooting at something else.

Shoulders sagging, the sorceress yanked her hood over her head, deflated. I tried to pull her close, but she stiffened in place, hesitant to be caught cuddling.

"Drunks are idiots, especially drunks wearing Croakies," I said.

She zipped up her hoodie-vest. The ocean howled.

"On Tuesday, when I was the only one still wearing a T-shirt," she said eventually, "girls from Delaware were like, 'What's there to hide, dorky ginger dyke?' Whatever that means. An hour later, everyone was jumping to music, arms up. Some man pulled me aside, like, 'Your loose shirt exposed your naked abdomen! A pastor's niece should know better!' His freshman son was standing there, ashamed because my body made him sin. So tie me to a millstone, thrown into that ocean …"

As she stared into sand, I asked, with violent intent, for that man's description.

"So the repressed tomboy's also a porno skank," she sniffed. "Then another rando said *the pastor's niece* shouldn't pout with crossed arms while everyone worships. I dunno how else to disappear! Without girl bodies, nobody'd ever sin, so nobody'd go to H-e-l-l. Wanna know why I quit cross-country? Because my huge bouncing butt stole the eyes of an unsaved neighborhood dad. I'd barely started my pathetic little puberty."

As she kept hand-gesturing like she was somehow both Jessica Rabbit and Steve Urkel, I was shocked to realize the oracle's mind was a battlefield. *Shouldn't she feel good about trying to protect me from lust?* **"YES! SHE JUST WANTS MORE POWER OVER YOU!"** *More? Sounds fun!* **"REGRET!"** *Sorry.*

"I feel the h-word for Dave-Tony," she growled: hate. "Gah, why not spill it all! The actual reason I buzzed my frickin' head is: Some deacon's wife called my stupid curls vain, according to First Timothy. But after I cut my hair, she said I'm disgraced, according to First Corinthians!"

"Soph," I said, furious at everything, wishing to carry her somewhere safe, "you're perfect."

"I miss nobody caring whether I'm too girly or not girly enough. I played tackle sports with boys all day, totally innocent, until I was suddenly this stared-at thing, preparing to be impregnated whenever Brio Magazine approves, even though babies terrify me, unless I ruin someone's bubblegum before I'm married and die a lonely s-l-u-t. Well, I can't ruin anyone if I'm a bald skull who never hugs, jogs, writes love letters, dresses like it's summer … thinks … reads … speaks … exists …"

I'd heard that before, inside my own head. I'd been trained to hate part of my body, but couldn't imagine having to hate the entire thing. I wanted to reject whatever had installed that in her. **"YOU'LL REGR–"** *Shut up! Sorry. Not now!*

"I shouldn't whine," she mumbled. "Grownups glare at PG like she chose her figure. At least Alexa's from planet who-cares. She's like, 'I stole you a gee-darn bikini. We'll look s-e-x-y while we kick the ship outta motherfriending Delaware c-words.' The thought counts. Thanks for listening to boring drama, dude."

I'd listen all night, if it helped. "Dare you," I said, nodding toward the endless shoreline. "Tackle sports? Kidding. Or …"

She laughed! "But curfew's now," she said, gazing at forbidden horizons. We walked toward the hotel, releasing our hands in lobby light and rejoining them on the empty elevator. I did a movie thing, tapping a knuckle under her chin.

"I'll run with you, across the whole country if you want."

"No, you deserve a girl who'll do curfew dares," she mumbled at her sandy feet. "Pastor's niece is no fun."

"Well, you deserve Mr. Awesome Christian," I said, slumping. "Mr. Everything I'm Not."

Her eyes jolted up. We started to speak, then laughed, unsure whose turn it was for self-hatred.

"I hate me, but I love you," I said, front-hugging her so snugly, I lifted her nose-to-nose and smelled only beach skin. "So stop hating you."

"No, you stop hating my love-person."

My innards tingled like I'd been lined with tinsel. "See? We need each other. Be my … whatever, okay? In secret?"

"Gimme your blue Further Seems Forever hoodie," she said, sliding down to her feet, "and I'll make you a, like, secret whatever bracelet."

Now do I kiss her? Well, she's singing "Man! I Feel Like a Woman," so yes. Go!

Ding. The elevator door opened. *Nosy eyeballs could be anywhere on her floor. Gosh-fucking-dangit! Sorry.*

Walking her to her room, I explained the d-y-k-e-word, so she wouldn't repeat it.

"Oh," she said. "People think wearing Dickies makes me less boy-crazy. As frickin' if!" Looking over her shoulder, she whispered, "Do you think g-a-y is bad?"

"No," I said, hoping she disagreed with her uncle. "Jerry Falwell vs. my gay friend? Easy call."

She clapped her hands. "Aww, we chose our gay friends over outta-context Bible stuff, huh?"

Whoa. My mind started guessing through all the Graces.

We said our goodbye: "Me and Jesus love you."

Once I deliver my FSF hoodie, we'll officially be secretly … something! I'm getting a job at Pep Boys, then buying Eli's p.o.s. Jeep, then I'll drive her to Pizza Hut forever!

Victorious, I found a glow-in-the-dark frisbee and herded noisy idiots toward the beach. Calebs, Graces, Omaha Burrito Rebeckah, strangers, and even Josiah snuck out.

Funnest week ever, full of dumb mischief, and new AIM friends from six states. Couldn't find Sophie or Josiah all getaway day, though. Pastor family business, probably.

The ride home was so dark that I didn't know which Caleb was snoring on my shoulder. At least we'd remain pure on the Lust Bus, unlike the sinners in the back.

Alexa stormed forth, jabbing Caleb's rectangular forehead and hissing until he lumbered away. She plopped and said, "Listen fast. Last night, Pastor Jack drove here and took Josiah and Sophie home. Said she's a bad influence. Apparently, Josiah got caught [details I couldn't process]. Sounds fun, but w–"

"What?"

"Late last night, Josiah and [details]. Got it?"

"With who?"

"Fucking listen! The pastor's son got caught under a pier, shorts off with two guys."

Brain rebooting.

Sophie's "friend," her cousin. **"YUCK! ROMANS 1:27!"** My role model. "**BAD! FIRST TIMOTHY 1:10!**" Our Simba. "**DOOMED! JUDE VERSE 7!**"

Memories reshuffled themselves. Small moments that might've suggested something he couldn't have said. *What happened last night? I'd led him outside, directly into the notorious beach's temptations, too distracted by my own.* In the bus, I pictured Pastor Jack's rolled-sleeve arms wielding James Dobson books against my embarrassed friend. *Bus, go faster.*

"Just wrestling some fellas?" I asked. "Shorts have minds of their own."

"Dude. Three people told me the same story."

"Three? Tell them to shut up," I said, fighting panic.

Alexa popped bubblegum, smoke-bombed into darkness, and reappeared. "Done, maybe. Blackmail, threats, the usual."

She tried texting an email to Sophie. No service. We peered into darkness, machine-muffled chatter, and Third Day covers.

"Did you know?" she whispered.

"I was blind." I rethought the times Josiah hadn't seemed awestruck by Sara Beth, we'd called each other fruity as an insult, or he'd asked for unspoken prayer requests. I felt guilty for not perceiving enough to defend him. *Did I ever make him stumble during wrestling? I hope so. Otherwise, I'm ugly.*

"Typical pastor's-kid hypocrite," said Alexa.

"Stop. It's not wrong. Other than the shorts-off-edness."

"Duh, everybody likes guys and girls, so who gives a shit?" she said, something I'd later ponder. "I just mean Josiah judges me like I'm screwing everything in sight!" Then again, she bragged whenever guys warned each other about her. "Fuck, his dad's gotta be spazzing. Gay people terrify that man."

"Exactly," I whisper-shouted. "Our friends need help."

"And how's sweet-ass Sophie a bad influence? Bullshit."

"They think she's weird, which is craz–"

"She's weird as shit! She calls 'shut up' 'the other S-word!' She's the fucking world's best person! I tried to offend the pastor's niece, but she claimed me so huge, I babbled secrets I'd never even thought about. She's my only friend who's sweet to my weird-ass dad," she said, slapping a teardrop like a mosquito. "Ugh! You're all weird as shit. Fuck, I'm pissed as motherfuck. Geez!"

"Language," I said, side-hugging her. "That's short for Jesus."

"News flash: You're staying out late with me," she said, hugging her knees like an enraged roly-poly. "I gotta know my best friend's okay."

If someone had told me I'd lie to Mom about my whereabouts while shattering curfew after Beach Fest with Alexandra Giovanni, I would've assumed sophomore year would go perfectly. But hiding behind our pastor's backyard fence, waiting for his upstairs lights to turn off, everything sucked.

Alexa had parked at Josiah's neighborhood pool, then followed me through trees. We planned to check on him before driving to Sophie's. Camo status: pathetic, all from Pacific Sunwear. At least we'd stopped for supplies.

"How fucking long do pastors stay awake?" she said as I passed the Funyuns.

"How long can we wait? Do you, like, *have* a curfew?"

"Dad struggles with basics," she sighed. "I'ma stay outta trouble, starting any day now."

Broken-home buddies. Her mom, some author, left years prior. So Alexa had long been managing her dad's therapy schedule.

As a sprinkler threw walls of water between us and Jack's house, we talked summer plans. I revealed I'd just spent my life savings on two $25 tickets to Warped Tour, so I could take my semi-girlfriend on a three-hour road trip in my hand-me-down Jeep. Alexa approved, but threatened consequences if I either did or didn't misbehave.

"Gonna keep doing church?" I asked. *And get saved from Hell?*

"Whoa, I just realized my year's up. Guess I'm in too deep to quit now."

We sang Sum 41 semi-mockingly. Sprinkler done. Upstairs lights seemed steady, without dancing TV reflections. We snuck through wet grass toward the porch rock hiding the key. I twisted the lock as she played lookout.

"No security?" she whispered.

Oh right. I snatched the Funyuns, creaked the door, and dumped crumbs on the kitchen floor beside Bundles' bed. The fat bulldog rolled over, crunching snacks quietly.

"Chunky monkey," Alexa gasped, kneeling to snuggle him. Smart. Dog occupied.

All else was silent. I tiptoed into the hallway. Second door on the left. Tap tap tap. Rustling. Door opened. Josiah, still in beach shorts, stared at the floor, probably expecting his dad. Hard to tell in darkness, but I saw no black eyes.

I whispered words of assurance: "Sup, dawg."

He looked up. "What the … how'd …?"

With no better ideas, I offered what he'd given me when I'd been drowning in shame two summers earlier: hugging arms and a "snuggle up, tough guy."

He hung his head. I talked him into meeting us behind the bushes. I didn't see a limp, bruised arms, or split lips.

Words tumbled fast. I offered to sneak him into my house, because I couldn't shake stories of things super-religious men did. James Dobson had once bragged about beating up a freaking dachshund!

"Come with us," said Alexa, cradling bulldog tonnage. "I'ma take Bundles home wiff me, doe. Him will love my lady Lucky," her pit bull.

Josiah laughed once. "If they woke up and I was gone, I'd be in even bigger trouble."

"Is bigger trouble even possible?" asked our trouble expert.

"Nah. Leaving a note first." He led Bundles back inside.

"A rule-follower's agreeing to this?" Alexa said, rattling her head. "What the fuck is he escaping?"

She dropped us off, then left for Sophie's, where she'd sneak through the usual window.

"Things have been worse," I said on my enormous couch. "No Rapture this time!"

He'd only had that one laugh in him. He slumped on his side, staring at the floor, so I activated my First Chronicles attention span and sat criss-cross.

"I'm such a fraud," he muttered. "Treating sin like a scoreboard. Like I could …"

"It's okay."

"It's not. I judged you. And everyone. Knowing all along …"

"It's okay."

That lasted several rounds.

"Lots of people did boy-girl beach stuff," I said. "Are they horrible now? I wished for sin. That's just as bad. Some drank! That's way worse!"

"Does everyone know?" he asked the floor.

"I dunno anyone besides Alexa who knows details." Technically.

"I'm sorry … wasn't trying anything, crashing here … pretending to be normal …"

"Dude, without you, I'd have like zero friends," I said, perturbed by his self-loathing. "Maybe we like the Spice Girls for different reasons, but God loves you."

"How can you say that?" he said, finally looking up. "You think God hates *you*, and you haven't even done anything."

No fair! I'm allowed to say God loves everyone without including myself. Change the subject! "So, when you kissed Sara Beth, did that … feel …?"

He called her a beloved friend, whose affection was "nice." Lightbulb! Whenever Bobbi described being "born gay," I'd always nodded along, but never understood. Suddenly, it was crystal clear.

"Nice? If Sara Beth kissed me, I would've jizzed myself paralyzed. See? Clearly, God created you and me different! Case closed!"

"Leviticus 18:22," he replied, clobbering me with the Bible's harshest supposed condemnation of homosexuality.

So I countered with "fearfully and wonderfully," Psalm 139's description of God meticulously creating Josiah.

"Sodom and Gomorrah," he shot back.

"Wrong, that's about selfish people, not gay people! Ezekiel 16:49!"

"Romans 1:27."

Two could play that Paul-quoting game. "Galatians 3:28. Guys, girls, no difference!"

"Ridiculous. Paul clearly sai–"

"Fuck Paul," I yelled. "If Jesus gives a shit about this, he'll say so in red fucking ink."

Josiah rolled onto floor. "Abomination. That's me."

"You know, a wise man named Paul said all fall short, not *Josiah* fell short."

He pursed his lips at me. After a lull, I squeezed forth the question: "You fucking swear your dad didn't hit you today?"

"Matthew 5:33–37. I'd scold your language … but … golly."

Thinking of my lowest moment a year earlier, an even bigger worry seized me. "You're not gonna hurt yourself, are you?"

"Dude," he grimaced, "I'm not *that* big of an abomination."

He didn't know I'd tried to hurt myself, but by his math, I was the basement's biggest sinner. Therefore, he wasn't. Therefore, mission accomplished.

He stared at the ceiling, breathing like a sleeper.

> xSHARKSWITHRABIESx: he's safe

xOneGirlArmy86x (Sophie): thank you [hug]x99999999

xSHARKSWITHRABIESx: [hug]x99999999 so you knew, huh

xOneGirlArmy86x: mhmm

xSHARKSWITHRABIESx: wait why are YOU in trouble??

xOneGirlArmy86x: davetony banged on my door at 3 am, grilling me. i panicked and said maybe king david, paul, cs lewis, and rich mullins were gay. davetony yelped like id shot him. i couldnt stop saying Jesus snuggled with 12 guys every night. he was yelling but i was crying too hard to avoid mentioning God's partly a WomanSpirit. eli appeared so i froze and they made me pack my stuff

xOneGirlArmy86x: brb

xOneGirlArmy86x: me and my humble wife alexa are so fucking pissed we're putting on fucking rainbow temp tattoos. ima plant weed on davetony. ima tell pastor jackass he'll never be megachurch rich, so he should die screaming. hail satan. lets cybersex ;-P

Thank you, Jesus. Everyone's settled in for the night anyway. I typed, "yeah," but paused, to avoid looking overly enthusiastic. *Pressing enter in three, two …*

xOneGirlArmy86x: ALEXA TYPED THAT

xSHARKSWITHRABIESx: yeah

xSHARKSWITHRABIESx: yeah obviously haha

xOneGirlArmy86x: DELETE YOUR COMPUTER WHILE I MURDER HER

xSHARKSWITHRABIESx: nbd, let's focus

xSHARKSWITHRABIESx: is he gonna be in worse trouble if he's not home

xOneGirlArmy86x: maybe

xSHARKSWITHRABIESx: his dad wont hit him, will he

xOneGirlArmy86x: i really doubt it

xSHARKSWITHRABIESx: should we put him back before his dad wakes up

xOneGirlArmy86x: ask him

xSHARKSWITHRABIESx: he swears he's safe there

xSHARKSWITHRABIESx: doesnt want his mom to worry

xOneGirlArmy86x: we're on our way

Twenty-four hours after the pier, we crept in black hoodies through shadows.

"Thank you guys," Josiah mumbled. "I'll remember this. I'm sorry."

"Please be okay," said Sophie, on tiptoes to kiss his cheek, tear glazing the rainbow on hers.

"Not that I deserv–"

"Fuck that self-hater bullshit," said Alexa, hugging him with Sophie squeezed between. Out of words, I joined the group hug, in case we didn't make it.

Josiah walked across his floodlit back yard, past bushes, and onto steps.

And we saw the doorway silhouette.

"Boy," thundered Pastor Jack, "get your butt inside before neighbors see you fled your own mess."

My friend slumped even lower and passed beyond floodlight. We mumble-yelled protests as Josiah waved us back.

"Sophia Primrose, enabler, your parents will hear from me immediately," said my pastor. "Isaac Siena, Jr., and Alexa Giovanni, kidnappers, you're lucky I haven't called law enforcement. I won't let depravity impede my ministry, but choices have consequences. Turning my niece into a skinhead and my son into … You're forever cut off from my family and my church, you two broken-home demons."

PART THREE
THE BOOK OF JUNIORS

He punishes the children
for the sin of the parents

— The Book of Numbers

NINETEEN
WAYFARING STRANGER

JUNE 2002

"MAYBE JOSIAH WAS BORN LIKE THAT," MOM SAID AT OUR KITCHEN TABLE, after I'd deployed every gay fact I knew. "But that'd mean either Pastor Jack or his wife has battled same-sex attraction. Surely that would've come up in a sermon at some poi–"

"You seriously think it's hereditary?" asked Eli, gulping coffee. "Mother. It's like left-handedness. A cross for some to bear. You sure you grew up in California?"

"Apples don't fall far from trees," Mom sighed. "We hear about selfish millionaires who raise selfish kids, promiscuous mothers whose children chase love, fathers ..." *who die depressed, blind-drunk, and maybe-suicidal in 1993.* "But maybe that has nothing to do with Josiah. Besides, the looks I get at church because I'm not little miss lily-white? I don't want my son's friend getting those!"

She asked who Josiah's "beach compadres" were. Eli didn't know and wouldn't reveal the snitch. Then Mom's detective questions included: "Isaac, were we out late on that beach?"

"Sure. Why?"

Oh. I was shocked enough to almost stop eating. *That's why Jack called me a demon? People think I was a shorts-off guy?*

"Mom, I love girls so much, I almost gouged out my eyes."

I did finger guns at Eli, who knew I wasn't joking. He grumbled.

Undaunted, Mom mentioned my constant sleepover MMA and the gay facts I'd shared after smuggling Josiah. "Angel, scientists recently discovered something called bisexuality. Er, *being born with* both-sex attraction? Is that the cool term? Brother Ricardo at church was born that way, until therapy. You know, there's this idea called mixed-orientation marriage, where gay men and lesbians can just marry each other."

"Mom, do you wanna marry a lesbian?" I asked, reaching for the dumbest question I could think of.

"Only if it's Oprah. A zillionaire!"

"Well if you don't, why should Josiah have to? More lesbians for me to marry. Everybody's happy."

Eli grunted his first laugh in a thousand years.

I expected Mom to hit me with the handful of Bible verses that use the word "homosexuality" in some translations, but not in others. Instead, she grinned like she thought my dumb question was clever, maybe remembering California things from before she'd joined Young Life church camp to impress Dad, assuming he was a holy roller (actually, he was just nice).

Build on the positives: Despite how they conditioned her, she's trying to accept that people are born differently. **"IN ETERNAL TORMENT, YOU'LL REGRET TURNING YOUR MOTHER BISEXUAL!"**

"I don't like guys, but liking guys is okay," I said anyway.

"Nope, acting on SSA is sin," Eli rumbled. "Reality isn't your anything-goes basement Bible study."

"Just don't tell your friends I'm some uncool bigot," said Mom. She wanted to be a Rush Limbaugh, but needed to be liked by people who reminded her of adolescence. "Born-that-way relations don't make babies, but as long as others are making babies — Eli — maybe it's not my business."

By then, Eli was sick of people reminding him that his wife wasn't pregnant. He yelled, but Mom kept riling herself up, eventually saying, "I'm leaving that man's church. Rejecting my son is rejecting me."

She's just choosing cool youths over people who'd side-eyed her complexion, but whoa.

"Eli?" she asked. "You quitting their youth ministry?"

"If keeping people outta Hell is objective one, I gotta keep volunteering," he said, rubbing his temples just like her. "Of course Isaac's in trouble for breaking and freaking entering. This is not 'Nam. But going forward, does Jack's church wanna do prosperity-gospel crap? Is the attendance explosion just yay-Republicans stuff? Bump all that. Starving Hell is all I care about."

I hated some things he said, but appreciated others. I assured Mom that things would blow over, and then we could return. Jack would admit God had crafted Josiah, then embrace me, the prodigal son surely only considered demonic because of my old Christmas pageant role.

We arranged one last Men's Accountability Synod. I beheld my Calebs, their precious faces bursting with pizza.

And I decided to try something. I banged a fist on the table so hard, they jumped.

"Listen up, you rectangular virgins. In five minutes, we're gonna give Josiah the normal-est hug possible. Make fun of his boring-ass clothes and Michael W. Smith albums all you want, but gay jokes are fucking done."

Best Caleb said, "But it's sin." Thus, he became Worst Caleb.

"Shut up or I'ma tell everyone you've drawn Miss Frizzle naked."

Worst Caleb pouted as five Calebs giggled. It's called doing discipleship.

"If Josiah wants to talk, we listen. We're all equally wretched here. Questions?"

"Sick speech, Big Bro," said another Caleb. "Most bad a-words gotta do more church. You're so bad a-word, you can't do any. Excommunication is sick."

Blown away, I realized they really viewed me as an elder, similar to how I viewed Josiah and Amir. I felt shame for having squandered that power until then.

Josiah entered, dragged there by Sophie, smiling like he'd suspected he'd been lured into a forbidden hangout. He tried to apologize, though he'd done nothing-ish wrong. I'd convinced him to sneak out! Both times!

"Not barging in on guy time, so I'll go next door," Sophie said, wearing a newsboy hat, looking church-preppy, like somebody'd scrubbed the *me* off her. "Gotta eat veggies anyway."

"What's next door?" wondered a Caleb.

"Gotta eat what?" wondered another.

"Women, why such mystery is?" wondered a third.

"What's wrong with Pizza Hut's veggies?" wondered a fourth. "Ranch, croutons, everything the body needs."

A fifth, singing about talking to tomatoes, wandered toward croutons.

"Josiah, how's your heart?" wondered Worst Caleb, restored to Best Caleb.

Our Simba looked up from his hands. "Thanks for caring. I deeply covet your prayers. Day at a time, I guess. Me and Dad finally had a talk that went both ways. This is a lot for him."

Calebs crunched massive fistfuls of rock-solid croutons, but were otherwise silent.

"Prayed a lot. Nothing's changed. No surprise. But there's a few older church guys who've battled SSA, an–"

"Who's gay besides Ricardo?" blurted the dumbest Caleb.

"Um … ex-gay. Don't speculate. Apparently, they've known about me longer than I have. For years, telling me God loves everyone, quoting The Birdcage in front of Dad. Speaking of, I've now seen an R-rated movie. Ha! People knew. Miss Esther. Baby Cuz, wannabe matchmaker. Sara Beth, lifesaver."

We scrambled to apologize for jokes. He said our "constant grab-butt" had been his best camo.

"You gotta do gay rehab?" asked a Caleb. I punched his arm, but Josiah patted me like I was trigger-happy Peter attacking Romans.

"Yep, but since private school doesn't want me now, I'll finish at public school like you cool kids," he said, smiling with too many teeth and glitching a little. "The guys say therapy's … iffy. Bottom line, if I never act on temptations, mine are just like yours. I'll coast into Heaven, monk-style."

"Bullshit," I said. "We don't have to never fall in love or whatever."

"Life's not fair," he shrugged, frustrated with us. "Paul says some things aren't right for some people."

That did it. I vowed to mash Bible verses together until Josiah got gay married.

"One time, Lilyanne Grace wrestled me, which owned," said a Caleb, lip quivering, "but you're my best wrestle friend, Simba. Nobody forced you to care about us butthead jabronis."

Hugging Josiah again, the bawling Calebs revealed they'd be turbo-grounded for being there. We were really splitting up. How would those goofballs tie their freaking shoes without Josiah or me?

Before the world fell apart, I had to discover what was next door, apparently on the side opposite the Calvinist church.

She sat at a back corner booth, looking out a window. A whole song played. Most of another, too, as her head rested on my shoulder.

"I'm ultra-grounded," she said, "and lying to my parents just by being here. First time I've done that, ever. Dad's saying mean stuff, and he's mad at Mom letting her brother ground me. One cousin said such dumb garbage, I called her s-t-u-p-i-d! Alexa called me crying. They made me hang up on her! Josiah feels guilty for everything. And ..."

Lying for me, partly! I pressed my face against the sinner's forehead.

She hugged me tight. "Stay outta trouble until you're back, okay? I'm scared I won't see you for forever, maybe a whole entire month."

I showed her my new hand-me-down cellphone, complete with "Get Ur Freak On" ringtone. "Ten text messages a month! Once things chill in like three weeks, send me one. Then I'll hand you the hoodie of kinda-datingness?"

"Yes! Kinda! Oh, Uncle Jack's firing Dave-Tony for being a dork. Er, technically because Beach Fest was hanky-pankyville. Whoaaa, your cellphone has a camera?"

Her cheek was soft against mine. I did some bared-teeth snarl as she stuck her tongue out. Click. In grainy black and white, she was eating my chin. Squinting, we declared our photo probably cute. She wanted a copy, meaning I'd have to transfer it to my computer somehow.

"Radio Shack's gotta have a cord," I said. "I love you so much I'ma pass out."

"This photo will get us through these weeks apart. I love you so much I'm gonna barf."

"Here goes the fastest ten days ever," I panted in her face.

"Every day apart, I'll burn you a CD of outrageously secular songs," she said, breathing up my nose. "I have seven blank CDs. That's plenty."

Time to reveal my incredible road-trip plan. From my wallet, I pulled Warped Tour tickets. Six weeks away. She caught her breath and ... tackled me into the booth.

"We'll road trip, Ize. I swear," she said, gray eyes shining inches above me, "to ... to God."

Bro, if this is what awaits, exile will be a 72-hour breeze. I'm Jacob in Genesis, whistlin' away time until I'm re-chosen by my father figure.

"Just the stud I was looking for."

Weeks later, I was walking home from Target on a Friday afternoon, phone-to-computer cord finally in hand. Cutting across church's unusually empty parking lot, I was being shouted at by some guy in a pickup full of lumber.

Then I realized: Timmy!

As we hugged, he explained he was home from his band's tour.

"You're a natural handyman," he said, remembering I'd helped him build a ropes course at camp. "Whatever construction project Jack's starting up, this wood was technically on Grandma Esther's land, so I say we do some useful mischief."

With tithes raining down, Jack had begun clearing land for an enormous new sanctuary, bragging about doing so before obtaining permits.

"I'm, like, not allowed to be here," I said.

"Amigo," Timmy said, winking, "me neither."

"If we follow directions," he said, adopting Miss Esther's Appalachian accent, "we'll finish quicker'n a hummingbird's honeymoon, a'ight?"

Standing in the church campground's tiny parking lot, he handed me gloves. One measurement, cut, or swing at a time. Directions. Precise. Words with definite meaning. There weren't slightly contradictory construction plans. No mystery, thank God.

While mimicking his put-on accent, I found myself speaking increasingly honestly. Still a praise musician, he used as much Christian lingo as ever, but was holding back details about why he'd left Jack's church.

I collapsed on my couch that night, woke up early the next morning, and found Timmy already back at it. Causes had concrete effects, and then we stood atop a skateboard half-pipe, having improved a church camp for Jesus. I felt needed.

Plus, he handed me enough money for a really cheap new phone. Fortunate, because mine had fallen out of my pocket. Er, *almost* a new phone. I had to tithe, plus make up for tithes I'd skipped — I worried my selfishness meant church couldn't afford both its Christlike objectives (feeding orphans and constructing Jack's buildings).

I lost my old phone's unsent photo, but that was okay. Warped Tour was in three weeks, and exile was surely almost over.

TWENTY
SONGS FROM THE PENALTY BOX, VOLUME ONE
SUMMER 2002

"No cursing," Coach Jackson said when we asked about playing MP3s over the stadium's speakers during voluntary workouts. Coach trusted rising-senior Amir a lot.

Nelly, "#1 [Edited]." The Trapt song. phish-ginandjuice.mp3.

Beside empty parking lots, Amir and I threw, caught, kicked, and ran.

Some country song. Panjabi MC [Edited].

I'd downloaded / deleted / re-downloaded all those songs before, except the country, which was for the 280-pound linemen. Amir's playlists accounted for every teammate.

"We Ready [Edited]." "In the Air Tonight."

He said teaching me route-running helped him understand it better. He was a patient coach.

"Bia Bia [Edited]." "Down With the Sickness [Edited]."

Throughout that summer, I got good at punting, way stronger than in middle school. Simple. Stance, hands, step, swing, repeat. Either my foot touched the ball correctly, or it didn't.

Eminem, "Til I Collapse [Edited]." Linkin Park.

No unseen mysteries. No unwritten rules. Only objective truth.

"Bodies." OutKast, "B.O.B. [Edited]." "Chop Suey."

Did leaving Jack's church mean quitting church? LMAO, good one. Sunday morning, Sunday night, and Wednesday night remained mandatory, though Mom let me choose *where*, since I could drive myself.

I'd forgotten how much her megachurch felt like a college campus. Between billboards displaying the megapastor's quotes about "unlocking potential," a thirty-foot Jesus statue overlooked a diner bigger than *my* church's sanctuary. I'd been a middle-schooler there, lost among hundreds of youth-group regulars, sometimes even thousands watching bands like Caedmon's Call or Big Tent Revival. It was a big, big house, and I'd been a weird, weird kid.

As a rising junior, I made friends there while waiting for Jack to get a grip. One look around a room that big and you see where you fit. At *my* church, the robotics girl and the poetry girl hung out, because there were limited options. But at the megachurch, I could scan past lacrosse guys and bluegrass girls to the Ninety Pound Wuss and Mars Ill shirts, the corner of Hot Topic and Zondervan.

The youth pastor, a fauxhawked semi-pro snowboarder, followed a nine-member praise band. He joked about Xanga, A Walk to Remember, and Shakira, then reminded us to tithe.

We split up by grade level. In the juniors room alone, there were fifty girls, all Christians and therefore dateable, though that was irrelevant info for me, a semi-boyfriend. Seven of my classmates were there, including two who'd told me they liked Christian bands, which I'd interpreted as mockery. Smooth.

"I've kissed her, kinda kissed her, crushed on her, but was busy dating her," the landscaping guys' leader explained, pointing around the ecosystem.

Squads of ushers guided traffic toward the giant sanctuary. The pastor's smile adorned merch displays. I'd remembered the stadium-style seating, but not the swirling lights and goshdamn lasers. The huge youth group filled only a fourth of the balcony, where a skater girl with an eyebrow ring sat beside me. In the choir wall, Mom was a tiny brown dot.

The sanctuary band deployed smoke machines, space-whale guitars, forty-foot-wide HumbleTron graphics, and newlywed lead singers who eye-fucked each other throughout Coldplay ripoffs called things like:

"Galaxy Hands (C'mon, Let Us Worship in This Place)"

After the offering, the pastor took the circular stage …

Lenny Kravitz, "Are You Gonna Go My Way"

… and talked for eleven minutes about how people should let Jesus make them happy. Then, a video promoted his marriage-advice book, followed by a call for volunteers and a reminder that donation boxes were by the exits — near the "Galaxy Hands" CDs.

"That place rules," I said after Sunday night's service, an hour of radio DJs roasting the pastor's humility. "There's a bowling alley!"

"That place is … something," said Mom, clipping coupons.

"We timed it just right," Amir said at noon on July's hottest day.

We always finished with the suckiest part: sprinting ten yards, sprinting back, and repeating with an additional ten until we sprinted the full field (and back). They're called suicides.

We lined up, the last song started, Amir took off, and over the speakers was … *What? That's not allowed at school!*

Kirk Franklin, "Melodies from Heaven"

Working out to gospel was churchier than even I'd thought possible. But three minutes in, when I was ready to die, the music dropped to just angel-trumpet voices pleading for rain. And I was running, but not growing weary. *Not only gonna make the team, I'm going pro! Why didn't we play this for Alexa at Harvest Season? We don't need Christian bands copying Pearl Jam! We got better shit already!*

Finishing mere steps behind Amir, I tumbled into grass.

After a minute of listening to birds, lazy mid-day traffic, and our brutalized lungs, he panted, "Coach got mad once. Replaced our music with old gospel ish. But man, it's secret sauce. I saw pastors' grandkids and choir boys lighting up, waving hands, catching the Ghost or whatever for fun. And eff it, me too! It's music! Who cares whether it's hitting your body or soul or both?"

Beneath the punishing sun, I creaked upright and hobbled upstairs. He thanked me, thinking I was gonna retrieve his iPod.

"Nah," I said, smile bursting forth, "we're gonna sing one more verse."

Another afternoon, Coach stopped by, baffled to hear …

Whitney Houston, The Preacher's Wife soundtrack

… blasting from the PA. He invited us to his tiny church near the airport.

There, we saw robes, candles, and incense like churches in movies, but office-type windows, not stained-glass. Ladies wore fancy hats.

Coach's daughter, the only high school girl, played violin. She was dating some nerd, not that I was available. Right?

The lady pastor (whoa) said we shouldn't overly obsess with saving souls and forget Jesus spent his earthly time saving lives. *I don't follow that math. Souls outlast lives.*

But everyone was nice, thanking me for visiting. It was obvious I was a visitor. I was the white (half-Greek, FWIW) person.

The megachurch pastor told oceans of (white, I suddenly noticed) faces about the abundance Jesus offers. MP3s of "Galaxy Hands" remixes, 99 cents. Hot chocolate machines in the primary youth building. Eyebrow Ring Girl was surprised to learn of my semi-girlfriend, because my semi-girlfriend was one of Earth's few inhabitants who didn't attend that megachurch.

"I forgot how much that place loves money," Mom said in our (modest) home. "I feel like a failed Christian for being middle class!"

During a sermon about Jesus depositing blessings, a painter created a waterfall mural on stage. Me and the post-hardcore guys camped near the skater girls. The pastor's internet show hired its own band. The snowboarder joked about Juwanna Mann, Space Ghost Coast to Coast, and "dude, you're getting a Dell," then reminded us to tithe.

There was a newspaper article. Three choir ladies and two secretaries accused the pastor of sexual harassment. Some people wanted him fired. Some said the women traded virtue for attention. Some worried the whole church was based on his personality. Seemed crazy, because I would've attended just for the waterslide. He tearfully confessed "a bygone season of marital trials," announced a book about restored innocence, and pledged proceeds to the rehab facility that'd recently cured his "porn addiction." (His church owned the facility.)

"Galaxy Hands (Vindication Remix)"

Mom believed the choir ladies, so we quit the megachurch again. Photos of me camping still remain on their LiveJournal. Years later, anyone on earth can see 2002 me, tan and swole beside some girl with an eyebrow ring.

I already regretted skipping Warped Tour, but what was I supposed to do? Regift Sophie's ticket? Go alone? I sat on my roof in emo poses.

After talking to me nearly daily for two years, Sophie hadn't replied to emails or been on AIM for six weeks.

Josiah guessed she wasn't allowed. I didn't want to make him play messenger, and he was hard to contact at "rehab" anyway. (Yeah, same facility.) Declining my offer to Ocean's Eleven him out of there, he said, "Ex-gay celibacy seems doable, now that I understand what activates my attraction is ..."

"Jiggly-glistening hot guys?"

"... skipping morning prayer."

I missed Josiah, the Calebs' harebrained wisdom, PG's unstoppable honesty, all my other church oddballs, and even Alexa's personality. It was like we'd grown up together, but I'd only been involved for a year or two. *That wasn't enough for them to miss me. I might as well not exist.* At least I no longer meant that literally, thanks to them.

At Pizza Hut, I told the megachurch story to Amir, who said, "You know how, when a team fires its coach, they hire the opposite kinda guy? I've heard of an opposite kinda church."

At 4 a.m., fifty miles from home, we saw a woman's ghost beside a water tower. "No way my folks would've let me drive out here," Amir said, grateful for my tinted windows. Out in the hills, he was the obvious visitor.

We passed cows and you're-all-going-to-Hell billboards. Asphalt became gravel. He sampled my binder of burned CDs, surprised to find Switchfoot in the Christian half, and moved my carefully mislabeled DMX albums there too.

We followed MONASTERY signs onto dirt roads and saw four stone buildings in a square. We sat on planks in something like a cave. It was only summer-morning chilly, but our bones shivered. A dozen bald men filed into a choir-like area. Nobody explained anything.

Slow and cutting singing, maybe in Latin

Something old and important surrounded us. *Don't break the spell. Don't fart.*

"This is dope," I whispered, watching guys moan pre-sunrise syllables. "Once."

"Hella glad we came," Amir said. "Once."

He closed his eyes. He always got good grades, minded his business, and was fine practicing by himself. Of course he liked it there. Once.

We wandered into another stone building. In daybreak light, we saw rows of painted honey jars and a cash register. A bald man with glasses, brown robes, and a soft smile appeared. We asked, delicately, if we could buy honey.

"Buy it all so we can afford PlayStations," he honked in a Boston accent. He explained they had jobs, including beekeepers and brewers. "The four Bs: Beatitudes, Baldness, Beer, and actual Bees. The fifth would be Babes, but Saint Mary's is 102 miles thattaway."

I'd always heard pastors say drinking is sinful ninety-nine percent of the time (the one percent: Jesus making special grape juice), and I knew it was the sin that might've damned my dad. Yet this monk survived thanks to beer. *Therefore, monks should die.*

"Can … we … um …" I said anyway, *not that I'll drink it, because that's evil.*

" … like … buy …" Amir said.

"You puppies have IDs? Laws are real, even in monk land."

Of course we're joking! Anyone who chooses alcoholic-ness hates themselves, God, and everything. At least the megachurch doesn't sell literal poison! You know, Mom smoked weed as a kid, and she turned out fine …

We drove home, dipping Taco Bell cinnamon twists into monk honey, talking about cool silences rich with warm somethings.

Bob Marley, "Could You Be Loved?"

I walked toward fall football practice, heard a soul-deflating thump, and saw a ball booming higher than any I'd ever punted. Then another towering heartbreaker. I saw the kid launching those bombs, and learned a ringer had transferred to my school.

The Trapt song.

You'd think I would've known, but nobody ever talks about punters. Coach had been honest when he'd said I might only play as a garbage-time tackling dummy. I saluted the mercenary and bounced up outta there.

Fun summer. Got in shape and helped a friend. I planned to spend Friday nights doing odd jobs with Timmy, to stay out of trouble until my church family brought me back.

"When life gives ya nails, get to hammerin'," Timmy said in our joke accent. "And whenever you feel lower'n a bow-legged bedbug, talk to me about it, y'hear?"

My junior year uniform: Allen Iverson shirsey and flip flops with socks, just like the football players.

That year's See You at the Pole crowd proved my so-called secular-indoctrination school actually included zillions of non-persecuted Christians. **"YOU CAN'T QUESTION YOUR TRAINING! YOU W–"** *The principal's singing along with Steven Curtis Chapman songs! How's that gonna make non-Christians feel?* **"… WTF DID YOU JUST SAY?"** *Fuck. Sorry.*

And every time I awoke from Hell nightmares, Church Tour continued, as I stormed Diablo II's final-boss sanctuary in a really stupid way, armed with only Acts 3:21, First Corinthians 15:22, Revelation 21:5, and …

Natalie Merchant, "Sympathy for the Devil"

TWENTY-ONE
HELL IS FOR CHILDREN
HALLOWEEN 2002

"THIS'LL BE WAY SCARIER THAN OUR EX-CHURCH'S SPOOKY SHIT, RIGHT?" Alexa asked, wearing cutout leather pants with a mostly see-through top, tossing a cigarette, and climbing into my Jeep. "Somebody said it was on the news!"

Our friends still weren't allowed to see either of us, so we were driving forty minutes away. I staple-gunned my eyes to the road as we talked horror movies. Her boyfriend, busy at football practice, took her to R-rated movies all the time. Yeah, well, I was good at downloading stuff.

She said her dad had been through so much, divorce and illness and whatever, that she'd never told him about our banishment. I told her about churches I'd visited with Amir.

"We both found lady preachers?" she interrupted. "Pastor Jackass would freak. I joined the Unitarian Uni-whatever Oasis of Acceptance and … fuck, I forget the whole name." That little shack had become the butt of Pastor Jack's jokes about liberal Christians. "It's nine grandmas who sing 'Love Train,' draw cartoons about Buddhist squirrels, and never yell at me! We protest jail, the concept. Did you know all prisoners are in for shit like smoking weed? We Uni-whatevers learn about society. Way better than learning about Psalm 2,000,008. Besides, Jesus said good sheeps are nice to criminals!"

We passed a HELL HOUSE: 25 MILES AWAY billboard. I hoped the show would startle her into getting saved. *That'll impress our church into taking me back!*

But I warned her, "There's no way this place allows 'Dirrty' Christina Aguilera costumes."

"This is the modestest outfit in the entire video," she groaned, digging around, finding my bloody-switchblade Converge hoodie. Goodbye to another one! Three different Graces still had hoodies of mine. Megachurch Eyebrow Ring Girl had slept in one throughout August camp. Sometimes this is a claiming-her-territory thing, but mainly, every woman is always freezing. Whatever.

Mad about her costume, Alexa said, "Church weirdos think if a guy likes a girl, that's the girl's fault. Girl likes a guy? That's also the girl's fault! Girls like each other? Two girls' faults! If guys like each other, is that a girl's fault?"

"Church dudes taught me feminist moms turn their sons gay."

"Fuck, I was joking! Our Sunday teacher lady once pointed at you guys like, 'God created boys to be visual, to appreciate their brides revealing motherly enchantments or whatever the fuck. But because you little whores grew boobs, those horndogs can't stop spank-banking! You're splattering their splooge on your Heavenly report cards, you skanks!' I'm para-quoting."

HELL HOUSE: 15 MILES AWAY.

I argued, amid my fourth Santa Fe Gordita from our Taco Bell stop, that church guys faced challenges too. "We beat ourselves up for beating ourselves up."

My gripped-fist gesture didn't faze her. She was busy eating the lettuce from her tacos and handing me the rest.

"Dude, the churchiest girls feel guilty for bathing too thoroughly," she said, her fingers doing educational motions. "Before banishment, I asked some dweeb why masturbating is bad. He's like, 'Durr-dee-hurr-hurr, because in Genesis, God murdered some guy who jizzed everywhere.' I'm like, 'Girls don't jizz, dumbass, so I'ma treat myself!' That's called interpreting scripture. Then Sophie started explaining Jewish genders or something nerdy. He got mad, which made her sad, so I went mama bear until he kicked me out. Aww ... she'd be jealous I'm wearing your hoodie."

"Jealous? She remembers me? What'd she say?"

"Ugh, I'd love to meddle in forbidden romance, like Ro–"

"Rogue and Gambit. Got it. Just tell me."

"Dork! She got in so many arguments with her family, she's still mega-grounded from everything. I can't even sneak in her window anymore! I used the Graces as gossip middlepeople — until they got rededicated big-time. They only share secondhand messages if you call them prayer requests. Asking my best friend about her weekend takes ninety goddamn weirdos!"

Impatient, I bugged my eyes.

"What I've heard," Alexa huffed, "could mean either she's gonna marry some Church Dynasty asshole or she hopes you burst into her bedroom naked like the Kool-Aid Man."

"The Kool-Aid Man wears glass."

"No, Kool-Aid's his blood," she said, extending a palm, seeking a response.

"I got a new phone. If she's text-messaged me, I didn't get it." *And I love her, but …*

"Man, it's Halloween. Just show up! Church boys won't even break rules in costume."

"I already broke into the pastor's house! What, break into hers? You're steering clear too!"

She slumped and groaned, "Fine. We can't get her homeschool-jailed forever. Gah, that pastor fucked everything up by being scared."

From the line of cars, as Alexa wailed along with her horrendous Saliva CD, we saw roadside HELL HOUSE 2002 signs painted with flaming goat skulls. Metal as fuck! We parked in gravel, and somebody made me leave my cardboard sword, which had been my entire costume.

"Evening, I'm Shane, serving as pastor here," said a man with a plaid shirt and soft South Park *mmmkay* voice as our group entered a medium-sized sanctuary. Corn dogs in hand, we snickered about nerdy Shane running a haunted house that'd made USA Today.

"You might've heard this event's nothing but cruel scare tactics," he said, like a doctor delivering bad news, "meant to terrify people toward our opinions. Well, the media makes mistakes. After all, we're not the ones pushing cocaine-laced Snickers at rainbow parties — don't worry, I'm teasing. Guess who invented those hoaxes? The media."

"For fifteen dollars, I demand scare tactics," Alexa whispered.

"What you'll see tonight isn't a Wes Craven fantasy." Beside Shane's stage, a man in black-and-white camo waved us toward an open door. "Believe me, we'd rather carve pumpkins. But every year, the world's jadedness forces us to escalate our wakeup calls."

An hour later, returning to my Jeep, I only thought, *We shouldn't have come here.*

When you're a little kid, attending a Hell house fucks you up, sure, and on a level beyond the average haunted house. The church experience is about horrors that don't end when you leave, but follow you into eternity.

Attending years later while bringing an unsaved friend might've been even worse. At that point, nothing went over our heads.

As one scene depicted a gay teenager being dragged from his hospital bed into Hell, I wanted to hurt whoever believed Josiah or Bobbi deserved that fate. When another showed a free-spirited church girl becoming demon-possessed by "dabbling in the occult" (meditating), I felt defensive of Sophie and Amir, who liked learning about religions. The scene that implied a drunk girl deserved to be gang-raped made me sick to have brought Alexa, a frequent partier. The only scene that didn't feel like it'd declared war on my friends: the room in which Satan claimed a grieving heroin addict.

There was even an "I attend church every Sunday morning, Sunday night, and Wednesday night" character who considered herself so full of "satanic depression," she chugged from a vodka bottle, cut her wrists, and left with car keys. As we walked toward the parking lot, the drunk girl's car was arranged like it'd plowed into a minivan full of children.

Right beside the smoke-spewing van lacquered with gore, church counselors mobbed our group's crying middle-schoolers.

"Tonight's your chance to avoid ending up like these people," said the counselors while the kids nodded. "Now repeat this prayer after me …"

As I pumped gas for the drive home, Alexa's dark eyes glared past me.

A horn honked.

Oh, great, my brother was walking over. She locked her door, rolled up her window, and slumped beneath the dash.

"Now, that was the gospel," Eli hooted. "After Jack's rah-rah-America crap, it's nice to remember God's heart for the lost!" He raved about how many kids he'd seen praying with counselors. "I get giddy watching people show up cocky, then crumbling as reality sinks in. I just told Pastor Shane the exit should be a maze, so kids can't duck counselors."

I rambled about how bad I felt for those middle-schoolers.

"Every teenager needs a butt-kick," he scoffed. "Got mine around seventeen! You remember? The potatoes! Seriously, I adore your gift of protectiveness. Use it! Kids crying now beats kids crying forever!"

"Dude. The car wreck? That's what they'd think of me — and your freaking father."

His smile faded into steel, and he stared through my eyes, nodding like we were teammates. "Motivation."

On the highway, Alexa was so silent, not even Limp Bizkit's "Break Stuff" cheered her up. Doing seventy, inches from an eighteen-wheeler and therefore inches from eternity, I worried about the unsaved girl beside me. Beyond the gore, we'd glimpsed good news, right?

"That shit was fucked up," I said, steering onto her eerily empty street. "Every scene seemed like it was picking on our friends. Except the druggie thing, I guess. But ..."

Staring at her unlit house, she spoke in a flat drone. "I've only told one person this. She trusted you, so I'm trusting you. If you spill anything ... fuck threats. I'll fucking hate you."

She looked up, her face stone. I nodded.

"When Mom bailed and told me I'd wind up a wreck like Dad, he fought to keep me, like I wanted. Except now I'm raising him. I have his checkbook, so bills get paid. If I don't get him to work or VA therapy, he doesn't go. He has this, like, condition called CMI. It means *everything sucks, nobody cares*. Everybody thinks '91 was some easy war. He had to kill people, then dreamed about them, then felt weak for doubting himself. Can you imagine how hard they gotta brainwash you just to make you point a gun at somebody?"

I second-guessed every time I'd mocked her criticisms of the War on Terror. Exhaling so hard she shook, she revealed his addiction to pills.

As one tear betrayed her, she curled a lip. "School people use my house for parties, since Dad's always zonked out or gone. And I'm a pushover, scared to make them clean up, because they won't like me anymore. My mother took my brothers, even though I was their better mom. My best friend's grounded from me. I suck at church, but ... fine, church was my family! Now all I have is my puppy and my daddy. And I just paid fifteen dollars to hear my daddy deserves torture."

"I'm really sorry we went," I mumbled, already **regretting** backing down. "I hadn't been since I was six. I only remembered special effects."

"All that Hell shit," she said, unzipping my hoodie and handing it back, "isn't afterlife panic. It's excuses to abuse people now, like addicts and victims need more bad shit. Let's create middle-school self-haters! Then call them sluts who'll get boys damned! Because we're the only way outta Hell, everyone better agree with us on everything. Hell is a world without God? Hell is a Christian president bombing Iraqi babies!"

"Dirrty" Christina stood in freezing air, shivering with rage.

"Anything that keeps people outta Hell's justified, huh? That's what Eli thinks? While he mind-fucks fourteen-year-olds at our church, kids we're supposed to protect? But nobody cares what the heathen bitch thinks. You really think that shit was fucked up?"

I nodded, bewildered. *Protect church kids from … church?*

"Our friends need us," she huffed, "and somebody's gotta confront your brother."

TWENTY-TWO
WHEN YOUR HEART GLOWED THE HOPE

NOVEMBER 2002

I HADN'T EXACTLY PLANNED TO TRY WEED, AND DEFINITELY NOT IN AN INSANE Clown Posse fan's RV. It's the gateway drug to being ensnared by demons at fifteen dollar Hell houses, but juggalos are just that friendly.

Many hours earlier, I'd been at Bobbi's StarCraft-themed birthday party. When the juggalo, her jovial nineteen-year-old cousin, had invited her to smoke with his friends, she'd wanted to try it — if she had someone she could bail with. (Coincidentally, I'd volunteered right after the juggalo told me his "candy goth" roommate thought I was cute.)

After hours in his crowded RV — watching the Queen of the Damned DVD loading screen, devouring Flamin' Hot Cheetos, and playing Acid Tetris — I retroactively learned the concept of hotboxing. My gooey eyes and sprawling giggle-arguments revealed I'd partaken without intentionally inhaling, meaning I'd done the worst sin: emulating a Democrat, Bill Clinton.

Beside me on my Jeep's hood in brisk night air, Bobbi sat wide-eyed, commenting on being high as if she was conducting a study.

"I'm willing myself to have supermassive versions of any emotion I want," she said. "Engage sadness, 200 percent. Go! Whoa. Bad choice."

"The galaxy's my face blanket," I said, striving to drown in the stars above. My mind was kinda trying to rationalize law-breaking — *I'm showing an atheist how cool Christians are and bodyguarding a 105-pound anime nerd* — but mostly didn't care.

Pointing at the horizon's brightest light, I said, "Bet you don't know that random star's name, Know-It-All."

"That's not a star," she said, the funniest joke I'd ever heard. "That's Venus. Some cultures called it the Evening Star *and* Morning Star, like it was two friends separated forever, even though they couldn't possibly part. That dot's a whole numinous poem, maaan."

I appreciated her love for space. It's fun when atheists resort to the word "numinous" to describe blatantly spiritual feelings, and it's fun when atheists admit there are things they'll never know.

"In the Bible, Venus is the enemy falling from Heaven," I said.

"We're looking at Satan right now? That owns!"

"Well, the Bible also calls Jesus the Morning Star."

"See, if *I* said Jesus and Satan are the same, I'd get burned at the stake."

By then, we rarely argued about religion, but still tried to push each other toward uncertainty. Otherwise, we got protective. On one field trip, I'd told some HELL IS REAL sign guys to leave her alone, even though that meant endangering souls. And when two non-believers had looked up from worshiping Tool lyrics to accuse me of believing in Space Teapot, she'd called them the most hurtful words any atheist can hear: "Not clever."

"But what if it's not about Jesus defeating Satan?" I said, gazing at pearly Venus, a morning thing disguised as an evening thing. "What if the coolest way to beat Diablo II is without any weapons? What if I wanna save Diablo, not kill him?"

"You definitely inhaled more than me."

As we spotted shooting stars, I asked her how things were going with the ladies. Not exactly out at school, but not exactly hiding, she'd grown frustrated by girls who hinted at wanting to experiment. "How about they experiment with each other, then report back?"

"Word. Hey, did you know I used to believe all men are missing a rib because God took one of Adam's to make Eve?"

"Whoa, that's why I have an extra rib?"

Once I realized she was trying to catch me being gullible, I said, "Really? Lemme see."

"A., it's freezing, and B., aren't you dating Miss Homeschool or whatever? She was all you talked about for like a year."

"Enh," I said, projecting my weed emotions toward apathy. "Lost touch. Wouldn't have worked anyway. She's a Dynasty child, mega-attuned to the Spirit. I can't attune to anything deeper than, like, sports."

That made Bobbi recite the endless plot of Final Fantasy X, tearfully detailing a love story about a jock protecting a sorceress from his dead father, who was also God or something. I zoned out, then countered with a story she wouldn't care about: Amir's football heroics from the night before, when he'd nailed a forty-yard kick to beat our archrival.

Then we stared at Venus.

"I think the candy goth would deflower you, if you asked," she said. "Then she'd brag about it at school. Jesus Boy, conquered by a Marilyn Manson fan."

Actually, the candy goth had said that to my face, and she hadn't been the first. At school, rumors about my DUI dad and boiling-brimstone brother painted me as barely restrained danger. Whichever girl could finalize the goodie-goodie's downfall would win badass status. Sometimes, queen badass Alexa snarled wannabe renegades away from my locker. (I pretended that was possessiveness, though it was probably protectiveness.) Turns out that labelling every girl a temptress meant some decided to play along.

"I'd let the candy goth do whatever," I said, blandly amazed to hear myself saying so. "But walking inside sounds like work."

"Weed saved your V-card," Bobbi laughed.

"Speaking of cards," I said, digging in my pocket and handing her a coupon from the Pep Boys where I'd worked for a year, "happy birthday, dear."

"Free oil change. Good one, dear." Though her folks were wealthy, she didn't care to drive.

"Borrow your parents' car? I could introduce you to this cashier. She's nice, pretty ..."

Bobbi froze with nerves at the thought of initiating public interactions. I listed anime things they had in common and said, "You don't gotta propose! It's just ... you wanted friends who know what it's like to be you."

"No way I'll go blurt at a stranger. But fine. Just for that, I won't tell anybody what Jesus Boy did tonight."

Huh, Mom texted me four times. Weighing options, I responded, "fell asleep at caleb's roflmaoooooooo," the lie that almost always worked. I'd need a way to change out of my weed clothes before church in a few hours.

Bobbi, hopping down to go sleep on her cousin's couch, dared me to crash wherever the candy goth was. *It'd be simple. Just walk inside, become a man, and accept that she'll brag about her church-assigned caricature: soul-stealing enchantress.*

I watched my breath float past the moonless sky's brightest light. From outside the RV, I could hear universally beloved Christian shoegaze band Starflyer 59 on loop. My recommendation, yeah. I felt **regret** for lying to Mom, but nothing else. Surreal.

Oh well, at least I'll never drink, because drinkers are family-abandoning lowlifes beyond redemption.

Unless ...

Asking my body to feel all the hope that could be mustered by a fading contact high, I reached lazy fingers toward Venus. Caressing the night sky's so-called Devil in my hand, I wondered: If some of us evening things can still reach morning, can't all of us?

"Let's say I, like, accidentally smoked weed," I said to my church's only attendee I was allowed to see. "Would you tell Mom? She's never technically forbidden it."

Eli stepped away from the wall and rubbed paint-splotched fingers against his temples. I could *see* him weighing "God made seed plants for people (Genesis 1:29)" against "Everyone must submit to authorities (Romans 13:1)" against "Don't call God's creations unclean (Acts 10:15)."

"America and Jamaica have different laws, but the Bible says nothing about weed," he said. "Therefore, I don't care what America thinks. But since you know Mother wouldn't want you doing it, you dishonored her — whether or not she listed it as one of the many crimes you obviously shouldn't do."

"You gonna tell on me or not?"

"Do you want me to?"

"For what? It was accidental."

He chuckled, not believing me. We got back to work, painting our aunt's porch in Saturday silence.

Later, sitting in the grass, he said, "You ever think about why you're the Isaac Jr. and I'm some other guy? In the Bible, Eli sucks. Corrupt. Sexist. Deadbeat. Unprincipled."

"At least you're not some guy only known for almost getting killed."

"There are cool Abraham-and-Isaac interpretations," he said, listing ones he'd learned in college. "When Isaac laid down, ready for Abraham to kill him, I've always pictured Isaac as a defiant martyr."

"Defiant of what? Abraham was God's main guy."

"God's main guys were wrong all the time."

"You're not even God's main guy," I said, more harshly than I'd intended, "so what if you're wrong about Dad? About if we can all make it home together?"

He looked down and shook his head. "I'm not."

"Says who?" I barked, slamming my gloves onto soil. "Did you put a fucking tracking device on his soul?"

He chugged water and watched birds. "Scripture's clear. Sorry. If you're asking why I'm so resolute, well … you remember that night when I was seventeen."

That Wednesday night. I was nine.

At that small church, K-12 students gathered in one room before dispersing. A few dozen of us sat in folding chairs, singing Jesus songs. The hallway door slammed open.

"Deny Christ or die," barked a ski-masked man, pointing a semiautomatic rifle. He stormed up the middle aisle, followed by three even burlier gunmen in Oakleys and fingerless gloves. One screamed, "I'll paint the walls with you little Jesus-lovers."

We froze as they thundered toward the front row, where they grabbed a seventeen-year-old by his red hoodie, dragged him into the hall, closed the door, and roared at him to renounce his faith. He yelled, "Please don't kill me! I hate Jesus!"

"Too late!"

We heard a gunshot and a heavy object thudding onto the floor.

I believed my seventeen-year-old big brother had just joined my father in death.

Moments later, Eli walked back in, bawling. I darted to hug him, but he shoved me away in shame. The men, dads from a neighboring church, explained it'd been a skit about standing up for faith. The thud had been a potato sack.

But they'd never warned Eli. With all his heart, he'd blasphemed.

(Yep, that happened *before* Columbine.)

A day later, Eli told me he'd endangered every child's soul by shouting about God being fake. He told nine-year-old me, "What if a kid had believed me, when I'd renounced Christianity? Jesus said it's better to be killed than to endanger young souls! Those cowards should've protected you kids by blasting me to Hell."

My brother was no longer the goofball who snuck me hip-hop tapes. After watching the "I Pledge Allegiance to the Lamb" music video about a father who'd rather orphan his son than change religions, he ditched his Division I-AA football scholarship, applied to Bible college, and told Mom, "I owe Jesus my life, and I intend to pay."

Riding back from our aunt's house with sunset in our eyes, he said, "Maybe I'm not an Eli. Birth certificate aside, maybe I'm an Elijah."

"Guy who listened to silent mountains?"

Lowering his sunglasses from his forehead, he said, "Guy who did whatever it takes. He could've let 450 false teachers live, but he counted the cost of letting their message spread. So he killed them."

"Lemme guess, some church rando disagreed with you about something, so you're stewing," I said, rolling my eyes. "Killing is, like, super Old Testament behavior."

"I'm sick of hearing about nicey-nice New Testament God," he said, stirred all the way up. "In Revelation, Jesus kills more people than the whole Old Testament combined. Which Old Testament people stood beside Jesus at the transfiguration? The killer Elijah and ...?"

"Moses."

"Another killer. Both claimed by the New Testament."

Watching him clench his jaw at the road because of some debate I didn't care to learn about, I could only laugh.

"You should smoke weed," I advised.

Caught looking overly intense, he grunted and softened. "That'll fix me right up, huh?"

TWENTY-THREE
SNOWBIRDS AND TOWNIES
NEW YEAR'S 2003

As Pastor Jack's ever-expanding praise band blasted Voldemort's theme throughout the remodeled sanctuary, lit by the expanded HumbleTron's lightning graphics, the Demon General donned a spiked Nazgûl helmet (drama minister Ricardo really crammed *everything* into Christmas pageants). For 2002, the General commanded not just a squad, but an army. The new light system flashed red, revealing the bigger-than-ever youth group clad in black. The General raised his armor-plated arms as upgraded speakers bellowed his prerecorded boasts.

But handsome idiot Gabe appeared in his stupid archangel costume and botched some victory speech while silent Mary smiled.

Backstage, demon minions removed their helmets and hugged genius Ricardo.

The General planned to remain in costume until reaching the loading dock, where I'd sneak out of the suit and return it to Best Caleb. In a gesture of loyalty, he'd decided the role was mine, whether I was allowed at church or not. Gabe never knew, not even while smirking past my locker the Friday before.

I couldn't see much through the General's headgear. I heard a door bang open and felt a stern shove.

"Couldn't get Christmas canceled, Caleb?" someone shrieked in character at me. "Been too busy telling me Gandalf out-Jesus'd Frodo? Well, never send a demon to do the Peace-freak Hollywood Feminist's job!"

Lumbering around, I saw Sophie barreling toward the stage, warning everyone to avoid eye contact or she'd call the ACLU. Grownups chuckled, hopping out of her warpath. Idiot archangel Gabe, terrible at staying in character, acted like her security guard.

I had the phone numbers of girls from school, and planned to ask one out for New Year's. But the Demon General had made a promise to a weird feminist in a wig of streaky Kelly Clarkson hair, even if she looked so much happier in that devout mob than she'd been a lifetime earlier, sitting on the beach with me.

BadBoys5318008 (Amir): YOOOO YA BOY'S A D1 KICKER!!! SCHOLLY TO YOUNGSTOWN!!!

BadBoys531800: AT MY CEREMONY IMA THANK COACH, GOD, FAM, AND YOU, BIG BOY!!!!

xSHARKSWITHRABIESx: [Away message: blink-182 - i miss you]

Whoa, awesome. I might've been destined to follow him one year later, if I hadn't quit football twice. Squandering talents is yet another sin (Matthew 25).

Pastor Jack's church added a coffee shop, where Caleb worked, nosing around and "acquiring documents" like a bored Solid Snake. He found lists of rejected coffee shop names (Heaven & Earthiness, Robust In The Lord Always, Steamy Grindin' Xtr3me, etc.), charts showing the newly retitled *Senior* Pastor Jack had started overseeing seven newly promoted sub-pastors (plus talk of launching satellite churches in other cities), and plans for the much larger sanctuary being built in the woods.

More interesting was the list of other churches soon to attend the New Year's tourist-town youth retreat, including the tiny Calvinist church near Pizza Hut.

Sure, Calvinists believe we're tainted by our fathers' sins, but joining the Calvinists' youth group for a week would get me to my friends without getting my friends in trouble.

To avoid overhearing Calvinism during the van ride, I kept my headphones in, with one Further Seems Forever song on loop: "New Year's Project," about two people waiting to share the future.

I hadn't told even Caleb I was coming. During the first lunch break, at the knife store, he hugged me in surprise. Beside him, PG said her new band, called Wearing Nothing But Eyeballs, played "post-West-Coast pre-hardcore." Hugging other folks I hadn't seen in months, I was shocked to find they remembered me, let alone missed me. I met Misfits-patch freshmen who considered me a criminal legend, plus tons of other new people. *Whoa, we're the biggest church here.*

Then I saw a rainbow beanie on a girl walking alone toward ski lifts, holding mittens out wide, still daydreaming of snow.

Steps away, seven hundred feet tall, I called out, "Foxy?"

I glimpsed pinkish hair and gray eyes before a warm, swaying hug that lasted through several giddy questions and explanations.

"Where'd these muchachos come from?" she said, stepping back, patting my upper arm.

"Oh. Football, I guess. Pink hair?"

She revealed an adorable short bob, with bangs swooping across her freckly face. "You played this year? Awesome!"

"Your hair's dope. Like …"

"… please say Pink."

I nodded. She fist-pumped. Her big smile convinced me that we'd easily resumed being BFFs-and-more.

"I gotta wash it out," she grimaced. "So happy you're here!"

"Why get rid of it?"

"Ehh, people hate it. Oh, I'm getting a job! Farmer's market! How's your mom?"

"The one near my work? We could take breaks together?"

"Aww, the one downtown, but that'd be awesome! I miss you constantly. I'm so sorry I couldn't get you unbanned yet. Things sucked, bad. How was Warped Tour?"

"Everything's okay now. We got three days here."

"Yayyy! Oh emm gee, now we can talk about Two Towers! When Gandalf came back on the hill! With the light! Gah, so perfect! Oh! I left you a painted rock! Like … months ago, on your Jeep. Did you find it?"

"No, sorry," I said, handing her a CD case. "Here's one song seventeen times. This is your coolest hair ever. Whoever doesn't like it sucks."

"Thank you. I made you … a lotta CDs," she said, clearing her throat. "So …"

"Could I have kissed you at the veggie restaurant?"

Yeah, it was sudden, but I was done waiting. Her smile collapsed. Uh-oh.

"Um … yes," she said, quiet. "I …" Her eyebrows did the thing that meant somebody was hurting.

"Head-shaving day?"

"Ize …"

It wasn't going how I'd hoped. *NBD, of course things are awkward.*

"Paintball day?"

"Lemme …"

"Snow day?" I said, presenting white stuff in my glove. "Now it's a real snow day. See?"

She squeezed her eyes shut. "You're so special to me. But … I kinda dated somebody, an–"

"All good," I said, swallowing pangs. "Dabbled too, kinda."

"Still?"

"Nope!"

Eyebrows trembled. Gray eyes shone.

Nobody'd ever warned me it'd feel so much like nausea.

I asked, "Still?"

She nodded. It hurt so fast, I laughed. She mumbled about pageant rehearsals with … *be not afraid* … the archangel Gabe.

"He's a nice guy," I lied through my collapsing throat.

Christian comedian Mark Lowry once said ancient people described emotions as happening in bowels, not hearts. Standing in the cold, I realized the ancients were correct.

She babbled an explanation, indicating she thought I'd given up first. "I heard gossip … some church LiveJournal, some eyebrow ring girl in my FSF hoodie … my photo, I never got …"

As my guts shoved themselves upward like a Push Pop, I heard footsteps. *Lord, smite me. Hurry.*

"What up, Christmas nemesis?" said the assistant pastor's son in a Lakers rugby shirt and a black blazer, looking like Paul Walker had evolved into John Cena, patting my chest and playfully tugging Sophie's hat past her forehead.

When, Lord, will you hurl me into the sun?

Well? You gonna weigh in, Coward? On anything? Ever?

"Me and Jesus love you, Ize," she said from the infinite space between.

"Guess what, princess?" he said. "I can finally rap and play guitar at the same time."

How the fuck does sadness cause bubbleguts?

I really thought the pastor's niece would choose me over multi-talented princes who wear blazers on purpose? I was gonna crash the Church Dynasty, some broken-homed, foul-mouthed, salvation-doubting rabble-rouser who inspired her to lie, break curfew, and dress like Ozzfest?

I'm stuck in this town? With Calvinists?

Slumped in a Wendy's bathroom, I realized discussing my plans would've changed things. Caleb or Alexa would've warned me. But in case there was any doubt I'd die alone, the snow on my glove was bird poop.

TWENTY-FOUR
SAY THE WORDS

JANUARY 2003

I SAT BENEATH A CRAP-GRAY TWENTY-DEGREE SKY, HOLDING A YEAR-OLD PHOTO of her saying ILY with her hand. I imagined wind carrying that photo seaward, but it plopped onto roof tiles and skittered into the damp gutter. *Wwwhhhyyy'd I open that wound? Obviously, things should always stay buried.*

Over Radiohead's "Creep" in my headphones, I heard someone climbing my ladder. Mom sat and said, "A breakup veteran's here to listen, angel."

"Wasn't a breakup," I snorted. "It was zillionty-billionteen times worse than everything that's ever happened, all because that pastor's an uncool bigot."

Mom grimaced, keeping her promise to listen. I hadn't told her what'd caused my infirmity, but she'd learned from Eli, who'd bellowed about my "season of singleness" being a blessing. "Hard to save souls and suck face at the same time." *Challenge accepted, dork. Actually, never mind. I'm doomed to die alone with my face unsucked.*

"Does this stupid hurt end?" I groaned at Mom.

"The Bible says this too shall pass," she said. It doesn't, but I was too sad to correct her. Damn, that's sad.

"How can anything suck this bad?" *Like, when Dad died, I felt blank denial, dawning despair, and confused guilt. Why's this feel more intense than that? People are joining my dad in Hell every minute, yet I'm sick over some girl? What the fuck's wrong with me?*

"So potent and vivid. That's adolescence," Mom said with eye-smile wrinkles, gazing across our neighborhood. "Every moment's the end of the world, something you'll remember forever, or both."

"I never agreed to remember anything!"

"It was a Wednesday," she said airily, counting details on her fingers. "Afternoon. 1975. May eighteenth. ABBA on his radio. Ellis Moribaldi, in a blue robot shirt, said his mother was making him dump me. I thought I'd die in that driveway! But suddenly, it's been years since I've thought about anyone from high school. Then again, I still remember Moribaldi's address in Pomona." She laughed, like I'd mock her. "Part of my mind's fifteen forever. Same goes for every other former teenager. Such deep marks, feelings too big for bodies, and then ... where'd all that potent and vivid go?"

That wasn't Republican Mom. That was Weird Mom, as glimpsed in breezy-haired photos buried within forgotten shoeboxes.

"It gets worse?" I grumbled. "Guess I'll kill myself now."

She slapped my arm, apologized, and scolded my "terrible humor." I was joking, but shivered to imagine her learning that I'd contemplated impaling my brain two years earlier. (I'd never told anyone besides Eli. I also felt sick for being flippant with someone whose spouse might've intentionally driven into a tree, not that anyone ever spoke about that.)

"Life doesn't end when you're sixteen, is the point," she said, patting my tummy. *Easy for you to say, weirdo! Bring back Republican Mom, who understands all my potential Christian wives will be claimed within three years!*

"Life is pieces that come and go. We decide which pieces we hope to keep. And speaking of things staying, your buddies downstairs insist they won't leave until you cry on their shoulders. That probably means they live here now. I'll order pizza."

I gallumphed into the basement, where Caleb and PG were playing my PS2, and harrumphed onto the floor beside the ottoman.

"Wanna taco bout it?" said PG, scooting across fake leather. She looked down at me, squinted awkwardly, and said, "Are you ... mad at ...?"

Mad? Sophie promised things. How long did she wait? But was she supposed to wait forever? The LiveJournal! The hoodie! Did Alexa's telephone game fuck something up? Wasn't Sophie destined to love Dynasty sons? Was getting closure worth stomachaches? I should've let the candy goth annihilate me. On and on, the same echoes for days. Just be honest.

"Enh."

"Without you and Josiah and Alexa and me and our whole little family, she got lonel–"

"Enh!"

"This basement was our home," PG sighed. "Pastor Jack broke it."

"Speaking of, uh, our fallible shepherd," said Caleb, plopping beside me, "we're still unhappy about Josiah and you guys. Wanna help us respectfully confront Pastor Jack? We even found an unbelievably powerful grownup ally."

Once I stepped foot back onto Jack's campus and saw how much of Miss Esther's land had been cleared for his new sanctuary, I expected forest-guardian Ents to start hurling boulders.

Caleb texted "Bravo Papa en route" as I sat curbside, wearing a clip-on tie. Alexa, smoking behind a dumpster, had agreed to "dress like a Hufflepuff, ugh."

Senior Pastor Jack strode forth in orange-tan skin, jet-black hair, and freaking Air Force Ones despite being unfathomably old (forty-one). I extended my right hand, making manly eye contact. When Alexa stepped beside me, gnawing gum, his half-smirk faded.

Once, I'd looked up to him. Standing eye-to-eye, I discovered what the Fresh Prince meant by saying, "He don't want me."

"Sir," I said, "we request five minutes of your time at the All Will Be Made Brew."

"Hmm," he grunted, lips pursed. "You two missing your friends enough to apologize for troubling my son and his mother?"

Rage flash. My jaw clenched. I'd written a gently persuasive speech, but fuck it. "You gotta say it's okay, from the pulpit, for people like Josiah to be themselves." I sounded mad. Alexa flinched.

"Okay?" he said, forehead scrunched. "As in ...?"

"Like ... guy-guy stuff. And you have to tell Alexa she's not a demon," *unless you want the unsaved girl to actually become one.*

"I'll be praying for you both," he snorted, turning and talking over his shoulder. "Your brother's surely disappointed. I'd hoped time without community would wake you both up."

I looked to the west. "It'd be easy, sir."

"Find another Bible-believing church," he said, digging for keys. "Mine's failed you."

I looked to the remnants of Miss Esther's trees. "You just say words into the mic."

To the west, sunlight slipped behind hills.

Alexa popped bubblegum. "Your salary's worth selling out your kid, you spray-tanned bitch?"

One foot in his Charger, my replacement dad stared like we'd pooped on his pulpit.

The day has gone down in the west, behind the hill into shadow. How'd it come to this?

And in the last light appeared a white-clad rider in a packed church trolley driven by Caleb. At the turn of the tide, puttering at fifteen miles per hour, was our old youth pastor Timmy.

I left, embarrassed by having gone off script.

LetsTalkAboutLexBaby (Alexa): timmy's like "my homies are right! throw the doors open! welcome our gay familia"

LetsTalkAboutLexBaby: jackass was laughing. apparently former youth pastors arent powerful allies :-/

LetsTalkAboutLexBaby: sophie jumped out like "this is about ALL the josiahs, thousands whove felt unwelcome. dont you want them filling pews, uncle jack?"

LetsTalkAboutLexBaby: they waved a banner PG designed. big rainbow church logo. she's so talented!

LetsTalkAboutLexBaby: timmy was bummed you left. whyd you leave

xSHARKSWITHRABIESx: is this gonna work or did i blow it

"Good news first," said Josiah at Pizza Hut. "Isaac and Alexa, Dad conceded you're … dramatically prone to well-intentioned gestures. Long story short, you're welcome to come home."

Caleb led a cheering hug mob around me. Alexa and Sophie somehow sat on each other's laps, squeal-hugging. When Gabe wedged himself between them, Alexa recoiled.

PG barreled into stories about their recent youth pastors, including some guy who'd let her "borrow his GameCube, but then quit after two weeks and was like, 'Keep it, I'm agnostic now,' so I have a GameCube and tried doing Video Games Church, but nobody came. Can we use your enormous couch again, Isaac?"

I shrugged, not exactly feeling like a freaking spiritual leader.

"But, obviously, Dad's not changing church doctrine," said Josiah, lips pursed. "No gay weddings, to say the least."

All around the table, shoulders slumped mid-hug.

"That was never gonna happen," he laughed.

After turning eighteen days prior, he'd left "rehab" and crashed in my basement because he "didn't feel like" going home. ("Does ex-gay mean you like boobs now?" I'd asked. "I appreciate sweater silhouettes," he'd said, mystifying me. Days later, he left to roadie for praise musicians, planning on getting a GED before college.)

"Can't you just beat your uncle at Bible arguments?" PG wailed at Sophie.

"I was the speckled sheep even before the trolley stunt," she mumbled as Gabe palmed the back of her neck. *She says "speckled" instead of "black" because it's more biblical and doesn't sound racist. Ooh, so smart and moral, yayyy.*

"Dad said, for the sake of family harmony, he'd consider resigning as senior pastor and overseeing interims," said Josiah. "He asked if that's what I want. Heavy, man."

"He's such a bullshitter," snorted Alexa, who theorized that Jack already knew his son wouldn't ask a pastor to stop winning souls, no matter the cost.

Josiah tried to uplift us, talking us into picking winnable battles after his exit to the conservative college we'd nicknamed Church Dynasty U would remove "a distraction."

Wearing a Brainwash Projects shirt at a secular coffee shop's open mic, Caleb was about to rap about Jesus battle-rapping Satan to death, every Christian rapper's first song idea.

"You know how our parents write notes to get us out of health class?" he asked me at our table.

"Uh, Mom's only letting me skip class if I go to church instead."

"Well, I found a pamphlet by a Left Behind author on how learning about syphilis and hymens in government health class turns you into a depressed atheist. But he also said gay people are liars, and Josiah's not a liar, so ..."

So Christian bigots are liars! Say it! Why can't he ever admit when grownups suck?

"Here's what you missed in health class," I said, with hand gestures. "When two people love each othe–"

"Dawg, I learned that from Lil Kim lyrics," he grunted, sitting up tall, then slumping back down. "I'm asking because ... say I wanna ask PG out and join her music ministry ... but I dunno if it's the right time of month to ask ...?"

She sat on a stool, playing guitar in secular public for the first time. When she grinned at the bleach-haired lunk, he straight-up tittered. I explained that "time of month" didn't mean whatever he thought it meant — not that I knew either.

"In that case," he said, "I'ma go spit that ancient DC Talk song about saying I love you."

"Wait, nobody's gonna kill Satan?"

"But first: love potion," he said, squeezing chocolate syrup into his Mountain Dew and reciting radio-edited Jay-Z lyrics about cognac.

Then, Caleb moped on my enormous couch all night. Whatever he'd said, PG had interpreted as him wanting to be just friends, making him too sad to rap.

The next morning at church, he was raring to unload his heart for real — but she'd brought a guest, some drummer named O'Connor whom she'd met at the open mic.

"He's wearing the same dingy clothes as last night," Caleb chortled. "Meanwhile, my cargs were washed recently. I'll tell him grunge is dead. Dunno what grunge is. Something my uncles were into."

On stage, our latest adult was a lineman-sized Church Dynasty son. Most youth pastors dressed like Stiffler, but that bozo wore a suit. Everyone knew he held the local shrimp-eating record, with a plaque and everything.

"We shouldn't roll off a couch and into God's house," Bozo preached to a hundred-plus teens. "Pretend Jesus walked in! Would you want him seeing ratty sandals? Fellas, put on some slacks. Reflect what's inside!"

(Thus Bozo inspired weeks of both defiant under-dressing and sarcastic over-dressing.)

As we were leaving, PG asked for help. "That guy I brought is literally homeless, a traveling poet, and I promised nobody would judge him. But Bozo's crap made him leave! I gotta find him, but first gotta confront Bozo. I'm bad at expressing myself! Somebody come with me!"

I sensed Caleb's wheels turning. He was mad that someone had made PG sad, but afraid that defending O'Connor would keep his rival near PG. Then something broke the deadlock. His hand hovered toward her elbow. "Say the words, Peej."

After she informed Bozo she'd begin gossiping about him and dashed to find O'Connor, Caleb poked Bozo in the chest, challenging him to "a shrimp-eating contest, Saturday night, winner gets the mic next Sunday."

"Dummy, he outweighs you by eighty pounds," I warned the husky sophomore.

"Numbnuts, you said we stand up for people," he said, rectangular eyes intense. "WWJD? Jesus would humble the shrimp champ. That's WT-fork-JWD."

Saturday at 11 p.m., Caleb sat in my bathroom with a to-go box, figuring he had until midnight to catch up to Bozo's outrageous shrimp total.

The boy finished nine short. Badass, but grody.

"It's not what's outside that matters," Bozo preached hours later. "Folks say you gotta dress fancy. That's worldly! After all, Jesus didn't wear designer threads. Robe, sandals, lookin' fly!"

Our group high-fived Caleb, who tumbled onto teal carpet having surrendered his body for the poor.

Minutes later in old-person church, Senior Pastor Jack announced God had approved even bigger plans for the construction project replacing the woods. Jack shared HumbleTron depictions of the eight-figure sanctuary featuring a big white dome, saying it was "a financial leap of faith," so we "shouldn't accept less than God's best."

(Translation: Here come the offering plates again.)

Sub-pastors swiped the mic, announcing God had approved them using church funds to thank Jack for leading "this outpouring of the Spirit." The HumbleTron revealed a red 1968 Mustang GT, engine revving — in the freaking foyer. *We'll remember this, next time they tell us we're being too rowdy in church hallways after hours!*

I saw Mom clapping along until her semi-boyfriend mouthed, "$50,000 car."

Caleb looked sick. Passing the plate again, our whole pew looked sick. Our eyes remained locked onto one part of the HumbleTron map, where Miss Esther's house was doomed to be replaced by a parking deck.

TWENTY-FIVE
SCHISM

SPRING 2003

"YOU GUYS INTO CONSPIRACY THEORIES?" SAID SOME TOOL FAN, SPEWING NEW World Order crap as if he was one of those GeoCities websites full of twirling crucifix GIFs.

Undead Kennedys! Bohemian Grove! 2Pac! September 11 was fake, deserved, *and* "phase one!" You know, Christian wackos and secular wackos sound the same, except when …

"… that brings us to Israel," the Tool fan said. Oh, Lord.

"This is science class," I said, rubbing my temples. "We just need a presentation topic."

He squinted. "Methinks … Jewish?" And he muttered some other stuff.

Ugh. As a Pat Robertson veteran, I knew all about Christian wackos having a creepy Jerusalem obsession, but had never before encountered an explicitly anti-Semitic wacko.

"You know that movie Contact?" I said. "How it starts with Hitler's radio message at the Olympics he lost by sucking ass? Let's do a science presentation on that."

"At least Hitler killed the guy who killed Hitler's killer," said our partner Chloe, the tennis team's weirdo, wearing a Gettin' Lucky in Kentucky shirt to protest girls getting sent home for suggestive shirts. Watching me untangle her statement, she winked. *Chemicals!*

"Next idea," huffed Tool. "Psyoppers say global warming's real, bu–"

"That's totally what they want you to think," said Chloe with an eager smirk, plus long hair so wavy that I was on her side regardless.

"Stay outta this, airhead," he said.

"During the so-called Cold War, Russia and America totally worked together, gobbling up poor countries," she said with documentary-voiceover gravitas. "Now they're turning Russia into the world's farm, but Russia will make America hand over NASA, then nuke America from orbit and escape to the moon. Psyoppers want you obsessed with how many rich people are Jewish so you never notice how many rich people are on the moon, which is totally fake."

Help, I'm in love again.

"The moon's bullshit," I agreed.

Maybe her smile's crooked because she grew up hiding her gapped teeth. Well, she should keep pointing it at me, because I'm kinda allowed to smile back!

Chloe and me saw Final Destination 2 on a Friday, so our second date was on a Sunday. She assigned me a costume: my grayest sweater, combed-est hair, and brownest shoes. It's funny: If Pastor Jack hadn't sent me wandering, not even Chloe's smile could've convinced me to visit a Catholic church.

Just like every movie's church scene, a uniformed guy waved his hands and recited stuff. The bulletin included ads for local businesses, and the service lacked jokes, tangents, guitars, volleyballs, lasers, or hugs. *Why's every church movie about Catholics, anyway? Someone should write a Protestant lock-in horror.* I'd learned the word "Protestant" from Chloe.

Suddenly, she was tugging my arm. "We gotta go study," she said, which meant creating MS Paint evidence of the moon's fakeness until Tool Kid's head exploded.

Forty minutes after we'd arrived, I followed the small crowd toward chilly sunshine. That church included somber families who attended regularly, but she was the class-clown sibling from a one-Sunday-per-month household.

"What about confession or whatever?" I asked, playing dumb.

"But we haven't sinned," she said, grinning like she was teeing up a reply.

I shouldn't say it, according to the purity pledge card in my wallet. Being near her is already … **"A SLIPPERY SLOPE TOWARD HER POLYTHEIST LAIR'S HELLFIRE."**

Openly hoping for sloping, I whispered, "Not yet."

We saw Cradle 2 the Grave on a Friday, so the next Sunday was our fourth date. At my church, Chloe dressed "totally Protestant" in a Jesus Is My Homeboy shirt and huge side ponytail. Every sugar-rushing hug made me want to believe the kiss-away-the-brainwashing theory proposed by Alexa months earlier.

"Children abandoned, an unprecedented epidemic," Pastor Jack wailed as heads nodded. "Parents scared to parent! Ever since the '60s, when the Devil's henchmen — multiculturalists, the Supreme Court, the Department of *Re*-Education — feminized the Church into silence. While Hollywood's convincing a generation to replace parenthood with perversions, you know what they're doing in Iran? Spawning heterosexual Muslim babies, then indoctrinating them to keep spawning!"

I felt sick of, among other things, hysteria about single-parent criminals. *Wild Things is about Denise Richards being ruined by her dad's suicide, and church's nuclear-family obsession says the same about me. Sorry I've watched Wild Things. Twice. This weekend.*

"Long ago, we birthed Christian multitudes," Jack groaned, "but now our few coddled offspring are ripe for purple-haired-freak indoctrination."

"When's one-man improv end?" whispered Chloe.

We played hangman on offering envelopes. She solved "Chloe's butt is pretty." I solved "The song from She's All That."

"Kiss Me"? Huh. Wonder what she means by that.

We polluted envelopes with flirt words, leaning in so tightly, I smelled pineapple Jolly Rancher.

"… and I got an email," Jack guffawed, in a better mood. "Some she-pastor, whose church has better attendance in its cemetery than its sanctuary … "

Somehow, Jack mocking the harmlessly anarchist Uni-whatever grandmas improved the mood. *I'm glad Josiah's on the road, free of Jack's shit, never to think about it ever again. Right?*

"… told me we're destroying the environment. Those old woods out back! I said, 'Lecture appreciated, Captain Planet, but …'"

As everyone laughed, I hoped the global-warming believer beside me wasn't offended, but she cackled at "Captain Planet."

"My beautiful trophy's giving me the stink-eye in the front row," Pastor whimpered, pointing at his wife as everyone laughed. "Look, she's smiling! I'm not kicked outta the house yet, folks. Anyway, I said, 'Captain

Planet, you think this world's our home? Not since a righteous Father banished Eden's tarnished offspring!'"

Everyone amen'd the man who'd formerly preached about God's wondrous sparrows and glaciers. Environmentalism started to sound appealing. **"YOU'LL REGRET IDOLIZING CREATION OVER ITS CREATOR!"** *Sorry.*

"During this season before the earth melts with fervent heat," Jack snarled, "Jesus says we mustn't leave investments buried! Dig that oil up! Don't waste your life, or your planet! Ecclesiastes commands us to work, consume, and once it's consumed? Rapture blastoff, destination: Gold Street, baby!"

Huge cheers. Two years earlier, he'd handed me books that said the Rapture was invented in the 1830s.

"I'd glorify every acre on earth with Bible-believing sanctuaries if Father God commanded. And, if you can't steward your land, She-Pastor Baghdad Bob, maybe once we've cultivated what God's given us, we'll keep going, you hippie-dippies with empty pews."

Giant laughs. Shit, me and Chloe were laughing!

"Lord, I'm in the doghouse now! Mama, write a check and save some whales! She's gonna make this hurt, folks. Hurt me, mama! Whatever number keeps me from getting kicked out next!"

Crossing the street after church, Chloe asked, "What was that sermon, like, about?"

"'Kiss Me,' then 'hurt me, mama.'"

"Okily dokily, but answer my question."

Whoa. Did she just ...?

At Pizza Hut, she believed Caleb was joking when he taught her how to pray to God instead of Mary. As I drove her to the mall, she slid Christian CDs in and out, awed by "Protestant alternate reality."

"Name a secular band, and I'll tell you the Christian music shop's recommended replacement," I said. My friends played that game sometimes, but I'd never tried it with school people, who assumed born-again kids didn't realize our own multiverse was funny.

"My favorite band's Sublime," she said, like a question.

"The Dingees are Christian Sublime."

"Oh, I get it. Help, Satan hooked me on Eminem!"

"Listen to KJ-52 instead."

"Destiny's Child?"

"... is the secular Out of Eden."

"Nickelback? For a friend."

"Kutless, you Nickelback lover."

She belted the Nickelback lyric everybody knows. "Boy bands?"

"Relient K," I laughed. "Plus One, technically."

Many rounds later, she said, "Are all Christian bands ripoffs?"

"Nah. It's how they're advertised to parents. Secular bands sound similar to each other, too."

"Who's the least similar?"

At the mall's Family Christian Store, I played her some Danielson, the squeaky indie band Sesame Street could've hired for a cults episode. She loved it. As she explored Christian math games, umbrellas, and stuffed animals, I swiped the official band-substitution chart as a gift.

"I'm totally framing this," she said, hugging me.

Despite standing beside a Max Lucado display while holding a chart that claimed Marilyn Manson fans would like Rackets & Drapes, she gave me a uranium-green greenlight. Thanks to Amir's bragging, third base sounded simple, but nobody'd ever explained first.

So my lips attempted something on hers, time fast-forwarded / paused, my faceskin flared, my heart gushed ice cream, and I saw a crooked smile, unhidden as could be. *Fun!* **"YOU REGRET THIS ALREADY."** *How about this one!* **"ALSO YES, ALREADY."** We got banned from Family Christian Store.

With my thumb glued to her millimeter of midriff, I asked, "Which Catholic saint gives, like, +50% poison resistance?" We looked it up at Borders bookstore: Saint Benedict of Nursia. *Sugar-rushing makeout!* **"REGRET."** Banned from Borders. **"REGRET."** With her hand in my back pocket, she asked if Pentecostalism was real, and soon we were banned from Yankee Candle for speaking in tongues. **"REGRET."** *Wow, the kiss-away-brainwashing thing is working!* **"LMAO."**

In the food court, I felt weird for sincerely asking, "Is praying for dead people real?"

"Totally. And, in Heaven, Auntie Rosalie's praying for me."

Since we were still pawing at each other, I asked, "Should we have six kids, Catholic-style?"

"Twelve, Quiverfull-style." She'd even learned about those missionary-spamming families? It was like we were each doing research projects. My turn.

"Do you pray for people in ... not-Heaven?"

"Purgatory or whatever? Totally."

"Why isn't purgatory in the Bible?"

"Oh, it's not? Well, Orange Julius totally isn't either," she said, slurping our shared PDA straw.

"If the Bible's whatever, people end up preaching crusades and indulgences."

"True. Real Bible-thumpers preach Iraq invasions and construction tithes."

We laughed, but I felt ashamed of the pastor she'd heard.

I said, "So I should, like, talk to my dad?"

She boggled like I'd just alleged the moon is real. "You don't?"

"Even if he could hear me, he's either perfectly happy in Heaven or beyond help in Hell."

She thought. "I don't get how people put up with a God like that."

I laughed. *I bet all Catholics are just like her, too nice to believe demons are real.*

We debated Sheetz menu rankings while drooling our eyes into each other's skulls. I'd heard puppy love is Satan's simplest purity-stealing strategy, but I merrily snatched my heart from my future wife and shoved it toward Chloe. *When I drop her off, I'm gonna ask her to be my girlfriend!*

Driving her home, I felt talons descend from the clouds. The guy who'd banned us from Borders was a classmate, one I'd scolded about partying. Not only had my animal hand approached her boob, it'd covered her shirt's Jesus face. And if her baptism hadn't counted because she'd never chosen it, I'd steered her further from legit salvation.

"Sorry about today," I said.

She stopped singing along with Danielson. "I totally liked today."

"Me too."

"What's the problemo?"

"The problemo's I totally liked today."

Rapidly, I explained slippery slopes, unverified salvation, eternal torment, and depraved hypocrisy.

Her confusion surrendered to laughter. "Ohh, I get it! I'm Protestant today, so now you're doing Catholic guilt."

"Wait, people on Comedy Central use that term. You have custom guilt?"

"Confession, penance, grruuughh. Not like you guys, singing sins away."

What?!

We didn't know whether to fix our guilt by praying silently, making private amends, doing public performances, or puking shame onto other teenagers. After trying all that, Best Caleb once drew a blueprint for a penis guillotine. Another Caleb once thought his parents hadn't Dobson'd him enough, so he'd head-butted his driveway. Josiah still blamed himself for his dad's bigotry. Mom still apologized for leaving the house to earn mortgage money. On December 17, 1993, I could've begged Dad to get saved, but instead I'd been playing Micro Machines.

Only Catholics have guilt, huh?

I high-fived Chloe bye.

---

xSHARKSWITHRABIESx: then again, maybe catholic confession is the right idea

hearitinmyghost (Bobbi): en.wikipedia.org/wiki/Catholic_Church_sexual_abuse_cases

xSHARKSWITHRABIESx: ah

As people filed in for night church, Caleb pointed up front. Ten Graces marched past the stage in tie-dye shirts, handing out flowers. Apparently, they'd spent the afternoon mad at Pastor Jack's slash-and-burn message.

"Maybe environmentalism's not that evil," said Caleb, climbing over me toward PG's emo-black tie-dye. I followed.

They sat in the Sign Language section, where Sophie wore a floofy dress. They handed her two of their vaguely explained protest flowers, she put one in her hair, she handed one to Gabe, he scoffed, and she handed both flowers back. Graces fluttered around Caleb, adorning his rectangular head with flowers. I sat, and as Graces flowered me, I confession-bragged about Borders.

"Get her all-the-way baptized before defiling Waldenbooks," advised Kayleih Grace.

During the hug-a-neighbor intermission, the pastor's niece's boyfriend told me and Caleb, "You sweeties look metrosexual," with a cartoon lisp.

"Yeah, well, today I got banned from Gadzooks," I said.

Gabe raised an arm, dangling his wrist. "You're mocking this Captain Planet sissiness, right?"

"No, Mother Earth's beautiful," said Caleb, hand-projecting his voice toward PG.

It's wrong to hate Gabe, but not weird, right? I'm too sexy for the Thomas Kinkade Gallery, so it's not like I'm jealous of his dating situation. He shut up once Sophie appeared. We almost waved, but he turned her toward sub-pastor sons who needed to be greeted.

I adjusted my laurel crown, unsure whether this was sincere protest, general obnoxiousness, or teen drama. *Regardless, I belong with tacky troublemakers, not Dynasty offspring.*

Pastor Jack again preached about our disgusting planet's broken homes. His niece stood without petals, signing her assigned words.

MyPlaceInThisWorld (Josiah): Sup.

xSHARKSWITHRABIESx: ehh

MyPlaceInThisWorld: Yeah.

xSHARKSWITHRABIESx: u?

MyPlaceInThisWorld: Ugh.

xSHARKSWITHRABIESx: <3

MyPlaceInThisWorld: [Away message: ♬ You did not have a home ♬]

MyPlaceInThisWorld: <3

TWENTY-SIX
THAT'S WHAT YOU GET

SPRING, SUMMER, WHATEVER

TUESDAY NIGHT BIBLE STUDY ATTENDANCE: ELEVEN

I BOUGHT TWELVE DOLLARS WORTH OF WEED FROM BOBBI'S JUGGALO. IT burned in a cereal bowl like incense as fans blew smells out of the window. I didn't think it'd work, but hoped it'd offend somebody, once the Video Games Church crowd arrived in my basement.

"Man, I'm spent," said Caleb. "Powerbombed five girls into the pool all day. They pinned me on Nevaeh Grace's floor and tested Nair on my legs. Feel how smooth."

"I'm good, player," said Amir, finishing up a game of Madden as church kids arrived. "Sounds like you got some smoochies?"

"What? No. I'm a Christian."

TUESDAY NIGHT ATTENDANCE, ONE WEEK LATER: NINE

PG attempted her first VGC sermon. She unspooled tangents within tangents, making us laugh despite wondering where she could possibly be going, then somehow ended with, "Therefore, God sent the flood because Noah's friends stumbled over sex demons! Profound, huh?"

"The Book of Tobit has sex demons," exclaimed Chloe, having tentatively sampled scripture. (Catholic Bibles include an extra hundred pages of bonus lore, meaning an extra hundred pages go unread.)

PG did jazz hands at me, challenging me to connect those verses from entirely different biblical canons, the kinda game VGC used to play. Eh, that sounded like work.

"Okayyy, lemme try something else," PG said, tuning her guitar. "I wrote this after I got yelled at for writing un-biblical songs. I really miss everybody hanging here, man. If my spiritual gift of guitar can't get us back together, I give up. Anyway, here's 'Sex Demons.'"

Music? Frivolous. More importantly, I preached through my updated list of things Pastor Jack said in 2003 that contradicted things he'd said in 2000. Was Braveheart "the best movie ever" or merely "one of the best?"

TUESDAY NIGHT ATTENDANCE: EIGHT

Bobbi showed up immediately after my weekly Jack corrections, excited to reveal she'd customized a Rapture-themed Dungeons & Dragons game. The bespectacled atheist arranged papers on the ottoman and said, "Anyway, you've played RPG video games, right? You'll catch on. People born before 1980 figured it out."

"People born before 1980," said Caleb, blank-staring at giraffe-print carpet, "always tell us it's easy to avoid porn, but we're the first humans to attempt growing up pure while also having the internet. If you showed King David even a Maxim cover, he'd faint. The 'Crazy in Love' video would kill him in 9.6 seconds. Life's impossible!"

I'd hissed "dude" at him like fifty times, to no avail.

Bobbi stared at him with a sour frown. "What the fuck? You been looking at sicko shit?"

He stammered. I cringed because Chloe was nearby, but explained, "Jerking off means feeling ashamed afterward. Um, Caleb, we're not at church."

He muttered apologies, but I felt responsible for never resuming accountability group after Josiah's exit. Chloe looked at me, then at Caleb, putting things together.

"Whatever," Bobbi laughed, rattling her head. "I'm not some repressed Puritan."

TUESDAY NIGHT ATTENDANCE: FOUR

"Why's it evil to be sad?" said PG, strumming her guitar. "I always get yelled at, about my lyrics not being cheerful. People say, 'Stop pretending God's given you more than you can handle.'"

Doing my Pastor Jack impersonation, I rasped, "If I caught myself moping like Eeyore, I'd question whether I'd really accepted Christ. Folks, how's the world gonna want salvation if the Chosen look frozen?"

Maybe that was why I liked Christian music that got away with being unhappy. If church guys didn't want me blaring metal in the parking lot, they should've let somebody besides Zao write Christian songs about mourning suicide.

"Emotions are bad?" said Amir, playing Madden, clearly sticking around because of PG's cuteness.

"I was flipping through our hymnal, seeing these anguished songs we never sing," said PG. "But if I'm sad, some church lady squawks, 'Smile! Make 'em jealous of your Jesus!'"

Sometimes, Mom was that church lady.

"As if Jesus, man of constant sorrows or whatever, never had a breakup," scoffed Amir, who'd just gone through a breakup.

"The Bible's sad and scared and everything," shrugged PG. "But we're only ever happy about Jesus or mad about liberals."

The door burst open. Bopping in a swishy skirt, Chloe chirped a church song: "I got the joy, joy, joy, joy, down in my heart!" Feeling uplifted, I viewed PG and Amir as grumblers who'd failed to simply choose joy.

TUESDAY NIGHT ATTENDANCE: ?

Me and Chloe did stupid stuff like telling our parents we'd crash with friends, while actually attempting to get locked inside Target together.

Oops, apparently overnight workers exist. We found ourselves loitering in the parking lot outside my neighborhood after midnight, each of us down to our last cellphone minute and out of texts.

"Can't go home, 'cause I totally broke curfew," she said. "Couuuld I borrow a shweepin' bag?"

Sneak her into my basement! No, Calebs are there. (Without me, yes.)

Our eyes panned across the street, above black woods, and up at a giant moonlit dome. We scampered past streetlights and shrubbery, hand-in-hand toward Pastor Jack's nine-month-old construction project.

"Name it and effing claim it," she gasped, beholding the skeleton of the future three-story megachurch.

We tiptoed between fencing, over cinderblocks, and into a cavern. Beneath a walkway, in the near-black lobby, she said, "If anybody murders me, I'm done trusting you." As we frolicked, moonbeams flashed across the SAVED on her teal sweatpants' butt. We entered the March Madness-sized sanctuary, shining our phones into endless darkness.

Holding my belt loop as we navigated debris, she asked, "Where's the tub or whatever?"

We found stairs to climb. Staring down into a cavern lit only by stray moonlight, we were emperors. We tumbled and giggled, zooming past affectionate fun and into greedy grasping, speeding past things I'd promised God I'd never try — all while in the baptismal. **"YOU KNOW YOU'RE RACKING UP SHAME FOR LATER, RIGHT?"** *Yes.*

Her phone rang. Her dad asked why she wasn't at whoever's house.

"Sowwyyy, we fell asweep at Pwotestant chuwch," she said on my lap at a construction site. "Um, no, she's gonna stay here and keep praising."

I'm creation's filthiest mistake. As we retraced our steps, I said, "I feel terrible."

"Yeah, lying sucks," she said. "I'll come clean without snitchin'."

"I meant ... we ... in a holy place ..."

"Holy? How? There was no water!"

"I found some," I bragged. **"PERVERT!"** *Sorry.*

She snickered. "All we did was canoodle. Fun word!"

We slipped through whispering shadows. Passing lights, I dug my purity pledge card from my wallet. "Here. Protestant lore."

She read while rounding the old building, then stopped still. "You were supposed to save kissing for marriage? Geez, I'm a nasty succubus."

"What? No way. Why's everybody keep saying bad stuff about themselves?"

"If kissing's bad, are sex people evil?"

"Well, I can't date somebody who's been dirtied by some other guy."

"I'll probably wait," she said, watching the street. "But since the Bible's not my supplemental brain, which verse says God hates premarital doin'-it?"

It occurred to me: There's no thou-shalt-not-premaritally-do-it verse. Fortunately, I knew which bits to combine into the answer. I so dazzled her with knowledge, she shoved me against a wall. *Nice! Oh, she's hiding me from her dad's headlights.*

I'm officially the sexy danger man. Sneaking home while using my last text to send her a joke about virginity loopholes, I was officially desperate to cheat God's sex detectors, just like those seniors I'd judged as an underclassman. **"HEY CHAMP, WHO WAS RIGHT ABOUT YOUR SIN-UNTIL-SIN-FEELS-OK PLAN, HUH?"**

TUESDAY NIGHT ATTENDANCE: FIVE

"Hark, I bringeth tales of sex and violence," PG said, entering the basement. "Chooseth!"

"S-e-x," said Caleb, clearing his throat after realizing how hurriedly he'd answered.

She sat beside him. "So, two more church friends had sex ..."

"How's this keep happening?" Caleb said. "Christians acting worldly!"

"... and they feel terrible, so let's pray for reconciliation. Ta-daa, I'm not gossiping!"

Gossip was PG's pet peeve, partly due to other Graces "prayerfully" alleging she'd banged her bandmates. ("That'd be way unprofessional," PG had commented.) Church worked the same as school: Everybody was supposedly doing somebody, and Alexa was supposedly doing everybody. ("High schoolers? Ew," Alexa had commented.) The hottest news: Not only did kids at church believe Sophie and Gabe had become totally impure, someone at school likewise alleged he'd defiled "that dickhead pastor's niece." *Absurd and crass. I was robbed of my chance to be the guy in these rumors. Not that I care.*

"The s-e-xer wasn't me," Caleb said, hand hovering near PG's shoulder. "Promise."

"Oh, me no sexing either," she giggled, leaning toward him.

Amir, focused on Madden, grinned to himself. "Me neither. Today. So far." He'd kept hanging around later, amused by my church weirdos.

"Me neither," I said, wanting to brag-confess tub sins but ashamed and wary of spreading the temptation. If people stole my sinning-in-the-tub idea, crowds might ruin my summer plans, ruin them like my soul.

"All this sexy talk, mama mia pizzeria!" PG said, fanning her face. "Maybe if somebody preached hot stuff, we'd get full crowds in here again? We gotta try something to get booties in seats! I actually don't have a violence story. I'm a lubber, not a fighter."

"No violence stories? Darn, guess we're talking sex," Caleb voice-cracked. "So, point blank, I'm on a three-week streak of wet d–"

"I'll talk about violence," I shouted, triggered by "point blank."

"Anything but what he was finna say," groaned Amir.

"Once upon a time," I said, "there was a boy singing Jesus songs."

PG and Caleb made oOoOo ghost-story noises, hands hovering near each other's knees, as I told the story of four riflemen threatening seventeen-year-old Eli into blaspheming Christ.

When I finished, Amir's eyes bugged out at me. "Are you for fucking real?"

"Normal church crap," groaned PG. "Scary skits. Pew-pew-pew stories. The Antichrist's here! Blah-bitty-blahblah."

"Isaac's brother thought he was gonna die," Amir shouted, "then thought he'd damned himself."

"Sounds like a valuable lesson," said Caleb, drunk off PG glancing at him.

After a movie, the semi-lovebirds left.

Amir and I played Madden until we crashed. Awaking with arms around each other's legs, we sat up in darkness and accidentally held each other, then fired up Madden.

Blue lights dancing on his brown eyes, he said, "Man, that story effed me up. Then those terrorists got in trouble for threatening children, right?"

"Nah, we played foursquare. Just another day of hearing we were gonna be killed by Democrats."

"Man, if Christians need persecuted that badly," Amir said, "they could just walk my mom through TSA." He hugged me again, leaving to pack for college.

TUESDAY NIGHT ATTENDANCE: FIVE

At our basement fantasy football draft, Chloe and Caleb were having fun making normal picks. Bobbi had fun preaching about sports being another opiate of the masses. PG, clueless about sports despite proposing the idea to boost attendance, had fun attempting to draft "the guy from Space Jam?" And my advisor had fun warning me of **"ETERNAL REGRET"** for tenderly hugging Amir, for how Chloe and I had spent her break from work at Walgreen's, and for the usual sins. Fun for everybody!

The upstairs door opened. The deep voice from above hushed my friends. "Isaac, could I borrow you?" said Eli. I asked them to draft me another running back.

Walking toward the kitchen in a loosened necktie, his face was downcast. Mom sat at the table, kneading her hands.

"Lemme bring you up to speed, chief," he said as she breathed theatrically. "First, I'm quitting my job. Real estate isn't biblical: Leviticus 25. Second, I sinned by getting married."

Whoa! And wwwhoa!

As Mom grumbled, Eli explained. When he'd married an eighteen-year-old college dropout, as prescribed by Christian men, both bride and groom had believed instant romance would follow.

"For the last five years, I wondered why we couldn't connect," Eli said, eyes intense. "Well, when she was younger, church elders treated her like a hellion. And she's found a way to tell me she kept all that shame inflicted by men like me." He glanced at Mom. "So, why no grandkids? Because I sinned against her by marrying her without knowing her heart. Meanwhile, that marriage counselor, you know how he advised her to fix my sin? He said First Peter means she should dress flirtier around the house, so I don't cheat. Sorry, what do tiny pajamas have to do with saving souls?"

Man, if the Hell prophet can admit church is wrong sometimes, can't anybody? Mom apologized for hassling him, but worried he shouldn't spew anti-marriage propaganda at me, as if one opinion could overrule the million guys telling me to become a father-disciple-patriot. *Whatever, I'm just curious how he plans to justify this. Pastors constantly denounce divorce!*

"Matthew 10:35 says discard family, if need be," he sighed, wincing. "Luke 16:18 says the sin is remarrying, not divorce. Plus, lifelong singleness means focusing on evangelism. She's free to restart. Win-win."

"Like Pastor Jack says, broken homes create broken homes," Mom sniffed. (She'd re-liked Jack since the minute he'd unbanned me. Hmph.) "You boys have lacked household role models ..."

Eli took her hand and said, "I don't blame you. I blame Christians who say men ruling women is mission-critical." His eyes sparkled with mischief. "Hey, Jesus wasn't married! If Paul wanted men bossing around wives, why'd he say marriage is for weaklings?"

LOL, I love when he says heresies! But hey, he's chilling out for once!

"Besides," Eli said, "think about the cold, hard math."

LOL, sike!

"Say I had four children," he said, "and did everything right: McGee & Me, catechisms, Adventures in Odyssey, homeschooling, Campus Crusade, the whole kit. What are the odds one of those four would backslide into non-belief? Be honest! Even the most rock-solid church has kids falling prey to deceit! Then, what if my one non-believing kid has three non-believing grandkids, and on and on? During my honeymoon night, I pictured hundreds of my descendants in Hell."

I was again astounded by his godliness, to say the least.

"What if your other three kids became missionaries?" I asked, grabbing a pencil. We estimated costs and benefits, trading one Hell-bound child for 30 Heaven-bound converts.

Mom wadded my napkin. "You need coun-se-ling," she seethed. "Speak with our pastor about this Hell obsession."

"He knows I'm right," Eli chuckled. "He's busy parroting Bill O'Reilly, but why does he have a half-dozen altar calls per week, if he's not obsessed with salvation? Salvation from what?"

"Why are you like this?" she yelled, slapping the table.

He weighed his response. "Because I accept eternal torment is real."

"I believe that too, but I live a normal life!"

"Then do you really believe it?" he said, standing up, twice her size. "Half your co-workers are Hell-bound while you gripe about salaries …"

I put a hand on his forearm. She banged her chair against the wall and stormed past. "Those are good people! You can't judge everyone!"

"I don't judge. That's God's job," he said, soft and slow. "But good people go to Hell too. Very good. In fact …"

Our father … who art in …

Nope, nope, nope. I plugged fingers in my ears, all the way downstairs. I asked my friends which running back they'd drafted, but we heard Mom yelling, "Are you seriously justifying the Spanish goshdarn Inquisition?"

Yikes. If Eli stormed down there, he would've terrified Bobbi, and not just her. Chloe, never tub-dunked, barely believed in Hell. PG was so full of doubt, she'd been dunked three times. And Caleb might've taken Eli's side.

I shooed them toward Pizza Hut, but first, they heard my brother reply, "Mama, anything's better than Hell, right? Please say yes. Children can hear you."

TUESDAY NIGHT ATTENDANCE: THREE

Caleb walked in and asked me, in front of Bobbi, "What's the most messed-up church thing you've ever hea–"

"The Calvinists beside Pizza Hut say the age of accountability's fake," I said, not caring what Bobbi heard, "meaning stillborn babies go to Hell."

Gathering D&D stuff, Bobbi groaned, "C'mon, John Calvin killed somebody! Who cares what he thinks?"

"Who?" Caleb asked, sitting down.

"You guys seriously know nothing about your own religion," she scoffed, cramming papers into her backpack. "It changed during the time between Jesus and George Bush, actually!"

"Yo, she admitted Jesus existed," I said, offering Caleb a high five.

"Well, that stillborn thing tops what I was gonna say," he said, already standing to leave.

I grabbed his elbow. "What was it?"

He exhaled hard and said, "Well, our sixth-grade youth pastor was intense. When he blew a bugle at 3 a.m., we had to hustle outside, ready for the Rapture. But girls were in PJs, and we had sleepytime boners, so ... we didn't exactly pay attention to him reading Thessalonians."

He smiled, kind of. I laughed.

"Um ... like an hour after Rapture practice, I was peeing in the woods," he half-whispered. "Some loser decided I wasn't peeing, so my whole cabin called me Buddy Whack-It. Next day, I asked the counselor what it meant, and he called me Buddy Whack-It in front of older girls, who called me dirty. So I was ashamed of jerking off before I'd ever tried it. After four days, I asked him to make everyone stop calling me that. He grabbed my balls like, 'Buddy Whack-It, even if you didn't sin this time, remember all the sins you've gotten away with, and call it even.'"

"Eww," I said. "Isn't that ... like the priests on the news?"

He bolted toward the door with shocking speed. "I kept my shorts on, pervo," he shouted, barreling outside before I could round the couch. He slammed his car door and drove off. *Do I, like, call him? Give him time? Help.*

Bobbi, fidgeting in a corner, had been trying to leave silently. She spent a minute trying to delicately ask if Caleb's story explained his "prudishness."

Seemed like it might, except I remembered sixth grade too, when Halle Berry had been my first crush. Normal, right? Well, how about me worrying God would never forgive me for watching the Flintstones movie twice, just to see her again? Less normal.

Bobbi stalled at the door and mumbled, "I never really thought about it, but ... nobody chooses to be indoctrinated, huh? Nobody chooses to be repressed."

Repressed. Something about that word ignited my insides. It called to mind the comet cultists who'd poisoned themselves while wearing Nikes. Well, I was clearly wearing Airwalks.

"People assume we think we're better than everyone, but it's the opposite," I snapped. "You and me tried weed together, then did the same stuff with girls. Everybody tries stuff, but nobody else has to feel like they're failing God in the process. Feeling regret doesn't make me repressed!"

That word described me, but I resented it because it said I'd been weak enough to be controlled.

"Man," she sighed, "don't try to prove me wrong by committing some huge sin or whatever."

TUESDAY NIGHT ATTENDANCE: WHATEVER

Lights off. Venus Williams posters on Chloe's walls. Walgreens polo and khakis on her body. We were bored, lonely, curious, and double-checking purity fine print.

I want someone to care about me — sinful words, according to I Kissed Dating Goodbye. But I wanna be beloved and accepted, more than I deserve. I'll risk Heaven's rage if need be.

Ugh, so emo, you supposedly non-repressed, red-blooded male.

I worked up the courage to mention those legendary near-sex activities that were said to preserve juuust enough virginity. She mentioned others she'd learned about. We discussed body logistics we'd overheard in cafeterias. Going for alluring, assertive, and non-threatening, I mumbled, "Which should we try?"

"I like you a lot," she said, sitting up. "But this stuff sounds like too much for me right now, and ..."

"Okay, maybe later," I said, pretending I'd planned that far ahead.

"... it's not just me," she said, scooting against her wall. "When we've done stuff, and maybe you weren't ready ..."

"Oh, I'm not normal-manly-guy enough for you."

"That's totally not ... I'd have fun cuddling! Listen, a couple things we talked about, maybe one day. But when you feel bad because we did stuff, I feel responsible. So ..."

Something was wrong.

"If we're friends who do stuff, but doing stuff feels bad," she said, looking away. "Aw, man ..."

Crushed into silence and rocked out of my mood, I sat up, knees against my chest, too embarrassed for eye contact. We talked a while, seeking familiar magic, but it was halting, fragile, and gone.

At her door, she said, "I know Catholic kids who've literally beaten themselves up, but my Catholic guilt's like ... we ran the world for a thousand years, and we might've made it worse. Anyway. I don't wanna kick you out, but if you see me crying, you'll totally hug me, and ..."

"Can I say how bad I feel about making you feel bad, without making you feel bad?"

She half-smiled. We high-fived goodbye.

It's bad enough when big sins happen. Asking to plan them, without even being committed, let alone married? That was a fling, and it feels idiotic. **"INTERESTING. WHO'S RIGHT AGAIN, HUH?"**

At home, I found that chart made by older church kids, explaining how much virginity various activities cost. I tallied my summer failures, calculating I was a 35% virgin who'd been trying my hardest to reach 5%. Worm. Cancer. Hell-bound namesake.

Listen to yourself! Jerry Springer, 50 Cent, and everyone at school would die laughing at a guy too fragile for girls!

Wait, this is worldly shame, which I Kissed Dating Goodbye says is self-centered. Unless I feel supernaturally shitty, I'm even shittier for feeling shitty.

Plus, Chloe's words rang out. *I care more about which shame I feel than about global poverty! What a scumbag!*

There was never enough time in the day for all the reasons I hated myself.

The basement, once so alive, had become just TV glow. With nobody left for me to face, Madden's soundtrack played Thrice's "All That's Left" a hundred times.

"Stop crying, or I'll give you something to cry about," Dad once said, summoning James Dobson to impress Mom.

It made sense that he'd been desperate to regulate my emotions. He hadn't known how else to keep me from becoming him. He'd been sad, and next thing you know, that alcoholic had been in Hell for nine years, seven months, and twenty-five days. **"I'M SORRY, BUDDY."** *Me too.* **"YOU'RE IMAGINING ME SAYING THAT."** *I know.* **"I'M NOT REALLY HIM."** *I know.* **"HE WAS TOO EASY ON YOU ANYWAY. A FEW SPANKINGS? PATHETIC."** *Sorry.*

"What the world calls depression," preached Pastor Jack, "I call by its real name: the Devil."

Aha. That's who I can face. Diablo II, max difficulty, as my unarmed paladin dies for eight hours a night. This is my lock-in now, and nothing can stop me from harrowing Hell.

One way or the other, I will recover the only person who ever got me: a self-hating drunk named Isaac Siena, Sr.

TWENTY-SEVEN
THE ONLY THING

JUNE 2003

"No way I'm the first goddamn one to Bible study," snarled a girl voice from the blinding doorway.

"Turn light back off," I howled, digging around the couch for pants, my brain bursting skull-ward like fist-bound firecrackers. The Madden soundtrack blared Big Boi's "Church."

Alexa kicked cans into a pile. "You did this? You?"

Me. That morning, I'd stood up, driven to Wal-Mart, stolen a case, returned home, drunk my first beer, endured a few more, laugh-sung Madden songs, gotten dizzy, and ... yeah. **"YOU'LL REGRET,"** my insides yelled. "So will you," I'd replied out loud.

"Party nurse mode," Alexa sighed, venturing upstairs and back with a mug. "You look like shit, rookie. Talk."

Dirt-water coffee was even grosser than corn-water beer. I said nothing. She waited. I waited. She did her nails. I whined about summer. I was supposed to be the leader, with Josiah gone, but couldn't keep the gang together. Kind of had a breakup. And then there was the big stuff, li–

"Chloe spilled glitter on me in fourth grade," she said, "but that's no excuse for doing whatever boy shit you must've done. What'd you do?"

Finally, someone who'll call me a shitstain! I shared the basics.

She replied, "Ooh, game time! I do this with the church girls, not that they listen. Tell me everything you did this summer. I'll tell you whether it's actually bad or just church-bad. Go!"

I unloaded. "Normal," she kept repeating. I emphasized my betrayed elders, ruined future, and befouled shrines. "Normaaal," she sing-songed. I confessed shit I was proud of, like hating strange porn videos.

"Normal! If you didn't get anybody jailed or pregnant or sick … well, you're sick, but who cares. You and your former friend-with-bennies don't hate each other? Geez, congrats!"

"But w–"

"Did you bare souls, trade promise rings, all that dorky shit?"

"No, b–"

"You'll never call her a hoochie temptress, right?"

"Right, b–"

"Did you learn about lady parts?"

"Yeah! B–"

"Great! They program you guys into thinking affection is evil, but …" She paused and slumped all the way back, staring at the ceiling. "I'll stop playing love doctor. Love is bullshit made up by the government." She said she was equally sick of guys who acted like porn was real and guys who pretended to be flawless.

"Guess you're stuck with me. Sucks for you."

"People at school bet that'll happen, ya know," she said, side-eying me. "When you hug me, they're like, psp psp, he's gonna save her soul."

Yeah, right. Imagine me at her parties. "Hey, I'm a beer veteran now," I said. Imagine her at Christian concerts. "I'd go see your Deftones-ripoff band," she said. Satan helped me envision sneaking out of lock-ins with the girl who attended lock-ins just to sneak out. *I like you, Satan. There's hope for you.*

I laughed, "I'd be so cool at school, dating Not Another Teen Movie's mean cheerleader, except she's secretly nice."

"Bullshit, her eyes are blue."

Yeah, someone *tired* of hearing she looked like Jaime Pressly didn't need me.

But she kept going. "People'd say you're making an honest woman of me. I'd hide behind you like, 'My tall-ish, dark-ish, handsome-ish boyfriend knows Bible verses.' For real, if you got asked out by some girl who hangs with Christians but isn't one, you'd say no?"

I figured she meant it rhetorically. I knew embracing her would fuel **"REGRET."** Still, I instantly regretted saying, "Christians can't date non-Christians."

"Geez, they convinced you goodie-goodies heathen-ness is contagious," she said, smirking. "Sucks for you."

I cleaned my beer mess, and we walked to Pizza Hut. Passing a cop car,

I ducked my face. My head throbbed, but the evening sun wasn't unkind. Alexa was her usual self, asking me to interpret two-word texts from some baseball player.

"Why are you acting like me being a drunk hypocrite's no big deal?"

"Ooh, lemme try a Bible answer," she said. "When shitheads were throwing rocks at some lady, Jesus was like, 'Eat my chode, mothafuckaaas,' right?"

"Sure."

"Sunday teachers say that story means people shouldn't judge each other. Which, ha! But why stop there? When he's like, 'Only perfect saints can judge her,' she ain't perfect either, so she's included! He's like, 'Nobody gets to hate on you, not even you. Try better tomorrow or whatever, hottie.'"

I was impressed by her interpretation, but lost in worries about the CIA finding Wal-Mart's surveillance footage and my twenty dollar theft tipping my Judgment Day scales.

"Besides, chillax, you've let me spill shit too," she said as I opened the door platonically. "Speaking of ..."

"Hey, why'd you show up for Bible study tonight? You've never done that."

"Yeah, I'm still the actual fuckup. I just wanted to hug some church dorks, but Sophie's with her new fake-smiles crew, and ..."

We gathered salads and found an empty corner. "Bet you think I'ma admit some party-slut shit. Every bitch at school thinks I f–"

"Dude, fuck your chorus of high-school-movie enemies! You're too good for that shit."

She slumped. I slid beside her and asked what was really wrong. Glaring around for unseen gossipers, she said, "My dad. They took him to jail for the night."

Man. Imagine hiding that during an hour of snarky chitchat.

"It's my fault," she whispered. "I'd look at bank numbers and think, okay, I can pay bills and get him something helpful like Oprah books and, fine, maybe some stupid shit for me too. So many medical bills. I fucked up so bad, it five-tupled his stress, until he ... ugh. People look at me and say, psp psp, she's too adult. Well, I fucking suck at it!"

Trying to block out her invisible rivals and swirling demons, I leaned forward.

"Dad doesn't believe in rehab, not that I can afford it anyway," she said. "I'm mortified to go near school people, because ... fine! I can't magically ignore poisonous bitches."

"I get it," I said, sharing things Christians had said about the doomed children of DUI fathers and non-nuclear mothers. "Maybe I owe you a secret. I wanted to kill myself, a few years ago. I thought God hated me. Now I dunno if he cares. Don't tell anybody."

There. Told the truth. Her eyes flashed concern, but then narrowed. "Dumbass, if you kill yourself, I'm gonna get blamed. Everyone knows I'm your worst influence."

I laughed. Walking back, dirty-blonde bangs hid her eyes. Under streetlights, her well-worn sneer surrendered to a frown. Seeing Mom's car in the driveway, Alexa chuckled, "Guess I can't crash here tonight." For once, I almost believed she wasn't messing with me.

"NOT ONLY HAVE YOU ALREADY SQUANDERED YOUR HEART, A CHRISTIAN CANNOT LOVE A NON-VIRGIN OR A NON-CHRISTIAN, LET ALONE BOTH!" *I really, really, really hate you. But I believe you.*

Inside, Mom noticed something was wrong and sat us at the kitchen table. Gulping air, Alexa explained her family history from the 1991 Gulf War onward, blaming herself for every step.

"Young lady, show yourself some grace," Mom said in her warmest voice. "You're not leaving without raiding our pantry like you're the prettiest Caleb. And I can throw woman-of-the-house advice at you, like …"

I witnessed a thing never before seen: Alexa nodding at a list of homework assignments.

"But for now," Mom said, "I recommend ice cream, Hallmark movies, and us locking the stinky boys downstairs. If a girl needs a a mama, sweetheart, she's got one."

World's coolest mom! Even though she called me stinky, as if I regularly puke up beers, as if she even knows about that.

Clenching and shuddering, Alexa croaked worries about leaving her dog alone all night. Mom, a neat freak who'd seen too many pit bull news reports, grimaced.

"Lucky's stinky enough to crash downstairs with me," I argued, and Mom smiled just enough for the tough girl to tumble onto her interim mother's lap.

Sitting in backyard grass, where we'd hidden Alexa's car to avoid rumors, I threw a one-eyed pit bull's mangled wiffle ball. Sipping tea behind me, Mom said, "Goodness, that poor child cried herself to sleep."

"Most grownups hate her," I said, dreading my own impending confession.

"It takes honesty, to look back at who we were before we learned to hide," Mom said, hopefully in weirdo mode. "But seeing our younger versions can freak us out. She snorted when I said she reminds me of teenage Katherine, but ..."

"Of you? Yeah, right."

"... she kept confessing behavior at me, maybe using her reputation to test whether I'll reject her. That was my teenage move!" *Uh-oh, Mom's in detective mode.* "When your perfectly behaved ladyfriends visit our house, I think, 'Wonderful daughter-in-law candidates!' Then I think, 'These lil miracles would've been warned about sixteen-year-old me.' Whenever those innocent cherubs love on Alexa despite her demonstrations, it warms me to death."

I threw the ball for Lucky, a dog at one with the universe.

"Angel, that girl doesn't trust anybody easily. I'm proud she said maybe you're the guy filling in for her brothers. I hope that doesn't hurt, though."

Hey, clarity's awesome. "Guess I have a sister. Weird."

"And when she was trying to appall me with her misdeeds, I told her about," her voice hardened, "sixteen-year-old Katherine puking up booze." I turned to see a cocky smirk, but also worried eyes. "Young man, God made sure I happened upon some evidence."

I deflated, outraced to my own confession. She sat behind me, resting crossed arms on my hunched back. *Go ahead, call me a failure seeking excuses to fail even harder. Tell me I'm acting like I wish to be unborn. Speak truth.*

"Why'd we decide to drink?" she asked.

"It's not we. You didn't."

"I've been we since your brother was born. Do we wanna drink again?"

"No."

"Who'd we drink with?"

"Nobody."

"Hmm. Which friends are we protecting?"

"Nobody."

"Hmm. Which girls?"

"None. Stop hmming."

"Were we upset about Miss Chloe?"

"Sure, and whatever else."

"You two were cute, even if you talked like those comedy shows where nobody's laughing. Would talking about feelings be smarter than drinking?"

"Maybe," *unless they're feelings about religion being exhausting. No, stop.*

"Who bought that beer for us?"

"Nobody."

"We stole?"

"I did."

She tapped my spine, making me shiver. "I'm scared, angel. It's like hearing echoes. Jesus saved me from that path, but your father struggled. Now, for a decade, I've heard stories about him. I'm sure you have, too."

Finally. Tell me which story to choose: loving father, raging DUI, or psychotic breakdown? Maybe that choice would decide whether Heaven or Hell is the story I'll tell myself. Then again, some kid at school once decided Dad died as a fugitive bank robber. That's the cool story, at least.

Mom said, "We'll never know which is true, but …"

I gasped. I'd never heard her invoke the mystery that'd haunted me for almost half my life: Had he risked the lives of other drivers, or had he abandoned me on purpose? I realized I'd always hoped for the latter. A car full of lives vs. one soul. Cold, hard math.

"Teenagers try things," Mom said, already moving on. "Maybe I'm a pushover, or maybe my work schedule gives you unfair freedom. But sometimes, I trust you to make good choices and learn from bad ones. I overlooked you trying pot once …"

"What?"

"Child, my ears are failing, but my nose isn't. Some things I'll monitor, hopefully nudging you correctly. Other things mortify me. This is the thing. So many good ways to emulate your daddy. You do not have permission to damage yourself."

Unless the Apostle Paul tells me to! No, stop. Priorities. "I'm allowed to smoke weed?"

"Ears failing all over! I overlooked it once."

"I'ma smoke so hard, you'll be a hippie again."

"You can't afford to."

"I have twenty-seven dollars."

"You had twenty-seven dollars. You're paying back Wal-Mart, writing the manager a letter, and donating two paychecks to charity."

Concrete atonement, no matter how dorky, sounded better than interminable groveling. Without quoting Proverbs, televangelists, or horror-movie monsters who kill slutty drunks, she made me want to be better tomorrow. Really, she had me at "we."

"Did I ever tell you the moment I fell in love with Isaac Sr.?" she said. "We were smoking with the burnouts, watching children race box cars. This lonely boy nicknamed World B Fat asked if he could drive one. No way he'd fit! Everyone laughed! But your daddy wandered off, returned with a hammer, and helped the kids make an XL car. I was flustered, discovering I liked a good guy. And poof, Eli existed. Conceived *in* wedlo–"

"Mother."

I spotted a bright star and guessed it was Heaven's prodigal, Venus. I said, "The least alone I've ever felt wasn't at school, work, football, or even church, but when my couch was World B Full. I've been so mad at Pastor Jack, I kinda threw away my friends who never even voted for him."

"Anybody else miss fellowship?"

"PG says so. Caleb, I gotta call. Alexa's a lonely World B Popular. I miss … everybody."

"What God joined together, let nobody separate."

"Anything that can be built can be rebuilt better?"

"Now there's Isaac Jr.!"

"Rapcore was played out in middle school," PG sighed, bangs angling beneath her lopsided trucker hat, reading Caleb's book of lyrics. "What if you said these lines, but not as hippity-hop? Like, can you scream? Do you know our song 'As Angels Vomit Themselves to Sleep'?"

"I miiight know that one," he lied, pretending he listened to anything but her demo CD. Around her, the rising junior in a backwards trucker hat strained so hard to act like a senior, he transformed into a large freshman. I was rooting for my boy to finally ascend her list of suitors.

"Also … we don't outright say Jesus anymore," she said, suddenly surfacing an old argument with who-knows-which adults. "We never asked to be a ministry! 'You owe God your talents.' No, we're Christians who like banging drums! When MxPx got shunned for crossing over, I was like, go MxPx!"

Caleb looked wounded. They argued a little. I suggested other Bible words for Jesus. They liked Morning Star so much, they started a song with that name. Adorable!

Finding Caleb at her band practice was fortunate. *I gotta talk to him anyway, maybe? Or wait until he brings up his sixth-grade memories again? I dunno.*

First, I'd gone there to propose an idea. "We should get the Tuesday night gang back together. I've learned stuff from other churches, but it doesn't have to be me talking. PG could be in charge. I just miss you guys."

"Other churches? Being wishy-washy leads people astray," said Caleb, paraphrasing Jack's warning against attending non-Jack churches.

I was frustrated by his fear of broadened horizons, but I understood it. Still, between mild-mannered Methodists, rowdy Charismatics, popeless-Catholic Lutherans, Alexa's Uni-whatever communist grandmothers (*Karl Marx kinda sounds like Jesu–* **"REGRET!"**), Amir's mom's temple, Bobbi's telescope, and the synagogue where questioning God is an inside joke with God, "it's like everybody's onto something. Everybody except Calvinists."

"Oh man, I stopped by to hear my homegirl sing," said someone in the doorway, "but now I have a surprise for y'all."

We turned to see a grinning Timmy, who was about to leave on tour again. PG scrambled to hug him. His wink made me feel like I'd been caught stealing candy.

I explained, "All Calvinists are assholes who think God rigged a Hell lottery. Worst part is, they might be correct." PG nodded. Caleb argued.

Timmy laughed, threw an arm across my shoulder, and said, "Been a'ight, boy?"

"Gettin' there, old-timer."

Outside, we followed him to the path between condemned strips of trees. On a little rocking chair, half-smiling at an empty cup in her hands, sat Miss Esther, withered from chemo. She didn't notice we'd stepped onto her porch until Timmy tapped her hand. He reminded her of our names, but she scoffed, claiming her memory was perfect. We'd learned to play along.

"These ragamuffins tickled me," he told her, slow and loud. "They said Calvinists are bullies who worship a cruel God."

Slowly, her eyes lingered on each of us. A grin surfaced.

"My daddy's daddy's daddy was a Calvinist, much as he disliked that term. Primitive Baptist, to be precise," she chuckled, with heavy breaths every few words. "Daddy's daddy too, plus Daddy. I don't figure I ever stopped bein' one. Preacher's daughter. I remember it all, seventy … Lord, eighty years later. We're born completely depraved … "

My heart sank, hearing somebody in our non-denominational mishmash take sides with people who'd declared salvation impossible for some of us. *She's the last light of the church that chose me, yet she believes she's in a special tribe, so fuck everybody else? WTF is Primitive Baptist? Cavemen who can't dance?*

"Tell 'em what they called your particular kinfolk," Timmy said.

Slowly, she told us about cry-laughing preachers, Spirit-filled women interrupting them, and ten-hour riverside theology debates. "They ran Daddy outta so many one-room churches. Down there, every hill's got its own flavor of Baptist. Bitter grudges over flea-sized stuff."

"The name, honey," he said. "What'd they call you?"

"I was about yay-high," she said, dangling her hand inches off the porch, "when a man struck my daddy, tellin' him he's wrong about this, that, and the third. That's the first time I heard the name, most likely."

"What was it?"

"Why, they ridiculed us by calling us the No-Hellers."

What, they didn't wanna go to Hell? Big deal. Join the club.

"God pre-arranged our lives, sure enough," she said, closer to naptime by the breath. "But, in the end, God wants every creature home, Psalm 145:21, don't he? First Timothy 2:4? Second Peter 3:9?"

Hair stood on my neck.

"And if God controls everything," she said, "would God choose an ending God don't want?"

I realized her No-Hellers believed in literally *no Hell*.

"We used to tell it like this," she said, summoning fundamental memories. "There's a lake of fire for the abominable, says Revelation 20. But after a season of cleansing, that old description might not fit anyone, says Revelation 21:4. Only the chosen enter Heaven, sure enough. Well, who informed God he can't choose all his children?"

No. Freaking. Way. Caveman Calvinists said everyone goes to Heaven?

PG wept, saying girls clearly could preach. Caleb was horrified by a saint disputing everything we'd ever been taught.

Hair stood on my neck because that Revelation thing was exactly what'd scandalized my brain on my fifteenth birthday, the day we'd founded Video Games Church.

What if love so thoroughly conquers all, there's a sunrise for Lucifer and sympathy for Diablo? What if it's not about confronting Eli, but burying what haunts him? What if Jack's mightiest weapon was formed from nothing? What if the Bible's right when it says all will be made new, and that includes my father?

I gotta talk to Sophie about this. Wait, we're not friends. But what if ...

"WHAT IF YOU'LL REGRET ASKING WHAT IF?" *What if Miss Esther's a Great Depression West Virginian who believes women must wear dresses, not a scripture genius? What if questioning the necessity of salvation leads to accepting damnation? What if doubting the men who taught me proves those men right?*

During hugs, Miss Esther said, "Gumdrop, once I'm gone, keep leadin' my babies out here."

I agreed, queasily. *She understands the parking deck's gonna replace her house, right?*

"Acts 3:21," she said. "We ain't finished 'til that's his will."

PART FOUR
THE BOOK OF SENIORS

Set me as a seal upon your heart,
for love is as strong as death

— The Song of Songs

TWENTY-EIGHT
TAKING BACK SUNDAY

JULY 2003

"ONE LAST STORY," PASTOR JACK SAID, WHICH ALWAYS MEANT FIFTEEN minutes remained until the final altar call began.

Give him this much: The man preached his ass off. With attendance overflowing, he was adding a *fourth* Sunday morning service each week, providing capacity for swelling crowds ahead of the bigger sanctuary's completion.

"July 1992," he rasp-boomed, "some twerp from New York, a gangster's grandson, visited a suburban church surrounded by sleepy maples and said, 'Here, Father God? There's more bodies in the cemetery than the sanctuary!'"

I hated that joke about dead people no longer counting.

"The Lord replied, 'Smartypants, did I stutter? My anointing will descend here. Say yes, then I'll ask the questions.' That's been the vision ever since."

When I was 13.9, that sounded humble, like Jack was calling himself dumb. At seventeen, I heard a man bragging about his talents turning God into a determined recruiter.

Jack trumpeted attendance statistics, comparing 1992 to 2003, and shared twenty-year "total souls touched" projections for his satellite-church network, which would require funding more projects — even before the new sanctuary's 2005 completion.

"But bigger isn't always better," he said, telling a sprawling story about his wife's "packrat" tendencies. I watched the redhead ASL translator's whirling hands repeat the usual women-be-shopping jokes about her aunt.

"The point is, we all let junk gather," Jack said, bass-boosted. "We throw the doors open but fail to discard trash. Think about our hearts, dissuaded by false prophets and humanly approval. Our households' various agendas and perversions. Our cities, welfare-spewing Gomorrahs!"

Okay, I'd known as a sophomore that, according to the Bible, the crime of Sodom and Gomorrah was *withholding* welfare. Surely that M.Div on stage did as well. (Why was I listening to somebody I could no longer stomach, if I was allowed to leave for another church? Wait, you're really asking? All my friends were there. Duh.)

"Even this house itself is marred, Father God forgive me! As is our nation, which some would surrender to terrorism, socialism, atheism, feminism, humanism, modernism, and Mohammedism — I repeat myself, because I already said terrorism. No -ism but baptism!"

I couldn't help scanning the sea of laughing faces. A few summers earlier, the place had included brown faces. The congregation had since boomed, yet PG was its last dark-skinned teenage girl. The Calebs always changed their minds on their own ethnic descriptions, but by then, everybody else's seemed obvious.

And, right around "agendas," Sophie's ASL hands had frozen.

"Men, we guard this house against anyone, foreign or domestic," Jack continued. "My beautiful bride in the front row, I adore beyond description. But if perversion emerged in my home and she defended it? In that scenario, God's commanded me, as his steward, to discipline her unmistakably. As a woman of God, she accepts that."

Sophie awkwardly kneaded her knuckles.

"Men of God, we are the ramparts," he rasp-roared. "We thank Father God for our modern Teddy Roosevelts, including one I can't name without IRS persecution: our wild-hearted William Wallace staring down demon-emasculated cowards who'd surrender God's nation to darkness. Our Gandalf the White informs the righteous we must fight with our lives for America's souls! We thank Father God for our modern Moses, our Judeo-Christian deliverer, our burning Bush."

He winked in response to booming laughter. Two years prior, wizard Harry Potter had been "satanic." Then, wizard Gandalf became the president Jack couldn't praise without paying taxes. Shit, I'd grown up learning European-American allies would be on the Antichrist's side in the

Middle East, yet we'd said the opposite each time a Bush had invaded Iraq.

The youth group murmured. Sophie shuffled off stage, clutching her hands to her chest. Something too good to be true made me climb over my Calebs and slip out a back door. That something: Miss Esther's revelation.

Speed-walking through halls, I turned a corner and found picturesque homophobe Gabe whining at Sophie about having caused a scene.

"But it's like Uncle Jack was talking about my cousin," she mumbled. "And George Bush isn't Gandalf! Gandalf can read."

"Well, if you're clocking out early, nobody's at my crib," he said, grabbing her butt. I couldn't judge him, because I'd said that stuff to Chloe. *But without sitting up front, doing deacon-son stuff,* I reasoned.

He saw me approaching, chuckled, and started walking, drawing her along by the upper arm.

"That sermon sucked," I said.

Her high heels gained traction against the magenta carpet. "I just keep hoping Uncle Jack's gonna go back to my childhood hero, instead of this character," she said, staring at her hands. "I've gone along with so many things, I'm tainted."

"Aww, princess," Gabe mewled, as I heard Jack's voice more loudly through a briefly opened door. "Let's get you outta here."

"Nobody's leaving," rumbled Eli's wood-grained voice, entering our hall. "Some people in there can only get the altar call from your hands, Primrose. Get in gear."

Sophie shrank. *Gabe's silenced for once! Siena brothers, mount up! Wait, Eli's not on my side.*

"You can't make her repeat Jack's politics crap," I muttered.

"Well, skip the politics crap," Eli whisper-shouted. "The altar call's critical!"

"I can't do it anymore," she sniffed, looking frantic as Gabe massaged her shoulders.

Eli, fists on hips, grunted, "If you're injured or something, teach me how to do it."

Slack-jawed, she gasp-laughed, fluttering her chin-length hair. "That's so many words!"

"Just teach me how to say this," he said, urgent eyes bearing down. "Everyone must be saved from Hell, declaring with their mouths, 'Jesus is Lord,' in front of oth–"

"Mouths?" I laughed.

"Hands, whatever," he groaned.

"Let's start with 'Jesus,'" she said, tapping her palms with her fingers. He repeated the motion hurriedly, and her eyebrows said she felt pressured.

I told Eli to write on a sign like a roadside John 3:16 lunatic. His mountainous face revealed delight as he hustled to find posterboard. *Dude, if I ever tell him what Miss Esther said, he'll shoot me. That zealot's everything I need to become.*

"Now let's getcha outta here," Gabe said, clasping Sophie's hip.

She glanced back at me. My palms decided to press themselves together — "prayer" — and tip forward — "request." Once she reached the end of the hall, she glanced again.

She'd been my best friend. I'd ignored her since January just because of jealousy-turned-bitterness, even though she'd once saved me from hurting myself.

Yeah, our semi-dating promise failed, but I'd neglected a far more sacred pact: Freshman year, I'd vowed she'd speak with her own voice, her own hands. I'd fucking pinkie sworn it.

And if that wasn't the last straw, I heard Gabe singing Creed.

Eli told me he'd smoothed things over with Pastor Jack. "I said she's having a hard time, so I stepped in. And I recommended he relieve his niece, even though that used to be cute, and use trained adults instead."

"That was cool of you."

"What? How? Her meltdown endangered souls."

> xSHARKSWITHRABIESx: not trying to start drama.
> uhh do you think gabe is good or bad

LetsTalkAboutLexBaby (Alexa): fuck that fakeass prick

> xSHARKSWITHRABIESx: ah

LetsTalkAboutLexBaby: answer your fucking phone

Alexa cussed for 11.7 minutes (stopwatch) without specifying why.

"She barely trusts anyone. She's convinced she's going to fucking Hell. You're a ginormous dork, but you're, ugh, a good dude. You're part of my plan, okay? Don't fuck it up."

I'd clearly missed a lot. "Uh, on it?"

"If this doesn't get his ass booted, I'ma curb-stomp his nutsack. Hug your mom for me!"

One Wednesday night, some church lady asked if any student bands could open for NewSong at the county fair. We recommended PG's band. The lady approved, no questions asked. That was awesome because:

1. NewSong, founded before I was born, is what people assume all Christian music sounds like: mega-bland, typified by the melodramatic "Christmas Shoes."
2. PG played some six-word emocore sub-genre, wailing nonsense over clanking guitars as Caleb shrieked. It ruled, we thought.

Two days later, our group snickered at adults in patriotic gear who didn't know they were about to be howled at for thirty minutes. As I carried band gear, PG critiqued my armload, so I caveman-hoisted her over my half-Eli-sized shoulder as laughing Graces wrestled her free. (Being outnumbered was typical. Church's senior class was two-thirds female, so I planned to never leave church.)

"Howdy, we're Make Me Your Blood Bank," she said into the mic with a white belt on her black jeans. Confused grownups applauded, muttering about her androgynous drummer. Caleb, hair matching PG's swoopy black bangs, screamed whatever. Grownups shared cotton candy. A dozen teenagers moshed. Grownups tanned themselves, only minimally offended. Heartbreaking!

"Surpriiise, my homies are tight again," Alexa suddenly said, shoving Sophie to stand beside me. "Aww, so awkward! Too bad. Get to it! Icebreaker queen, out!"

She kissed Sophie's cheek, then spun to leave with some tattooed golfer. Sophie shouted, "I'm locking my window at 1 a.m., whether you're home or not."

For the first time in months, I stood inches from my former soulmate, with an acre of awkwardness and non-flat Jesus in the space between. All the things I'd wanted to say were bubbling up like beer vomit.

So I said, "You like Creed now?"

In a preppy yellow dress, she laughed through her nose, like she'd expected that. As she tucked hair behind her ear, I saw chewed-up fingernails. She answered: probably "enh," but I hoped it was "ugh."

Tensing the bold eyebrows that'd once controlled me, she thanked me for supporting Alexa. Surely dazzling her with my leveled-up social skills, I bragged about exaggerated misdemeanors and "a girl I dated." We fidgeted and sweated through agonizing small talk and into tentative nostalgia from a time before promises, when we'd been two freshmen on speakerphones wishing we were actually playing Mario Kart together.

I told her about the recent day when I'd wandered into an Eastern Orthodox church, maybe drawn by Mom's Greek heritage. I described the chants, scents, and painted-dome ceiling, things forgotten by two-thirds of Jesus world. Orthodox sacraments are called mysteries, and they're so mysterious, not even the priest knew how many there might be — not even after the service lasted 150 minutes.

"The part I wanted to tell you was he also said maybe the Bible's scary stuff," *the stuff that used to make you call me in tears at 2 a.m.,* "isn't about damnation, but about, like, love. God's, I guess. Like, maybe Hell is ..."

She blinked so fast, I shut up. Emotion glistened the gray eyes that'd once drowned me. Something was raw.

On stage, PG introduced her finale. No chance we'd keep standing there for NewSong. *Marrying that walking polo shirt is Sophie's path, sure. But what if some villain leads her astray?*

I hummed the Offspring's "Want You Bad," then said, "Bet your boyfriend won't let you do the Ferris wheel with me."

She gave me a scolding smirk. *I once feared I'd corrupt her, but now that's the funnest ambition imaginable. Oh, this is how the "deflower" girls view me.* **"REGRET!"** *I said "imaginable." Rhetorical!*

"Nobody tells me who I can split fried pickles with," she said. "After this song?"

"I think Alexa wants you to cheat with me," I said, like a monumental dare.

"She said if I don't, she'll beat me up. She could try, I guess."

"Guess you're in trouble. I just wanna tell you forbidden secrets, though. About, ya know, salvation."

"Hush up," she laughed, turning away but staying. "Everybody's staring at the pastor's niece, as per frickin' usual."

Settle down, Republicans, clearly I only want to tell her Miss Esther believes Hillary Clinton goes to Heaven!

By then, all along the grassy hill, adults outnumbered moshers. PG's band launched into a bizarre emocore cover of a country song I didn't know: "Sin Wagon," about being sick of behaving. Couldn't agree more.

"Uh-oh," Sophie said, pointing at beefy men in shirts with crosses and guns. "They'll recognize this is the Dixie Chicks."

Uh-oh. For months, conservatives had been outraged by that band opposing the Iraq invasion.

Soon, I saw scowling confusion. The beefmen stomped toward PG's stage, shouting about "feminazi peace-freak garbage" wrecking "a Christian event" (at a public park).

I used to believe Christian men weren't actually saying peace was anti-Christian, until I watched Christian men rage at my brown-skinned friend because she was implying she didn't like bloodshed. *Fuck th–* **"INFIDEL, YOU'LL REGRET OPPOSING GOD'S CHOSEN NATION!"**

As patriots neared the stage, PG backed away from her mic. Caleb pulled her toward their van. We hustled to load their stuff.

Riding back to town, she mumbled, "Told you that wasn't the place for that song."

"Well, nobody told me that's who wrote it," Caleb yelled.

Quoting things Rush Limbaugh taught us in middle school, he quit the band and made his dream girl cry.

TWENTY-NINE
DID IT HURT? WHEN YOU FELL FROM HEAVEN?

AUGUST 2003

> xSHARKSWITHRABIESx: dare you to come over and let me show you a video game. promise you'll maybe like it even tho its about uhhh satan

Seriously? That was my move? Blew it.

> xOneGirlArmy86x (Sophie): i love dares! tuesday like old times?

Whoa.

"Her name's Vandalf," said Sophie in my driveway, patting a purple Ford Econoline older than either of us. I'd never given my vehicle a name, so I dubbed it "Samwise GamJeep."

My social skills further dazzled her as I pointed at her little rainbow-plaid button-up and said, "Shirt, uh, good."

Glancing me up and down, she fidgeted with her tiny ponytail. "Your messy hair's, like, neat or whatever." She paused for a ground-stare mumble. "Please don't think you have to lemme be your goofy sidekick again. Alexa means well."

As rain started to fall, the reply that escaped my mouth was, "Cool!"

In my basement, she sat in a folding chair beside mine. As iTunes happened to play emo she liked, I beelined to Diablo II like a dork, dumped handfuls of Skittles onto her lap, and handed her room-temperature Mountain Dew.

"Who dared your guy to fight without a sword?" she said as I clicked my unarmed paladin through Hell, demons splattering against him. "He's a walking bug zapper. Citronella candles are nicer."

"No weapon. I've powered up only his defensive auras and stuff. Tested combos. I've spent, uh, hours on this. We're halfway to showtime."

As fat demons exploded into goop, we talked families. I told her Mom was worried about Eli's volatile temper.

Sophie said, "Dare me to tell my family God's calling me to college instead of missions?" She was considering Penn State and women's colleges in Georgia, Massachusetts, and North Carolina, plus the obvious choice, the Dynasty's recommended Bible college. *College starts in a hundred years! Go State or whoever!*

She also revealed she was again in trouble with her family. "They assume I'm at Bible study right now." It kept dawning on me, how big a deal it was for the church's most visible youth to walk off stage.

"You're a bad mammerjammer," I said. There's no non-cuss way to say "badass."

"Well, you're the one who dared me to," she said. "Years ago."

A little too much eye contact. Outside, thunder chastised us.

As my paladin approached the final seal, I said, "Dare you to summon Satan."

She hunched forward, narrowed her eyes into all-business mode, and reached to click. "Pshh. I dare him to show up."

Atop a flaming pentagram, our paladin stood as empty-handed as Rage Against the Machine's fire monk. Behemoth Diablo growled, "Not even death can save you from me," and attacked. My fingers clattered, draining health potions but forming no weapons, only laying hands on a sick being. She cheered as I dodged lightning, shrieked as I almost died, and shouted, "Go! Go! Yes!" once a blue soul floated free from Diablo's red body.

I wiped sweat, hopefully subtly. She sat criss-cross and said, "Did Satan have a good-guy soul leaving him? Did death save Satan from himself?"

One step ahead already! I nodded, cleared my throat, and launched in. "So, one night years ago, you were upset about … the afterlife."

"Just one?"

"True. I talked to Eli after that. And he cried about it, too," I said, making her eyes bug out. "I realized you two were like me, believing in Hell as totally, actually, for-real true."

The first time we talked in months was also becoming the first time we'd talked about our biggest fear. She sipped Dew.

"It makes me … I dunno. Mad? Especially when Eli said …" I gulped nerves. "He believes our dad's in Hell."

Her jaw dropped. One hand floated near my arm, nearly touching my skin for the first time in fourteen months. *Focus. She has a boyfriend anyway. But he sucks! Focus.*

"I wanted to prove Eli wrong," I said. "But it's not like I have Hell's sign-in sheet. I just refused to believe Dad's hurting forever."

I was daring her to let me continue. Considering God's punishments unjust was way more blasphemous than disliking them. She shrug-grimaced, grabbing her purple backpack off the floor.

"Salvation is when life beats death," I said. "So we try to picture that. We listened to songs about slaughtering Satan. Christian novels say this basement's full of angels stabbing demons. In wrestling games, we created Jesus to beat up the Devil. I've murdered Diablo a zillion times. Satan gets his a– … butt kicked in Dante's Inferno, plus stuff by this guy John Milton," I said, boldly implying I'd read beyond the CliffsNotes. "There's a story about Jesus invading Hell, conquering Satan. With weapons? Really? Jesus said to love enemies! Isn't that love more powerful, the more hateable the enemy? What if, when Eli told us we're equal to Satan, Eli was right, but …?"

"I'm listening," she said, holding a little notepad, surely ready to shoot me down.

"When my paladin convicted Diablo, saving him without stabbing him, I really wondered: Maybe nobody's beyond hope. Literally nobody. Alive, dead, or worse."

"Holyyy gosh, I got something to tell you," she said, hands jittering, surely about to bury me with book reports.

"And then I read PG's Dixie Chicks lyrics. Flying away while dragging feet! Like, Satan doesn't wanna love Jesus, but the Bible says everybody will. That includes the little blue soul escaping Satan's body, right? If even Satan goes home, all people do, right?"

She sat, quiet as a sunflower, raring to speak but making sure I was done. I stared at her lime-green nails to avoid eye-drowning. I felt proud. Maybe I'd finally schooled her on Bible stuff.

She stood, paced, and said, "Ize, I've been desperate to tell this stuff to somebody. You know that scary Zao album we loved as freshmen?"

Liberate te ex Inferis, loaded with clips from Event Horizon, is the rare Christian-world art genuinely empathetic toward the fallen.

She made a metalhead face, sticking out her Skittles-rainbow tongue, and said, "Well, their 'Hell is only a word' thing from some movie made me wonder, so I learned the word. In the Bible, 'Hell' often means 'grave.' Like, Psalm 139 doesn't say God watches me in Hell! It says God still cares after I die! Sometimes 'Hell' actually means 'Hades,' some guy the Hercules movie made mean. My parents are sick of homeschooling me, so I'm gonna do a mythology elective!" She kept listing biblical words translated as "Hell" despite not necessarily being meant to imply a fiery prison for the undead. "My uncle called this comparative-religions hoo-ha, back when he still spoke to me. During his sermons, I sometimes replaced 'Hell' with these other words, but ..."

I sat more stunned by the second. Her mini-assembly's custom sermons offered hope. At issue: whether it was false hope.

She lingered near me, then took three big steps away. "This summer, I messed up mega-bad. You've, um, probably heard." *Whatever you did, it was nowhere near the rumors.* "I camped in my uncle's study, trying to find hope. Turns out, some smart Christians have argued Hell is an instant, not forever. Others think saved people get resurrected while the unsaved just stay asleep. Even C.S. Lewis, right under our parents' noses, wrote like Hell isn't eternal!" She waved her notepad, arms wide. "Anyone can make the Bible say anything! Also, you know how Milton's Satan is weirdly sympathetic?" she asked, and, thanks to CliffsNotes, I had the confidence to shrug.

I'd assumed that asking a pretty girl to watch me play Diablo II would make me the basement's biggest nerd, but the pretty girl was rapid-firing infodumps about whoever Clement of Alexandria was. *Me schooling her? LOL.* Flipping pages, she said, "1,800 years ago, one of the most important Christians, this guy Origen, who Catholics got mad at once they showed up, after he died ... Anyway, he believed — you ready? — everyone, even Satan, will be saved."

No wonder they'd sensed they should keep us apart. We'd been cooking versions of the same reckless heresy. Things were going better than I'd hoped, even better than the dirty hopes.

"Frickin' yesterday, I snuck to your Orthodox church, and I asked stuff," she said, sitting on our couch for the first time in ages. "It's gorgeous, ahh! Their guy Gregory of Nyssa, from the year 300-whatever? He said all things below God are equally below God, because God's infinitely great, right? Satan's no worse than me, because we're equally not-God. So because we're all equally bad anyway, if anyone's saved ..."

Then everyone's saved, which would mean church men are wrong about everything. She didn't dare finish her sentence. Still, I bragged, harder than ever, about being half-Greek. *Oops, my weight on this old couch made you lean toward my screaming skin. Dare you to keep leaning.*

"I miss this place," she said, playing with her ponytail, tangible, totally huggable. *Go. No, she has a boyfriend. Go. No, my summer sins would pollute her. Good!*

No, stare at the ceiling and say the unsexiest words imaginable: "You know Calvinism?"

She blinked. "Like, God already decided who won't go to Heaven?"

And I told her what Miss Esther had said.

She blinked. With rainy wind swishing against my windows, she slumped against my couch and grinned at the ceiling.

We've assembled something, right? Literally all will be made new, according to ancient desert Christians, musical hillside Christians, some pastor-approved Christians, and ... more? Who else can we dare to discover? And if they're right, what breaks? **"If they're wrong, you break."** *What if we dare to break together?*

"What if," she whispered, smooth knees screaming near my leg, "being created is being chosen?"

"What if we're allowed to say what if?"

I leaned back, shoulder under her propped elbow. Gray eyes shimmering, she said, "What if everyone reaches Heaven, but the reason isn't that they recited correct words before they died? Maybe the reason is that ... um, I dare you say it. Maybe ..."

"Denying the need for salvation and fooling her into joining you? Commit to this bullshit together, and you'll be damned apart forever."

Forever? I wasn't thinking that far ahead.

"Exactly. Recant. Atone. Eternity's a long time to be wrong."

Huh? I meant I was only thinking ahead to touching her leg. Skin! So! Shiny!

"Boy, not even death can save her from you."

"... Hell ends up empty anyway," I whispered.

We both felt chills, sitting inches apart. Co-conspirator giggles. Trinity and Neo. '03 Bonnie and Clyde. Did I believe our outrageousness about churches telling the biggest lie imaginable, or was I just in love with a deviant? Something rampaged around my mind, jostling the columns upholding everything I'd ever believed.

"Maybe we can become good," she told my eyes, "after we do evil things."

"Maybe I'm your evil thing," I said, unable to hide a grin.

Looking away, she sigh-laughed, "No, I'm ..."

As Dashboard Confessional's makeout song faded from my speakers, we listened for especially pissed-off thunder, but heard only our alarmingly heavy breaths. She lifted her arm, showing me freckly goosebumps, and my fingers skimmed along tiny hairs, closer and closer and ...

Jolting away, she grabbed her cellphone and punched someone's number. *Gah! Calling church cops on me!*

Actually, she recorded a voicemail. "Gabriel, God laid something on my heart. Um, we're breaking up."

Dare! You! To! Move!

My chest burst into flames as my hands shot toward her. She stammered scripture-based breakup rationale into her phone while letting me scoot her closer.

Christians are taught this argument: "If Hell wasn't real, everybody would do whatever they want." In that moment, it felt true.

It was like when praise concerts send emotions soaring, when on-fire Christians dive into backseats, colliding like rainbows crisscrossing into plaid because bodies can't distinguish love from Love. Maybe when you teach people they're one neglected prayer away from damnation, but they discover you know nothing, their celebration is your fault. Or maybe youth pastors worry too much about Britney Spears' wardrobe and not enough about C.S. Lewis.

She tossed her phone, and we lunged so urgently, our long-delayed first kiss was a forehead-bonking nose-lick. "ACT EXPERIENCED," screamed my mind. Tumbling to the floor, I somehow kissed her earhole. "MAKE BABIES," screamed my body. Digesting her Skittles tongue, I pondered her fingernail-digging ferocity. "I'D DIE FOR YOU," screamed my heart. The person most paranoid about anyone glimpsing her sports bra's straps found me worthy of the whole orange-with-white-stars thing.

We'll be flattened by guilt once we stop. So why stop?

But, from atop the stairs, shouting my entire name, was my mother's voice.

Hours later, Sophie finally answered her phone. "Your mom hates me. And she should, because I attacked you."

"My who? I miss you and your boobs I almost saw. B-words."

"Your mom. She was mad."

"Oh. She thought we were doing satanic stuff."

"We were. It was my fault."

"No, she thought you were teaching me yoga."

Sophie kept hoarding the blame for something called "sin." Never heard of it. I was on baby-blue Neptune, building her a library shaded by palm trees, but returned to reality when she whispered, "Ize?"

I argued Mom had been surprised, not angry. "She was like, 'Be careful with that sweet girl,' blahblahblah."

"I'm not sweet," Sophie yelped. "You've heard what I did, right? And then I dragged you down too!"

"Let's take stuff slow," I suggested, feeling like I'd become Chloe.

Sophie sighed, probably studying stormclouds for signs of God's disapproval. After always worrying that I'd soil the priceless girl, I had. *Plus I'll feel stupid once the Taliban bombs our Pizza Hut and we awake in the Hell we denied. Was that really worth a makeout? Yeah!* **"REGRET!"** *We'll see!*

"You've heard, right?" she repeated, more quietly.

"Heard what?"

"You don't want me. I made my former person stumble majorly, and now I'm a love addict or something, trying to refill my ruined heart. Just like they warned us."

A self-hate contest? Let's go. I tried out-confessing her: "This summer, I wanted to 95% do sex, and that counts. So don't feel bad. If I'm too garbage for you, I understand."

"I should've told you," she whisper-rattled. "Please don't hate me. Please forget me. I didn't just make Gabe sin. We had actual, demonic, legs-apart ..."

Brain rebooting.

" ... s-e-x."

Gut somersaulting.

"Did I learn my lesson?" she said with ragged breath. "No! Now I'm ruining you! I can't be a wife somebody deserves. I'm a nast–"

"Stop," I said, throat clenching. **"WHOREMONGER, CALL HER A DECEITFUL HARLOT!"**

"Chewed-up bubblegum doesn't deserve love," she sobbed, hanging up.

I stood, feeling all emotions until one emerged. Mad at something old and vast, I threw stuff into my backpack, drove 9.1 miles, ignored Mom's texts, tiptoed between rose bushes toward the window Alexa always snuck through, and stood in the rain. **"REGRET."** Balled on the floor, Sophie wore her rainbow shirt, restored after a villain parted it, with "Face:Face" by Norma Jean blasting. I tapped. **"REGRET."** She shook her head. I signed, "Request prayer." **"REGRET."** She dragged herself to her window.

I'd always loved that band. But they were screaming at Sophie about female abominations, so right then, I hated them. Eyes ringed with reddened skin, she fidgeted with a purity ring, a disguise that embarrassed her. I knew the rain made her want to invite me in, despite how much we believed we shouldn't be near each other, so I liked the rain.

Hanging my head, I kicked a rock, but nudged it back into its puddle because she liked nature. *She's caught in my self-hatred auras.* **"FOOL, SHE'S LURING YOU!"** *Delete them.*

I told her, "I'm sorry I called myself garbage. I'd never imagine meaning it about you. You're the opposite."

"CHRIST'S SUFFERING, ISAAC! YOU CAUSED IT!" *I'd give anything for her to see herself how I see her.* She sniffed, arms crossed.

"If we're unhappy, let's talk to friends," I said. "That can be me, if you want. Today, we agreed God likes us forever, right?"

"GOD ABHORS YOU, FUCKING WORM!" I shoved as much tranquility faceward as I could. She was still sad. *I'd give everything.*

I said, "If I'm lying about thinking you're good, I want it counted as me blaspheming the Holy Spi–"

"Frickin' ... you're gonna get struck by lightning!"

She pulled my arm and found a towel. We sat criss-cross on her floor. For the first time, I saw her Homeschool Yodeling Tournament participation trophy, stacks of 7ball magazines, chair-sized stuffed dragon, cardboard box labeled Alexa's Emotion Cubicle, and bulletin boards of friend photos, including me, the sophomore Christmas demon.

Slumping into her crossed arms, she said, "I can't talk about it. Definitely not to you, the guy I broke promises to."

We stared at walls. *Get her talking. Whatever it takes.* Feeling a sting, I asked, "Did you love him like that?"

Soft and slow, she mumbled, "I thought so. Uncle-approved Dynasty guy. My future felt settled, a minister's wife. You don't wanna hear."

Nope. But: "I wanna listen."

She inhaled, sprinting through basics about him having been nice at first. "Months later, he said if we leapt to that level, we'd be together forever, because sex is what spouses do. After weeks of freaking out, I decided him getting it from somebody besides his future wife would be even worse for him. I accepted the sin of failing to guard his heart from lust, which seemed better than becoming single and having church ladies nag me about lacking a baby-making plan."

Maybe that mental-gymnastics story had been edited to sound like she'd been forced to like him — c'mon, he was pretty, talented, and grownup-endorsed — but how could a smart person have believed such a shithead was her only option?

From her rapid mumbles, I gathered Gabe had done a vague rededication performance before leaving for college as a redeemed voyager, while Sophie kept torturing herself for his idea.

I just wanted her to be okay. **"NO, YOU'RE DISGUSTED! SHE'S DISEASE-ROTTED!"** *Shut. The. Mother. Fucking. Gosh. Damn. Fuck. Up. In. The. Name. Of. Jesus.*

She sniffed and wiped snot. I played with her shoestrings. According to every adult who'd educated me, God wanted me to flee like Joseph had from Potiphar's wife, leaving Sophie mired in guilt so we wouldn't multiply it together.

Call me a bleeding-heart sucker, but that's fucking batshit. Desperately, I rambled about her sweetness, filling the air with evidence she was still wonderful, going back to the day she'd let a lonely freshman invent algae characters with her.

Her reddened face twisted like something wasn't adding up. We both knew I was supposed to be appalled. Yet all my training, from Hell fear to lust shame, kept crumbling before one fact: *Me like lady.*

"Your bubblegum's perfect to me," I said, before realizing bubblegum's squishy pinkness was why youth pastors chose it for sex parables. "Personality-wise."

I offered a pinkie, and she hooked it.

"Please be honest," she said, trying to tolerate being loved. "If you'd known, you wouldn't have kissed me."

"How honest?"

"Brutally."

So I pulled her into a sloppy face-smash. She squawked, "I have snotface, psycho!"

While wiping mess off both our faces, she laughed for real. *Hell yes!* Leaning back, she grinned her puffed cheeks and said, "Anyway, how ya been?"

I laughed hard.

But she meant it. Ugh. I shared the gist of my gripes. She said, gentle as a meadow, "Alexa told me patience got you to finally emote. Guess who waits *her* out?"

"Fine, Dr. Phil," I mumbled. "I'm sorry I wasn't there for you during family stuff. You did nothing wrong, dating somebody. I hated you looking happy with the guy I wanted to be, and I had no idea who I was. I've never known. I've always chased the moment when I don't gotta be me anymore. I hate ... "

Breathing got difficult. I shook a little. She nodded, soft and seeking. *Ugh, I forgot about her powers.* I reached for her, we crumpled onto carpet, and she bundled herself against my chest, curling her arms like a T-rex.

"I don't think I can be okay without you," we each said.

We brightened, reassessing nostalgia until she laughed, changed CDs, and rummaged for documents hidden years earlier (because I Kissed Dating Goodbye said love letters are evil). I grabbed my backpack and offered a trade.

As Zao snarled about protecting a wingless angel, two hearts thumped through one Further Seems Forever hoodie, finally where it belonged, adorning Sophia Grace Primrose.

"Everybody will think you're dirty," she said, "dating the typical-pastor's-kid niece."

"Everybody will think you're dirtier, dumping the archangel for the demon."

"Me and Jesus love you."

"Me and Jesus love you more."

"No, me and ..." (Etc.)

After I drove home through cartoon comet-hearts and actual rainbows, Mom smiled and said, "If she shaves her head again, you're grounded."

LetsTalkAboutLexBaby (Alexa): god im good at this. say "thank u, matchmaker queen"

xSHARKSWITHRABIESx: YOURE BEAUTIFUL ON THE INSIDE, SIS!!!!!

LetsTalkAboutLexBaby: make me regret trusting u with her, and ill icepick ur dickhole, bro

---

xSHARKSWITHRABIESx: CALL ALEXA! LET'S DO DOUBLE WEDDING!!!!!!

BadBoys5318008 (Amir): dawg first of all good evening and secondly wtf

---

MyPlaceInThisWorld (Josiah): Take care of my baby cousin. That's an order.

xSHARKSWITHRABIESx: WE FIGURED OUT HELL IS FAKE! LUKE 3:6!!!!

MyPlaceInThisWorld: Incredibly reckless statement, Isaac.

---

xSHARKSWITHRABIESx: I LOVE YOU MY FRIEND!!!!

hearitinmyghost (Bobbi): goddammit ... 9/11 happened again??

---

g00dbyeskyharb0r (PG): gang back together for realsies????? ʕ⊙ᴥ⊙ʔ

xSHARKSWITHRABIESx: YES WE ADORE YOU SO MUCH!!!

g00dbyeskyharb0r: tell me mah fren, among todaysz spiritual breakthrus, which was most wonderful???

xSHARKSWITHRABIESx: THE ANSWER'S OBVIOUS!!!

---

xSHARKSWITHRABIESx: BOOBS ALMOST!!!

BigDog699999999999 (Best Caleb): describe

BigDog699999999999: hurry

xSHARKSWITHRABIESx: ARE YOU TYPING ONE HANDED!!!!!

BigDog699999999999: r u not

Everyone will love our Very Nice Calvinist opinions, our brains are completely fixed, and we'll be together forever. Seriously, what could bring me dow– My phone rang.

"Sounds like we're both in the spotlight," Eli chuckled. "Mom said you swiped Jack's niece from an elder's son? All eyes on you, chief! Anyway, just got awesome news. I'm the full-time youth pastor responsible for your whole crew."

Eww. Or, actually, what an opportunity! I'll fix Eli with the power of love, equipping the superior evangelist to fix everybody! "Hey, did you ever hear Miss Esther's ideas about Hell?"

"Crackpot."

"Oh."

"Everybody-goes-to-Heaven Universalism is feel-good BS for desert weirdos. I wrote college papers on it being shot down for centuries, even though tender hearts fall for heretics like George MacDonald swaying the freaking Narnia guy astray. Seriously, those wackos want Hitler in Heaven!"

"Oh."

"If anybody I'm responsible for spreads that crap, I'll get fired for beating their ass. Anyway, did Mom ever give you the sex talk?"

What a transition. I realized, "Wait, *you're* gonna give me the talk? Too late. I've demolished my don't-touch-anybody card."

"Congrats, Don Juan," he grunted. "Here's the speech: I know they tell you virginity's sacred, but the Bible's sex rules have nothing to do with troublemakers fooling around. Plus, I'm realistic. Things will happen. Don't get anybody pregnant, but don't waste all day frustration-humping like you're sneaking it past God. Efficiently getting each other's little rocks off, wham bam, over and done ..."

I held my breath, in awe as always.

"... will free up time for clearer-minded evangelism."

Nobody warned me I'd feel love in my skull. It was like waking up with my brain tied to balloons. Potent and vivid minutes flashed past.

Painted toes rested on my dashboard as we memorized Relient K's "Gibberish." The first chance we got, hands beelined into shorts. (Guilt followed.)

At church, I became prayer-requests-gossip subject number one. *Sexiest danger man!*

At least her parents liked me, maybe because I gave them business handshakes and could adequately discuss the Buffalo Sabres. Her dad handed me maps, quizzed me on traffic routes, and wrote, "I'm supposed to be cleaning my gun, to scare you into behaving. It's already clean."

No longer advising the Calebs against touching themselves, I was instead sharing all my lady-parts knowledge: "It's just like Diablo II. Click the button until something kabooms." (Surreal experience: teaching that to Sophie, who'd never dared to try. Massive guilt, pride, and everything in between.) Jay-Z's "Sunshine."

xSHARKSWITHRABIESx: save file back to you

MyPlaceInThisWorld (Josiah): We declared war on Gandhi??

xSHARKSWITHRABIESx: he took our uranium!

MyPlaceInThisWorld: So? We have plenty. He's Gandhi.

xSHARKSWITHRABIESx: its the principals

Video Games Church grew every week, and at 9:45, we shooed people out (leading to double guilt, because the two ranking Bible-knowers definitely shouldn't round third base). We were still wary about teaching Very Nice Calvinism to anyone in Eli's youth group.

Me and the Calebs tried junkyard paintball, highway bumper cars, technically drug-dealing, and TP'ing a principal's house, recording everything on semi-stolen camcorders (all guilt-free). Me and Sophie were alone for nine minutes. (Guilt. But we started talking about it. She craved affection despite knowing shame would follow, while I worried I was Gabe's sequel. To stop sinning, we "broke up," then watched a movie. Success. For seventy-four minutes.)

Every August day: drive to Pizza Hut, the church parking lot, a random Caleb's house, and Taco Bell, bumping into a dozen equally aimless friends along the way.

When the ladies formed a baking club, Alexa learned about my freshman crushes on an atheist lesbian and a senior pretend-dating Josiah. She laughed so hard, Mom shared every embarrassing Isaac fact. (Sophie play-consoled me downstairs, and soon, guilt stuff happened.) Grits, "My Life Be Like."

MyPlaceInThisWorld (Josiah): If I give Gandhi all our gold, will he stop nuking us?

xSHARKSWITHRABIESx: see we shouldve laid low

Senior-year uniform: whatever was still mine. All girls borrow boy clothes, but dating an Avril Lavigne fan meant enduring identity theft. At school, I emerged in rumors about someone befouling "that dickhead pastor's niece." *How crass. It's about time.*

One morning, I noticed a singing crowd. Oh, right, See You at the Pole. A fired-up freshman wailed, "We'll shine the gospel into that liberal cesspool." *Man, who programmed these kids' heads?*

Apparently, Church Dynasty boyfriends must attend discipleship conferences, AKA take-this-nation-for-Christ camps minus any actual camping. Sophie physically removed some woman's hand from my knee, because men aren't the only creepily huggy church adults.

We took the whole gang to concerts like Between the Buried and Me, PG's coffee-shop Phantom of the Opera, and Five Iron Frenzy's breakup tour. For Sophie's first-ever actual Halloween, she was Frodo, and I was Sam. (Hobbit snuggling led to human guilt.)

xSHARKSWITHRABIESx: on a 1-10 scale, Dude Horniness is either 8 or 9 at all times, but she goes from sub-0 to GET OVER HERE. its awesome!!! we gotta stop

BadBoys5318008 (Amir): much you are discovering, padawan

When Sean Hannity freaked out about jelly bracelets supposedly being sex things, Sophie ditched hers, so Alexa started wearing twice as many. We got watched closely at church, but hid by volunteering in the nursery even though toddler chaos annoyed her. I learned I love goofing off with kids. She and I snuck out of Harvest Season, ranked national parks to visit, and generated guilt after our lists matched. MxPx's "Do Your Feet Hurt?"

I started closing shop at Pep Boys, which pushed my non-school-night curfew to eleven, plus whatever I could negotiate for being wholesome enough to date a pastor's niece. Sophie's parents, spooked by two of her older sisters rebelling, essentially gave up on parenting. Sophie made me eat vegetables she'd gardened and sang Kelis' "Milkshake" while I made her shitty van less hazardous. (And then I explained that song's lyrics, leading to van-based guilt.)

Every month, she had a new research fixation. I once listened, while playing Madden, to every fact about Joan of Arc. One day, from under her mattress, she revealed library contraband: a scholarly commentary on Bible romance. We tee-heed at academic explanations of boob metaphors, but gawked when the professor argued Song of Songs 5:1–6's shove-your-hand-into-my-wet-hole couple ... wasn't married. Taking the Bible literally, we play-wrestle 69'ed. When we sat up, she said, "I think I'm dirty, but I know I'm adored." Feeling daybreak, I said, "You can only pick one. Say it." She admitted, "adored," and made me answer, too. It physically hurt to call myself beloved. We tested our anti-guilt mantra with some winner-gets-head Mario Kart, then drove to the hills and shouted Queen's "Who Wants to Live Forever?" at the clouds, convinced we'd become invincible.

Doing Saturday shit like driving to Ohio just to take one inside-joke Polaroid, then returning without telling anyone we'd left the neighborhood, we were dirt-broke immortal, both called "baby girl" by our favorite graveyard-shift diner waiter, who considered himself "the mother hen of night owls." New Found Glory's "I Don't Want to Miss a Thing."

Every night, by the time I made it home, fifteen dudes who'd gathered each other from jobs at various Applebee'ses were quoting the Pork Chop Sandwiches video on my enormous couch. *If Heaven isn't exactly this forever, I'll take my business elsewhere.* Saviour Machine's "Love Never Dies."

School remained boring. *WTF, December already?*

Miss Esther died of cancer, age eighty-eight.

At her funeral, old people gathered in her barn and sang sacred harp music, a cappella mountain hymns. Timmy hugged me on his grandma's porch, whispering, "There's no such thing as an ending."

Beside her casket, Pastor Jack preached, "Miss Esther would surely ask you to speak with a counselor urgently, to avoid the lick of eternal flame."

In his entourage stood Eli. Rare status for a youth pastor, especially a lowborn divorcee. Evidently, I'd missed a lot during my season of potent and vivid minutes.

Afterward at dinner, Sophie worked up the nerve to semi-challenge Eli to an eggheaded debate about the Trinity's composition. As their jargon sailed over my head, he refused to yield an inch, predicting her arguments like Matt Damon in Good Will Hunting.

Either stimulated or exasperated, she asked, "Aren't you ever curious, though? It's supposed to be a mystery!"

"I know that I know that I know," he said. "I'm certain."

And around that time, she and I became months away from parting again, this time forever. God removed State from her list of colleges, but had still never spoken to me.

THIRTY
NO ONE EVER REALLY DIES

DECEMBER 2003

03:00

"It's so dark out here. Set your phone to military time, dickfart."

"Guzzle my gooch, butt-horn," Caleb replied in my passenger seat, digging through Wal-Mart bags. "Crap, we forgot duct tape."

04:00

Another Wal-Mart run, with the Clipse's "Grindin'" on loop. Taco Bell on the way there. And back.

05:00-06:00

We infiltrated the nearly finished new sanctuary and hustled through darkness onto the stage in Jack's soon-to-be throne room.

We were scheming to affix Miss Esther's shawl to the ceiling. Like enshrining a basketball legend's retired jersey. Like claiming Jack's bigass abomination in the name of Miss Esther's Very Nice Calvinism (my sentiment, at least, but not Caleb's).

The plan: Let a balloon lift her thin garment up into the rafters, then yank a long piece of yarn, hopefully popping the balloon but leaving the shawl up there, thanks to Gorilla tape.

Well, the yarn tumbled down, but the balloon didn't pop, so we scurried for equipment. After endless hours at that compound — Sundays, Wednesdays, holidays, camps, lock-ins, scavenger hunts, odd jobs, mischievous loitering, etc. — I knew where to find a BB gun in the old building.

"Try aiming at the bright pink thing," Caleb said, his flashlight illuminating the new sanctuary's cavernous ceiling as my BBs doinked off rafters. "That's what your mom told me. Hey, don't you feel anti-Semitic for thinking Hitler's in Heaven?"

"Jews think Hell's bullshit, dumbass."

As Caleb recited the Jews-are-wrong-about-how-God-works-now argument, my assistant chimed in: **"Hey buddy, you're being pretty obstinate, aren't you? Let's say Caleb's wrong, even though he's right. You'd still regret risking your friendship by sowing discord, wouldn't you? TTYL!"**

So I interrupted Caleb's speech with, "Fine, maybe Hitler's in Hell for a billion-kajillion years. C.S. Lewis said Hell is basically purgatory."

"Oh, now C.S. Lewis is Jesus?"

"No, Aslan the Lion is Jesus."

"Idiot, you let your ex-girlfriend slobber Catholicism into you. Catholics aren't Christians."

"A thousand years ago, they would've killed you for saying *you* are," I said, summarizing a half-remembered Sophie rant. "And whatever, Catholics love Hell. Dante was Catholic!"

"That book rocks my face off," he said while drawing flashlight pictures on the ceiling.

"Metal. So dark. Dude, I can't aim if you keep wanking the flashlight."

"Oh, am I leading you astray? Sucks, doesn't it, Hell-denier?"

07:00

Mission successful. Happy-go-lucky custodian Björn saw us celebrating by pointing skyward like Sammy Sosa, then joined in, assuming we were saluting Jesus.

Returning the BB gun, I got caught by seen-it-all secretary Miss Stacie. She grumbled, "I don't wanna know. Gimme a hug, then scram."

"Boys, why'd we leave the house while it was still dark on the last day of finals?" Mom said on speakerphone as I drove Caleb to his school.

"Mourning Miss Esther," he said, wiping tears.

08:00-11:00

School. Early release!

12:00-1700

"You and Sophie will feel like a-holes when people get damned for listening to you," Caleb said as we played Grand Theft Auto. "You'll be like, 'My b, Jesus. We humped each other into thinking your sacrifice was pointless.'"

"You're pointless, except for your four-pointed skull."

"I'm dead serious," Caleb said, launching a speedboat over a bridge. "You're telling people in a burning building they don't need water because the fire's imaginary!"

"What if there's more to Christianity than eternal l–"

"More than eternity? Dawg, I failed algebra, but you're the math idiot. How come you never say any of this to Eli?"

18:00

I checked on Miss Esther's sweater before strutting past pageant rehearsals, making sure everybody remembered I was protesting Jack's Christmas. Because he was a warmonger and/or uncool.

19:00

Ignoring Eli's boring sermon, I drew red staplers on Sophie's Chucks.

20:00

At Pizza Hut, I bragged to easily impressed sophomores about Operation: Sweater. Sophie rolled her eyes, half-expecting to be the one blamed for it.

One sophomore named Sanctity Grace liked her nickname because she believed it protected boys from "thinking a sin word," presumably "Titty." As a freshman, I would've found that thoughtful (and fallen in love, thereby sinning). As a senior, I wished she could just enjoy how fun it was to say "Sanky."

21:00

"People whisper about me anyway," Sophie said in the makeout parking lot, "so I imagine making them watch me earn whispers. I imagine us getting caught doing stuff on stage at church. There. Out-pervert that."

"Two chicks at the same time, man. They're both you."

"Eww. Wait, I got a dirtier one!"

"Wanna do stuff in the new baptismal?"

"Never mind, you win."

Oh. Finally, I confessed the previous summer's baptismal befouling.

"Sorry," she said. "I judged."

"There wasn't water in it, at least."

"Tap water's not special anyway. Jesus was baptized in a river. Genesis 1:2 means ocean water is the holiest. So deep, mysterious, dark ..."

"Nerd."

"Shut up! Get over here."

22:00

Alexa's empty car sat beside Sophie's curb.

"What's your wife do until you're home?" I asked.

"Sits on my computer, typing cuss words. Or talks to my folks. She cried because Mom called her the tallest Primrose sister. Big ol' softie."

"Then, once you walk inside, underwear pillow-fight time?"

"Ooh, kissing practice and everything! Just like your sneaky adventures with Caleb."

"That was for Miss Esther."

"Hey, call me when you get home tonight. I wish I could hold your hand out there. It's gonna be so dark."

23:00

Mom was texting her latest semi-boyfriend goodnight as Eli walked in. He poured cereal and grunted, "Youth ministry's bullcrap." *LOL, now we're cooking!* She swatted his arm so hard, he giggled.

"I work eighty hours a week on side quests," he said, pretend-flinching away from her. "Sorry, I'm not nagging sixteen-year-olds about shorts when it's ninety degrees! 'Hey Eli, forget your day off, today's the old-folks potluck.' Pastor Jack wants me hyping summer camp all year and posting stupid videos, so lonely boys wanna come meet counselor girls."

That made me remember being a lonely 13.9-year-old, when one smile from seventeen-year-old Sara Beth had made me believe God was finally directing my path.

"Church camps are just bug spray, guitar, and Fear Factor stunts," Eli ranted. "How corny am I, trying to do quiet-storm-radio youth-pastor voice? Ooh, carry this fire, y'all, even though you turds are planning to go pee on the Target once it's dark. Girl, let's sing 'I Could Sing of Your Love Forever' literally forever. Ooh baby, Republican Supreme Court, yeah ..."

I died laughing. Apparently, Jack wanted Eli to have Timmy's attendance-boosting personality, but also a version of Dave-Tony's law-and-order gimmick. Freshmen weren't afraid to smack Eli's tummy and run away. The grizzly bear was stuck being a teddy bear.

"Isaac, ignore this divorced sadsack," Mom said.

"Let's get going," Eli said. "They say nothing good happens after midnight. That's why we're doing this, actually. C'mon, Dad would've laughed at that!"

As Mom rubbed her temples, Eli looked for backup. I agreed, "He's laughing."

Eli said, "Rhetorically."

MIDNIGHT

Tired-giddy, Mom sang "Shining Star" in the car.

"Ricardo the drama minister, that guy's incredible," Eli rambled while driving. "He's working on a skit about Jesus saving this girl from STDs, anorexia, and killing herself. It's set to some band called Lifehouse. Makes 'em bawl. Really feels so dark, like she's in constant immortal danger. Which she is, because everybody is."

Entertained by his boundless grumpiness, I asked for his personnel assessments, none of which felt like gossip because he'd said them all face-to-face. Sophie: "Spacebrain." PG: "Frustrating." Alexa: "Unsaved." Calebs one through five: "Duds." Me: "Distracted." Himself: "Half-assed." Best/Worst Caleb: "Potential."

01:00

Isaac Siena, Sr.
11/20/1959-12/17/1993
Dad, Husband, Handyman

The police report said it'd been exactly ten years, to the minute. I didn't know how I'd feel, seeing that headstone for the first time since elementary school. Eli was quiet, slowly pacing. Mom hummed and arranged lilies. *They say grief's a process. Have I done all of it? Any of it? Am I supposed to feel something? Anything? Ever?*

"It's so dark out here, I worried it'd feel morbid," Mom said, dabbing a tear beneath heavy clouds, "but he was a night owl anyway, like his namesake. Anybody have words?"

"All you, namesake," Eli smiled, patting my shoulder.

Oh man. Deep breath.

"Our father, who art in Heaven," I said, nerves rattling. "That's all."

"Poetic," cheered Mom.

We stood for a long time while she talked to the dirt hiding his abandoned bones.

As Eli and I followed her to the car, he grumbled at me, "Our capital-F Father in Heaven?"

No. I was twisting Jesus' words, daring you to discuss Dad's soul in front of Mom. And you didn't, so I felt victorious. But then you counter-dared me, so I'm imagining an hour-long car ride of arguments, me slamming my little Bible-study brain against your whole Bible-college brain.

So I shrugged.

"The one verse I remember Dad enjoying," he said, "was 'speak the truth in love.' He'd say, 'Truth hurts, lies kill.' Lately, I think I've been afraid to hurt feelings. I've let distractions delay Dad's mission."

Aglow in white lamplight, backed by black branches, Eli said, "Getting eager for summer camps after all. Big crowd like Jack wants, all mine for five nights. Then go old-school shock and awe."

02:00

"Please don't keep Sophie and me alive in pain forever, if we're wrong," I prayed that night with my forehead on my shower floor. "Just erase us."

In my closet, I found a book I'd first read at age six.

The author had experienced a near-death experience at fifteen, being dragged by his arm toward the gates of Hell.

After later becoming a preacher, he'd witnessed an unsaved woman die. Telling the story, he wrote, "She died and went to Hell, crying, 'It's so dark! It's so dark!'"

THIRTY-ONE
MARY, DID YOU KNOW?
CHRISTMAS 2003

In the catacombs under the booming church's parking lot, dozens of rabble-rousers were skipping the pageant, our little protest against Pastor Jack.

The Calebs were debating Lord of the Rings with Sophie, the only person expecting to get in trouble for being down there. She was several minutes into arguing Liv Tyler's Arwen is just as Jesus-y as Gandalf, Frodo, or Aragorn.

"No, the gospel doesn't matter if Jesus didn't resurrect like Gandalf," a Caleb retorted, to echoing cheers. "Liv Tyler's belly button is awesome, but Gandalf's the Jesus!"

"It mattered what Jesus did before dying," Sophie said to higher-pitched cheers. "Just like Arwen — movie Arwen — rescuing Frodo and healing Aragorn before she gave up immortality to unite elves with humans! Jesus and Arwen both did that! To show mortals how to treat each other! His life was more than just the crucifixion!"

Calebs huddled, ultimately agreeing to disagree. Earning a tie while arguing against freaking Gandalf was a win, but I was biased.

"Of course Gandalf's partly Jesus, but being a *whole* Jesus takes a fellowship," she said, tapping her palms and orbiting her thumbs around each other, breaking First Timothy's sexist heart by preaching on church property.

The Calebs lifted me so that my arm could reach out toward cell service. Josiah, spending Christmas with college friends, answered. We all wailed "Christmas Shoes," making up tear-jerkier lyrics because the only non-grandparent who knew the actual words was our Simba. From the choppy speaker, he said, "Dumbest thing that's ever made me cry."

We lit candles, exchanged priceless garbage from thrift stores, and nominated PG, our lead vocalist, to deliver the Christmas story. She read Mother Mary's one-girl-army declaration of joyful war.

"'My soul glorifies the Lord ..."

Throughout the tunnel where she'd won Paintball War, her strong-sweet voice echoed.

"'... He has brought down rulers from their thrones, but has lifted up the humble. He has filled the hungry with good things, but has sent the rich away ... empty.' Wait, Mary said that? Since when?"

It's a disorienting moment, when you realize the Christmas story you've read a hundred times has always included, hidden in plain sight, an anarchist manifesto. Eyes turned toward our ranking bookworm.

"You guys know how so much of the Bible seems to say wealth is bad, but we're told those parts are metaphors?" Sophie said, grabbing my hand for backup. "You're not crazy. The Bible says wealth is bad."

We looked up, like we could see through dirt, at a sprawling compound's parking lot full of SUVs with Fox News bumper stickers.

PG, still staring at the Bible in her mittens, said, "So that's why pageant Mary never gets any lines?"

BigDog699999999999 (Best Caleb): we gotta stop trashing everything we believe

xSHARKSWITHRABIESx: wut?

BigDog699999999999: mocking christmas. hating the greatest country. griping about everything. what about our church's food banks? missions? saving souls?

BigDog699999999999: guess you never actually cared

xSHARKSWITHRABIESx: fuck you. ive cared as hard as i possibly CAN

xSHARKSWITHRABIESx: hop in your masturbation-fueled car and fight me

BigDog699999999999: whoa dang dude easy

xSHARKSWITHRABIESx: everybody says i have a doubtful spirit and need to TRUST HARDER and im corrupting the pastors niece and blahblahblah

xSHARKSWITHRABIESx: if im not somebody else yet, its not for lack of fucking effort

xSHARKSWITHRABIESx: wanna play nba street

BigDog699999999999: busy. giving your mom da slam dunkalicious

---

Mom told me to spend Saturday ranking six college preferences so that we could assemble applications. It was the most we'd ever talked about school.

1. *State. Duh. Fifty minutes away, balanced between leaving and not leaving. Got columns, trees, trumpets, bars, squirrels, chants, ice cream, etc. Great program for my major. What's my major?*
2. *Miami, near where they filmed Wild Things.*
3. *San Diego State, where they filmed Bring It On.*
4. …

I searched MapQuest, made an MS Paint map, shot three BBs, and listed colleges accordingly. Done. It took nineteen minutes, mostly spent waiting on the printer.

Then Mom added the Christian college Eli and half the Church Dynasty had attended. That's the school I spent time researching. *The student manual regulates hugs? Rejected.*

I sensed that I was lucky to only be slightly pressured to attend there, since church kids are often heaved toward it or its bigger counterparts like Liberty ("DC Talk met there" was how it'd always been pitched to me), Hillsdale (no rap-rock groups whatsoever), or Bob Jones (LOL factor: earning a "BJU" degree).

xSHARKSWITHRABIESx: did you read that article yet

LetsTalkAboutLexBaby (Alexa): of course not

xSHARKSWITHRABIESx: it says girls cant sue that school over assaults. is that normal

LetsTalkAboutLexBaby: wtf we cant let sophie go there

xSHARKSWITHRABIESx: we cant let sophie go there

LetsTalkAboutLexBaby: jinx!

LetsTalkAboutLexBaby: diet coke!

And I kept Googling.

Apparently, schools like this opposed racial integration into the freaking '80s. Aha, they were friends with the people who made school prayer a controversy in the '60s and discovered abortion was bad in the '70s.

Why don't we learn any of this in church? We pretend our ideas were set in stone 2,000 years ago, even though things changed within Mom's lifetime!

And I read what white Christians, the ones who'd molded the men who'd molded me, had said during the Civil Rights Movement.

And I found MLK quotes very different from the dreamy go-tos. Like: "Any religion that professes to be concerned about the souls of men and is not concerned about the slums that damn them, the economic conditions that strangle them, and the social conditions that cripple them is a spiritually moribund religion awaiting burial."

And I realized this: Some of the verses interpreted to justify sexism had long been interpreted by Protestants and Catholics to justify enslavement.

WTF, man. Mary, did you know? When you called for the last to be first, that it'd somehow be used against the last?

THIRTY-TWO
CONTROL

FEBRUARY 2004

"REMEMBER WHEN I BROKE INTO YOUR UNCLE'S OLD HOUSE?" I ASKED AGAIN.

She nodded, showing me her doodles of an overalls-clad Athena bursting through Zeus' skull and flying away on a giant owl. (She'd learned more about my half-Greek heritage than I had. I countered by depicting her ancestors' Scottish mythology: a drunk golf ball.)

We were watching football on Pastor Jack's big new couch. After years of competing against the Super Bowl, he'd compromised, rescheduling Sunday night service to take place before kickoff.

"Church Dynasty" had been just a joke, but with traveling musicians, sub-pastors, and a billion other button-ups in that house, it fit.

After the national anthem, Jack lifted a hand — interrupting back-slapping, roared stories, and rafter-shattering laughter — and prayed for "your protection around all our brothers in Iraq, Father God. Not just American servicemen …"

Whoa! He's praying for Muslims!

" … but also Iraqi Christians suffering the Caliphate persecution headed America's way."

Sike.

Anyway, I was supporting Carolina with an old Charlotte Hornets shirsey, because after Tom Brady's bullshit against my semi-beloved Raiders, I'd root for James Dobson over the Patriots. Sophie, a lapsed Bills fan, repped Carolina with sky-blue streaks in her dyed-black hair.

Someone's farts-and-elbows nephews climbed on me. She said I could shoo them, but they were the only beings there I understood.

We were busy dodging questions from adults. "Youth ministry," I answered, whenever asked about life plans. She kept claiming she'd major in Home Ec at Dynasty U, though I whispered that she shouldn't even joke about going there.

That night, the follow-up question adults asked me was whether Brady could win again. "No, the Panthers have the better punter and kicker."

But the follow-up they asked Sophie had her saying, "After college, I'll grow here where I'm planted, raising my successful husband's many children."

She was telling people what they wanted to hear — the churchier the girl, the more frequently she's asked when she'll start birthing missionaries — but it still sucked that her answer didn't include me. Successful?

"You had such flawless Judy Garland hair," squalled the queen of the blonde trophy wives, xenomorph-smiling in Sophie's face. "Don't you worry about the type of males you'll attract by damaging it? At least no more Sinead O'Connor meltdowns!"

With ruby-red lips and smoke-ringed eyes like the Distillers' lead singer, Sophie's face was already a sarcastic-punk reaction to church women urging her toward makeup. They were always so comfortable competing for attention, satisfied with un-weirdness, and confident they'd never need different modes, unaware their speckled sheep might bite somebody.

I told the Smiler, "I like her hair."

The Smiler studied me, surprised that I existed. "I meant husband-type males, not high school sweethearts," she said, squeezing my shoulder like she owned it before whirling to machine-gun laugh at men howling stories about outwitting atheist car salesmen.

"She's jealous," I said. "You aren't stuck dying your hair the only color old guys like. Yellow's overrated."

Sophie growled, "How dare she treat you ..."

Dynasty members believed things about me. Some still suspected I'd turned Josiah gay on the beach. They whispered about Dad's contagious legacy and Mom's tragic singleness — because I wasn't Eli, who'd "overcome" that stuff. And Sophie had gone from repeating sermons in gray turtlenecks to yammering with her hands about the Kabbalah at my Bible study, where we led church oddballs astray. People believed she must've dumped Dynasty prince Gabe in a demonic lust frenzy. (Ridiculous. The lust frenzy involved Bible verses.)

As more Smilers descended, I looked for backup. Sophie's introvert parents were inching outside. Eli was bellowing, "Wrong, America was founded on lackadaisical Deism, not Christianity," at four guys who'd become his brimstone sidekicks. *Help.*

Just in time. Shimmying through the door was drama minister Ricardo, acting all the way up while various Gene Hackmans clapped his shoulders and quoted his every zinger. They loved him performing Ex-Gay Theater Guy, but only if he swore he'd die alone. Charming his way around, he called my purple child's-XXXL shirt spicier than his velvet blazer and make Sophie glow: "My gosh, she's 'Just Like a Pill' Pink!"

The halftime show started with Beyonce and Frodo urging us to make serious choices (Jessica Simpson screamed, "Choose to party"). Church men guffawed as Ricardo danced to Nelly.

"Is that a real piercing in your nose? My son's nineteen, but easily intimidated," another Smiler asked Sophie, leaning over our couch. *Gah, was this the pressure on Eli's eighteen-year-old wife, on Sophie a year ago?* Kidnapping her from Dynasty U started to seem like my calling.

Two other women smiled questions at Sophie, encouraging her to wear thirty-seven pieces of Christian flair and sample guys who were versions of Gabe. If I made a peep, it'd confirm everything they thought about me. *Somebody do something!*

And Ricardo yelped at the TV, "Sweet cheeses, a naked titty!"

Huh. Accurate.

Somebody screamed, "Hell in a hand-basket!" Somebody dropped a punch bowl, scaring the nephews. Two babies were crying. Bundles was barking. A deacon's hand was bleeding.

"Turn that crap off!" roared Pastor Jack from the kitchen. "Children can see! I shouldn't have compromised with this dirtbag world! Anyone with concern for this nation, follow me to our sanctuary! Mama, let's roll!"

Assembling emergency church was his latest gimmick. During the scramble toward the driveway, I worried I'd die if I couldn't laugh out loud soon.

"Such a shame what that woman on TV did, huh?" said the Queen Smiler in Sophie's ear.

In the street, Sophie gritted her teeth. "Justin monster-trucking Timberlake did it! So now my OshKosh B'goshdarn husband-type boyfriend's taking me to watch our mud-or-fudge-ing Panthers at … at," she shuddered her fists, "at Hooters!"

We'd once waited thirty minutes at TGI Friday's instead of taking two open seats at the bar, hesitant to be seen among drinkers. Now we were squeezed into the bar at a restaurant I believed to be a brothel.

"I like our waitress," said Sophie, sitting tall, wanting to be seen on a dirtbag's lap in a den of iniquity. "Kyrsta flirts with single guys, but doesn't look at you, 'cause she's my new friend."

The man beside us snorted, "Like she's sincerely asking how to copy your Joan Jett hair? You're the mark, sweetie. She knows he won't tip if you're jealous."

Sophie, crunching carrot sticks, glared until he grinned into his beer. "Ize, this Patriots fan said Kyrsta's hiding her love for you. Guess this is goodbye."

"Sorry, all things end. Except you called me husband-type."

"That b-word hated it!"

The Patriots fan groan-laughed. Waving from her fake nose ring to her fishnets peeking beneath cuffed jeans, he said, "Typical pastor's-kid rebellion."

He explained his second ex-wife once dragged him to church, where Sophie had stood up front in red curls. Warning her against following pastors' kids who rebelled too hard, he rambled disastrous stories while leaning on me all drunk-mopey. *Am I just a rebellion thing?*

"Pastor's *niece,*" she said.

Our Panthers tied it with a minute left, surely meaning overtime, a delayed end. In mere months, college would be the end of all things, unless ...

"How husband-type are we talking?" I asked. She always could've chosen somebody holier than me. But her smokey eyes proved she could've also chosen somebody way unholier than me. *Am I ENOUGH of a rebellion thing?*

"Dude, don't propose at Hooters," honked the ever-drunker Patriots fan. "What are you two, eleven?"

"This guy's got love advice?" she shouted, making his friends hoot. "Focus on your team losing, sir."

"Oh yeah? Make a bet. Panthers win, you say yes. He ain't joking, cutie."

His friends goaded her. She looked at me, wide-eyed. My face maybe said: *I was, but ... go Panthers*?

"Deal," said the center of attention, more comfortable around strangers than her own Dynasty. "Patriots win, you tip my homie Kyrsta double."

Mugs clinked together, beer and Mountain Dew.

"We're gonna win, boo," she said, leaning back. "Bars are rad. I see why Jesus partied with big-time lowlifes like us."

"Under control, boo," I said, arms around her. "We got the better punter and better kicke– … ah, shit."

Carolina's kickoff went out of bounds, setting up New England's game-winning score. Our friend kept his word, despite rambling about love being fake. Sophie dug my wallet from my pocket and paid, pretend-feministly.

"By not looking at you," she said, watching confetti on TVs, "Kyrsta acknowledged a choice I made. I chose not to court some fake-holy dillweed. She sees me as just another person, not a floofy princess or pastor's-kid time bomb." Mythology sketchbook in one hand, my hand in the other, she said, "Maybe I'll keep making choices."

She bought us exit music and flipped to the J discs.

"Please take Dynasty U off your college list forever," I said.

"Me and Josiah always wanted to go to the same school," she sighed, "but I think he's miserable there. Maybe I would be, too."

"State it is, then?"

"College with you is my dream," she said, trying to convince at least one of us it could happen. "I just gotta discern whether God wants me there …" or the women's college far away, where she'd also been accepted, and where the patriarchy couldn't decide who she'd become. Sounded awesome, except I was in the patriarchy.

As we stepped outside, Janet Jackson sang about being seventeen, about being controlled.

THIRTY-THREE
ACQUIRE THE FIRE

FEBRUARY 2004

On the youth group's right side sat my ragamuffin family, an authentic first-century Video Games Church. We rolled our eyes whenever someone played Rich Mullins' "Awesome God" again, but we blasted Mullins' songs about Jesus being too poor for things like car stereos. At school, we made sure to snort loudly when fundies asked if Gilgamesh copied Noah, not that we knew the answer. Our stance on abortion was vague, fluid, and very Sun Tzu. Our Anti-Flag stickers and Psalters patches would've impressed Thomas Merton.

On the left sat the cymbal-clanging goodie-goodies who always worshiped with one eye open, spying to see who wasn't worshiping with both eyes closed. (I saw them.) They prayed for "this nation," ignoring El Salvador, Iceland, and Azerbaijan due to jingoism, a word I knew because I was in the world, as Jesus commanded. Their Bible performances happened at a park, allegedly so they could avoid electronic distractions, but really so they could be seen, we discerned. They used the terminology of old people, who were bad, except ones I liked.

Between our sides were kids who maybe paid attention to Eli, maybe partied on Fridays, and sometimes kissed, fence-sitters who never weighed in on which side featured better Christians.

And then there was Sophie, who had to appease both sides, and Caleb, who just grew closer and closer to Eli.

Nine hours before the lock-in at the go-karts arcade, we saw The Passion of the Christ. Reviews included Caleb saluting, one kid puking, and Sophie complaining yet again about Hollywood diverging from source material. I kept laughing about Mel Gibson's Satan having a Mini-Me, which was more fun than remembering the good news: Romans flayed Jesus' ribmeat because seventeen-year-olds did hands-in-pants stuff behind a putt-putt brontosaurus 1,974 years later.

At 5 a.m., we learned that the overnight battle of the bands' Guitar Center gift certificate wouldn't go to PG's latest emocore band, !AndCountTheStars(ThenOpenFire)!. Also not winners: the Toby Mac cover rapper, country girl singing about geography, eight-dude prog band that'd spent its set explaining its own lore, Rebecca St. James interpretive puppeteer, or electronica guy who'd pushed one laptop button (for Jesus).

The winners were stupid-hatted funk-jazz dweebs who sang two words: "Got faith?"

Fuck, that does it. Church is officially too dorky. Eli chuckled into a mic, defusing the boos. He paid up on some bet, letting sophomores shave his beard, then sent everybody out for hot dogs.

"Is Eli, like, cool?" asked a nearby junior.

"At least he doesn't do secular bonfires," shrugged a sophomore.

The herd filed back toward laser tag, grabbing unlit candles from a table by the door. But Eli pulled me and Caleb into a huddle with some brimstone-sidekick dads.

"Men, a couple helpers fell asleep, so you gotta step up," he said, handing us black bundles of cloth. *Ugh, I'm not here to work. A robe and a Scream mask, like those goofy-ass nail buckets at freshman camp? Fine, whatever. I'm an adult, according to movie theaters.*

Eli lit one candle, handed it to me, and whispered instructions to Caleb. We followed my brother into the black-lit room floor full of dark-neon kids in bright-neon clothes. Through the mask, I couldn't distinguish faces.

"It's 6 a.m., boys and girls," Eli roared, snapping almost everyone to attention.

Oh, this'll be so corny. Some kids snickered. In the mirrored walls, I saw my orange fire and Scream mask differently than 13.9-year-old me had seen confession bucket reapers. *What a dumb kid I was!*

"You have a choice to make," Eli growled, silencing the snickerers. "Are you in? Or are you out?"

He couldn't save this silly garbage until summer camp, after I've graduated from youth-group theatrics forever?

"I'd be a poor steward if I only oversaw rock music, hot dogs, and

Spider-Man's-like-Jesus dogcrap," he yelled. "Let's get serious, fast. I need you to understand consequences. You either accept the entire truth, or none of it."

Fortunately, this mask means nobody knows I'm participating.

"My helper, Brother Isaac, has the only lit candle ..."

Goshdammit.

"... which represents gospel salvation: John 3:18. Students with unlit candles, you're representing Hell-bound flesh: Matthew 23:33. If our missionary can light your candle, you're saved: Romans 6:23. Once you're saved, you're blood-bound to spread that fire: Revelation 2:11."

Some kids jostled for sitting space.

"Lit candle, going to Heaven: Revelation 20:15! Unlit candle, going to Hell: Second Thessalonians 1:9! Three minutes to salvage what you can! Oh, and thank Brother Isaac for the accompaniment. Found this CD his crew left in a church office."

The speakers blasted Demon Hunter's "Screams of the Undead."

Dark-neon faces laughed, lifting candles. I tried to hold mine steady enough, which took forever. Finally, a second light.

"Better get moving," Eli yelled. "Satan sure is."

I handed someone my candle and told them to keep evangelizing while I discarded my stupid costume. *Half-dozen candles lit, not that I care.*

"Two minutes until unlit candles represent Hell-bound souls," Eli roared. "We're on pace to bust Hell wide open!"

Just win the stupid game. Hell fear is for fundie morons.

"Ninety seconds! Heaven or Hell! Choose!"

Murmuring became chattering.

A hand grabbed my arm.

"Light me," some kid yelled, eyes orange-black with firelight.

A scared freshman. And finally, I saw him.

Now do you see what I see?

I see a wretch like me.

"Sixty seconds!" yelled Eli. "Mercy Seat's a-smokin'!"

Calls of "over here." Enough lit candles to distinguish orange-shadow faces. Fireflies flitting from wick to wick. *Freshmen, haunted like I was. Was?*

"Book of life's slamming shut! Thirty seconds!"

Chattering became shrieking. Calls of "hurry." Firefly whirlwind. Lighting candles wasn't enough. A girl screamed. I shoved aside a reaper reaching to snuff one of my souls.

"Twenty seconds! Knock knock, he's here!"

"Eli's wrong about Hell," I whispered at faces, for the first time hissing heresies in the accuser's midst. "Colossians 1:20, everybody will be God's. Ephesians 1:10, everything will be one."

"Five! Four! Three!"

Kids screamed. Faces flashed orange. I'd spent months as a detached senior, too cool to care about church kids.

"One!"

The room burst bright. I was surrounded by children, some giddy, some hiding red eyes.

"About half of you made it," Eli said. "Hey, if only half of humanity went to Hell, we'd be making progress!"

My body deflated as I watched those kids buy it. How could they not?

"YOU STILL DO, AFTER ALL!"

"Can't save 'em all, but we'd better try. Intensity! Purpose! Whether your lost buddies like it or not. Building's burning! Start shoving! Now, if you need to be saved, your gut's begging for it. Meet me by the fountain. If you're saved beyond a shadow of a doubt, stay put for … ugh … laser tag."

In blacklight, some scrambled for guns and vests. Others plodded behind Eli, either weeping or smirking.

Sophie appeared, giggling, "I think I punched Caleb."

"I should've been telling them it's okay to question," I said, feeling an all-consuming need to save kids from fear, far stronger than the need I'd desperately faked as a freshman evangelist. "I can't win a fast-moving argument with Eli. Man, he picks tough verses. What happens if I confront him and lose?"

"Hey," she said, her hands on my face. "Let's walk."

So we spent four hours sneaking around a lock-in, committing the dirtiest sin of all: telling young people God literally loves literally everyone, literally forever. I sidled beside that scared freshman, playing NBA Jam by himself, and asked, "Can I share some good news?"

We gathered seven kids by the air hockey tables, delivering the Gospel of Hell That Maybe Ends Eventually. Four called us deceivers, but three begged to know more. Candle-snuffer Caleb said, "Dare you to keep talking. Eli's coming." We played air hockey.

> xSHARKSWITHRABIESx: damn look whos online.
> how u doin

MyPlaceInThisWorld (Josiah): Honestly? Decent. Maybe done with self-destructive business. My aunt said I was being a Pastor's Kid cliche. Took the fun out of things.

The most exciting thing he'd told me: He'd bought a shitty Taurus, totaled it, walked away, and gone swimming. He said, "Honestly, that relieved something. I know that's stupid." Otherwise, he was evasive, confessing vaguely so that I wouldn't be tempted to emulate him, which I took to mean he'd gotten drunk.

MyPlaceInThisWorld: How about you?

xSHARKSWITHRABIESx: wanting high school to end now/never

MyPlaceInThisWorld: Thinking about helping at our campus church fall semester. Could use help! Might preach Paul. ;-P

xSHARKSWITHRABIESx: fuck paul

MyPlaceInThisWorld: Haha. I'm angry at Paul all the time. But I'm also seeing a guy with an impossible task. The first person who ever had to explain grace! Meanwhile, he had friends to argue with and struggles to fixate on, just like anybody.

MyPlaceInThisWorld: Besides, find me a Roman man besides Paul who considered women co-leaders. Matter of fact, sell me on your no-hell theories without quoting Paul.

xSHARKSWITHRABIESx: >:|

MyPlaceInThisWorld: ;)

xSHARKSWITHRABIESx: im just amazed youre all resolute after what they did to you

MyPlaceInThisWorld: Pffft! I'm no saint. I hope my dad drops dead.

MyPlaceInThisWorld: Isaac I shouldn't have said that to you. I'm incredibly sorry.

xSHARKSWITHRABIESx: its fine

MyPlaceInThisWorld: I don't hope that anyway. That was stupid to say.

xSHARKSWITHRABIESx: you didnt put a hex on him lol

xSHARKSWITHRABIESx: i just meant youre kinda still you, despite all this

MyPlaceInThisWorld: At my lowest, I can't shake the feeling Jesus loves me anyway. Sometimes, He's told me through you and my baby cousin. I disagree with your theories, but know you're seeking with love. You're my favorite people.

xSHARKSWITHRABIESx: come home this summer, dude. mi casa su casa

MyPlaceInThisWorld: Got a better idea. Details TBD. How's the wannabe megachurch?

xSHARKSWITHRABIESx: weird. eli's your dad's righthand man wtf

MyPlaceInThisWorld: Not that weird. They believe the same thing.

xSHARKSWITHRABIESx: what

MyPlaceInThisWorld: Men owe God numbers, no matter the cost.

THIRTY-FOUR
THIS LITTLE LIGHT OF MINE
MARCH 2004

One Sunday a year, the youth pastor filled in during Pastor Jack's semi-vacation. Freshman year, all the kids had cheered for Timmy. We'd even cheered for Dave-Tony sweatily preaching Song of Songs. In 2003, my friends had cheered a Messianic Jewish former dentist whose pet peeve was movies using the word "goddamn."

From a recording played on the new sanctuary's 40.1-foot-wide HumbleTron, Eli was being introduced by Jack, who joked about needing help getting the file to us.

Sophie whispered that her uncle's computer aptitude actually included constantly checking his sermon downloads, "a junkie for stats going up." By then, the internet was full of napalm recipes, LiveJournal photos of me looking swole in 2002, and MP3s of Jack saying the Antichrist was probably an effeminate Frenchman.

"Nobody's more passionate about Christ's commission than Eli Siena," said Jack's video. "I love this rascal like he's my own. When he sported that lion mane, I nicknamed him my Simba."

Ugh. In the 99% finished mega-auditorium, opened a year before the rest of the mega-facility would be completed, seven thousand people applauded. *Yeah, well, I'm still the coolest Siena brother. I've canoodled in that baptismal.*

My brother's big bones looked trim, packed into a suit. Despite having spoken to crowds basically that huge before, like at Beach Fest the previous summer, he kept chuckling nervously. He joked about wishing he'd stayed in real estate, in case God kept blessing Jack's church with land. He thanked the youth group for loving him through "a season of reconciliation," AKA divorce.

He preached from Luke 16.

"The damned rich man shouts: Father Abraham, I'm suffering in fire. Send Lazarus to fetch me water! Abraham says: Nope, you had your chance to avoid Hell. When you were alive, you had scripture."

My brother's deep voice weighed like concrete on the hushed 7,000. *It's a parable, dumbass!* Still, Jesus' story sounded scalded, especially with Eli's grim emphasis.

Dwarfing the pulpit, Eli said, "I'll share another warning from the fire where that rich man still burns, 2,000 years later. Lemme tell you about my hero, who taught me to study, tinker, protect, and always be truthful, even if it hurts. December 17, 1993 ..."

It's not true, so I'm not scared, right? Eli glanced back at the choir, nodding at Mom. She seemed stone-faced, but from the balcony, it was hard to tell. And he told his story. Our father, who art in ...

Hands started touching me. *I'm fine. Nobody buys this pathetic shit, right? Sophie and me told like forty of these seven thousand people that Hell's temporary, and at least a dozen kinda believed it. That's enough to ruin Eli's fear-mongering. Everyone notice how nonchalantly I'm playing Dope Wars?*

The crowd was silent while Eli said, "Daddy cared about people. So right this second, in that torture chamber, he's begging me to warn you."

Stop touching me. This doesn't concern me. Right? First Timothy says God wants everybody saved, right? Wait, First Timothy's the book I reject because it's mean to girls and also a book I stake my soul on? Right.

"Some say the gospel's harsh, dark, and bloody," Eli said, locking his eyes onto faces. "Well, it's infinitely nicer than the alternative. My father's spent ten years, two months, and twenty-six days in conscious separation from light, joy, and security, enduring the opposite, every second, including this one. Once he's been there ten thousand years, he'll face no less time than when he first began. Folks, we can't ignite with purpose unless we acknowledge the stakes. Ready for objective truth?"

People dabbed their eyes and looked away from him.

"I love my family," said the thunder. "I love my mother's toughness, my brother's heart. But family pales before the mission: Luke 14:26. My father's situation is God's will, the consequence of rejecting a gift. So do I believe my hero — along with everyone in this building who chooses the same — deserves Hell?"

Long after his echo, he let silence linger.

"Yes, I believe the kindest person I've ever known will never stop deserving agony."

Congregants gasped at the thing they believed, said out loud. Eli made his side sound ridiculous — but undeniable. The cost of disagreeing with him, if he was right, was infinitely higher than any reward for agreeing with me.

"I know youth pastors quote Keanu Reeves, not Catholic theologians, but here goes," he said, trying comic relief. Nobody laughed. I belted, "HA HA." Sophie squeezed my hand.

"The brilliant Thomas Aquinas said, as citizens of Heaven, we'll 'rejoice in the punishment of the wicked' damned. Believe it or not, we'll consider their suffering 'divine justice,' our 'direct cause of joy.' Joyful or wicked — folks, those are the two choices," Eli said, voice crackling. "Now command your feet to make the choice my wonderful, wicked father didn't."

Instead of asking for heart-yanking hymns, he flashed a palm at the music minister, asking for silence. He then pointed at the altar. *Interesting showmanship. Played the dead-dad card, then threw a curveball. Everybody's surely confused to see a youth pastor playing badass.*

Yet entire pews of teenagers stood, holding hands with heads down. Adults streamed down stairs and up aisles. Someone screamed prayers for a hospitalized relative to accept Christ before it was too late. *Shit, Eli's awesome at this.* Masses gathered, signing up to do anything Jack's church said because the alternative was being boiled alongside Isaac Siena, Sr.

"I'm gonna get called a hard-heart," whispered Jack's niece, who was supposed to lead revivals, not stay seated. "But I'm not leaving you alone after that."

I said the reverse. Going forward to rededicate would've felt like admitting my brother was right, like surrendering my claim to Dad's soul. But staying put would've gotten her judged even harder. So many people mobbed the stage, the crowd swelled near … *oh right, the big-ass sanctuary has hella side doors.*

In labyrinth shadows, she said, "My heart's breaking for everyone who's been taught God's just a huge bully. It's not like Eli *wants* to be certain it's hopeless."

I drove out of town before wondering where we were going, because 6,990-something people had just decided justice had been served for ten years, two months, twenty-six days, and counting.

G00dbyeskyharb0r (PG): if i lose faith

G00dbyeskyharb0r: but still try

G00dbyeskyharb0r: does it count less

G00dbyeskyharb0r: or count twice

xSHARKSWITHRABIESx: is that a lyric

G00dbyeskyharb0r: it is now

xSHARKSWITHRABIESx: u dont do emoticons anymore

G00dbyeskyharb0r: oh right

G00dbyeskyharb0r: (◡ˠ◡) yayy

xSHARKSWITHRABIESx: lol (◡ˠ◡)

G00dbyeskyharb0r: rofl (◡ˠ◡)

Eli was "humbled and encouraged" by how quickly his divorce had blown over. Jack even put him on course to lead the church-planting expansion campaign.

I felt obligated to protect fourteen-year-olds from my brother, but he'd already grown wildly beyond my control. *How was I supposed to stop him anyway? I don't have dirt on somebody who's publicly announced every rule he's ever broken! If I somehow manage to out-Bible him, he'll consider it rational to protect souls by body-slamming me into silence. C'mon, if I complain about a future associate pastor quoting intense Bible verses, I'll be the one in trouble!*

Jack wasn't a fire-and-brimstone guy at heart, but he wanted Christian soldiers to retake America. And maybe that's easier with an attack dog threatening eternal consequences for failure. Because the only thing more important than getting butts into seats is scaring butts into never leaving.

THIRTY-FIVE
BIGGER THAN THE BOOGIE MAN
SPRING BREAK 2004

THE TWELVE-DUDE PROG BAND ASSEMBLED ON MY ENORMOUS COUCH, beginning a 24-hour Gran Turismo race.

I left them, headed to my last-ever church camp, my first as a counselor. I'd found Dad's tattered Randy Savage tank top, faded purple, an heirloom that showed off my semi-swole guns.

"Sup, let's go to camp just like Satan goes to Heaven," I said, lazily trolling Caleb while climbing into his huge truck.

"Dude! Not in front of little kids," he said, again demoted back to Worst Caleb.

We collected six campers named Micah, crammed them behind the front seat, and added five more bonking around in the back.

When "B.O.B." played, one Micah said, "Eww, classic rap" — about a song from 2000 A.D. I surrendered the iPod, and the pipsqueaks found "Jesus Walks," the billionth Christian rap song (though it considered itself the first). I welcomed the nervous newbs how Josiah had once welcomed me, by requesting testimonies.

One 13.9-year-old, a basketball player with a baby mohawk, warbled about having been a vile hellion — breaking hearts, lording debts, spreading false witness, addicted to Surge soda, and hurtling toward damnation — until he'd seen Veggie Tales' Jonah movie. The others amen'd, thanking Jesus for halting the carnage. *Who convinced them the only way to make God sound cool is to call yourself shined-up shit?*

"You were created good, Surge," I told the convert. "Genesis 1. Psalm 139."

"Nuh-uh," said another Micah, adjusting his glasses, "Romans says because of Adam, we're born dead."

"Bible fiiight!" squealed Surge, fists spasming. "Careful, Brother Isaac. We're Bible sword drill champions! I got next!"

I felt a smile splitting my face as my heart broke for those innocent sinners. "Then, Romans says because of Jesus, everyone's alive. I'm a two-time Awana champ dating a five-time Calvinettes champ. You sure you got next, Surge?"

They blinked, then argued like wild. Being a counselor was gonna be fun, and not just because I'd pass along the sacrament of peeing on the Target.

"Back in my day, we debated boobs and farts," Worst Caleb whined. "Now we just hope Isaac runs into somebody even more stubborn."

PG led all forty-two children, armed with water guns, on a hunt for Caleb. The middle-school pastor wasn't there, but we didn't need him. We'd found tons of refrigerated lunchmeat.

Me and Sophie ate lunch last since she was the only legal adult there. Wearing my stolen hat backwards, she rambled about feeling like a failed den mom because the kids had warmed up to PG more quickly. Then she said I'd be a better parent than her, WTF.

"Like, say you and your wife had kids" she said, "and y–",

"Who's this wife who isn't you? You married some seminary guy with male role models and shit?"

She paused. "Boo, when you joke about that stuff, are you actually insecure?"

I shrugged.

She pouted. "Aw. C'mon. Good Christian guy, that's all I'll need."

Time to test those three traits, one by one. "Would you marry a *bad* Christian guy?"

"Eww. Dated one."

"What about a good Christian *girl*?"

"Only if that somehow convinced Josiah to marry a good Christian guy."

"Would you marry a good *non-Christian* guy?"

"Never. Three non-negotiables."

It felt awesome, soaking up sunshine and being pre-qualified for each other.

"Anyway," she giggled, "if Mrs. Siena got some awesome job, I bet you'd love staying home with the kids."

"Sure, home's where I play Madden. Oh, you mean would I ... what do they call it? Wear the skirt?"

She bumped a thigh against mine and said, "What if I find you a teensy-weensy one?"

We scheduled a midnight meeting, snickering about becoming the horny counselors we'd once judged. For me, stuff like swapping clothes was flirty mischief. For her, boy garments granted +10 imperviousness or something. Church people nagged her to "grow outta the tomboy phase," making it us-against-the-world fun. When they demanded my deep thoughts on why I condoned gender rebellion, I was like: *Most boys are dogs, most girls are cats, some people are foxes, and my lady's foxy. Deep, huh?*

"Those boss-husband families are weird," I said. "Even big hairy Eli hated that shit. What's wrong with tag teams? What makes some guy your warrior-pastor-superdad, except at opening jars? Like I know shit about dadding."

She smiled, tracing her finger across the wooden table, writing in mystery languages. *Hope she doesn't want a boss-husband enforcing the Deuteronomy 22:5 patriarchy. The skirt dare was a test I failed! Get manly! Rule women! Attend Reformed seminary!*

"Okay, new one," I said. "Say you and me live in sin ... at, say, State ..."

"Well, speaking of school," she said, smile fading, "after prayerfully considering with all my heart ..."

Fidgeting with bracelets, she was hesitant to tell me her college decision. That made me realize it'd never been a dilemma. The faraway women's college, where one of her favorite religion scholars was a professor, would soon put essentially infinite space between us.

"It's where God's calling me," she stammered. "I feel led. Let go and let God."

"Perfect," I said, swallowing fears of distance, influence, and the boxer-briefs lady discovering things about herself among women. **"BIBLICAL GENDER ROLES AIN'T SO BAD NOW, HUH?"**

She told me how much she needed that place, continually glancing to check my reaction. "God wants me nowhere near this town. I believe God wants us together, but is long-distance too much? You're gonna meet cool college girls who aren't a kajillion miles away. Tell me what God's putting on your heart, okay?"

She'd never stopped deluding herself into believing I was the God-contacting guy she'd always wanted. Her choosing a liberal hamlet over a fratty land-grant wasn't a surprise, let alone one requiring God's introductory consultation with me.

Church couples got married by age twenty, but we'd become suspicious of church tendencies, and marriage wouldn't change the distance anyway. School couples broke up while splitting to different colleges, which also sounded bad. We threw around ideas, but the only options were to end things or to trust in 250 texts per month and cameras that let you AIM shirtlessly. She panicked and blamed herself.

"No stressing over it until the last day of the best summer ever," I said. We pinkie swore.

Then she twinkled. "Speaking of summer! Forever ago, I promised you a road trip. You thought that was only good for Warped Tour '02! Ha! Vandalf and I are hitting national parks and stuff. Josiah's idea! He's buying gas. And more good news! He's transferring to State — heck yes! — so you and him could fly back for fall semester. We'll do Cornerstone Festival, get piercings, hike waterfalls … I'll try weed!" Her hands showed me mountains, music, and stars. "I've done the math. We'll live stupid cheap. Road trip, boo?"

Blown away by everything, especially Josiah fleeing Dynasty U for the same school as me, I squeezed her tight and agreed, "Road trip, foxy." I was eager for a summer full of guys-vs.-Graces prank wars and easily ignored problems.

She smiled at the woods' explosive laughter. "If we survive being the only grownups here."

"God made Adam and Eve, not Adam and Steve," yelled a Micah.

Excellent choice.

Sophie and I had claimed half the kids, and, thanks to walkie-talkies, we knew the other twenty-one were accounted for.

I punted the football high, watching them scramble for made-up points. Standing among them and helping those who couldn't throw it all the way back, she replied, "God made Adam as God's companion, right?"

The kids nodded as she punted the ball toward me.

"God wanted Adam to feel companionship, too, right?"

They nodded.

"God was disappointed when Adam didn't feel it, even though the only figures so far were Adam and God, right?"

They nodded, looking at each other.

"And then what made God sad? Adam shared a sweet time with someone besides God!"

Now watch middle-school imaginations finish the story. They cackled about Eden's "snake shaped like a dingaling" and "fruit that's juicy like yo mama's v-word," imagery acknowledged by scholars and ignored by pastors.

Surge squealed, "Yooo, the reason God didn't make Adam and Steve … is … God *was* Steve?"

"Our God," a Micah sang, "is the gayest God."

"I think God's above being just boy or girl," said Sophie between punts. "The Bible says God's a womb, mommy bird, and girly Spirit. But if the Bible's gotta be about Father God loving guys, that's okay for human guys too, huh?"

She continued. Half the rugrats were awed, while the other half had been conditioned to hear that as Satanism. (One kid ran to pee.)

God being a RuPaul tomboy is Sophie's favorite argument. What's mine? Do I even care anymore?

Kids kept yelling ingrained churchisms for us to debunk, a la MythBusters: "God helps those who help themselves!" "Cleanliness is next to godliness!" "A gate in Jerusalem was named Eye of a Needle, so it's fine to be rich!"

And Surge shouted, "If I'm scared of missing the Rapture, does that mean I'm going to Hell?"

And there it is.

"WAIT."

I dare you to move. Say the words. All of them.

"ISAAC, YOU'VE IGNORED ME OVER AND OVER …"

For weeks now, listening to these kids has meant hearing my younger self, a kid scared of his shadow because it verifies his body obscures light.

"… BUT THIS IS THE BIG ONE."

I'm convinced nobody's sending Surge to Hell. Over my dead body.

"THERE IS NO COSTLIER SIN THAN FOOLING CHILDREN."

But still, I might be wrong about that, the biggest thing imaginable. It's irresponsible to sway kids this impressionable, right?

"DON'T MAKE ME CITE THE VERSE. YOU KNOW THE ONE."

Football in hand, I gulped nerves. I watched preteens bounce beneath a stunning sky. Imagine everything those kids had been taught, plus four incoming years of chasing one flawless set of certainties. They must snuff every doubt while choosing the correct pastor's life blueprint, or else. *How do we stop being guided by fear disguised as mercy?*

Bits of dirt fell away as I turned sun-warmed fake leather in my hands. I pictured Micahs and Mikayla Graces with hearts full of nails and heads full of nightmares.

I could plant a seed and be the senior 13.9-year-old Isaac had needed. It felt worth risking my soul. Because a stiletto knife in my basement proved lives were at stake.

"MATTHEW 18:6, YOU NIHILISTIC WORM. THESE CHILDREN HAVE BEEN TRAINED. IF YOU LEAD THEM FROM THEIR PATH, A MILLSTONE AROUND YOUR THROAT WILL SINK YOUR WRITHING CARCASS FOREVER. LISTEN TO YOUR BODY! IT FEARS CENTURY AFTER CENTURY OF REGRETTING THE 'EVEN IF YOU'RE CORRECT' ARGUMENT YOU'RE FORMING AGAINST ME, DOESN'T IT? EVERY TIME YOU DESCRIBE THIS MOMENT IN PAST TENSE, YOU'LL STILL FEEL IT!"

It's true. When you tell me the universe funnels children with incorrect opinions toward torture, my body urges me to apologize. Sure, I think flawed humans spent thousands of hours programming you into me, but what if you're correct?

What if God really is a final boss, one not even death can save us from? Considering the stakes, shouldn't we kneel before the ultimate Caesar?

But in a universe with eternal Hell, wouldn't God be the worst bully, someone the righteous should oppose no matter the cost? Shit, even if you're correct about how the universe works, you're wrong for condoning it!

"Your entire being already regrets this."

Yeah, but you guys told me I should die for what I believe, right? C'mon, if one martyrdom merits a crown of righteousness, imagine the loot I'd collect by getting slaughtered forever!

"Farewell, Isaac Siena."

"Church guys made up words to scare you," I told children, pushing the argument farther than we'd ever dared. "You're not going. Nobody's going. Not atheists. Not satanists. It doesn't exist. Jesus loves you. Like Event Horizon said: Hell is only a word."

I kicked the football and found it smashed into my forehead by the big hand of Eli.

He wasn't supposed to be there. Angry body warmth. Forearms bigger than my biceps. Mouth spewing hot rage into my eyes.

"A young man informed me you two idiots were doing your shtick," he seethed, his surging chest knocking me backward. "I thought, Isaac needs sent home."

My whole face stung. My eyes watered.

"But now, I hear you putting little souls in danger of eternal Hellfire, you millstone," he roared. "You're the one spreading heresies under my nose for months? Tell me I misheard you!"

I glimpsed Sophie ushering kids away.

"Glad I tagged in to run this camp," Eli said, clenching his sweaty hair and scouring my eyes for something redeemable. "I'd already planned on giving these kids hard facts, but … Lord … no …"

On my white sneakers, I saw two blood drops become three.

"Isaac, take it back right now. Tell them. Please! We'll make this right. If you explain to those kids you were wrong. We'll atone for this, buddy."

For once, I held his stare, seeing sweat, terror, and a blood-red line in the dirt.

"Please take it back," he said, paws clenching my shoulders. "I did this once. Same age as you. Remember? Never say that crap again. Go tell those kids they must be saved today or else!"

For years, OutKast's firearms advice had rang in my head: Don't point a gun unless you're prepared to fire it. Don't tell children Hell is real unless you want them becoming adults who act like it's true. And don't tell me to memorize my Bible unless you've accepted I'll use it against yours.

I gritted my teeth, tried to look big, and breathed, "No."

He inhaled sharply and blinked away tears. "Go check on dinner. Do it quickly. No …"

As he tromped toward a storage building, I walked past kids and counselors milling around PG's guitar. My walkie-talkie crackled. Caleb needed help lugging food across the long path from the parking lot.

I walked through the remains of Miss Esther's woods, past trees that'd watched 13.9-year-old me dig into fear and find love inside. *Kid-by-kid, I can undo whatever damage Eli's about to do.*

My walkie-talkie crackled again.

"… got a …"

Garbled girl voice.

"He's … toward us …"

"What?"

"… got … hands …"

"Got what?"

The word registered. I started sprinting back.

"Gun."

Clambering over a hill, I saw screaming kids crowded behind PG. Eli stepped onto the bridge with a semi-automatic rifle in his hands. He'd already planned to replicate the moment that'd broken him, that Wednesday skit from when he was seventeen, but I'd given him cause to make that skit real.

"This ain't some fucking camp game," he echoed. "Denial's a lie from the Devil's mouth! It's not too late, but it's getting close!"

Stepping onto the opposite side of the bridge, twenty feet in front of him, was Sophie. I ran even harder. He roared at her to recant. Close enough to see his red cheeks and her palms upward, I knew she was praying with eyes clenched.

For years, he's told me he'll do it.

"Discard family, if need be."

"It's rational to eliminate anyone who endangers the unsaved."

"If you ever try to damn my baby brother, I'll fucking kill you."

And when has he ever lied?

I tumbled down the hill, scrambled to my feet, and prayed for speed. Almost to the bridge.

"I've prayed for both of you," he called at me. "But I swore on my soul I'd never deny truth again."

When those men had pulled guns on seventeen-year-old Eli, he'd wilted, failing to call their bluff. As I neared the bridge, I wondered if he was bluffing, since his rifle lacked a magazine, but I imagined a round in the chamber.

Her prayer hands clasped above her head: *You shall not pass.*

"Stand down," he howled at her.

Steps away, his free hand raised to his barrel grip. Stomping onto the bridge, I had to somehow shut down a guy twice my size before Caleb arrived — because I worried he'd assume it was typical church theater and take Eli's side.

"You touch her … you gotta kill me," I wheezed, my feet pounding to a stop within his punching range, my palms raised in a basketball defensive stance, and my heart thumping so hard it thrummed my ears.

"Isaac, I love you," he said, twitching his finger onto the trigger, like a lion baring its fangs. "But I've failed to protect you. Please let me start now. Don't make me threaten you."

"You got one bullet," I panted, convinced he'd use it, but determined to tank all the damage myself. "It's mine, or I'll tell every kid … everyone's just guessing about God."

I tried to match his height, knowing I never would. Heart thump-thump. PG screamed at kids, "Cabin! Move! It's not a game!"

"Let that damned man go," Eli roared, grabbing my shirt, ripping tattered fabric like cobwebs and jabbing cool metal into my bare chest. Now I couldn't even be buried in Dad's shirt.

No one ever really dies. Fear orbited me, but wasn't within me. I thought of the martyr who'd clapped his hands while burning alive. *Peace that surpasses understanding.*

"The Spirit's working in those kids, and you're obstructing that Spirit," he said, stone-jawed. "I'll hate myself until I rot, if you make me. You're putting forty-two souls in jeopardy."

His math was simple: Their forty-two souls outweighed mine.

Mine was simpler: He only had one bullet.

"You promised you'd never let anybody challenge you," I said, forming no weapons, just paladin auras. "But I promised stuff too."

Rifle barrel. Sweating red face. Squinted eye. Sophie screaming. Trigger finger. Thump-thump-thump.

"Eli, Dad's in Heaven …"

Thumping, louder and louder.

"… and …"

Tears in hazel eyes. Thumping.

"… I'll see you when you get there."

When I was fourteen, I pinkie-swore she'd never again be silenced.

All I want is my best-summer-ever road trip. But I surrender all.

Believing what they taught us made us all crazy.

If you kill me, you'll prove me righ–

THIRTY-SIX
ALL THAT'S LEFT
THE END OF THE AGE

It's so dark.

Swimming through shadow.
Brain boiling. Burning inside.
Red voices. Talons.

---

*I **regret** that.*

Transporting me.
Body somewhere beneath.
Music, lights, and eyes.

And all the devils are here.

Surfacing. Spine still submerged.
Blinding glare. Black holes.
Air rushing in. Oceans receding.

Please choose me.

Song on high.

Humming.

Five Iron Frenzy's "Every New Day."

"Ize?"

"… Halle Berry?"

"Aww, you wish," said the gentle voice. "Back again, babe?"

I had a hand, being held. I grunted noises at the backlit red-pink ghost.

"You've got a bad concussion," the person said, nuzzling me.

My breathparts shook, and my hurtface worrybadded.

"The kids are safe," Sophie said, patting my thumpchest. "An hour later, half of them were goofing off. It was insane. One was like, 'Anywho, why's premarital nookie allowed for animals but not people?'"

I couldn't remember my name, but remembered exactly how a pastor would answer that. I asked, "How long …"

"For three days and nights, you fell! You're coming back more, though. One of these times, you'll stay! You've said you remember the bridge?" Maybe I nodded. "Well, Caleb hustled toward the walkie-talkies. From Paintball War a zillion years ago, he remembered the creek-bed's a shortcut, thumped across the bridge, and did a harebrained gainer attack into Eli. Two big boys, your poor noggin, wood railing."

Caleb had saved my life … with a Street Fighter flash kick. He wasn't just Best Caleb, but the Best of All Possible Calebs.

"And, um, I dunno how many more times I have to tell you this," she said, fidgeting. "The doctor says you'll be fine, but a bullet kinda, like, got you."

Oh. My left arm was elevated, with heavy bandages near my shoulder. Sophie insisted Eli hadn't meant to shoot me and the collision had bumped the trigger "on accident." I laughed. She said I'd laughed every time.

"Blood was everywhere," she said, resting an elbow on my chest, looking like she'd cried more than slept. "You know that wrestling hold you always do, when you're done letting me win?" She giggled. "In the pile-up, you did it to Eli for real."

"Which one? Lay it on me, so I know."

"You've said that every time, perv. I grabbed the gun while Micahs piled on him like ants. Surge found duct tape and yelled, 'Don't f-word with the Homeschool Illuminati.' While we hogtied a terrorist, I'm like, 'Language.'"

She detailed trying to wrangle kids, talk to cops, and keep me alive while everyone yelled questions at her, the legal-adult boss. "Do you remember my dad showing up and blubbering on you?"

That part I didn't believe. "You've sat here for three days?"

"Me and your mom have bonded like crazy! She knows astrology? Whaaat? Church folks keep visiting. I've gone to your house for stuff. The prog band said hi."

Mom inched into the room, hugging me like I was made of dandelion. A nurse asked if I wanted solid food. "Pizza Hut, please." He assumed I was joking.

"Our Pizza Hut's gone, angel," Mom whispered, holding Sophie tight. "As soon as you two took eyes off it. They say it'll become a goofy-shaped funeral home."

I shook my head, seeking happier topics. "Where's Eli?"

"You're back long enough to ask, so that's good," Mom said, exhaling hard. "I'm not bailing him out, obviously. We've filed restraining orders. Alexa's finding me a big, tough dog. I never should've let Eli get this sick, I know. I'll keep him away from you two. I'm so sorry."

"Well," I said, "I know what he's sick with."

At homeschool prom, I got lectured about jai alai, falconry, and throat singing. When the metallurgy kid said God approved of America's colonization, I yelled, "You sound like my brother! Bring your sword to the parking lot!" Sophie rerouted me to Dairy Queen. When we reached my wonderfully secular school's prom, all eyes were on Alexa kissing the prom queen. But once I walked in the door, all eyes turned to me. *I'm stealing attention from THAT?*

Reporters explored my school, photographing Eli's all-county football plaque and trying to interview me. Internet commenters blamed Dad, Mom, God, Satan, Republicans, Democrats, etc. In hallways, every kid watched me. "Hero." *Fuck off, I'm Eli's biggest enabler and evolution's biggest mistake.*

After reporters questioned Jack, he bitched in sermons about "the liberal media" blaming "this ministry" for "one deranged individual." Pastors could contort any story — from Columbine to Eli — into evidence that they were the kinda Christians who would've been persecuted by Romans.

At my middle-class house, Jack and his entourage put filthy hands on my single parent's shoulders. He hugged me, weeping, for defending his niece against "a lone wolf gone rogue." He requested the four camp counselors join him Sunday, on stage. "But I'm a demon, according to you," I said. "Wear jeans, whatever you like," he replied. I grabbed some skater shirt with a beheaded Statue of Liberty, planning to unload into the mic with my badass gunshot bandage on display.

Two steps into the parking lot, I saw the sanctuary's big white dome above treetops and felt Sauron's crosshairs stealing breaths from my chest. In that building, seven days a week, people prescribed limitless suffering for outsiders, and I'd never really been an insider. PG found me hiding behind bushes and diagnosed me as having "the chronic uh-ohs."

I blasted Bad Religion and declared Dogma the best movie ever, while my girlfriend leaned further into spirituality, planning a tattoo of the Kabbalah's Sefirot symbol. I got her van ready-ish, like nothing had changed. She declared my road-trip maps perfect, then added a couple religious destinations. "Stop dragging me to church!" Our first-ever actual argument. Yuck. Mom said, "She's recovering too, angel. She was jumping outta her skin in the hospital. I wish you two would visit the church counselor. Caleb said it helped, right?" I told Mom church creates hypocrites and the Bible lies about when camels were domesticated. She said, "We can't expect church to have perfect people. It's a hospital for sinners, not a museum of saints. You'd regret quitting!"

The counselor said, "Set this season of turmoil at the foot of the cross. Let's ensure your relationship with Miss Sophia is Christ-centered. Any unconfessed sexual regrets?"

After that, I told Mom I was done. "Sorry I'm too big to spank." I ripped Christian band patches off my backpack, almost attempted whispering the word "goddamn," and even ... bought a Tool shirt.

Thank fuck, seniors could leave school early. I wouldn't have been able to eat lunch alone otherwise. Endless Christian missionaries paraded past my locker like I was a gazelle among cheetahs or a girl among boys. One listened to me rant for twenty minutes, then said, "When people quit church, it's because they want an excuse to sin. Try my church instead. We're so chilled-out, our pastor has a lip ring! Let's get coffee? Maybe invite Bobbi Birdsong? Or gimme her digits?"

At our graduation party in some rich kid's neighborhood, Division I athlete Amir stopped by, commandeering the music and blasting Kirk Franklin. Football players acted up with praise hands raised, which seemed fascinating, except I was fending off FCA nutjobs. Cops showed up: "Gospel soundtrack. That's a new one." We bolted to the theater and saw Saved!, about Evangelical misfits. "Finally, there's a movie about us," my Christian friends said. "Good for you," I said, still drunk.

"I wanted some big sermon showdown with my uncle," Sophie said as we played Mario Kart with our phones off. "I'd preach about Eve, humanity claiming a role in creation, no matter the cost. Both testaments start with a woman confronting power, you know? But I'm so broken, I can barely move. Counting seconds until I leave forever. Can we pray together?"

"Go for it."

The only person who wasn't in denial about me: Caleb. Facing death together only made us feel forced to ignore that we'd grown apart.

But the thing I resented most about getting shot? Drama delayed our road trip. Mid-summer, after Eli's arraignment, I imagined testifying at his trial: *You people say you believe in eternal Hell, but aren't screaming about it on street corners? Then you don't believe in it! Eli believes in it so much, he'd send me to it!* Mom heard me ranting to myself and said she'd prayed I'd "stop hating God," like I could hate a stranger.

My prefabricated mind had never been mine. Whenever pieces like the Rapture stopped fitting, my skull had reverberated with regret. Having to believe Christians are morally superior, being gay is bad, science is fake, murder by Republicans is cool, and on and on? Those pieces slipped away, too. The day Hell became bullshit, I felt an earthquake, and then came Eli's Wormwood meltdown. As smoke spewed through clouds of ash, I wondered what remained.

While sifting through a closet of old books that'd created Eli, I found conservative shit he'd been too good for. My basement was full of Christian band posters, weird Bible drawings, and Christians walking in, playing Christian music, making Christian jokes, and constantly fucking praying for me. They helped me bonfire Eli's stuff, but gasped when I burned a book I'd spent years loading with highlighter ink and covering in Solid State Records stickers: his hand-me-down Bible.

Our last Tuesday, looking around my basement, I saw people with doubts displayed as scars. But I saw others who'd been church kids without really dwelling on why. And I saw people like Caleb, determined to revive America after my graduating class had failed to do so.

My anger faded into numbness. **"You'll, like, regret not caring."** *Fuck, you're still here?*

PG reminded everyone that it wasn't the place to discuss Eli *(thank you)* and led the sharing of joys, sorrows, and prayer requests. They sang her emo-pop versions of "Make It Happen," "Ain't No Mountain High

Enough," and "Maps." They split Little Caesars communion and collected soup kitchen donations. *Okay, whatever.*

She tossed the Talking Football toward Sophie, who handed it to a first-time speaker with a nicotine patch.

Alexa exhaled, rambled through nerves, and said, "You've all asked for years whether I'm saved. Well, no, I don't call myself a Christian. I haven't earned it."

I enjoyed watching lips whisper, "That's not how it works." Nervously, Alexa found Sophie's eyes, and they signed "breathe" to each other.

"All I know is, Jesus said anyone who helps poor people is in," Alexa said, looking down. "Give away everything, he said. I haven't, not even the million things I've shoplifted. So Jesus said I'm out."

Hands shot up, ready to correct her. She kept describing a gospel about saving lives, not souls.

"This is scary crap, man," Alexa gulped. "I'm about to disagree on Bible stuff with Cory." (Her nickname for Sophie. As in, the Boy Meets World nerd who adopts a popular loner.)

"Keep going, Precious," chirped Sophie.

Alexa inhaled, popped bubblegum, and snarled, "I hope Hell is real. Except Jesus didn't say Hell's for addicts, Muslims, atheists, gay guys, welfare people, or you pretty girls. He said Hell's for goddamn rich people. Luke fucking 16."

(Weeks earlier, her agnostic dad had accepted that he needed help. She'd borrowed a boring skirt and asked Pastor Jack for the church to fund non-faith-based rehab. Denied.)

She raged until those who disagreed with her applauded anyway, but I was numb even to that. She dialed down, embarrassed by sincerity.

"I know you guys wanted to save my soul," she mumbled at giraffe carpet. "You gotta settle for, like, saving me. Since I was twelve, I tried to be a grownup, but you let me be just some obnoxi–"

Mom pulled her by the arm, down into a sideways lap hug. "I treasure you, sweetheart, and my swear jar does, too." That loosed laugh-cheers as Alexa hid a huge smile.

Yay. I feel nothing.

With lead singer's authority, PG called for attention. "You guys were my high school, so I'm making a MySpace yearbook we'll share forever. Semi-circle up!"

They awarded each other superlatives, one by one. Bobbi, there for video games with her secret girlfriend, earned Smartest Except For Maybe Sophie. People chanted for a friendly debate to settle it. Bobbi asked why a perfect God would allow evil. Sophie imagined a God who's not one flawless being, but webs of goddesses so curious about humanity, they incarnated as an oppressed Jew. (Then the duelists traded hair-dye ideas.) Superlatives resumed. Caleb, who'd saved my stupid life, declared me Den Dad. Not a superlative, but whatever. Everyone cried and laughed. *I'm the numbest.*

Most people left, promising to never lose touch. In the yard, lying under sunset clouds, Alexa clung to Sophie, whose head rested on Josiah's chest. Sophie worried she'd never be bold like Alexa, who worried she'd never be deep like Sophie.

With an arm around them, Josiah said, in a tranquil version of his dad's rasp, "Just keep combining your powers, no matter who it ticks off."

"Your hot cousin said I compwetes you," Alexa said, snuggling Sophie tighter during our last day as anything like children.

A few others gathered. Alexa polled them on whether Sophie would "experiment" at women's college before Josiah finally kissed a guy.

I waited for a lull so I could say something. **"Whoa, you'll DEFINITELY regret that. It'd be simpler to keep faking everything until you die, so you don't die alone."**

But I mumbled, "Maybe I can't believe anything."

They grinned, waiting for my punchline.

Instead, I detailed my desperate nights beseeching silent ceilings and distant stars. "All my life, they promised if I cared hard enough, I'd have an experience. It'd turn me into who they wanted me to be. Chasing it nearly killed me," *in more ways than most of you know.*

Sophie sat up, chin trembling. *It's official. We're cosmically incompatible. She wants a (1) good (2) Christian (3) guy. "Non-negotiable." Her entire upbringing dictates we have zero future.*

"I was born in church world, but I'm not of it," I said. "Maybe the only time I felt honest was playing a Christmas demon. Maybe all I had left was hating Eli's certainty. Maybe I've spent four years chasing that camp singalong high. Maybe I'm scared of Hell because it's the world without you guys."

You should all dump me. Our friendship was based on things we never shared.

But the cuddle pile grew around me. PG said, "You're not alone." Caleb said, "Even Jesus doubted." Josiah said, "Even Jesus felt abandoned." Alexa said, "You too pussy to cry, bitch?"

People remained uncomfortable with my pent-up lack of breakdowns. *Sorry, but eleven years, five months, and twenty-nine days ago, God's spokesmen shuttered my tear ducts.* I wriggled through arms toward one pair, whispering, "Can I road trip anyway?"

"We pinkie swore," Sophie sniffed. "No stressing until after the best summer ever."

Out of nowhere, Timmy responded to the email I'd sent him on 9/11.

> "Brocephus! I'm so happy my homies are leaving Pastor J's bad juju. Come find me on the road! Let us breaketh bread! Also [hillbilly voice] a lawyer handed me a mighty interesting piece of paper. Reckon I'll need a hand with an even more mischievous construction project next summer. Be good out there, but not too good!"

My headlights revealed the ladder propped against our house. I climbed into warm night air, where Mom sat, gazing toward glimmering highways. We listened to bugs, cars, and wind.

She said, "He was right to insist you be named after him."

Oh, a big talk. "Is that bad?"

"Never. You both take things apart in ways I'll never understand, and that's okay. You're always in your own mysterious world, so I've never known how things affect you. While your brother, not to excuse him, has been an open wound since your father passed. Now I'm certain you've been hiding wounds all along, angel, and I'm so sorry. Maybe you'll tell me why."

Nah. You wouldn't like hearing why. "Eli chose. Dad made one mistake. There. Not your fault."

"I can't bear losing you next," she gasped, holding back tears, making me pause, ache, and actually listen. "If you're throwing away your childhood, the parts that hurt … keep what you can?"

"Like what?"

"Well … me, maybe … even though your father and I raised Eli and got talked into hitting you and …"

I shrugged, but still: Millions of parents read the James Dobson books that'd gotten my friends beaten. Now what? Should we beat our kids, on and on forever, long after Dobson dies rich? I can't totally understand anyone who's ever believed it's cool to assault small bodies, but my mother thought I viewed her and the angry Republicans' version of Jesus as identical. *She never knew half the shit they dumped into our skulls! How can I blame her? On the list of church people I love, Mom remains #1. Err, #2. Tied? Stop making me rank.*

"When you were four, we went to the Grand Canyon," she sighed. "Those pictures of you in a little cowboy hat? We strolled up for sunrise, expecting to point at rocks and leave for breakfast. But your father walked near the edge, froze, and said, 'Holy fucking shit!' I'm just quoting!"

She was cackling so hard, I shushed her.

"You were riding his shoulders. Eli'd wandered off to charm older girls, back when he was so funny. Your little face with my hair and your daddy's eyes, glowing like a tiny Charlton Heston. Thunderstruck. Blown away by a crack in the ground. I looked at you two, your jaws dropped. I thought, sure, it's a *large* crack."

I heard echoes of my own laughter.

"Bawling your little head off, you said, 'Mama, look at God's fingerprint!'"

She put a hand on my cheek. "I looked at you and said, 'Angel, I already am.'"

My breathing skipped.

"And your face registered what I'd just called you. And you replied, with all your four-year-old might, 'Holy fucking shit!'"

We had a big, hugging, laughing argument. I ranted about how pastors couldn't control her voting. "The TV's yelling about immigrants. Your grandparents were immigrants! Your Bible loves immigrants!"

"Young man, I'm voting pro-life. Period. There's an invisible war in this country."

"Maybe vote against visible war," I grumbled, still unsure how to weigh Bobbi's feminist arguments against all the dead-fetus photos I'd seen. "At least find a new church where women are humans."

"A new church? Duhhh," she groaned in her mock-teenager voice. "Kinda done hearing strangers' opinions about my family. Current and future, wink wink."

My laughter ran out. "Just gonna have a fun road trip. Then God'll announce she should marry a Jesus guy."

Mom didn't say the but-you-saved-her-life bullshit that I hated. She studied stars for a while, then told me to keep the family Glock nearby on the road. Ominous astrology. (No, I wasn't leaving her defenseless. She'd obtained a Rottweiler renamed Pomona.)

"Nobody'll bother a group rolling four deep," I assured her.

"Four?"

"Josiah's bringing some friend he won't admit he likes. Ex-gay status vs. road-trip romance: Something's gotta give!"

She watched more stars, either accepting what I'd said or ignoring it.

"By the time you get back, you'll legally be a man," she laughed, in disbelief. "I won't pretend you and Sophie will sleep in separate tents, bu–"

"The talk? Mom. Eli handled this. Then he gave this awesome scar. But still."

"Son, the world's lied to you about what a man is. A man listens for what others need, rather than taking whatever he wants. There, that was the talk. Don't tell your father I waited this long to do his job."

I'd been called a man before, like when a youth pastor had addressed me and other eleven-year-olds as "men of Christ who'll stamp out Mormonism." But the first time anyone said it with any legitimacy, she framed manhood not as a license to conquer, but as a duty to liberate.

After a long silence, she said, "I let so-called men of God raise you. I can't change that now. I can only hope I'm someone you'll talk to about everything that's hurt you, *especially* if those things are me. We'll never agree on everything, but angel, I'd choose Hell over a world where I'm not your mama."

PART FIVE

The heart burning
for the sake of all creation,
for humans, for birds,
for animals, for demons

— Saint Isaac of Ninevah

THIRTY-SEVEN
ME WITHOUT YOU
SUMMER

"EVERYBODY BACK HOME DESERVES THIS VIEW," SAID JOSIAH'S INTERNET FRIEND Daniel, strumming his guitar atop Vandalf beside the moonlit Atlantic Ocean.

After looping back into our time zone (albeit hundreds of miles south), we'd soon have to backtrack toward the airport near Sophie's college. But how could our road trip end without a beach night?

Constantly shaking hair from his face, Daniel was a husky Wilmer Valderrama whose frat stories lacked conviction. He was always climbing trees with Sophie, doing stupid pranks with me, and mocking the object of his poorly concealed crush.

As a smirking Daniel sang a way-too-familiar song, Sophie paced in the sand, checking her fifty-cent Cinderella watch bought at a Virginia Goodwill.

"Golly, these lyrics are decent theology. Did you write this?" Josiah asked, making Daniel laugh while cheerily salvaging the song church kids resented being accused of liking: Creed's "Higher."

Months earlier, Sophie and I had pinkie-sworn to ignore the future, but the future was hours away. I hoped our breakup would be on BFF terms, maybe after finding a spot for first sex and last sex. *After all, splitting is best for us both. I'd end up miserable, marrying a Bible-thumper.*

"Almost, almossst," she whispered as Daniel leaned back toward Josiah's chest, clearly singing to one person. We'd tried our hardest to make the trip a double date.

As random bystanders waved cell phones and sang along, her watch beeped, so I raced her toward the ocean.

"Got your phones?" Josiah shouted, still squeamish about his baby cousin running wild.

"Nope," we yelled.

"Do crimes," shouted Daniel, there at the end of all things.

This trip's memorial playlist, based on our most frequent highway singalongs:

1. Best summer ever. MxPx, "Doin' Time."
2. We visited twelve national parks. Fefe Dobson, "Take Me Away."
3. Fifty miles outside home, once nobody recognized us, Sophie molted, bopping into rest stops like she was Gwen Stefani in overalls and we were No Doubt. Stoic Josiah spoke with hints of melody in his hands, like he was testing it just to prove it wasn't a fit. JoJo, "Leave (Get Out)."
4. Near Tucson, he got bit by a snake, shook it into our campfire, kicked aside logs to save the snake, and resumed his boring speech. Daniel swooned, fruitlessly. Meat Loaf, "Out of the Frying Pan (And Into the Fire)."
5. In Fort Collins, we liberated friendly Mormons and Jehovah's Witnesses by chugging Baja Blast to celebrate Halle Berry's birthday. Further Seems Forever, "The Moon Is Down."
6. I turned eighteen in West Memphis and got a tattoo of a goat skull with a halo. Josiah got the Leviticus verse that forbids tattoos. Sophie pierced her nose for real. Gloria Estefan, "Everlasting Love."
7. Daniel scored weed near Shenandoah, knocking out my post-concussion headaches. Sophie's philosophy textbook revealed Plato invented Hell hundreds of years *after* somebody started writing the Bible. Pink Floyd, "Wish You Were Here."
8. In Nevada, we saw Mean Girls and hit a casino for money to see it again. There, we met a stripper who said he always responded to judgment with magical words: "Okay, thank you!" Houston, "I Like That."

9. We found shirtless-dude wrestling infinitely funny. "My boyfriend's gay like Johnny Knoxville," said Sophie. The Trapt song.
10. She invited me to a Greek cathedral, one she'd picked because of my mother's heritage. She kept nudging me toward religious stuff, scared to pressure me but tacitly giving me until the trip's end to re-become good-Christian-guy husband material. Pink, "Just Like a Pill."
11. Road game: spotting Hell billboards, cow pastures, dildo shops, and ammo shops. Needed ammo anyway, after we shot up Hell billboards on I-26. Stavesacre, "Sundown Motel."
12. Josiah admitted his dad hadn't just sent him to a "sex addiction" facility for six months. Jack had kicked him out and had never actually considered resigning as pastor — all while non-subtly bragging about "cleaning house." Howard Shore, "The Last March of the Ents."
13. I found Sophie crying, convinced that her family had disowned her for choosing what they called "lesbian college." She remembered being twelve, when her parents caught her reading Judy Blume and spanked her as she recited Proverbs 31 through tears. That made me remember fifth grade, when I punched some boy for saying Hell worms were eating my dad's guts. She and I yell-laughed about August 2003, when we'd declared our brains fixed, and stole champagne (sorry). The Distillers, "Dismantle Me."
14. When she little-spooned against me, I hoped she felt safe. In her hair, dyed lilac, I buried my face, hiding from nightmares about Psalty the Singing Songbook shooting up my high school. Underoath, "Reinventing Your Exit."
15. Best summer ever. Boyz II Men, "End of the Road."

We'd spent most of four years basically together, those last weeks round-the-clock inseparable. All summer, we'd fallen asleep scared of making any more promises sure to become jinxes.

And when I boarded my flight home the next morning, we'd be a memory.

"How far ya wanna go?" she asked, ankle-deep in waves, tying a ponytail.

"Wherever's past all the way." I chucked my tank top and checked my Velcro pocket for the just-in-case. One last night to test every promise.

"You're my witness, I did this," she said, inhaling hard and taking off her shirt. Crossing her arms over her sports bra and scanning darkness for furious youth pastors, she'd fulfilled half of her public two-piece vow to Alexa, leaving on jogging shorts. I stammered so badly — I'd seen that skin many times, yet in starlit blue, it was new — she did a hands-on-hips pose.

Dressed for speed, we hopped into sprinter stances.

Three, two, one, go. Bonking elbows. Feet smacking wet sand.

"I'm going forever," the experienced runner puffed beside the thundering ocean. "You'll bail on me, though."

"Forever," I wheezed.

The further we ran, the less chance there was that we'd return to Vandalf in time to tear ourselves hundreds of miles and one God apart, to admit we'd become adults. We slowed to a walk, alone in every direction, stepping through midnight waves.

As we passed sleeping beach houses and distant tankers, a wad of fabric smacked against me. She'd thrown her shorts, completing the two-piece dare. I retorted, becoming the naked beach guy until I worried about birds biting me.

Around 2 a.m., we found a trail into overgrown trees above a gentle cove.

"Unless we haul ass, we won't make it back until like 5 a.m." I said, stepping onto stones. "Except I'm keeping you out 'til 6."

"Boy, I'm never letting you leave," she said with moonlight eyes, climbing onto my piggyback and talking flirty trash as I ascended in delicate darkness.

For weeks in our tent, we'd … behaved like eighteen-year-olds far from oversight. Abstaining from nothing but the final rebellion, we'd teasingly dared each other to initiate it anyway, maximizing difficulty "for fun." One night's freedom-overdosed riskiness had startled us into buying a just-in-case condom, which kept looming like the One Ring.

Above the cove, we sat criss-cross. In hours, the sun's eye would find us. There at the end of all things, I felt a surging urgency, like a flag needed planting before she dated townies.

Over the cliff, she lifted her left hand and twisted a silver band free. Starlight glinted across the purity ring she'd agonized about bearing. And she placed it in my palm. "Keep it safe."

Wow. Uh … now what?

"Don't wanna look like a homeschooler at liberal college?" I said, so she could joke toward what I hoped she was saying.

She mumbled, "I've always wanted you as my actual first time. My body says go, and … it's either now, or … I picture you at State with … Do you have the, um, just-in-case?"

I tucked her ring into my Velcro pocket full of our seashells, swapping it for a square foil wrapper.

She'd once explained what virginity's *actual* significance was, 3,000 years ago in Canaan, yet wasn't free of True Love Waits. And I'd gathered she felt guilty about not technically saving it for marriage, like she owed me more than what Gabe had obtained. That'd always made me remember how I'd found her a year earlier, weeping after being used.

Obviously, there were things I wanted. But I couldn't. I frisbeed the unopened condom into a clearing. *She's changed so much, but she's not ready today, so we'll never be ready together. That's life.* **"Who says *you're* ready, playboy?"** *Shhh.*

Man-dude role models would mock me for remaining the world's oldest semi-virgin. Okay, thank you! And people who've never been screamed at for hand-holding would ridicule her for trying to believe her rose retained all its petals. Okay, fuck you.

Her eyebrows de-tensed. There. Worth it.

We stared heavenward. I pointed across the ocean at Venus, too bright to be a star. Soon, our eyes locked onto a particular airplane, maybe the one I'd soon leave on. Within an hour or two, the sun would find us, there at the end of all things.

"Now's when we promised we'd decide what's next," I croaked. "This might suck so bad."

"Dare you to say it," she crackled.

"We always swore we'd only date Christians," I said, as her falling face confirmed we'd been assigned the same non-negotiable. "We hated Green Day because they said Christians could date anybody. But I never became that godly guy for you. Now I can't even pretend."

I heard only the billion-year ocean just beyond the cove.

"I have an awful habit," she said. "I assume faith works the same for everybody. When I learn it doesn't, I feel pride. I always argued Alexa needed my Jesus, until she made me understand hers. I love you too much to chain you to somebody who reminds you of bad stuff."

"I picture you with somebody who can sing it and mean it. I'm so jealous I wanna die. But you deserve somebody as Spirit-filled as you."

"Obsessing over religion might become my, like, job. I so understand you need space from it and … me."

Before the Eli thing, we'd thought physical distance would be the hardest part. Yet Jesus had always been the space between us. We scooped handfuls of black dirt, let it go, and watched wind scatter it.

"I'm a fraud," she said, eyes bleary. "I hate the idea that Jesus being executed was good! I love Jesus! I'm a softie! What if we're saved not because Jesus died, but because Jesus lived? Pretty dumb, huh? And I let my uncle lie about God. Remember those guys at the fair last summer who wanted to hurt PG for America? Uncle Jack's building an army of those guys! I was so timid …"

"Jack's crowd watched his niece take back her hands," I said, rubbing her shoulders. "How many people realized, 'If she can do that, anybody can?' How many sophomores heard you every Tuesday, then listened differently on Sunday?"

Sometimes, only briefly, she brooded like Batman watching bank robbers. "Maybe I picked this college so I can train to humiliate him on his turf," she growled, teeth bared until her rage retreated. "But I should fly home and hide. Huge poser. Religious studies? Pathetic. You were the Christian I wanted to be."

"Oh, please."

"You say what the heck you mean! I can't even pray right."

"C'mon," I laughed.

"Seriously! Me, chitchatting with the All-Mystery? People think I'm some oracle. As if. I'm a space-brained ditz who babbles at the wind. Forever ago, summer after freshman year, I snuck outside and talked to the sky because you'd felt clouds reaching down to hurt you. It made me think of Psalm 139." She sang Rich Mullins' version, in fading falsetto, "The night's as bright as day …"

"Why 139?"

"For some reason, I remember it was exactly 1:39 a.m."

Oh my god.

At that exact minute, I was a fourteen-year-old pressing a knife against my eyelid, begging my free hand to punch its handle hard enough for God to like me. And not only had her words preserved me, she'd stayed awake with me the whole time?

I don't deserve feelings this big. Shake it off, Siena.

I kissed her salty forehead, leaning down because I was larger and therefore tougher than her. Right? *Don't think about old things. They hurt.*

Think about the future. Sure, let's do that. Imagine talking on the phone to a speckled sheep in a dorm many miles from home. Some homesick night, she'll feel lonelier than ever, this sacred person who grieved what I couldn't. I couldn't shake anything off. I felt old things welling up, things I'd never known how to bury.

I wasn't crumbling. I was sitting strong, so girl-woman could lean on boy-man. That's the ordained structure. *Shake it off, Siena.*

There at the end of all things, she said, "Four years ago, you let some creepy homeschooler babble about algae. Seconds after I shaved my head, trying to vanish, you hugged ginormous butterflies into me. My life changed when my tenth-grade crush said Mary Magdalene preached the Resurrection. Dude, way before you confronted Eli, you saved my life. Deal with it."

My lip quivered. My cheeks trembled. *Shake it the fuck off. Crying is for ungrateful denialists who want to unearth things that cannot be made new.*

"I can't lie, I feel a voice screaming it's wrong to love you, but I h-word … I *hate* that voice!" she said. "This whole trip, I hoped you'd decide you're still the same as before. That's stupid. Me and Jesus will always love you, and I'm sorry for taking too long to realize I only needed you to believe the *me* part."

But … but that doesn't add up …

"I'm sick of believing God loves us in a way that's basically hate," she said, tears streaming like snowmelt. "Jesus said the greatest commandments mean loving others *like* we love ourselves. Not *more than* or *instead of*. You know what *like* means?"

My breaths skipped. Shake it off.

"Do you? Babe, no matter what we were taught …"

My chest filled with hurricane feathers. Shake.

"… you're supposed to love yourself."

It felt like vomit rising. *Without love, nothing matters, said Paul.* I knew what was happening. *Love each other, said Jesus.* I couldn't stop it. *Love is greater than faith, said Paul.* Blessed are those who mourn, for not even death can stop them from fulfilling the commandment. *And we can't love unless we accept love, said Sophie's Jesus.* So I surrendered all.

Shields shattered. The child I'd hated for wanting to grieve had become an eighteen-year-old I hated for wanting at all. Fortresses failed.

So many scalding years of poison started pouring from my eyes, expelling plagues onto her sunburnt chest. As I tucked my hands against myself like a T-rex, the arms around me were small, but strong. I was limp, shaking, helpless, filthy, depraved, damned, disgusting, and adored.

But she whispered, "You can only choose one."

Maybe one minute. Maybe one forever. My everything hurt, like scratching soul-sized itches and digging the ache. I sat up, drained and full, there and floating. LMAO at my slobbery mess. She laughed, wiping herself like a windshield. I felt awesome! Fuck drugs, just cry!

I mocked her stories about me, telling her *she* was the cool hero in *my* memories, the princess who'd discarded royalty to slum with a wretch.

"Well, I'm so not-heroic, I wanna go home with you guys," she said, there at the end of all things. "My folks would buy a plane ticket over the phone or whatever, if I apologized for stuff. I can't abandon you, after all you've been through. I'm scared of the world."

And at the side of the sea, I finally told her about the night when, riding the wings of dawn, she'd talked a fourteen-year-old out of self-lobotomy.

"You owe me nothing, and you never did," I said. "You saved my life first. Ok?"

She nodded, wiping tears with the back of her hand.

"Don't let anybody, including me, decide who you become," I said. "You're going to that school, not because you're *called* or whatever, but because it's what you want. It'll suck at first. But I got your back, no matter what we are. And your insides, eventually, hopefully. I'm, like, excited to learn what I believe, starting from scratch." I paused for drama. "But I already believe in a goddess you should believe in too."

Nailed it. Wait, her smile kept anticipating. That nerd thought I was literally about to share mythology opinions.

"Foxy, she's you. Duh."

Josiah, doing jumping jacks in his dorkiest polo shirt, chuckled, "Just in time, half-naked insomniacs. Get some exercise? You smell like it. Coffee?"

Minutes before sunrise, we guzzled Mountain Dew, panting from our race back to the van.

"You didn't do crimes yet, right?" he asked like a fired-up Ned Flanders.

"Oops," Sophie said, showing her hip's hickey to the only person she enjoyed embarrassing.

"Swear I'm surrounded by Calebs forever," he muttered. "Anyway, we plotted a crime before we skedaddle, if the lazy man ever wakes up. It's a crime in most states, at least."

"What's a Josiah crime, playing Point of Grace too loudly?" I asked.

"Smelly lady, this crime requires a reverend," he said, handing Sophie his Bible. "First Corinthians 13, please. If Paul didn't wanna join the gay agenda, he shouldn't have written the wedding chapter."

He handed me two gold rings, saying, "And we need an even smellier best man."

He banged on Vandalf's door and turned to see us stunned. *Somebody's getting gay-married? Here? Now?*

"I can't be your reverend," Sophie said, fluttering every limb. "I'm your maid of honor!"

He stared, computing. Then he babbled, "Wait. Not me! Two older gals met us and gave us jobs. Sleepy guy's their musician. Guess I'm their wedding planner? Golly, you thought me and … erp."

Haaang on, why's he so chipper?

What happened here last night, by the ocean under the stars?

Was it like the last night of church camp, when rampant hormones …

"Josiah got some," I realized out loud. I swear, every time I let that guy stay out after curfew on the beach …

He turned away, blushing and mumbling about Creed singalongs. *Fuck, Creed did this? "Higher" has to go on my road-trip playlist? Brutal!*

Fidgeting like a freshman, he shushed Sophie's ecstatic demands for romance details. Vandalf's door opened, and Daniel strode forth like a 5'6" Achilles, guitar in hand, wearing swim trunks and a formal bolo tie. He stood on tiptoes to kiss a blushing Josiah twice, said, "Twenty minutes of summer left, slowpokes," and marched toward the ocean, where two brides-to-be were gathering seashells.

Hey, when was Josiah's actual thunderbolt conversion, the moment when he became the person God made? Was it that Promise Keepers rally when he was twelve? Or was it when he looked down, daydream-smiling as his cousin giddily punched his chest, and said, "There. Happy now, brat?"

At the waterline, Daniel was already charming onlookers. As we hustled toward them, Josiah explained those women had met decades earlier at Catholic school. Beside brides in a white sundress and white coverup, we hurried to assemble because their photographer was freaking out about timing the sunrise first kiss.

As sparks of daylight struck the sky, I held the Bible so our priestess could preach, with two hands and all, "If I speak in the tongues of men or of angels, but do not have love, I am only a resounding gong ..."

Behind me, the ocean swelled as it has for a zillion years. In front of me, a pastor's preppy son held a scraggly guitarist's hand, a perfect moment amid chaos.

Near the chapter's end, Sophie read, "When I became an adult, I put the ways of childhood behind me." She was cut short by the photographer losing his mind and ordering all non-brides to stand aside.

I hadn't acknowledged a sunrise since I was small, and never over the ocean. They said that light damned my father.

But finally I watched.

And finally I listened.

And do you hear what I hear?

I'm blessed by the breath of my constant crush, plus this rhythmic rush of waves breaking themselves anew. The endless ocean engine, ancient of chaos days, might be a mindless monster, but this blackened blanket began as our birthplace.

And do you see what I see?

Above the edge of emerging orange, the highest sky still smolders indigo, as so many stars scatter grace across gorgeous horror. Our lonely home's halo is an ageless forge so huge, it's never stopped making old things new, yet so painstaking, it engraved each grain of sand in our hands.

Roaring water. Wandering stars. Angels of the silence. Everyone craves visions, voices, and visual evidence. Even saints wait lifetimes, placing faith in prayers for faith.

But why plead for signs when we're surrounded by wonders?

Life's first fire ignites our hot-pink horizon. Scorched citrus clouds squeeze Skittles down the middle of our peach-streaked sea. The sudden sunbeam blushing our warm arms is part of our star, our hearth of everything we are, the heaven baked into ever-breaking, ever-remade hearts.

I've dreamed of fire lakes, my father's remains claimed by something like the sun. That dream's real, kinda.

Because do you know what I know?

We came from that sunrise, and we'll one day return. After we die, we rejoin earth, earth rejoins star, star becomes nebula, nebula becomes star, and star makes earths, again and again until maybe even the universe is made new. Works cited: Bobbi's science monologues, Sophie's Kabbalah fan-fiction, Revelation 22, and Venus, midnight's daylight.

So do you know what I wonder?

What if it was never about individual conversions, but about reparations unto restoration, in this universe or the next?

What if it ain't just about the ending? What if everything that happens beforehand matters too?

What if, amid Psalm 139's unbreakable communion between the buried and me, I join melodies from heaven, full of awe and trembling, in a prayer learned from my mother …

"Holy fucking shit."

EPILOGUE: MEANT TO LIVE

NOW

TIME FLIES. MY (LAS VEGAS) RAIDERS STILL SUCK, THOUGH.

Social media has obsoleted high school reunions, but I'm at a gathering anyway. Thirteen-year-old me would love learning I'm with Christians, while eighteen-year-old me would feel betrayed.

Sorry, kids. I wasn't cut out for high-control religion. I wasn't bad at it, though I thought so at the time. [Uncle Rico voice:] I was *awesome* at it. Too awesome!

I'm prone to depression, full of intrusive thoughts, comically self-critical, physically allergic to toxic positivity, stubbornly skeptical, addicted to worrying about my binge-and-purge indulgence, diagnosed by one acquaintance as neuroatypical, and uncertain who asked me to volunteer for existence. I was primed for what we think of as Christianity to kill me, either by my brother's hand or my own.

So my salvation testimony is this:

I'm alive because of Christians.

That list started with college football journalist Josiah, here with his husband, a Mennonite minister in Philly. After spending his twenties pretending to be ok, my big brother's known on TikTok as the scandal-proof pastor's hot son who preaches, "Christians can't make Jesus stop loving you."

They rode here with my sister PG, an Atlanta mother of three who spent seventeen adult years ignoring her childhood, then visited her birthplace in India and started an exvangelical podcast (on which she teaches her Lutheran husband about hardcore churches, then giggles at his horrified reactions).

Most of my Calebs are here, ranging from a youth pastor to an "apathist," but I've lost my dearest little brother. In 2007, I was Best Caleb's best man. In 2016, desperate to believe in authority, he blocked our entire crew on Facebook.

I'll forever regret failing to steer him not just from January 6th, but from teaching his kids to fear humanity. Survivor's guilt.

He's who I would've become, if somebody hadn't steered *me* from the "God in America Again" path. That took so many, including some — like environmental engineer Bobbi, meteorologist Amir, and EMT Chloe — who thought we were just gaming. (They're not here, but I'll tag them in the photo anyway.)

Obviously, Eli's not here. He's one of those edgelord Idaho pastors with no parishioners, just tons of YouTube followers. He's funded dozens of Hell billboards nationwide, but lost his one-track-mindedness, occasionally bragging about shooting his "woke" brother.

As a small child, I considered seventeen-year-old Eli a man. Now that I've arguably been one for a while, I consider late-forties Eli ... a seventeen-year-old. I thought losing my daddy was the worst thing possible, but when Eli lost his *father*, men of God burdened him with becoming mine. And fathers possess certainty, we were taught, so Eli discarded curiosity. I was lucky to wander toward doubts and temporarily Christian rock bands.

I remember considering myself a badass because I'd conjured sympathy for the Devil, like it's difficult to root for cool villains. The challenge began once I realized my actual devils have never been red-pitchfork characters.

So hey, big-talking Isaac Siena, who feels rebellious for wanting Jesus to forgive Satan: Can you love Eli, the fallen angel who so loved the world, he'd sacrifice his baby brother to save it?

To a fault, I empathize with seventeen-year-olds. So I'm trying. As a display of moral superiority. (But I can't forgive Eli until he stops going viral for calling yoga pants promiscuous. Huge dork behavior. People would think I'm a huge dork, too.)

I kept more than I'd expected, at least. Timmy's another Christian at our reunion. A few years after high school, we helped him build an inclusive campground on some special land. Miss Esther had willed it to our church, until Pastor Jack's bigotry had changed her mind right before she died. Yep, my old church camp became an oasis reclaimed from Isengard.

(The globally syndicated Pastor Jack turned our camp into a lucrative persecution fantasy, of course. His church had already profited from Eli shooting me, once it was found not liable, since "legal fund" donations outweighed lawyer fees. My final tithe. I hope it funded a water slide.)

Also here is Mom, the "moderate conservative" mystery who believes women shouldn't preach, but terrorizes transphobic pastors on Instagram. She's about to levitate, once I reveal she's six months away from finally meeting her first grandchild.

For now, she's snarking with Alexa, a hometown grocery stock clerk. After bottoming out at thirty-three, she moved in with my mother, emerged as a marathoner fueled by junk food, and got matching demon tattoos with me. She's finishing a law degree because "the actual-ass gospel's about setting every captive free. Jesus fucking said so."

I can't believe in a virgin birth. Sorry, I tried. However, Alexa's never wrong — I haven't cracked a Bible in two decades, but I know Luke 4:18 fucking says so.

Millions of captives grew up so scared of eternal **regret**, we did everything the church machine asked. Now those of us who made it out owe something to captives still ensnared, don't we? Love always protects, doesn't it?

So we'll relentlessly oppose hypocrisy, no matter how pointless it feels. Nope, our facts and logic won't fix whoever the current Rush Limbaugh is. So fucking what? The point is planting seeds in the minds of onlookers who are only 99% indoctrinated.

In fact, we're the religion-industrial complex's worst nightmare. By grooming us to dread everything that'd de-groom us, it revealed its deepest fear: its nail-scarred star pupils realizing we hold not only a hammer but also the blueprints. By age six, we mastered their lingo. Humbling them at Bible trivia? Child's play, literally. Our machine created its own monsters, ones armed with this superpower: We cannot be fooled by charismatic men pantomiming certainty.

But that's only worth a damn if it benefits someone else. What men meant for evil, may God use for good. Leaving captivity would've been easier, if we'd had refugee elders loudly telling us deconstruction — the modern term for facing rejection in order to feel less insane — is worth it. So let's become those elders.

Nobody chooses to be indoctrinated, and nobody's entirely free of it. Maybe you've been drafted into a battle against a different machine of bigotry or poverty or injustice. Still, in our common war, each liberation leads to another. (Sorry for making all this sound like The Matrix. I was raised by Y2K youth pastors and Zack de la Rocha.)

The point:

People can change. Need proof?

Hi. :)

Need more?

Look around this shrine of renewal — our Pizza Hut-turned-funeral home-turned-combination Pizza Hut and Taco Bell — at church kids who became everything we were programmed against.

Leading our playful prayer is someone supposedly too curious to be a Christian and too spiritual to be an intellectual: Dr. Kori (she/they), adorned with undercut red frizz and a Jurassic Park thigh-sleeve tattoo.

(You've known her "past-tense childhood nickname," Sophia. In 2021, she came out as "demigirl, the femme side of non-binary.")

"They told us, 'Leave space for Jesus. Let Jesus separate you,'" she said in 2004, days after we'd split hundreds of miles apart. "But our souls are breaths of the Spirit who's feminine in Hebrew: Genesis 1. When we die, those breaths go back to her: Ecclesiastes. We're not actually separate souls! We're one Spirit breathing in and out! Jesus isn't the space *between*. Jesus is the space!"

"Sweet. What's your part of the Spirit wearing?"

"Ooh, for you? Capri pants."

After one year, I dropped out of college, taught myself web design, and moved to her. We vowed to live in sin until age twenty-five, but once we realized *how much* her extended family hated her semi-engagement to an apostate, the wedding became the funnier troll job.

Fond of blowing freshman minds with God-is-always-changing theology, Kori's endlessly patient with conservative homeschooling veterans who haven't yet found adolescent eye-openers, like a forbidden book kinda about a dinosaur theme park, but really about the folly of control.

I believe imperialists cannot be redeemed until they've prepared everlasting banquets for their victims, but otherwise I'll defer all religion thoughts to her. Meanwhile, she's surely the only Scottish-pink Buffalo Sabres fan in the Syriac Orthodox Church's 2,000-year history, but still asks me to talk her into being herself.

Original sin is faulty doctrine, she argues in her cute little romper, and not just because Augustine's invention of the concept is refuted by Ezekiel 18:20. After all my worries about becoming hopeless like my father, I realized he wasn't. "Anything that can be built can be rebuilt better," he said.

On my middle-school football team, I was the punter. My job was to surrender the ball, ending an opportunity. But to discard wasn't to dismay. It was to turn a failure into another chance. To turn yesterday into a bet on tomorrow.

I said all that in order to say this to a superbloom on a planet aflame, the presumably freckly-olive kid somehow already named Arwen Siena:

> If Hell is a world without God, and if we are all breaths of the Spirit, then do you know what I know?
>
> Then, beloved, Hell is a world without you.
>
> You will be born good. The same goes for everyone — yes, even James Dobson. Treat them accordingly.

ACKNOWLEDGMENTS

Thank you to my wife, Emily, for, among a million other things, her reaction to that time I revealed having witnessed gunplay at church in middle school. It made me start writing "YouthGroup.docx."

To our kid for coining "Sharks With Rabies."

To my editor, William Boggess, who convinced me to only write the story I'd set out to write.

To my cover artist, Emily Mahon. My reaction: "lmaooo genius."

To my copy editor, Nicole Fegan. Don't blame her for my choice to use non-italicized movie titles.

To Justin Ferguson and Andrew Klema, both far too generous for years with feedback and encouragement.

To crucial early readers Holly Anderson, Mike Altman, Danni Baker, Anthony Bales, Jonathan Beecher Field, Spencer Hall, Carden Hedelt, Alex Kirshner, Kalan Kucera, Hasan Masood, April Maxwell, Ben McCloskey, Shanda McCloskey, Travis Miller, Stephanie Newell, Van Newell, Jessica Nipp, Femi Omoni, Max Ornstein, Matthew Pierce, Jonathan Redding, Kacie Rowlette, Brigit Stadler, Jon Whittaker, Alex Y, and Josh Young.

To the Shutdown Fullcast Extended Universe. A decade ago, when I started unearthing this stuff (by posting Audio Adrenaline jokes with Jon Bois and Bill Hanstock, iirc), you told me to keep going.

To my fellow FBC breakaways. You saved my life. Deal with it.

And most importantly, thank you for reading — but now I'm gonna ask you for more. **Please leave a review online! Amazon and Goodreads are the most impactful at the moment, but all are dearly appreciated!** And search "Hell Is a World Without You" on Spotify for the chapter-by-chapter playlist! (And leave a review online!)

ABOUT THE AUTHOR

Jason Kirk, a longtime sports journalist, co-hosts the Vacation Bible School Podcast and the Shutdown Fullcast. He's contributed to The Athletic, This American Life, Penguin Random House's Hazlitt Magazine, Slate, USA Today, Vox, and many others. An Atlanta native, he grew up as a maximum-effort Southern Baptist and is now a lazy Christian pantheist. His non-fiction literary agent is Erik Hane of Headwater Literary Management.

All of the author's proceeds from *Hell Is a World Without You* preorders are being donated to the Trevor Project.

Subscribe to his free newsletter — jasonkirk.fyi — for more.

Made in the USA
Las Vegas, NV
24 January 2024